The Prophecy Chronicles: Prophecy Foretold

by

Ron Hartman

D1713367

Credits
Cover Artist: Designs by Ms. G
Editor: Christine Young

Printed in the United States of America

Dedication

For my wife Leslie, the real Ashley. Her love and devotion has always been unwavering. Without her I would truly be lost in a strange world.

"The Starburst Stranger will cross the Burning Sea and bring the Light to set the people free." -An ancient prophecy

BOOK ONE: ARRIVAL

Chapter One

Daniel Marten cringed after picking up the phone. It was reflex to answer whenever it rang, and unfortunately that reflex didn't stop when the store closed. He was exhausted. The day drained him. It was all he could do to muster friendly charm in his voice as he lifted the receiver and said, "Home Town Pharmacy, can I help you?"

"Hi, it's me," a woman's voice replied. "Why are you still answering the phone?"

Daniel's brown eyes lit up, the slight frown of irritation disappearing from his high forehead. "Hey, Baby! Don't ask, I'm a moron." Daniel considered her question and added, "Wait a minute, why'd you call if you didn't think I'd answer?"

Daniel's wife, Ashley, replied, "Because I knew you *would* answer."

No catchy comeback came to mind, so he just said, "Ah, I see. So, what's up?"

Ashley chuckled in that distracted way mothers have when their young children are milling about. "Well, I hate to bother you while you're at work, but do you think you'll be coming home soon?"

Daniel smiled and cradled the phone to his ear. "You're never a bother. After the day I've had, your sweet voice is like manna from heaven!"

A little overdone, sure, but Ashley graciously laughed anyway. "Uh-huh, sure it is."

Daniel grinned. The skin around his eyes crinkled into a nest of laugh lines, testament to a good life. He ran a hand through thin salt-and-pepper hair and replied, "I'm just about done. Did you need something?"

"No. Well, yes. We could use a gallon of milk. Mostly I just wanted to tell you to be careful. It's been snowing pretty hard…the weatherman said not to travel if you could avoid it."

"Well, I *could* avoid it, but my girlfriend told me not to come over tonight." He could almost see Ashley rolling her eyes when she snorted. He smiled again and said, "Don't worry, Honey, I'll be careful. Besides, I have my truck! Why'd we buy it if I couldn't go off-roading?"

Ashley chuckled again. "Why do you always call it a truck? It's an SUV, Dork." Her voice sounded a little more uncertain when she continued, "Okay, I'll see you when you get home. I love you."

"I love you too. See you soon."

Daniel hung up the phone and reached his hands above his head, lacing his fingers together. He groaned as his back popped. The pharmacy had closed a couple minutes before, and he was ready to call it quits for the day. He combed his fingers through his hair again, sighed, and rested his hands on top of his head. *Man, what a day.*

Most of his patients were low-income retirees, several well below the poverty level. Many hoped when the new Medicare prescription plans came out they would actually be able to afford both prescriptions and food again. Sadly, most were disillusioned with the whole program now. As with most good intentions, when the government got involved, the result was a quagmire of confusion and red tape. Once enrollees picked a plan and hoped it'd save them money, they were shocked to find that it really didn't save them much. Many were cajoled into joining, with the looming threat that if someday something happened, it would cost them more to sign up later. The looming specter of "The Worst Will Happen if You Don't Prepare" had certainly filled the pockets of plan providers but had done little to actually help people who needed it.

Many of Daniel's patients signed up with discount programs offered by pharmaceutical manufacturers prior to the Medicare plans. But when the government stepped in, the companies cancelled their plans, leaving the elderly to foot the bill of higher co-payments with little assistance. No one could blame the patients for getting upset about how they'd been treated; their fixed incomes were now being stretched even farther. Unfortunately for Daniel, like most pharmacists, he was there when they had to pay up, so he got to bear the brunt of their discontent.

He'd gone to pharmacy school to help people and be a source of information for the entire community. Now the bitter truth was that most of his days were spent arguing with insurance companies on the phone and patients in person. Add to that the fact that Medicare plans also cut back on what they paid the pharmacy for each prescription.

That meant Daniel had to fill more prescriptions with less help just to break even, meaning less time to help patients and less of a chance to actually make a difference in his community.

Not for the first time, he wondered if maybe he should sell the pharmacy and move on to something else. *There has to be more to life than this.* He felt genuinely sorry for patients that couldn't be helped. He was also disgusted with the state of healthcare in this, the most powerful country in the world. *How powerful are we really, if we can't even take care of our mothers and fathers? Once they've given everything for our country, they're worth little to politicians. Besides being a voting block, that is.* Daniel sighed and combed hands through his hair again. *Maybe tomorrow will be better.*

He glanced down at the pictures on his desk and his worries seemed to lessen, at least temporarily. Four smiling faces stared back at him from the largest frame: Ashley and their kids. Ashley's dark blonde hair was pulled back in a pony-tail, her blue eyes shining as she sat surrounded by her children. She wore a light blue sundress and sat in a large over-stuffed leather chair. Elizabeth, their oldest, stood beside her mom, the spitting image of her mother. She wore a pink dress with little yellow flowers around the hem, and her head was tilted slightly to the side. It looked like the picture was taken while she was in the act of resting her head on her mother's shoulder.

Next was Nate. He stood on the other side of Ashley in blue trousers and a khaki-colored shirt. His hair was blonder than his sister and Mom, his eyes a slightly darker shade of blue. Even in a posed professional photo, Nate couldn't hide his ornery smile. He looked like he was just waiting to find some mischief the second Mom looked away. His little brother Ethan sat on Mom's lap, and if not for the two years separating them, they could pass for twins. His smile was sweeter and he tended to not play as rough as his brother, but Ethan adored Nate and would follow him anywhere…which usually meant into trouble.

Well, enough of this. It's time to get home to my little monsters before they drive their mom nuts. He chuckled at the thought. Certainly they were a handful, but he wouldn't have it any other way. Let the pharmacy worry about itself for tonight; he had kids to wrestle.

He grabbed his coat, making one last trip around the pharmacy to make sure everything was locked up tight before setting the alarm on his way out. As soon as the door was shut, Daniel realized that he forgot his gloves and hat inside. "Oh, well, I'm not going that far," he grumbled. He stuffed hands in his coat and hunched his head inside the lapel to block some of the wind that blew snow in every direction.

The temperature must have dropped twenty degrees since lunch, and snow was piling up in the parking lot. *I can see why the weatherman said to stay inside*, Daniel thought as he scraped the rapidly accumulating snow off of his SUV. *Man, I should've gone back to get the damn gloves!* His fingers were blocks of ice by the time he finished. He jumped inside, shivers running through him as the car warmed up.

Daniel's tires spun as he pulled out, exposing a thin layer of ice under new snow. "Another day in paradise," Daniel Marten said to the dark snow-choked streets as he left the parking lot.

~ * ~

The ride out of town was a white-knuckle affair. There were vehicles in ditches lining both sides of the road, the snow blowing harder. Wind and snow made white-out conditions that frequently blocked his view of the road completely. Every time that happened Daniel's heart jumped into his throat and he feathered the brakes, feeling how little control he had on the hidden ice. Even though he'd lived all his life in the Midwest, Daniel never got used to winter driving. He hated the cold and the feeling of doom that pervaded him whenever he had to drive in bad weather. He and Ashley dreamed of moving to Hawaii, but right now being close to family was more important.

Both wanted the kids to know their grandparents, so they moved back to their hometown after college, even though most of their friends had gone and opportunities were limited. The town had seen better days, and many of the residents struggled to get by. He worked at the local pharmacy for five years before Daniel's boss retired and offered to sell the business to him. After a lot of soul searching, Daniel and Ashley took the plunge, and now they really were tied to the town. Dreams of Hawaii took a back seat while they made the pharmacy a success.

A huge gust of wind threw snow in the air, making Daniel swear under his breath. For the tenth time in five minutes, Daniel caught himself wondering why they ever moved to the country. He could hear his own voice, arguing for the move to Ashley. *"The kids need room to run. Besides, we both love the country!"* Now, of course, Daniel was thinking, *What a load of crap! Country living's gonna kill me!* Ashley and

Daniel both grew up in the country and both knew eventually they'd return to the wide-open spaces. It was just nights like this that it didn't seem like such a great idea.

Daniel slowed and turned onto a paved country road that led home, skirting a semi lying on its side. He raked his eyes from the road as he passed the truck, even though his panicked mind insisted he'd crash if he did. He heaved a sigh of relief when he saw it was empty. Regardless of the weather, he would've stopped to help another in need, even if his instincts screamed against it.

Compared to the highway, the country road was like driving through a field. There was so much snow Daniel could barely make out where the pavement ended and the ditches began. Obviously, the over-worked road crews hadn't made it out that far yet, and there were no tracks for him to follow. *Evidently, everyone else had sense to stay home,* Daniel thought as he trudged along.

The road continued for about a mile, slowly rising up a long hill before skirting the other side in a series of s-curves. Daniel was almost to the first s-curve and nearly home when his cell phone rang. For a split second, he lost his focus and glanced down.

Black ice can be very unforgiving, and Daniel's momentary lapse was enough to doom him. His car slid to the left across the centerline. With a gasp, he frantically yanked the wheel in the opposite direction, but the vehicle didn't respond as it picked up speed, sliding downhill. Along the edge of the curve the ditch was very shallow. His SUV bounced right over the road's short curb and tore through a fence on the opposite side.

As wheels hit the greater resistance of frozen dirt, the top-heavy vehicle flipped over and smashed driver-side-first into the ground. Daniel was thrown into the window, cracking the glass. The impact split the skin of Daniel's cheek like an overripe melon, tearing his skin in every direction. Tendrils of broken flesh jutted below his left eye to his nose and down his cheek to his jaw. Another series of tears formed from his temple back to his ear and from his eyebrow up into his hair. Skin hung loosely from the grisly gashes as a sheet of blood fell down his face and neck. Intense pain overwhelmed him and he passed out, red mist fading to black.

Daniel's ride wasn't over, though. Momentum pushed his vehicle further as it rolled over, breaking through another fence and finally coming to rest again on its wheels. For the briefest of moments all motion stopped, but then the iced-over pond he was sitting on broke and the SUV sank.

Water poured through cracks in the windshield and passenger window, the freezing cold bringing Daniel back around with a jolt. It felt like his face was on fire, while his legs suffered a different kind of burning as the freezing water flowed in, now almost up to his waist. For the first time, Daniel really started to panic. He screamed and beat his fists against the fractured window. The broken glass gave, propelled back into Daniel's lap by the force of inrushing water.

Without the window to slow it, icy water came in like a tidal wave, and the vehicle sank faster. With his chest sinking below the surface, Daniel screamed again and threw himself toward the open window. Panic blinded him, though, and he didn't realize he was still buckled in. Ice splashed into Daniel's face, and he involuntarily sucked in a breath, pulling the freezing liquid down into his lungs. The fire that burned his skin now burned inside as well, and he felt himself sliding toward unconsciousness.

The last focused, panic-filled thought Daniel had before drifting off was, *Oh God, help!* Even that didn't have much emphasis, though, as his mind surrendered. His eyes closed a final time, and all faded to black.

Chapter Two

Sound came back first. Initially, it was muffled, as if people were talking (screaming, dying) through the thin walls of a cheap motel. Slowly, they became clearer, and eventually Daniel could make out distinct voices (gasping their last). It was obvious that the noise could only be one thing, but still Daniel's mind couldn't grasp what he was really hearing. It wasn't until it was as clear as if the people were standing beside him that he realized it was a battle.

At the same time the veil of darkness surrounding him lifted, the spectrum shifting from total black to subtler shades of gray and pink. Finally, Daniel realized his eyes were closed, and he apprehensively opened them.

He lay on a grass-covered bank, his feet nearly lying in a small stream, while he looked up at a blue sky punctuated by a full canopy of trees. Based on the foliage and temperature, it must be early summer. Daniel glanced down at his body, taking in his bare feet, dark trousers and blue dress shirt. A vague thought wandered through his mind, suggesting he should be wet and cold. He frowned, thinking that should be important.

A whisper of memory tickled the corners of his mind, and with a gasp Daniel sat up. The left side of his face throbbed, each heartbeat pulsing through his cheek. He lifted his left hand to his temple and gasped again when his fingers brushed the sensitive area. When the blood he expected wasn't on his fingers, he gently probed his cheek. There were no breaks in his skin, though the entire left side of his face felt swollen and bruised.

Carefully, he pulled legs under him and crawled to the edge of the stream, looking down at a distorted reflection that stared back with wide eyes. There was a large scar across the left side of his face. It was thickest right over his cheekbone, but thin tendrils ran across his nose, down to his jaw, back to his ear and past his eye up into his hairline. Daniel worked his jaw while fingers probed the rest of his face and neck, but he found no other injuries. Now that he'd explored it, the pain wasn't as bad as he'd thought, seeming more like a wound that was well on its way to healing.

Aside from the bubbling stream, Daniel had blocked out all other noise while he studied himself. He was distantly aware of (the clang of metal, the soft thump of arrows) sounds, but he was so focused on himself that he dismissed them. As he finished his inspection, however, recognition of what they were penetrated his mind. Daniel's stomach did a somersault as a man's shriek wailed over the cacophony of battle.

Eyes wide in fear, he forced himself to look over his shoulder, back toward the horrible sounds. The stream's bank was up a small rise dotted with saplings where he stared in horror as the breaking of branches announced someone running up the other side. Just when Daniel expected to see a person crest the hill, there was a whirring noise followed by a horrible thump like a wooden ball bouncing off concrete. His heart stopped yet he continued to stare, frozen in place, as a trickle of blood ran down the bank.

The blood brought Daniel out of his paralysis. Terror was forgotten as he darted to his feet, thinking, *I've got to help him!* Before he realized what he was doing, he'd climbed the bank, helping hands reaching out--until he crested the hill. An axe handle protruded from what had once been a young man's face. His hands started to shake as his mind shut down again. "No," he moaned, stumbling back a step as he distantly realized another man was running toward him. Some part of his mind screamed at him to get down, to hide, but it was too late. He'd completely surrendered to shock and was rooted to the spot.

The man running at him wore a red kilt and knee-high brown leather boots. A wide leather belt separated kilt from a bare chest that was thick with muscle and covered with red tattoos of stars and concentric circles. He had a black, short-cropped beard and long hair to match and was covered in blood, most of which didn't appear to be his own. His lips were pulled back in a snarl, revealing several broken teeth, while he gripped with both hands the largest sword Daniel had ever seen. He held it cocked over one shoulder as he ran, as if he were ready to hit a baseball out of a park.

Still unable to move, Daniel watched the man sprint up the bank, roaring a war cry. His fear melted away as the warrior closed and a detached part of his mind thought, *So, this is the end.* He made no effort to defend himself as the warrior reached the top of the hill and gathered himself to end Daniel's life. He pulled the mighty sword around and was just beginning to swing when he looked into Daniel's face and pulled up short. The rage evaporated from his face, replaced with awe as he gasped, "You!"

His momentum carried him forward and he stumbled to a halt beside Daniel, letting the blade fall to the ground while he stared dumbstruck at Daniel's face. Daniel opened his mouth to say something, *anything*, when there was a meaty thump and blood sprayed from the warrior's chest, making Daniel recoil in surprise. The two locked eyes for a second as the warrior slowly looked down at the barbed tip of an arrowhead sticking out of his chest. His vision clouded over and he toppled to the side, falling on top of the man he'd recently killed.

Daniel wiped bloody spray from his face as another soldier ran up to him, this one carrying a recurved bow with another arrow already notched. He had olive skin and dark hair and eyes and wore padded leather armor dyed dark blue with a silver mailed fist emblazoned over his chest. He skidded to a halt and glanced at the dead man in red with a look of smug satisfaction. "'E' git ya?" he asked, turning back to Daniel.

Daniel shrugged, unsure what to say. He managed to stammer, "Uhh," before the archer continued unperturbed, as if he hadn't expected a reply.

"'Tis goo' I caugh' sight o' ya. 'E woulda split ya like a keg, 'e would." He looked over his kill once more before sparing an unconcerned glance for the other dead man, a soldier wearing the same mailed fist as he did. When he returned his attention to Daniel, he did a double-take, only then realizing he wasn't a brother-in-arms. Silence stretched out as he chewed his lip, trying to decide what to do while he kept an arrow on the string. Finally, he let the bow drop. "Ya shouldn' be up 'ere, 'specially wit'out arms. Come wi' me."

Daniel was still trying to piece together what the archer said when he turned and stalked along the stream's high bank. Unsure what to do, he looked over the battlefield, hoping for inspiration. The stream ran through a small copse of trees which gave way to plowed fields and a narrow dirt road in the distance. The fields looked like they were just ready to be planted; but instead of crops, they'd been planted with bodies. Many were in dark blue uniforms like the man that saved Daniel, but many more wore red kilts, shirts, or headbands. The battle still raged in small pockets of resistance, but those wearing red were greatly out-numbered. Across the road blue-uniformed reinforcements rushed in to finish the battle.

Daniel blew out a heavy sigh and glanced down at himself, suddenly realizing why the archer spared him. His dark blue shirt and black pants looked similar to the winning side's uniforms. The archer must've thought he was a comrade when he rushed to save him. He looked to his savior, but he was already off the bank and moving toward the bulk of the blue army.

If I stay here, I'm dead, Daniel thought as he shook off the paralysis of indecision. *I need to get through this, one thing at a time.* First, he needed to get off the battlefield. Maybe someone, possibly the archer, could answer his questions later. With a final shudder at the carnage around him, Daniel ran after the archer.

Once he was moving, it was easier to keep hysteria at bay. Better to think about something he could control. With that in mind, Daniel latched on to the first thought that ran through his head, like a drowning man grabbing a preserver. *The last thing I want is to step on a sword. I could get cut...it could get infected!* With the thought running through his mind like a mantra, he focused on the ground and blocked out the horrors he was passing as he ran, curling his bare toes in fear of a hidden blade.

Soon the two were off the battlefield, marching their way into the army's forward camp. Periodically, the archer looked sidelong at Daniel, as if debating whether he should say anything. Prudence seemed to win out, though, so he remained silent until they reached a large tent in the camp's center.

Guards wearing blue tabards emblazoned with the mailed fist stood on either side of the tent's entrance. Both had long black hair with beards to match, the pale skin around their eyes the only visible flesh on their faces. Both held halberds in ready hands as they stared at Daniel and the archer. "Wha' 'ya want?" spat the guard on the left.

The archer took a step forward and motioned over his shoulder. "Foun' this'un near th' creek." His voice cracked, quavering with fear. The guards just glared at him, so he continued, his voice even quieter than before. "Thought he migh' be 'portant-like." Daniel saw beads of sweat dripping down his olive neck.

The two guards held their ground for another minute before sharing a glance filled with malicious delight. The one on the right growled, "So…you's the big 'portant man now, eh? Come 'ta show us yarn prize?"

The archer gave a fierce shake of his head and started to stammer a reply, but Daniel beat him to it, reacting before he had time to think. He stepped beside the archer and laid a hand on his shoulder, locking eyes with the guards. "Come on, they're not gonna help us."

The archer spun so fast it took Daniel by surprise. His face was contorted in a grimace of hatred as a bone-handled knife came out of nowhere and pressed against Daniel's throat. He froze as a gasp escaped him, feeling blood trickle down his neck.

The archer started to growl at Daniel, but it came out as a wheeze of pain as the guard on the right slammed the blunt end of his halberd into a kidney. The archer dropped to his knees as the other guard stepped up behind him and yanked his staff across his throat. He forced him upright as his friend came around front. The soldier held his halberd lengthwise in front of him, and casually leaned over the length of wood to look directly into the archer's eyes. "Ya Quarenie scum think you's better'n us," he growled. He leaned in closer and whispered, "Wha' if'n I cut off yarn thumbs? Yarn fancy bow wouldna help ya none then!"

The archer's eyes went wide with fear. He shook his head and opened his mouth to speak, but no sound came out. Daniel felt his bloody neck, but despite that he still wanted to help the man that saved him. "Stop this!"

Without even turning around, the guard in front swung his halberd, the staff hitting Daniel in the hip hard enough to knock him into the mud. He glared over his shoulder at Daniel and growled, "Shut it! We's no' done here!"

From the side a deep, stern voice said, "Yes, you are." The guards' pale faces became even paler as they jumped back to attention. The archer, whose face had gone from olive to ashen, fell to the ground, coughing and clutching his throat. Daniel looked over at a tall man with short silver hair and a close-cropped silver goatee. His breastplate bore the same insignia as the soldiers, but it was engraved in silver with gold lining the fist. A long dark blue cloak clasped with an elaborate golden tie trailed the ground behind him.

He glared at the guards before turning his gaze on Daniel. He nearly dismissed him until something made him do a double-take. His eyes narrowed as he studied Daniel in silence for nearly five minutes. Eventually, the archer stopped coughing and came to attention alongside his attackers, the fear in their faces mirrored in his own. The tall man ignored them as he pulled a black leather glove from his right hand and slowly stroked his goatee. "Where did you come from?" His voice was low and dangerous.

Daniel's skin crawled under the man's scrutiny. He shrugged and looked to the archer, who refused to return the glance. "I don't know," he replied. "I woke up by a stream." He pointed to the archer. "This man saved me and brought me here."

Daniel was held in the man's hard glare for a few more minutes until he finally said, "Put him in a tent. Give him food and drink." He paused and took in Daniel a final time before adding, "Find him some boots."

He walked away as one of the guards stepped forward and said, "Yar, Gen'ral."

He grabbed Daniel and pulled him toward a row of smaller tents. They had just reached the first when the General called over his shoulder. "When you're done, the three of you report to Captain Sturn for punishment."

The guard froze, and Daniel could feel the hand on his shoulder begin to shake. He shared a frightened look with his comrade before all three soldiers replied, "Yessir."

~ * ~

Daniel pulled on worn, knee-high black leather boots and walked around the tent, trying to get a feel for them. They were a bit too small, the leather lining the sole cutting into the edges of his feet as he walked. Daniel winced but continued to pace, in part trying to break them in, but also trying to think his way through what had happened. Why did the two soldiers turn on the third? And why did the men fear their commander so much? And just where the hell was he?

As Daniel turned he took in his surroundings again. The only furnishings in the small tent were a cot and a small flat-topped chest covered with a tray containing food and drink. Daniel glanced at the bread, stew, and the tankard of water and grimaced. The stew had large chunks of red meat floating in it, and Daniel's stomach rolled as he remembered the battlefield. *I have never been less hungry in my life*, he thought.

He continued pacing, wondering how long he'd be held, when he heard the horrible wail. Daniel gasped and spun toward the entrance. The scream came again, wafting over the distance, but this time higher pitched. Through the agonized sounds, Daniel could barely make out pleas for mercy, cut off by yet another scream. The voice sounded desperate as it moved up an octave. With every screech, Daniel's stomach dropped, and his blood ran cold. *What could make a man scream like that?*

Eventually, the screaming waned into sobbing, only to be started again by another voice, this one deeper. The deep tenor didn't last long, though, as scream after scream tore at the voice, making it reedy and high pitched. It resolved into a wheezy wail before the end. A third voice joined the chorus of pain, and Daniel didn't think he could take any more. His mouth was bone dry, his eyes burning from the strain of holding them open so long. He pulled his hands up to rest on his cheeks, his mouth open in an "O" of fear.

Daniel's hands moved up from his cheeks to cover his ears and he closed his eyes. He bent over at the waist, willing the horrible noise to end. Whoever was causing the pain did not capitulate, however, and the cacophony continued. Daniel dropped to his knees and retched on the grass that was the floor of the tent. He hadn't eaten in hours, and his stomach had nothing to give but acid, but he continued to retch, tears forced out the corners of his closed eyes.

Finally, the screaming stopped. The bustle of a busy camp that Daniel had been distantly aware of before had ceased. All was silent except for the beating of Daniel's heart, which hammered in his ears as he kneeled on the ground, resting his head on the grass. He sobbed quietly, thankful the torture was over but terrified it might start again. Eventually, the noises of camp life resumed long after the cries died away.

With a rough rub of his palms, Daniel wiped away the tears. He spit out the bile in his mouth and pulled shaky legs under him. He stumbled to the cot and collapsed on it. He lay there with one arm draped over his face, his nose in the crook of his elbow, and tried to force his breathing to slow, his hands to stop shaking. In time the hitching breaths of hysteria gave way as he felt more in control of himself. Daniel glanced at the tray beside the cot and reached for the water, his stomach doing a somersault at the sight of the (bloody) red stew. He took a dainty sip, the cool liquid flowing down his dry throat feeling like heaven, so he continued, forcing himself to take only small sips. He was so focused on keeping the water down that he didn't notice the absence of noise as a group of soldiers stopped marching outside.

"Bring him." Daniel felt his knees unhinge at the two growled words, and he would have fallen if he wasn't already sitting. His eyes as big as saucers, he looked to the tent flap as it opened and two soldiers entered. Daniel's heart was beating so fast it felt as if it was going to burst from his chest as the men closed on him, and he was vaguely aware that he helplessly shook his head.

"Come wi' us." When Daniel didn't immediately comply, the two looked at each other and shrugged. They grabbed Daniel by the armpits and yanked him to his feet, forcing him out of the tent and into late-afternoon sunlight.

Daniel's moan brought smirks to the soldiers' faces as they pulled him from the tent. He was powerless to stop them as he followed on leaden legs, his eyes searching for the torture chamber that must be nearby. He was surprised, then, when they turned him instead toward the command tent. Confusion and relief washed over him in waves until a cold voice in his mind said, *Not tortured yet, at least.* The relief evaporated and left Daniel staring warily at the large tent.

Two new soldiers guarded the tent flaps, which they opened when Daniel's retinue stopped before them. His guards started to hustle him forward but he jerked away from their grip, and so they released his arms, allowing him to walk under his own power. He was in the tent and the flaps were dropped back in place before he realized the guards didn't follow.

The interior was dark compared to the bright afternoon sunshine, and it took a moment for Daniel's eyes to adjust. There were doorways off to the right and left of the long tent, as well as partitions at the back of the main area that allowed dim light to illuminate a table and chairs set up at the far end of the hall.

A giant bear of a man sat in one of the chairs, turning to look at Daniel as he entered. He had a full red beard and long hair to match. The hair along the sides of his face was plated into braids, and the rest was pulled into a large braid that ran down his back. A long scar ran down the right side of his face, starting above his eye and continuing to his jaw, leaving a thick white gap in his beard. He wore a long navy cape that was edged with white wolf's pelt and over his massive chest he wore an intricate black breastplate. A silver mailed fist flashed on it, with two weapons crossing behind it: a sword and an axe. Rubies were set along the length of the weapons' edges, the craftsmanship so fine that they looked like blood dripping from the blades. The pommel of a sword rose before the man's left hip, and his cloak jutted out behind him in the shape of the unseen scabbard.

Scenes of the bloody battlefield flashed through Daniel's mind, and he couldn't help but shiver as he took in the giant's frightening appearance. Unsure what to do, Daniel opened his mouth to introduce himself just as the general entered the hall from the left. He gave Daniel a stern glance before moving around the table and sitting in the chair facing him. Without any preamble, he spoke in the same deep voice as before. "Who are you?"

Daniel felt like molten lead had been poured into him for how quickly his stomach dropped. *The interrogation begins,* he thought, as his rebellious mind returned to the tortured screams. His mind was not the only part of him rebelling, though, as his mouth was suddenly as dry as a desert. He opened it and tried to reply, but nothing came out. He swallowed past the hot lump in his throat as the general's scowl deepened at the delay. Panic setting in, Daniel stammered, "I...I'm...Daniel. My name is Daniel Marten."

Silence stretched out, Daniel's skin crawling under the men's intense glares. It was all he could do to keep from fidgeting as he endured the silence, willing himself not to drop into hysterics and babble uncontrollably. Finally, the general asked, "Where did you come from?"

The question hit him like a bucket of cold water. He hadn't even had time to consider such a fundamental question since he'd awakened on the battlefield, but now that he thought about it, Daniel realized he couldn't remember. He knew his name and had a vague understanding of his profession, but that was about it. And Daniel knew that wouldn't do. His heart raced and sweat ran down his back as he tried to think of an acceptable answer. The general's scowl deepened once more, and as panic set in, Daniel blurted out the truth. "I don't know." Fighting to keep hysteria at bay, Daniel continued before the general could say anything. "I woke up by the stream during the battle...I don't know how I got there."

The general's scowl didn't soften exactly, but it did change slightly as he shot a glance at the giant. He was a little less sure of himself when he looked back to Daniel and asked, "Are you the Stranger?"

With Daniel's pulse raging in his ears, he thought maybe he misunderstood the general. He tried to swallow and heard his throat click. "I...I'm sorry, what did you say?"

Daniel's timid reply was almost as if he'd thrown a bucket of water on the general. His uncertainty was replaced by rage as he stood and leaned forward, resting both hands on the table. He glared into Daniel's face and practically shouted, "Are you *the Stranger*?"

Daniel was completely at a loss. He had no idea what the man was talking about, but he was terrified of the consequences if the general didn't like his answers. He felt his face flushing, and a part of him knew that they would take that to mean that he was lying. Daniel looked down to the floor and quietly mumbled a reply, his voice quavering. "I...I don't know what you mean."

He was too terrified to look up as he stood there shaking, sweat flowing down his back. In his peripheral vision he could see the general closing on him, but he didn't have the courage to raise his eyes. He stopped in front of Daniel and bluntly poked a finger at the scar on his left cheek. Daniel had to stifle a cry, not from the contact, but rather from the much rougher treatment he expected to follow.

"How did you get this?"

Daniel could hear the barely contained menace in his voice, and his legs started to shake harder. He thought he would probably collapse if the general touched him again. Unshed tears built up in his eyes, threatening to overflow as he surrendered to the fear of torture. He would have told the general anything to prevent the pain, but he didn't have any answers. His voice was barely more than a whisper when he whimpered, "I…don't know."

He could smell onions on the general's breath he stood so close, but still Daniel couldn't raise his eyes to look him in the face. The seconds stretched out like hours while Daniel stared at the floor but didn't really focus on anything. *Please…please,* Daniel thought incoherently, not really sure whether he was begging for the interrogation to stop, or for the answers the general wanted.

After what felt like days, the general raised his voice. "Guards!"

In his fear Daniel did finally find the courage to look into the general's face. As the tent flaps opened behind him and the two guards entered, Daniel whimpered, "No…" He looked in vain for a sign of reprieve in the general's cold eyes as the men gripped his arms. Daniel's legs gave out completely as they pulled him backward, dragging him from the tent. The last Daniel ever saw of the general was his back, ramrod straight, as he walked to the table.

Daniel's fear was at a summit never before realized. He had no feeling in his legs, and all his mind could offer was a repetitive, *no…no!* If he'd drank more water he surely would have wet himself as they pulled him away, but as it was there was nothing to give. His mind shut down, his pleas limited to a terrified buzzing when he realized they were pulling him in the same direction as the screaming men.

He was so far gone into his fear that the relative darkness of his tent didn't even register until after the soldiers dropped him on the soft grass with a chuckle. When he finally realized he was not going to be tortured, tears of relief spilled from his eyes, muddying the ground beneath his face. Daniel lay in the mud and sobbed for some time, the terror and shock of the day leaving him completely drained.

~ * ~

The sun rose over blood-soaked fields, dawn light casting everything in red-tinted hues. It was as if the entire world were drenched in the blood spilled the day before. The fields were mercifully quiet as villagers and camp followers walked among the dead. They looked for lost loved ones, occasionally stopping to roll over a body to verify an identity. Here and there people kneeled along a prone form, weeping quietly for their loss. Others systematically worked their way through the fallen forms, searching for coins, weapons, and other treasures they may be able to sell later. The families gave the looters dark looks and some spat in their direction, but they moved indifferently on, intent on collecting the spoils of war.

The army was slow to wake, the men moving with exaggerated care after celebrating far into the night. Many had witnessed--and performed--horrible atrocities, but the visceral high of survival drove them on through the night. It pushed them to forget the deeds and welcome the oblivion of drink and song. Soon they would be looking after their fallen brethren, but not yet. Perhaps the next battle would be the one they would not return from, so they bore the after-effects of their revelry as a matter of course. The officers understood all too well and were lenient with them, at least for the day.

Daniel sat on the cot and watched the tent's east-facing wall shift from hues of black and grey to pink. He looked at the wall but didn't really see it. His mind was revisiting the horror of the battlefield and the terror of his interrogation. A line describing a conflict in another time and place came to him, and he distractedly thought, *Shock and awe, indeed.* As he sat in silence, he had his first chance to reflect on what he'd seen and done, to try and make sense of it all. The general's reaction was baffling. Try as he might, all his introspection only returned to the glaring holes in his memory.

There were small bits of memories, like flashes in the darkness, but they danced away from his grasp when he tried to focus on them. Everything, it seemed, all the essentials that made him who he was, were on the edge of his consciousness, but just out of reach. Like a tongue exploring an abscessed tooth, his mind kept coming back to the blanks. He tried to work around the block, to batter down the walls of forgetfulness, but to no avail.

He groaned in frustration, and reluctantly turned to where he was now. From what he'd seen, this world was vastly different than the one he came from. For one thing, it felt like early summer here, but he still had the vague feeling of icy cold from that other place. Then there was the battlefield. While he couldn't place what precisely was different, it seemed somehow wrong to him. The word that kept coming to mind was old-fashioned, but he couldn't really say why that seemed to fit. Not just the battlefield, but *everything* he'd seen seemed antiquated, as if his world had far surpassed this one. Things were done differently, faster somehow.

Then there was the problem with his understanding the soldiers. He distinctly remembered speaking a language called English, but that was definitely not what was spoken here. Even though he recognized that, he couldn't bring himself to utter a single phrase in his native tongue. Like most of his memory, the ability to speak it seemed to be just beyond reach, hidden behind the walls of his mind.

He heaved a deep sigh while he considered the inconsistencies, and the smells of the tent rushed into his nostrils again. The bile he vomited up the previous day had soaked into the ground but the odor remained. Adding to the stench was the stink of dried blood that coated his shirt and pants. The sharp tang of dried urine also wafted up, shaming him with the fact that he lost control of his bladder during the interrogation. His face and hands were covered with mud and his shirt was not only smelly, but also stiff and scratchy from dried mud and blood, making him yearn for clean clothes.

Daniel jumped as the tent flap opened and a soldier walked in. He wrinkled his nose at the pungent aromas, his lip curling to match the cold disdain in his eyes. He carried a tray with more of the same food Daniel was offered the night before along with another clay pitcher and mug of tepid water. He sat the tray down on the trunk, sliding the other to the side, and left without saying a word. Daniel cupped a hand and poured water from the pitcher into it, splashing his face. He wiped away the mud and tears and rinsed the mud from his hands. Just as he was wiping his hands on the filthy shirt, the tent flap opened and again Daniel jumped. The same soldier entered just long enough to toss a bundle on Daniel's cot.

Daniel opened the bundle to find a brown rough-spun cloth jerkin and faded blue trousers. He removed his filthy clothes and threw them into the farthest corner of the tent before pulling on the new clothes. The shirt was too large and the trousers a little long and baggy, but just being clean made him feel better about himself. Daniel sat down and looked at the mound of soiled clothing in the corner. *All I brought with me lies there.* The thought gave him a twinge of regret, but Daniel pushed it away and reached for the mug of water.

· When it hit his stomach, it was like waking a sleeping lion. His stomach gave a loud rumble, reminding him that he couldn't remember the last time he'd eaten. He patted his soft belly as it continued to knot and rumble. With a sigh, he picked up a piece of bread and delicately nibbled at the crust, tasting salt and yeast. Reassured, he chewed a few bites and swallowed. The bread's saltiness drove the moisture from his mouth, and he reached for the mug again. Within minutes the bread was gone, and when he tilted the mug to his lips, Daniel was surprised to find it empty.

He considered the pitcher but then remembered he used it to wash off the mud and blood. Remembering the blood made his stomach give a little flip, but he didn't think his meal was coming back up. Daniel gave a half-hearted grunt that would have been a chuckle had he not been pushed so far in the last few hours. *It's remarkable what you can adjust to,* he thought. Last night he could barely look at the food after walking through the battlefield; now the thought barely got a response from his stomach. Feeling encouraged, he turned to the stew, but the pink meat floating in congealed juices was too much. *Best not push my luck.*

Despite the queasiness, Daniel did feel much better with food in his stomach and wearing clean clothes. He rested his hands on the knees of his new trousers and closed his eyes, turning his attention to the camp around him. Daniel sensed its relaxed mood, so he assumed the battle was over. He let his mind wander, and inexorably it returned to his absence of memory, but before he could worry it too much, the guards outside his tent snapped to attention.

Daniel turned frightened eyes toward the flaps as the guard that brought him food and clothes entered. He glared at Daniel, resting a hand on the pommel of a short sword. "Come 'ere," he growled.

Taking a deep breath, Daniel pushed himself to his feet and walked to the soldier on numb legs, his heart racing. He was scared, but with food in his belly and clean clothes on his back, he resolved to face whatever came like a man. The guard motioned toward the entrance and he nodded as he bent to step through the flaps. Outside, the morning sun shined brightly from over Daniel's shoulder, throwing everything before him into sharp relief. Before him was a column of fifty armored men, and at the head of the column was the huge man from the general's tent the night before. In spite of his earlier resolve, Daniel gasped at the sight of the giant.

The word huge didn't do the soldier justice, and seeing him now, Daniel could tell that he didn't get a true gauge of his size when he was seated in the tent. He was at least seven feet tall, each arm easily larger than Daniel's waist. His legs looked like the trunks of trees, and the breastplate that he wore was so large the fist and weapons on it looked larger than life-size. A gap at the shoulders of the breastplate showed that the man wore a red vest under his armor, but his arms were bare, showing a road map of scars covering the ridged muscle there. He easily dwarfed the men around him. As if that weren't enough, he carried himself lightly on his feet, ready to spring into action at any moment. This was clearly a man who lived by violence, and wouldn't hesitate to use force.

As he faced Daniel the sunlight sparkled on the rubies encrusting his armor, and he seemed to glow in the bright glare, throwing everything else in silhouette. Daniel had to squint to see that he wore the same cloak from the night before. It was pulled back from his bare shoulders, displaying his massive arms to their best angle. If he wanted to impress and intimidate Daniel, he succeeded.

The guard following Daniel shoved him from behind. He hadn't realized he'd stopped moving, but when he glanced around he saw that he was only two steps from his tent. He took a ragged breath and forced himself forward, walking blindly into the glare from the man's armor. Daniel's resolve held until he was about two feet from the man, where he stopped and couldn't force his shaking legs to go farther. The giant didn't keep him waiting long, though. He'd been testing Daniel's nerve, and when he was satisfied that Daniel was cowed, he roughly cleared his throat and spat in the dirt. "Come with me, Stranger," he growled. Immediately after speaking realization came to him, and he forced a nervous chuckle, looking around to see if anyone reacted to his words.

Daniel frowned. Clearly that was supposed to mean something, but the import was lost on him. *What could make this guy afraid?*

The giant quickly regained his composure and stuck out his massive chest. He continued in a deep booming voice, "I'm Captain Gelnar, Commander of the Elite Imperial Guard. I will take you to the Emperor, on order of General Ignatius, Supreme Commander of the Imperial Army."

As his words died away, Daniel swallowed past a lump in his throat. "Oh...alright." He couldn't think of anything else to add, so he closed his mouth and tried to keep his nerves under control.

Gelnar grunted and turned to the column of men. "Come," he commanded. Without a backward glance, he set off through the camp. His troops fell into formation around Daniel and followed in Gelnar's wake.

As they marched Daniel took in the layout of the camp. Everywhere there were tents similar to the one he had been held in, most arranged around communal cooking fires. Armored soldiers in blue uniforms lounged before some, talking and playing cards. Off to their right beyond the tents was a large field where troops were assembled. There was a tall thin man walking before the troops, speaking to them. Whenever he reached the end of the line, he spun on his heel and marched back in the opposite direction. Without glasses, Daniel's vision wasn't great, but he could just make out the hint of gold glinting in the morning sun whenever the man turned. That and his silver hair led Daniel to believe it may be the general who interrogated him, presumably Ignatius.

Gelnar wound through the lines of tents and Daniel lost sight of the field. Eventually, the soldiers' tents became sparse as they moved toward the camp perimeter. Soon they left it behind entirely, entering a seedy and disorganized camp. The housing was much grimmer, comprised mostly of rickety shanties and lean-to's that looked like a strong breeze could knock them over. There were few soldiers, and most of the people wore dirty, well-worn clothing.

When they marched through the military camp, some troops idly watched them pass without much interest, but that wasn't the case for the camp followers. Daniel was surprised to see how many people stopped in their tracks, staring in wide-eyed wonder at them. Initially, he thought it must be Gelnar's size that drew their attention. *Men that big can't be normal.* But soon he got the feeling they were all looking at him. Any time he darted a glance at someone's face, they stared straight back into his own. Gelnar's presence didn't even seem to register for them.

Daniel frowned, but before he could ponder their reactions the troops arrived at a series of interconnected low buildings that smelled of manure and hay. Gelnar spoke to an old man standing outside then walked back to his troops. Soon the old man returned with several helpers, each leading a line of small sturdy horses. Each horse was equipped with a saddle and small pack of supplies.

Gelnar glared at the small mounts and growled, "Give me a *real* beast, fool!" The man's head bobbed as he wailed something, eyes round as saucers. He tried to bow low and run to the stable at the same time, nearly falling in the process. Soon he returned with a much larger steed that was covered with shaggy black hair. Its body looked like a large stallion, but it had thick curved horns like a mountain goat sprouting out of each side of its head. Sharp curved fangs protruded from its upper jaw, extending beyond a hairy chin. The small horses shied away from it, straining at their tethers.

It gave a low growl, and the hackles along its spine stood up when it was led to Gelnar. Daniel could see a momentary look of surprised pleasure and awe in Gelnar's face, but he quickly hid it with a frown. He yanked the bridle from the old man and forced the beast to look him directly in the eyes. The animal's eyes glowed green as the growling increased. The beast's upper lip rose, exposing more sharp teeth. Then the battle of wills ended, the animal looking to the ground. The growling continued, but it was much quieter and subdued. Gelnar grunted. "This'll do."

The old man looked sadly at the animal before bowing low. "Yar M'lord."

One of the younger stable hands led a brown mare, not much larger than a pony, to Daniel. He held the reigns out as Daniel took them with apprehension. He didn't like horses. The few times he'd ever ridden, he was constantly afraid of being thrown off, and the sense that he was surrendering control to another creature unsettled him.

He held the leather reigns in fingers that had gone numb and looked over the horse's equipment. The saddle was something like ones Daniel vaguely remembered, made of a layer of formed leather shaped to cover the animal's back. The leather was stitched into a thick blanket that made up the bulk of the seat. There was no pommel, and thin leather straps hung down from the saddle with small loops at the ends of them. If they were meant to be stirrups, Daniel wasn't likely to get more than the tip of his boot into each of the small holes. At the back of the saddle was a rolled up blanket with an overturned wooden bowl tied to its center, looking like a pyramid on a plain of rough cotton.

The stable hand saw the fear in Daniel's face. He was clearly frightened of the soldiers, and especially Gelnar, but he leaned toward Daniel just the same. "Don' worry none. She's goo'. Name's Blue Belle," he whispered. He didn't make eye contact and pretended to check the horse's harness as he spoke from the side of his mouth.

Daniel nodded imperceptibly. *Yeah, don't worry. That's easy for you to say.* He looked into Blue Belle's large dark brown eyes and murmured, "We're not going to have any trouble, are we Blue Belle?" The horse just looked docilely back and he thought, *A brown horse named Blue Belle...clever name.* He turned away to look at the other soldiers and Blue Belle nudged his shoulder with her muzzle. As he turned back, she bobbed her head once and nickered. Daniel did a double-take and patted her neck. "Good girl."

He looked to the young man and found him staring into Daniel's face, the same look of wonder pasted there as the other camp followers. Just then one of the soldiers growled, "Ya gonna kiss 'im, boy? Git back!" He clipped the young man on the side of the head with a mailed fist. The boy cried out and backed away, moving cautiously toward the stable. The soldier growled and spat in his direction as he sprinted into the shelter.

The soldier and his comrades laughed, but their entertainment was interrupted by Gelnar. He'd managed to mount the shaggy beast and ordered his men to do likewise. With a deep breath Daniel grasped the front edge of the saddle and pulled himself into the seat. Blue Belle didn't move a hair, patiently waiting for Daniel to get situated in the unfamiliar seat.

Once he was in place, he sighed and thought, *Well, that wasn't too bad.* He heard cursing behind him and looked over his shoulder to see three of the soldiers lying in the mud, their nickering horses prancing around them. Another tried to maintain his seat while his steed bucked ferociously, and several more of the troops were having various degrees of difficulty controlling their horses as well. Daniel looked back to the stable, but all of the hands had disappeared within. He stroked Blue Belle's mane and again murmured, "Good girl."

Gelnar jerked fiercely on his mount's reigns, forcing its head around to watch his men. Initially he laughed at their difficulties, but he soon grew irritated by the delay. "Mount up!" he roared, as if his men hadn't heard him the first time. The troops redoubled their efforts, and with a lot of sweating and brute force they were finally able to gain their seats. After a few more moments, they forced their steeds into some semblance of ranks around Daniel and his docile mare.

When Gelnar was satisfied, he looked around at the faces turned to him once more. His gaze stopped on a young soldier near the front of the ranks, who didn't seem to be having too much trouble with his horse. "Corporal Carmody, you are responsible for the Stra--our guest. Be by his side at all times."

Daniel noted Gelnar's hesitation, but before he could consider it, the young soldier nodded and replied, "Aye, Cap'n," his voice filled with awe. He maneuvered around the other troopers until he was alongside Daniel. He nodded to Daniel before turning his attention back to the captain. Gelnar surveyed the troops once more then yanked hard on his reigns and started off, continuing away from the camp. The men fell into formation behind Gelnar, with Daniel and Corporal Carmody near the front of the column.

While Daniel had no concrete memories of the few times he'd ridden horses in the past, as soon as he sat in the saddle he was overcome by a nagging sense of doom. His fear seemed to center around the thought of being thrown from such a great height that he would at least be paralyzed, if not killed outright. Blue Belle, however, quickly assuaged those fears. She was a gentle mount with a fluid step. Her stature also helped, as she was so short that Daniel's feet almost touched the ground while he rode.

Around Daniel the men either spoke to their fellows or cursed their mounts as the hovels became sparser near the edge of camp. They approached a large hill and Daniel saw what he initially thought was thick black smoke swirling in the air, but he soon realized that wasn't quite right. The way the black mass moved was somehow wrong, but he couldn't quite place it. He was still trying to puzzle through what he saw when he noticed that the murmuring of the soldiers had died away.

Their faces had gone completely white and they refused to look at him, instead staring straight ahead. Daniel turned to Carmody to ask what was going on when he was startled by a cacophony of bird cries. He looked back to the hill, and now that he could hear them, Daniel realized his mistake. What he mistook for smoke was actually a huge flock of black birds. They swirled around the other side of the hill, continually landing and rising again.

Daniel's stomach dropped along with his jaw as he took in the size of the flock. *Flock*, he thought, *more like a swarm!* The birds flew so thickly that they blocked out the sky, and the land around the hill was made unnaturally dark. As the troops crested the hill the winds changed, and a horrendous stench wafted over them, making Daniel's eyes water. He turned his head to blink away the tears, and when he looked back, he gasped in shock.

The valley beyond the hill was like a scene from a macabre nightmare. Everywhere Daniel looked, there were bodies stretched out to the sky, staked to the ground. Most had been stripped naked, their arms and legs pulled wide. The black birds lighted on the corpses and stripped away flesh with sharp beaks, gorging on the horrid feast.

Most had been men, but there were some women as well. As Gelnar's force advanced into the horror, Daniel also saw what could only have been a child staked out alongside a woman and man. Fortunately, Blue Belle was a sturdy mount, or Daniel would have surely fallen when he leaned to the side and vomited. Rather than rear, she nickered and side-stepped to maintain her balance until Daniel righted himself, wiping his mouth with the back of a shaking hand. None of the soldiers noticed Daniel's momentary delay as they moved through the valley (*the Valley of Death*, Daniel thought), as most only stared straight ahead. While they refused to look at the carnage around them, Daniel couldn't look away. He raised a shaking hand and ran fingers through his hair, wiping away cold sweat.

The column continued silently through the atrocities, following a road that had once been brown dirt but was now blood-red mud. While the soldiers were silent, the valley was anything but, as the carrion brayed loudly and fought over the choicest morsels. Along the outskirts of the Valley of Death, coyotes and wolves prowled, gnawing on remains. Occasionally, one would pull a limb free and run into the encircling forests. Among the other animals that came to forage Daniel saw a very large cat. It was as big as a lion and had a coat like a cheetah, but its fur was black, the spots white.

Fortunately--blessedly--all the people they passed were dead. It was difficult to tell much from the stripped bodies, but Daniel had a sickening feeling they were the red-garbed warriors who battled the soldiers the day before. He looked at a particularly large bird roosting on the forehead of what may have been a man. As he watched, the bird leaned forward and tore off the end of the corpse's nose. It raised its head to the sky and jerked up and down a few times. After it swallowed it looked to the soldiers and cawed shrilly as if scolding them for interrupting its lunch.

On the rise at the far side of the Valley of Death, the corpses were less picked over and more readily identifiable. Most had large bloody welts across their naked bodies, as if they had been cut or flogged after being staked to the ground. The terrible scenes overwhelmed Daniel's mind and all coherent thought ceased. His mind simply refused to process any more as it retreated into darkness. The only fragmented plea to remain was repeated: *Why? Why?*

They continued in silence until they reached the very edge of the valley where the quiet was broken by a coarse laugh. He looked up with tear-rimmed eyes to see Gelnar chuckling as he looked to the side of the road where fresh horrors awaited. Men had been tied to thick sturdy tree trunks that were sunk into the ground and crossed like a large letter "**X**". Their arms and legs had been lashed to the trunks, and they were stripped to the waist, their bodies drenched in blood. It wasn't until Daniel was even with the first of them that he realized their shirts weren't all that had been stripped from them: the men had been skinned from neck to waist. Gelnar continued to chuckle to himself, and as they reached the last of the bodies, he turned a hard stare to Daniel. Loudly enough that all could hear, he said, "Captain Sturn does take pride in his work."

Daniel eyed him blankly until Gelnar motioned his head toward the last of the skinned bodies. Daniel followed his gaze and looked into faces he vaguely recognized. He gasped when he finally realized he was looking at the archer that saved his life and the guards from the command tent. Just when he thought he was too numb to be shocked anymore, Daniel felt a new wave of horror wash over him when he realized that all the skinned men must have been soldiers from the army itself.

The words of General Ignatius echoed in his mind, and he reeled as understanding finally sank in. *"When you are done, the three of you report to Captain Sturn for punishment."* Punishment in the Empire was extreme.

Chapter Three

They marched the rest of the day through recently planted fields and sparse forests. Thankfully, there were no more horrors like the Valley of Death. The troops traveled in silence for several hours after the Valley, until finally they began to relax and banter returned. They acted almost as if they had never seen the inhuman atrocities.

Daniel was more shaken by the experience than the rest and he traveled in silence, lost in his own thoughts. Perhaps his reticence came from not experiencing the rigors of war, or perhaps the men were forcing the jocularity to hide how deeply they were affected. Eventually, Daniel was able to shake the horrible images, though they would follow him in his dreams for a long time. As the horrified numbness receded, he became aware of the men talking and laughing. He looked around and thought, *How can they even function, knowing they could be punished like that?*

He stole furtive glances at their faces, trying to tell if their casual attitudes were genuine or contrived. As he glanced over his shoulder, he saw from the corner of his eye that the young corporal was watching him closely. He turned to Carmody and saw that his face was still pale under the dirt, but his eyes were no longer haunted, as Daniel's undoubtedly were.

The Corporal held out a flask. "This'll 'elp."

Daniel reached out a shaky hand and accepted the flask. He pulled it to his mouth, but even before he tilted it back, the strong smell of alcohol wafted out. Just the smell made his eyes water, but he pulled it to his lips and took a small swig anyway. The hot liquid burned all the way down his throat, and it was all he could do to keep from coughing and sputtering. His eyes streamed and he grimaced at the horrible aftertaste.

When his eyes stopped watering enough to see again, he looked to the corporal who nodded sagely and said nothing. Daniel reached out to return the flask and was surprised to see that his hands weren't shaking anymore. He could feel his head clearing as if the beverage knocked the cobwebs from his mind. The young man stowed the flask and squinted toward the horizon, his eyes narrowed to slits to block out the afternoon's brightness. The day turned hot and clear, without a cloud in the sky, and the troops followed a path that avoided the relative cool of the nearby shady forests.

When Daniel felt he could talk without coughing, he motioned toward the corporal's saddlebag. "What was that?"

He turned a curious eye to Daniel. "Andor. It'll cure wha' ails ye, er kill 'ya!" He chuckled at his joke as he stroked his chin. Daniel gave him an uncertain smile and looked away, but Carmody had evidently only been waiting for an opening. "Wha's ye called?"

"My name is Daniel Martin." Daniel held out his right hand to the man. He looked at it closely for a moment then snorted and looked away, never offering his own. Daniel let his drop. "You're Corporal Carmody?"

He turned an uncertain look on Daniel, as if he was having second thoughts about starting a conversation. After hesitating, he gave a stiff nod. "Ya, tha's right." He glanced around nonchalantly, making sure they were unnoticed before he asked in a quieter voice, "Where ye from?"

Daniel's stomach did a flip and his mind shot back to the interrogation. He forced himself to shrug off the fear and look squarely into Carmody's eyes. "I can't remember...I wish I could. I woke up by the field during the battle."

Carmody's square face lit up at the mention of the battle. "Tha was some woopin' wa'n't it? We *showed* 'em!" He laughed again, sitting straighter in his saddle.

Daniel didn't really want to talk about the battle, but he also didn't want to lose the ground he'd gained with Carmody, so he asked, "Did you do much fighting?"

Carmody shrugged. "Nah, I wa' jus' cleanup. Ya know, finishin' thems that wernt done in."

Daniel felt a cold chill run up his spine. "Done in? What do you mean?"

Carmody gave Daniel an incredulous look. When he spoke he did so slowly, as if talking to a simpleton. "Ya know. Done in. Not kilt yet."

Daniel gave a slow nod, trying to keep the revulsion from his face. *He killed the wounded. My God.* He had no idea how to continue the conversation. He looked around for inspiration and noticed how most of the soldiers looked so much older than Carmody. He motioned to them and asked, "Were all of these men on cleanup?"

Carmody's eyes and mouth opened wide. "Are ye daff? 'Em's the Elite Imperial Guard. They led the charge!" His face glowed as he thought of their heroics. "I's jus' ordered ta foller along here."

Daniel nodded as he scanned the column of fifty men. "Is this all of the Elite Guard?"

Carmody grunted and shook his head. "'Is...is jus' the First Regimen'. I 'spect the rest're still in camp."

The column slowed to a halt with much cursing from the men riding unruly mounts. Even with a sturdy and patient mount like Blue Belle, Daniel's anxiety got the better of him as the horses ahead bunched up. Blue Belle took it in stride, though, and didn't offer any resistance when Daniel pulled, harder than he had to, on the reigns. Soon the order came that they were stopping to eat and rest the horses.

Putting his booted toes in the leather loops along the saddle, Daniel pushed himself to standing and swung a leg over Blue Belle's rump. As his feet touched the ground, he couldn't hold back a groan. Evidently without realizing it, he'd been gripping Blue Belle tightly with his legs the entire morning. His thighs felt like iron bars had been pushed through the muscles.

Daniel slowly turned at the sound of snickers behind him and saw that some men were in much worse shape than he. Those with spirited mounts could barely stand and were hobbling around in a bow-legged stance. One man lay on the ground, blood running down his face. His nose was broken when his horse's head crashed back into his face as he leaned forward to stand. When he swayed back with a curse, the horse bucked and threw him from the saddle.

The man's face was beet red as he pulled himself to his feet and yanked on the reigns. He ripped a dagger from his belt and leaned in, thrusting it toward the horse's throat. He was stopped in mid-stroke, though, by a deep voice from behind Daniel. "Hold! Lose your mount and lose your place in this unit, Sergeant. We move swiftly. We won't be slowed because you can't ride."

All laughter died away instantly as Daniel turned to see Gelnar coming back along the line. As he glowered at the soldier from the back of his frightening mount, the beast's eyes roamed over the troops, a low growl rolling from its throat. Tufts of hair were falling out along the lines of its bridle, and bloody foam crusted the corners of its mouth.

The sergeant paled and snapped to attention, fear in his eyes. Daniel's mind involuntarily returned to the Valley of Death, and he understood the man's fear. He didn't think his position in the unit would be the only thing the man would lose if he disobeyed. "Y-yessir, Cap'n, sir!" His gaze submissively dropped to the ground though he maintained his rigid posture. Gelnar glared at him for a moment longer then grunted and nodded. His steed's growl was cut off as Gelnar yanked on the reigns and spun toward the front of the column.

As soon as the captain rode away, he turned hate-filled eyes back to the horse. Gripping the dagger in a white fist, he yanked the horse's head down and swung the blade across, slicing the animal's ear off. A shrill scream rent the air as blood sprayed the sergeant. The horse tried to rear up, but the man's iron grip denied it. "Do et agin," he growled, teeth exposed in a feral grimace, "an' I take t'other." He tied the reigns to a tree so tightly that the horse couldn't reach the grass or a bucket of water and stalked away.

Daniel was frozen by fear. He wanted to go over and loosen the reigns, but he was afraid what the man might do if he interfered. On wooden legs he led Blue Belle to another tree and loosely tied off the reigns. He turned back and saw that Gelnar was watching the scene with an amused look on his face. He shook his head and grinned before giving his steed another rough turn of the reigns and racing to the front of the column.

~ * ~

Daniel couldn't bring himself to eat anything, not with the memories of the morning ride still fresh in his mind. He watched the men walk to a nearby stream and scoop water with their wooden bowls, drinking and rinsing off the dust of the road. He turned to Blue Belle and retrieved his own bowl then followed to the water's edge. Daniel filled his bowl and pulled the liquid into his mouth, experimentally rolling it around his teeth and tongue before swallowing. It had a slight metallic taste to it, but after the long ride in the hot sun, it felt wonderful sliding down his dry throat.

Daniel drained the bowl and grimaced as his stomach gave a warning clench. He squatted for a refill, but this time poured the water over his sweaty arms, rinsing the dust away. From another bowlful he cupped water in his hands and splashed it into his face before dumping the remainder over his head. Daniel sat back on his haunches and sighed, feeling clean and refreshed.

He glanced around and saw Corporal Carmody coming his way. The corporal walked with a swaying stride, his legs bowed slightly as if he'd spent most of his life in a saddle. He knelt by the stream and asked, "'Dja eat?" Daniel turned pale just at the mention of food, and shook his head. The corporal nodded as if he expected as much, and slurped water from the bowl.

When his bowl was empty, he sat beside Daniel and the two took in their surroundings. On the far side of the stream was a large meadow which meandered into a copse of trees. In the distance Daniel could see cultivated fields and the scattered roofs of farm buildings. To their right Daniel could just make out distant mountains, so far away they appeared purple in the intervening haze.

Daniel sighed, enjoying the silence and a breeze that cooled his brow. He could almost imagine he was home, standing in the yard and...nothing. Again that wall blocked him, keeping his memories just out of reach. He barely contained a growl of frustration and suddenly no longer enjoyed their break. He glanced at his companion and watched Carmody stare in open admiration at Captain Gelnar as he rode his beast up to a group of men. He said something and they all laughed before Gelnar yanked viciously on the reigns and turned the animal in the opposite direction.

Nodding toward them, Daniel asked, "Have you served with the captain before?"

Following Gelnar with his eyes, Carmody grunted and shook his head. "My cohort jus' joined th army a fortnigh' ago." In an awed voice he added, "Idn' he sumpun?" His tone and the awe-struck look in his eyes brought to Daniel's mind the image a little boy meeting his hero.

"He must be a very good soldier."

Carmody's mop of greasy hair bobbed. "He's the bes'! Used ta be leader o' th' Blood Guard." He motioned to Gelnar and continued, "Still wears they's armor. Now he leads th' Elite!" Squinting at the black, ruby-encrusted breastplate, Daniel grunted. "Once, ten men tried ta ambush 'im. Got tha' long scar on 'is face then. Killed 'em all, though. I hear it took some of 'em *days* ta die!"

The glee in his voice chilled Daniel almost as much as the words. What kind of world was he in? He looked back toward Gelnar and could see the pale break in the captain's thick beard. Still looking in his direction, Daniel swallowed and offered a quiet, "Wow."

Daniel's hesitance didn't faze Carmody as he continued in the same awed tone. "They say e's seen th' whole *world*! I 'spect 'e's been ever'where! I 'us jus' on local militia till this war wi' Naphthali…"

Carmody trailed off and when Daniel was sure he wasn't going to continue, he asked, "Naphthali? What's that?"

Carmody finally took his eyes off Gelnar to glance at Daniel, and then he motioned to their surroundings. "Naphthali. 'Tis all Naphthali."

"Naphthali…is this country?" Carmody shrugged and nodded. "Why are you at war with them?"

Carmody shrugged again and looked off to the distant mountains, squinting in the bright sunshine. "Don' know. Th' Empire don' share th' reasons wi' me, see?"

Daniel hesitated before nodding. The two sat in silence until Gelnar rode by again, not bothering to look in their direction as he made his way back to the front. Daniel glanced out of the corner of his eye and saw Carmody once more staring in wonder. He nodded in his direction and asked, "What's that beast the captain rides?"

"Tha's a Quarenian Waye...very rare...very *'spensive.*"

Daniel watched the mount, looking closely at the long fangs and curled horns. "It is magnificent," he offered. The Waye cast a look in their direction momentarily, its eyes glowing green, before Gelnar ripped its head forward and continued on his way. The Waye's long hair rustled in the breeze as it galloped to the head of the column.

Carmody nodded, his eyes shining with admiration. "'S *perfect* fer th' Cap'n!" Daniel noticed the other men finishing meals and gathering their supplies. Carmody snapped out of his adoration and said, "We gotta hurry! Time ta' go." He jumped to his feet and shuffled back to the horses.

Daniel kneeled by the water's edge one more time and filled his bowl, then followed the corporal. He looked around to make sure the angry sergeant hadn't returned yet. There was no sign of him and no one else paid him any attention, so he poured some of the water into his cupped hand and held it before the wounded horse's muzzle. It snuffled the water and drank thirstily, quickly draining Daniel's hand. He watched blood run from the horse's

missing ear as he held up handfuls of water until the bowl
was empty. With each handful Daniel's anxiety increased,
and he darted looks around, watching for the sergeant.

Finally, the horse finished the last of the water and
Daniel hurried over to Blue Belle and stowed his bowl. No
sooner had he fastened down the bowl than the sergeant
came back, growling curses under his breath as he swung
into the saddle. Daniel patted Blue Belle on the neck as he
undid her reigns and mounted up. There was a loud horn
blast from the front of the column and Corporal Carmody
fell in beside Daniel as they continued through Naphthali.

~ * ~

The rest of the day was uneventful. They traveled
north, always within sight of the distant mountains to their
left, and set up camp at dusk in the middle of a large field.
Daniel winced as he dismounted, his legs screaming. As he
stumbled away from the horse, it felt like there was a large
barrel between his legs. He tried and failed to walk
normally, so he settled for a painful swaying as he hobbled
toward the picket line, leading Blue Belle behind Carmody.

They untied the blankets and bowls from their
mounts and hitched the reigns to the picket lines. Carmody
showed Daniel how to remove the saddle and rub down the
horses, and then the two returned to camp. They went to a
tent that had open crates containing fruit, jerky, and turnips.
Carmody grabbed a couple of pieces of fruit and some jerky
and motioned for Daniel to do the same.

Daniel's stomach growled at him, and with grim
determination he pushed away thoughts of the Valley of

Death, forcing himself to take two apples and a piece of jerky. They sat on the ground in an unoccupied spot and ate in silence. To Daniel's surprise his hunger overrode his unease and he devoured all but half of one apple. He eyed it hungrily before deciding to save it for Blue Belle and placing it in his bowl for safe-keeping.

When they were finished eating, Carmody escorted Daniel to a small tent near the middle of the camp. He held the tent flap open and as Daniel made for the entrance, Carmody looked apologetically at him. "You's gotta stay 'ere till mornin'." He paused and then mumbled in a lower voice, "Cap'n's orders."

Daniel nodded and gave Carmody a timid smile. "I understand." Carmody motioned toward the flap and Daniel ducked and entered. The tent was much smaller than the one he'd been in that morning. He had to practically crawl in, and the tent was barely long enough for him to lay out flat. He unrolled his blanket and lay down with a groan.

Just as he was starting to relax, he heard men marching toward his tent. They stopped outside and his hands went clammy and started to shake. He sat up and scooted to the back wall, huddling as far from the entrance as possible. His meager dinner threatened to come up, and he clamped down with all his willpower to hold it in. As his terror rose, he felt himself winding tighter and tighter like an overtaxed spring. His breathing came in fast gasps, and he was nearly deafened by the rushing of blood in his ears. Through the cacophony of internal pressures he just barely heard a man outside say, "You and you, here. Shift change in four hours."

The rest of the soldiers marched away as the remaining two took up positions outside Daniel's tent. It was several minutes before he realized no new horrors awaited him that night, and several more minutes before he was finally able relax. He lay back down with a dry chuckle and another groan as he stretched out his legs.

Through the haze of his dim memory Daniel vaguely envisioned himself running in the past. Relying on those thoughts, he did a hurdler's stretch: one leg straight while the other foot rested against the inside of the knee. He tried to lean over his prone legs, but his paunch got in the way before he could stretch too far, and the burning pain told him his muscles hadn't been exercised in far too long. *If I did run, it hasn't been for quite a while,* he thought, looking down with disgust at his soft belly.

He continued stretching for as long as he could tolerate it before lying back down. The soft sounds of a crackling fire and his guards talking to one another wafted through his tent, but those sounds were nearly drowned out by the constant drone of insect song. As he lay there feeling his legs slowly relax, his last conscious thought was *I'll never be able to sleep with that noise.* Then he drifted off and slept without dreaming until morning.

~ * ~

Daniel jumped as the tent flap opened and a guard glared inside. "Git up." The flap closed as Daniel rubbed the sleep out of his eyes. He could barely make out the tent's interior in the gray of pre-dawn as he rolled to his side and hissed in pain. The muscles in his legs screamed when he moved as did his back and stomach. With a soft groan Daniel pulled first one leg then the other, before him and stretched. The overused muscles refused to relax, so when Daniel finally gave up, he rolled to his side and sat up with exaggerated care. He crawled to the tent's entrance and poked his head out to see Corporal Carmody waiting for him.

Daniel stumbled out of the tent and forced himself to stand, feeling as though his legs were at least as bowed as Carmody's looked. The corporal nodded and said, "Mornin'." Daniel nodded back and he and Carmody sauntered to the mess tent. They took some fruit and Daniel couldn't suppress a groan as they sat down to eat. Carmody grinned. "Ain't used ta ridin'."

It was more a statement than a question, but Daniel nodded anyway. "No, I guess not."

Carmody nodded again. His eyes wandered around the camp for a moment before they came back to light on Daniel. "Wha' d'ya do?"

It took Daniel a minute to put together what Carmody said, but finally he asked, "What do I do? For work?" Carmody grunted. "I'm a pharmacist." That was about the only thing Daniel knew for certain from his previous life, and his answer came with no hesitation.

Carmody frowned. "Ya' farm?"

Daniel shook his head. "No, a pharmacist. I help people with medicines..." He trailed off when he saw that Carmody was still frowning.

The corporal raised one eyebrow. "Ya' mash up plants fer people ta drink?"

Daniel sighed and shook his head again. He had the clear idea in his head of what a pharmacist was, but he couldn't think of a way to convey it in terms Carmody would understand. Again, he had the sense that he was somehow out of time with Naphthali; that it was old-fashioned in some way. He looked back to Carmody and with a shrug said, "I help people when they're sick."

Carmody brightened and said, "Ah. Yer a healer. Tha' is good news." He turned his attention to his breakfast and devoured the food with gusto.

Daniel felt uneasy. The words Carmody used weren't exactly right, but since he couldn't think of any other way to explain it, he let it drop. He worked on his own meager breakfast, and when he was finished, asked, "What do you do?"

Carmody sat up straighter and said, "Ah'm a Drombiere." His tone implied that his was an important job. When Daniel turned a confused glance his way, his shoulders sank and he frowned. "Ya' know, a *Drombiere*. Like 'n all th' songs?" Daniel's continued uncertainty nettled him. "A *Drombiere*...'master o' horses, cattle, an' women.'," he said in a dramatically deeper voice, as if he were repeating a catchphrase. He shrugged and finished simply, "Man o' th' plains."

Carmody gave an irritated growl at Daniel's continued blank stare, so he quickly nodded. "Ah, of course. I see." *Must be something like a cowboy.* Carmody nodded again in a self-important air and returned to his breakfast, finishing with a belch. He threw the scraps to the ground and stood up.

Daniel groaned as he climbed to his feet, which made Carmody grin. "Come on, let's stretch a bit." They made a large circuit of the camp, each step initially sending waves of fiery pain down Daniel's legs. After awhile, though, his muscles began to limber up and the pain receded.

They finished their circuit near the largest tent in camp. It had two central poles capped with dark blue pinions, embellished with black and red hashes. Daniel was just thinking about stretching his muscles again when a loud clash of steel on steel came from the tent's far side. He and Carmody shared a curious look before walking around to a large open area where fifteen men stood in a circle, all stripped to the waist and sweating. Each man was armed with a sword and shield, and all were breathing heavily. While none were seriously injured, several had small cuts on their arms and torsos.

Gelnar stood in the middle of the circle, sweat dripping off his naked body. The giant already intimidated Daniel, but seeing the smooth ripple of bunched muscle and the road map of scars that covered his body made him even more frightening. He gripped a huge sword in one hand, and though the corded muscles in that arm were bulging, the blade continually moved as if it were weightless. A normal man would have needed both hands to hold the massive blade aloft, but Gelnar moved it effortlessly through sweeps and curls, constantly shifting position, looking for weaknesses in the ring of men.

Gelnar attacked a man on the perimeter without warning, forcing him back. His blows rang down, playing a staccato rhythm on the man's shield and sword until the ferocity of the attack knocked him to the ground. He flicked his wrist and opened a shallow gash on the soldier's cheek before dancing back into the circle. The downed man winced as he climbed to his feet and returned to his place in the ring. Suddenly four men charged simultaneously, trying to overwhelm Gelnar with sheer numbers. The captain was a blur as he parried and spun, defeating all four in seconds. He nicked each with his blade before he danced away once more, drops of his victims' blood glistening on his massive chest. As the four returned to their places in the ring, Gelnar surveyed his exhausted troops and laughed. The sound was hard and arrogant. "Enough. Prepare to ride." The men saluted and turned away, their weapons nearly dragging the ground behind them as they shuffled to their tents.

Daniel glanced at Carmody who was staring in open-mouthed wonder at Gelnar as he toweled sweat from his body. His eyes flicked on them for a moment before they moved on in disinterest. Daniel was speechless and could only manage an amazed grunt at the display. "'E's amazin'!" Carmody breathed. Daniel could tell just by looking that Carmody was reliving in his mind every thrust and parry. A horn sounded on the far side of camp and brought Carmody out of his daze. He motioned his head toward Daniel's tent and said, "We gotta git our kit an' go."

When they got back to where Daniel's tent was, they found that it had already been taken down and stowed on the pack animals that followed the column. His blanket lay in a tangle, covered in boot prints. He grimaced as he shook the dirt off and grabbed his bowl, and Carmody returned with his gear just as Daniel stood up.

"C'mon," he said as they hurried to the picket line. Most of the men were already mounted and milling in small groups, waiting to get started. Daniel saddled Blue Belle, and as he mounted up he realized that his sore muscles were nothing compared to his sore seat. He gasped as he lowered himself onto the saddle and closed his eyes, hoping for a smooth ride. He took a couple deep breaths before he reached back and took the half apple from his bowl and offered it to Blue Belle.

Gelnar galloped by as she ate her snack, and when he reached the front of the column, there was another horn blast. With a jolt that made Daniel gasp, the column started moving, continuing north through the Naphthalian wilderness.

~ * ~

The day proved to be hot and humid, and Daniel was drenched in sweat by midmorning. It was also a painful day. Even though Blue Belle was a sure-footed and gentle mount, it felt like Daniel's hips were being ground to dust, and every swaying step felt like a red hot spike in his tailbone. After awhile, though, he became accustomed to her gait and Daniel was able to move along with her rather than resisting her swaying stride. Eventually, the fire in his hips and thighs diminished to a dull roar.

By midday Daniel's ability had improved enough that he could think beyond Blue Belle's next step. He looked at Carmody, who was gazing off in the distance, daydreaming. Daniel cleared his throat and asked, "Is your home far from here?"

A look of such profound sadness filled Carmody's eyes that Daniel wasn't sure he would answer. Finally, he nodded and replied, "Yar, 'tis a *grea'* distance... When our militia was called, t'was a fortnigh' ride jus' ta meet up wit' th' army...a *hard* ride." Carmody looked to the distant mountains on their left, sighed, and looked back ahead.

"Do you have family?" Daniel noticed for the first time how young Carmody was. Layers of dirt and armor hid him well, and the sparse scruff of beard he managed was spotty, but now that Daniel was looking behind the manly camouflage, he guessed Carmody to be no more than sixteen.

Daniel saw tears swimming in his young eyes before Carmody brushed them away. "Yar, me ma' and da'...an' Gertie..."

Daniel let the silence drag out before he asked, "Your girlfriend?"

Carmody shrugged. "I don' know tha' word... Gertie was ta be mine, an' I hers." His voice trailed off, as if it pained him to speak.

Daniel thought of all he had been forced to give up and gently asked, "Why did you leave?"

Carmody looked at him incredulously. "Are ye daft? They'd've staked me whole fam'ly if'n I tried ta run, everybody knows tha'!"

Daniel was lost again. "Staked?"

Carmody rolled his eyes and spoke more slowly. "Staked. Th' Rule O' Ten. Ya' musta' hert o' it!"

Daniel shook his head. "I'm not from around here."

Carmody's eyes narrowed. "Where ya' from ya' aint never hert o' the Rule O' Ten?" He looked around, making sure he wasn't the butt of a joke, but as usual the Elite troops were ignoring them. He turned back to Daniel's blank look and in barely more than a whisper said, "If'n anyone defies th' Empire, th' punishment comes back ten-fold on 'em. If'n I refused service, they'da kilt ten people closest ta me…Ma', Da', Gertie, neighbors."

Daniel's eyes popped open as the term "staked" finally sank in. In his mind's eye he saw the Valley of Death again, and his stomach did a somersault. *They even do this to their own people!* He tried to deny the idea even as it formed, but to no avail.

Carmody knew from the look on Daniel's face that he wasn't making fun of him. He solemnly said, "Ya' don't *never* defy th' will o' th' Emperor."

Daniel had to ask the question burning in his mind. He could barely force the words out past the large lump in his throat but he finally whispered, "What about those soldiers that…that were skinned?"

Carmody paled and took a long swig from his flask before answering. "Th' Emperor's will be done. All know th' punishments fer misdeeds. Do yer job, follow orders, an' nothin' bad happens. If'n ya' do wrong, th' punishment is severe." Carmody scratched his sparse stubble with a shaking hand and added, "Least ways, it's only me tha' pays if'n I'm here. Gertie's safe." He nodded, as if he were trying to reassure himself. After a moment he shook off the dark thoughts and glanced at Daniel, his eyes shining with pride. "Bu' if she could see me now! Travel'n wit' th' Elite!"

Daniel's hands were shaking again. Visions of the horrible punishments he'd seen whirled in his head, and he started to feel queasy. He couldn't shake off the unwelcome thoughts like Carmody had, so he forced a smile and a nod that felt as contrived as it was. Changing topic, he asked, "Why are we traveling with the Elite, Corporal? Are we in danger?"

Carmody gave a covert glance around before answering, "Nah, nobody'd be dumb enough ta attack th' Elite!" He paused for a moment before continuing, a look of uncertainty on his face. "'Course, they say th' Naphthalians ain't righ'. Ta' fight th' Empire like this? Stark mad!"

Considering the punishments meted out by the Empire, Daniel agreed whole-heartedly. Sweat trickled down his back, and he looked, as he often did, to the shady comfort of the nearby timber. It occurred to him that they'd been avoiding those cool oases, instead staying out in the open where the sun beat down relentlessly. As Daniel thought about it, he realized it wasn't just the tree line they avoided. The occasional farmstead was always circumnavigated as well. They were certainly going out of their way to travel unnoticed, or at least as unnoticed as fifty mounted men could. With a touch of dread, Daniel thought that perhaps the risk was greater than they knew.

For a time conversation with Corporal Carmody died, which was fine with Daniel. What he'd learned about the Empire's brutal tactics convinced him he had no choice but to continue in their company. Surely, they would not hesitate to use those punishments on him as well if he stepped out of line.

The day proved to be hot but uneventful. The troops followed the same routine they had the day before, traveling until midday when they stopped for a brief meal then continuing until nearly dusk. After his evening meal, Daniel was sequestered in his tent. He drifted off to sleep and almost immediately found himself in the Valley of Death. As he traveled through the terrifying landscape, he heard Carmody's voice repeating the same litany over and over again. *"Th' Emperor's will be done...all know th' punishments fer misdeeds."* He finally woke, covered in sweat, and sat huddled in his blanket until dawn.

Chapter Four

The troops set out before dawn, and by the time the sun was up, the land around them changed. It was as if the wilderness was a large blanket that had previously been lying flat but was now bunched up into a series of steep ridges. The rolling fields and meadows were gone, replaced by many deep gorges and ravines, and the sparse forests had grown together, frequently stretching right up to the narrow paths the horses followed. Even the rivers took on a wild cast; where previously there were meandering streams, now the soldiers had to ford swollen and swift-moving rapids.

The men gave the dark forest furtive glances as they passed and buckled their armor on more tightly. Shields, which had been slung on pack animals, were now carried by every man. When Daniel mentioned the men's change in mood, Carmody shrugged and tried to appear nonchalant. "Nothin' ta worry 'bout." He pulled his own shield a little higher as he spoke, as if he expected an attack any minute.

Daniel saw their grim faces and how tightly they gripped their weapons, and for the first time he felt naked without armor and a shield of his own. While the tension around him rose, the change in landscape slowed the column's progress to a near standstill. It was as if the Naphthalian wilderness itself was conspiring against the invaders, slowing them down just when they wanted to speed up. A sense of claustrophobia started to creep in as well. The closely-packed vegetation loomed overhead as they descended into narrow valleys and made the valley floors almost as dark as night.

Daniel tried to chalk it up to the dramatic change in scenery and the paranoia of the men, but as they plodded along, he got the feeling that they were being watched. Whenever he looked away from the forest, the hairs on his neck stood up, and he'd swear that he could see movement out of the corner of his eye. He'd dart a look in that direction only to see branches swaying in a light breeze.

As they ascended to the top of a particularly high ridge, Daniel stood in his saddle to get a better look at what was to come. While he looked ahead, he felt the now familiar sensation of being watched and spun toward the forest. This time Daniel did see large green eyes looking back at him. He could just make out a dark feline face with white spots. The cat's coloring was such a close match for the darkness of the forest that Daniel would not have seen it at all if not for the eyes. He leaned toward Carmody and whispered, "Hey."

Carmody darted fevered eyes at Daniel who nodded toward the cat. He sucked in a breath of surprise and had his short sword half way out of its scabbard before he realized he was looking at a wild animal. His tense overreaction caught his horse off guard and it reared, throwing his balance even farther off. He managed to stay in the saddle but just barely, as his horse side-stepped closer to the cat. In a panic, Carmody pulled hard on the reigns and shouted, "Haw! Git over!" The commotion spooked the cat which let out a tremendous roar that echoed off the walls of the gorge.

The entire line froze as men spun toward the two, pulling swords and axes, ready for a fight. The great cat came partially out of the dense foliage, its ears laid back and fangs exposed as it crouched. It swiped at Carmody's horse, but when the mount saw its attacker it, screamed and reared again, once more nearly throwing Carmody. He yanked out his sword and swung back and down, trying to swat away the massive claw.

Daniel heard another growl as something rushed down the trail at him. He cringed away from the new attack but saw it was Captain Gelnar charging his Quarenian Waye toward the beast. He held his massive sword high in one gigantic hand as he charged. The cat spun to its new adversary, but when it saw the size of the Waye, it sprang back toward the cover of the forest. Gelnar would not be denied though. With reflexes faster than the cat, he brought his weapon whistling down.

The cat screamed like a woman when the blade connected with its shoulder, nearly severing its front leg. It tried once more to lunge into the darkness, but the wounded leg would not support it and it stumbled sideways. Gelnar jumped from his steed and lunged straight ahead with the great blade. The cat growled deep in its throat and bared its fangs but to no avail. Gelnar's aim was true, and the lunge drove his sword into the cat's breast, burying it almost to the pommel in gore. The cat whimpered as it slumped to the side, already dead as blood pooled at Gelnar's feet.

With a mighty yank he pulled his blade free as shocked silence gave way to cheers, the men crowding around. He turned to them with a wild grin on his scarred face. He raised his arms in the air, one holding the bloody sword and the other closed in a fist. Gelnar vaulted into his saddle and looked around. "You see? There is nothing in these woods but overgrown kitties waiting for our swords! We will not be stopped!" He glared around at the men before smiling and adding, "Put this beast on the pack animals. I need a new rug!" The men roared their approval and Carmody joined in, though he was still shaken by the attack.

Gelnar raced back to the front of the column and the troops moved on, but the morale boost afforded by his antics didn't last long as the men were soon eyeing the forest again. Daniel looked to Carmody and saw that he was glaring into the darkness, refusing to look away lest he be caught unawares. Soon the sense of being watched returned, and like an oppressive blanket it suffocated all humor from the men. They continued silently throughout the morning, only managing two more deep gorges before the midday break.

~ * ~

The men were constantly on guard as they continued north and the dark forest continued to hug the trail. As the hours passed, their attention began to falter, and eventually even Daniel's mind wandered. He thought about the bloody trail they must be leaving behind them, what with that cat's carcass thrown over a pack animal. Surely that would bring more predators. Thinking about the cat brought back to mind Gelnar's attack. *His reflexes were even faster than the cat!* Daniel shook his head in wonder as his eyes flicked to the top of the next ridgeline, and he did a double take. For a second he saw a man peering out of the foliage, but when Daniel looked back, he was gone.

He snapped a glance at Carmody but saw that he was dozing in his saddle. Daniel shook his head as he reached out to him. *If a man eater tried to kill me, I think I'd stay awake, just in case he had friends!* His arm was half way to Carmody when a piercing scream made him jump. Carmody jerked awake and Daniel's arm fell to his side as another man fell from his saddle, an arrow in from his neck.

Daniel jumped again and pulled on his reigns, making the normally sturdy Blue Belle rear and nearly throw him from the saddle. As Daniel fought to keep his seat, the trail filled with screams and the sounds of combat. Men bringing up the rear surged forward, but the trail was too narrow to allow them to advance far. Several men emerged from the dark forest and hacked at the soldiers caught at the trail's narrowest point. The fighting was fierce and fast, and the attackers melted back into the darkness before the men at the head of the column had time to react.

Finally, Gelnar forced his way back to the scene of the battle, and all that could be heard were hoarse screams of the dying and the captain's curses. Daniel was frozen, shocked at the speed with which the day melted into violence. Distantly, he was aware that his name was being called, but his horror held sway until the rage in Gelnar's voice snapped him out of it. "Get up here, Stranger! Now!"

Daniel woodenly shook Blue Belle's reigns to get her moving forward through the throng of men. They made room for him to squeeze through, and when he got to the carnage, he gasped. It looked like the entire trail had been painted scarlet. The man he saw fall with an arrow in his throat lay in a pool of blood. Beyond him were four men lying on the ground, and past them was another corpse with four arrows in his chest. One soldier had lost an eye, his cheek flayed open to the bone. A wound in his chest had soaked his cloth armor, making it look black instead of navy. He stared at Daniel with a faint glimmer of hope in his remaining eye as a fine mist of blood sprayed from his mouth with every breath.

Daniel tore his gaze from that eye and looked to the other three men. One was already dead, his throat sliced so cleanly and his head thrown back so far that Daniel imagined he could see the white gleam of vertebrae at the back of his throat. Another man's arm was nearly severed. It hung loosely at his side while he stared stupidly at the gray hand that he gripped with his good arm. The final man's stomach was laid open. He failed to hold his intestines in as they spilled around his encircling arms and he stared on in bewildered silence.

Gelnar stood among his wounded men and glared at Daniel as Blue Belle came to a halt. "Do something," he growled.

Daniel glanced from the men to Gelnar. "What?"

Before Daniel registered any movement, Gelnar was at his side. He grabbed the front of Daniel's tunic in his massive fist and jerked him from his mount, pulling him to within inches of his face. "*Do...something.*"

Gelnar's breath was hot on Daniel's cheeks as he hung a full foot off the ground. He tried to shake his head as he stammered, "I...I don't kn--"

Gelnar threw him to the ground, right into the man that was trying to hold his guts in. The soldier's arms fell wide and there was a wet ripping sound as organs slid from his body. He screamed in a high-pitched piercing wail as he watched his innards fall to the dusty ground. "Heal them!" Gelnar roared. "You're a healer. Do it now!"

Daniel pulled away from the screaming man and shook his head helplessly.. Trying to sound calm he said, "I'm a pharmacist. I...I can't help them!" Tears stung his eyes as Gelnar glared at him. His voice a whimper, he said, "I give people medicine...to make them better."

Gelnar grabbed Daniel and pulled him up by his throat until the two were nose-to nose again. He shook with rage as he glared into Daniel's frightened face. "Then what good are you?" He dropped Daniel to the ground and took a steadying breath. "If they die, it's on you." He stormed out of the blood, mounted his steed and sped out of sight.

Daniel lay where he landed and looked with wild eyes at the wounded men. He could feel hysteria rising up in him like a wild animal; if he didn't act soon it would break loose and leave him cowering and blubbering on the ground. He took a deep breath and forced the thinning screams of the gutted man from his mind as a cold detachment took over. *I can't help him.* The man whose arm was nearly severed was drenched in blood and his breathing was very shallow. Daniel doubted he could be saved, either, and he swung to the last survivor.

There was definite doubt in the man's remaining eye, but at least it was still focusing on Daniel. His breathing came in watery gasps and he held his right arm tightly against his side, but since he was drenched in blood ,Daniel couldn't see his wound. In an unsteady voice he asked, "Where are you hurt?"

The man didn't even try to speak as he motioned toward his right armpit. Daniel pulled a hunting knife from the soldier's belt and cut the soaked tabard away, accidentally nicking the man twice in the process. *I don't want to see this*, he thought as the cloth fell away. But he gritted his teeth and said, "Raise your arm."

He slowly raised his arm and a torrent of blood gushed from a deep cut between his ribs. Daniel grimaced and grabbed the ruined tabard, pressing it tightly against the wound. He pushed the man's arm back to his side and cast around, desperate for something to apply pressure to the wound. In his mind the same mantra repeated over and over: *Oh man...Oh man...Oh man.* His frantic eyes landed on the soldier with the arrow in his neck. He darted to the corpse and ripped the man's belt off, nearly falling in a pool of blood in the process. When he turned back, he saw that the sole survivor was paler, his breathing raspy. Daniel helped him sit up, ignoring the man's pain-filled groan, and cinched the belt around his chest as tight as he dared.

He sat back and wiped sweat from his face, not realizing that he painted blood across his brow. He looked to his left and saw a bearded soldier walk up to the man whose guts were spilled. The man was barely alive, his cries no more than a whimper. The soldier looked to Daniel with impossible hope in his eyes. "Can ye 'elp 'im?" He hesitated before shaking his head and looking away. Hope died and the soldier's eyes turned cold as he cut his comrade's throat, ending his agony.

The man with the severed arm had already died, his eyes staring off into the void with a look of sad shock on his too-pale face. Daniel wrenched his gaze away and turned back to the final soldier. His breathing was more sporadic and the glare in his remaining eye was glassy and fixed. Daniel took a scrap of cloth that wasn't too soiled and gently stroked the ruined side of the man's face, wiping away blood and sweat. The man breathed his last and Daniel's head dipped, his chin resting on his chest as tears came. He cried in impotent misery, both because of what he couldn't do for the men and in fear of what would happen to him.

After a time, someone lightly kicked Daniel in the rump and he looked up into the blotchy red face of Carmody. "C'mon." Without waiting for a response, the corporal led their horses away. Daniel looked around at the circle of dead men one last time then pulled himself to his feet and followed Carmody.

The men were left to rot where they fell as the troops continued their mission. Tension ran high as the soldiers gripped their swords in one hand and their shields in the other, guiding mounts with their knees. Everyone silently stared into the darkness that surrounded them except Daniel, who was too lost in misery to care. His clothing was stiff and scratchy from dried blood and the smear on his forehead flaked off and blew away in the breeze.

Carmody refused to talk to Daniel as they rode, other than to give brief orders. He'd told the others that Daniel was a healer which proved disastrously untrue, and now he felt betrayed. The Elite troops refused to speak to Carmody, and the earlier looks of disinterest they gave Daniel were replaced with angry glares. Though he traveled with forty-four other men (*fifty no more*, he thought with a sigh), Daniel was isolated and lonely. He had nothing to keep him company but the scenes of the soldiers' last minutes, which continually replayed in his mind. The rest of the day proved uneventful, but death now stalked the company, and more misery would soon come their way.

~ * ~

Dawn arrived and met the troops already on the trail. As they crossed yet another ravine, they gradually became aware of a dull roar coming from the west. As they continued, the deep roar intensified until eventually it drowned out all other background noise. They climbed to the top of one last steep ridgeline and from there could see the land open up before them. The gorges and ravines dwindled away to a series of steppe plateaus in the distance.

Daniel looked to the west, searching for the cause of the deep-throated noise, but all that could be seen were low-hanging clouds that masked everything like a thick fog. Where the land flattened into steppes, the rocky shore of a large lake jutted out of the fog, and towering over all were the massive mountains, as indomitable as ever. The mountains jutted slightly closer along the line the troops were traveling, and their craggy peaks offered a hazy reflection on the surface of the lake.

As Daniel studied the land, Carmody momentarily forgot his anger and leaned toward him. "Th' Spirit Callin'." Carmody had to practically shout to be heard over the roar, and Daniel jumped in surprise before he raised a questioning eyebrow. He motioned toward the fog and said, "Them's th' bigges' falls in th' world! Never thought I'd see 'em."

Daniel nodded and looked back to the west. *Ah, a waterfall. You can't see it, though. Not really.* Daniel smiled at Carmody and said, "Very impressive!" Carmody nodded once in cold indifference as his amazement subsided and he returned to his new routine of ignoring Daniel.

From the tall ridge Daniel's poor eyesight couldn't make out much detail, but as they continued to descend, he realized why the mountains' reflection in the lake looked so imperfect and hazy. The entire lake was a frothing mass of white caps. The Spirit Calling Falls dumped into it with such force that the water raced through the lake before emptying into a river at the far end, which was also filled with white water rapids. The river looked to be at least a mile wide, and just looking at the foamy spray made Daniel's hands shake. How would they cross *that*?

Daniel absently scratched dried blood from his clothing as he studied the river during their midday break. *If we get there, I'm gonna wash these out*, he thought, grimacing at the feel of the stiff fabric. By then they were close enough to the falls that its roar drowned out everything, and Daniel didn't even realize what was happening until men ran past him. Startled, he turned and could just barely make out screams and the clang of weapons.

His stomach dropped at the thought of more bloodshed, but he ran in that direction along with the rest of the troops. When he arrived, the attackers were gone and fresh victims lay in their wake. Gelnar screamed in rage at the forest, challenging the gorilla fighters to return and face him. As fearless as Gelnar was, though, even he did not dare to go into the forest after them.

Daniel turned from Gelnar to the wounded men, and his stomach dropped when he recognized one in particular. Light brown hair blew in the breeze, and though he lay face down, Daniel could just make out the spotty tufts of a young man's first beard on his cheeks. With dread in his heart he rushed forward and turned the man over. Carmody's shocked eyes stared sightlessly, blood and dirt smeared on his cheeks and forehead. His body was criss-crossed with wounds. One ran from his throat to the inside of his left elbow, and the other looked as though he'd been run through. Rather than pulling back out, the attacker had slashed the sword sideways and nearly cut him in half. When Daniel pulled on his shoulder to turn him over, his lower body remained where it was, held to his upper body by only a thin strip of flesh.

He blinked back tears and gently lowered Carmody to the ground. A shadow fell over him and he glanced up to see Gelnar's rage focused on him. Spittle clung in droplets to his beard and a large vein pulsed on his forehead. He threw back his head and howled, spinning back to the forest and demanding that his enemies come forth.

Daniel saw that four other men had also been killed in the raid, their bodies lying in bloody mud similar to Carmody's. After a few minutes Gelnar turned and glared at Daniel before glancing to his left, where the sergeant that had cut off his horse's ear stood. "Sergeant, you have custody of the Stranger. See to it that he's kept...*safe*." Gelnar's lip curled as he growled the last and the Sergeant nodded.

The captain stalked away. When he was out of earshot, the sergeant glared at Daniel and cursed under his breath. "Git up!" he growled.

Daniel stood and looked down at the bodies. "What about them?"

The sergeant was reaching for Carmody's reigns when Daniel spoke and he turned back to look at him incredulously. "Wha' 'bout 'em?"

"We have to bury them...or build a pyre... or something." Daniel could feel hatred rolling in waves off the sergeant and his voice dropped away into a mumble.

The sergeant jabbed a finger at the corpses and said, "They's dead, an' they failed th' mission, so they stay where's they are! Now c'mon!"

Daniel looked at Carmody lying in the dust and sighed. He wasn't a friend exactly, but he was the closest thing to it Daniel had met since waking on the battlefield. He started to argue his point again, but he saw the murderous look in the soldier's eyes and dropped it. He walked away with the sergeant and the column moved on, leaving their dead for the carrion birds.

~ * ~

Before long the sergeant studiously ignored Daniel whenever he could, though he never strayed far from his side. It wasn't much of a change from how Carmody acted in the end, but Daniel still felt even more isolated and depressed than before. Granted, he barely knew Carmody, and they probably wouldn't have been friends had they met under other circumstances. But they made a bond. They were the only two in the company that weren't Elite veterans, and Daniel missed him.

Daniel glanced at the sergeant, who was riding Carmody's mount after abandoning his own. He was staring into the encroaching forest with mild curiosity, one hand on the reigns and one finger of the other stuck up his nose. He caught Daniel staring and turned a nasty glare on him. He started to say something, but the roar of the falls blocked out everything but a loud yell so he stopped. Instead, he made a rude gesture before turning back to the forest. Daniel sighed. *No doubt about it, he's not Carmody.*

They reached the last of the ridgelines, this one little more than a rounded hill, and stopped for the night. Gelnar eyed the fog warily as he ordered double guards. Soon Daniel was in his lonely tent and had only the raw roar of the waterfall to keep him company. He sat on his blanket and clapped his hands together, but he could barely hear the sound. Daniel idly wondered if his hearing was being damaged by the falls, but then he shrugged. In his current state of mind it didn't really matter. He lay down and tried to sleep, hoping the Valley of Death and Carmody wouldn't visit his dreams. He needn't have bothered hoping, though, for they soon found him as he drifted off.

~ * ~

The day dawned bright and windy, strong breezes tugging mightily on Daniel's tent. The troops got a slower start because the constant noise hampered all communication, and by the time Daniel's escort came, the sun was already well above the horizon. He kept his eyes on the ground as he followed the sergeant to the mess tent, mostly because he was tired of the angry glares everyone gave him. When the sergeant stopped, Daniel looked up for the first time and gasped.

The strong wind blew the fog away and the Spirit Calling Falls were finally revealed. The surrounding mountains broke off as if a giant hand had torn them and the result was a jagged line of cliffs at least two miles high. The vast falls were at least a half mile wide and plummeted down the cliffs until meeting a rocky abutment about a hundred yards up from the lake at its base. The falling water exploded onto the rocky plateau, accounting for the deafening roar. As Daniel stared in awe, he thought, *You should have seen this, Carmody!*

He could barely hear the sergeant yell something over the noise. He glanced over and saw him talking with the soldier manning the mess tent. "Now *tha'* is a sigh'!"

Daniel leaned in and shouted, "It's called the Spirit Calling Falls! The biggest in the world!" The two only offered Daniel glares as he nodded and smiled. They turned their backs on him while they ate, but Daniel didn't care. *Thanks, Carmody*, he thought with a sad smile.

~ * ~

The going was much faster once the column left the ridgelines behind, descending into a swampy delta. The water looked thick and muddy as it practically flew toward the river, but as they got closer, Daniel realized that he was actually seeing air bubbles forced into the lake by the lancing water. When Daniel saw past the bubbles, the water was so clear he could see all the way to its rocky bottom. The incredible flow of water stripped the lake clean, leaving no fish or plants, and nothing but sterile rocks remained. Along the eastern end of the lake three small islands jutted out of the water, dissecting its surface before it flowed into the river. The river itself was even more intimidating than the raw power of the falls. Its full width was a maze of whitecaps and eddies, and periodically jagged rocks jutted out of the flow, adding to the danger and chaos.

The roar of the falls was so loud it blocked out everything else, leaving Daniel in a cocoon of his own thoughts. He was so focused on studying the river that he didn't realize the column had come to a halt until Blue Belle pulled up to keep from running into the horse in front of her. They'd reached the delta. The column stopped alongside a pool and the men led their horses to the water's edge. Daniel tethered Blue Belle and walked to a large boulder that rose out of the water. He stripped off his bloody clothes and rinsed them out as best he could before laying them on the boulder to dry.

Daniel climbed onto the boulder and jumped into the pool, the cold water making his heart race. For a second the chill almost brought a memory to the fore, but the walls in his mind pushed it back at the last moment. The usual frustration came rushing in, but Daniel pushed it away and focused on the present. The water made him shiver, but it felt wonderful being clean and free. Daniel swam for awhile, just enjoying the feel of the cold flowing over his skin, when suddenly he was swamped by a splash.

The sergeant stood on the boulder, his arm cocked back and ready to launch another rock. When Daniel stopped sputtering and coughing enough to glare at him, the sergeant lowered his arm and motioned for Daniel to come back. He ignored the malicious grin as he nodded and got dressed at the boulder.

The troops were in their saddles again, but the going was slower, what with the streams and rivulets to ford. They reached a wooden lean-to near the water's edge just as the setting sun cast it in a reddish glow. Daniel glanced inside and saw that it was filled with skiffs. At the far end of the lean-to was a rack half-full of long spears that had a series of metal rings attached to each. Instead of a spearhead, they were equipped with curved hooks similar to a grappling hook, and large coils of rough rope were piled alongside the rack.

The company came to a halt outside the building and men dismounted. Daniel climbed out of the saddle alongside the sergeant and started to untie his bedroll when Gelnar rode up. "Get the horses ready! We cross now!"

The sergeant paled, his skin looking pink in the rays of the setting sun. He nodded to Gelnar and walked down the line yelling instructions to the men. Daniel frowned. *Cross? Cross what? The* river? Daniel practically shook with fear, but he couldn't stop himself from following Gelnar down to the water's edge.

On the shore a stone pier had been built, and on that pier stood a large ballista. Gelnar and his officers inspected the machine while men oiled the mechanism, readying it for use. Daniel came to a halt alongside the ballista and his legs nearly unhinged when he realized what Gelnar meant by crossing.

From the end of the pier the small islands Daniel had seen before stretched in a roughly straight line, the first about four hundred yards from shore. In the center of the island a wooden tower had been built of rough logs, and stretching from the tower to the pier was a thick rope, hanging low over the water. In the dying light Daniel could just make out another rope traveling from that tower to a similar tower on the next island.

Daniel was pushed out of the way as men wheeled skiffs on a low wagon to the pier. Each skiff had a metal pole at either end that had a large hinged ring on top. When the skiffs were put in place, the thick rope was laid in the rings and they were closed and locked, fastening the boats to the line. They were going to use the series of lines and the skiffs to ferry across the lake at its narrowest point before it became too choppy at the river mouth.

Once he saw how they planned to cross, Daniel shared the sergeant's trepidation. This would be tricky in full light at midday, let alone the half light of dusk. Daniel could feel his heart beating in his ears, but they were still so close to the waterfall it was impossible to hear the panicked beat. He kept hoping Gelnar would reconsider, but soon the pack animals were led to the pier, their eyes shielded so they couldn't see the skiffs. They were loaded two to a skiff and their legs were hobbled so they wouldn't panic in transit. Daniel saw a dark mass spread over the top of the second pack animal: the pelt of the cat Gelnar killed. Its sightless eyes stared toward the river as the horse was tied in place, as if it were awaiting doom to overtake the voyage.

Five men climbed onto the skiff and positioned themselves along the rope line that ran its length. Ten men stepped forward and used long poles to push it off the pier and into the waiting water. The men on board grasped the rope and worked hand-over-hand to pull the skiff into the void. Once it was ten feet from the pier, the powerful current caught the boat and the rope bowed out toward the river, stretched to the limits. When the rope bowed the boat was actually pulled beyond the first island, and only the single line kept them from falling into the hungry mouth of the river.

Daniel saw equal parts fear and determination in the men's faces as they heaved on the line. It wasn't until they were half-way to the island that he let out the breath he was holding. That was when the groaning started, a tension-filled sound that was more felt than heard. Men ran to the pier and stared helplessly at the taught rope as it thrummed like a guitar string. Soon the note changed as individual threads of the line began to separate. The men on the pier screamed to their colleagues to pull faster but their cries were wasted, lost in the roar of the falls. It was obvious the men on the boat knew something was amiss, though, as they pulled frantically on the line. With a loud twang the rope snapped and the skiff yanked off course, giving in to the current pulling toward the river.

The sudden jolt knocked the men over, and one fell into the churning water. The man at the front of the boat dove over the side of the skiff, making a grab for the rope as it shot through the ring on his end. He caught the last frayed strands and pulled himself to the island, finally lying gasping on the rocky shore. His friends were not as lucky. The boat spun sideways in the current and the leading edge dipped into an eddy. In the powerful flow a small dip was all that was needed to overbalance the boat, and the men and horses slipped to that side as the pounding current flipped it over. In Daniel's mind he could hear the screams of the men as they went into the water, but the roar of the falls made it impossible to truly hear anything. The skiff was sucked into the river and soon it was smashed to kindling. The last the troops saw was a bloody smear on a plank as it floated over a white water crest before being swallowed by the river.

Though it was impossible to hear, Daniel could sense the silence around him as men stared at the river. Gelnar ground his teeth and roared, "Get a spear! We go *now*!"

The men froze for a moment, but they couldn't disobey. They retrieved a bolt from the shed and fastened rope into the eye rings along its underside. Once it was loaded, they rotated the pins on the ballista to pull back its huge arms and fired the machine, launching the bolt at the island's tower. The spear sailed through the misty air, trailing thick rope behind it as it landed on target, slicing into rough wood. The man on the island shimmied up the tower and tied off the line while men on land did the same. Another skiff was attached to the new line and the last two supply horses were led onto the skiff and tied down. Five more men, their faces pale and eyes wide in terror, took their places on the boat.

It was pushed into the water and the men pulled with all their might against the current to fight for dry land. This time the line held and the boat crossed without incident, its landing met with cheers from the men still on shore. The men on the island scrambled off the boat, unfastened it from the line, and pulled it around to refasten it to another line on the other side of the island. The boat rested in deceptively calm shallows until the men resumed their positions and continued on to the next island.

When they were about half way to the second island, Gelnar ordered more men into the next skiff. Since there were no supplies left, four horses and five men were pushed into the water. As they pulled for the island, the half light of dusk quickly gave way to the gray that precedes night. The second skiff made it safely to the first island, and then a third skiff was pushed off. This time the boat was lost in darkness before it reached the halfway point. Daniel stared at the dark water, wondering how they would know if the boat made it, when finally a lantern was lit and hung on the first island.

The third skiff was the last in the shed, and so the men left on shore had nothing to do but watch the darkness until another lantern was lit on the second island, then finally on the distant third. After about an hour all three boats returned and the men rushed to drag them out of the water. Six men did not return, and Daniel had a momentary stab of fear before he realized they must have stayed with the horses and supplies on the far shore.

The boats were loaded and pushed off again. It was now completely dark, and there was no way to mark their progress once they were more than a few feet from the pier. The men left on shore tensely watched the lantern at the first island until it winked on and off twice, then stayed on. The crews on shore waited about fifteen minutes before launching the next boat and continued until all three were swallowed into darkness. After another hour, the boats returned and were pulled to shore. Horses were led to the second and third boats, but not the first.

Daniel frowned at that until the sergeant pushed him from behind and he stumbled toward the empty skiff. He swallowed his fear as he stepped with numb legs onto the wet planking. The only animal loaded on the boat was Gelnar's Quarenian Waye, which continually growled. The green glow of its eyes reflected back on its scalp and horns over the blindfold that covered its face. Gelnar stood at the lines in front of Daniel, his officers and the sergeant making up the boat's compliment.

As they were pushed into the water, he grasped the rough rope with all of his strength, his fingers going white. They hit the water with a muted splash, and Gelnar started to roar rhythmically, "Pull! Pull! Pull!" With every yell he reached hand-over-hand and the massive muscles in his arms bulged as he pulled the skiff across the water. Daniel woodenly followed Gelnar's example even though terror gripped him every time he let go of the rope, and he was certain he'd be swept overboard. When they were ten feet from shore, the current caught the boat and yanked it to the limits of the line. Even though he had seen this happen to the other boats, Daniel was not prepared and lost his balance. His feet slid on the wet planks and he nearly fell from the lines, but he caught his balance at the last minute and grasped panicky hands to the rope.

He risked a glance toward shore, but it was lost in the darkness and terror rose up inside, threatening to overwhelm him. He was trapped out in the void, nothing visible in any direction except for the rushing water, feet from his precarious safety. Daniel's footing was unstable, and the rope was damp from the constant pounding, making his grip questionable as well. His life hung on the razor's edge as they fought the current and pushed on to the first island.

Daniel was so lost in his terror that at first he didn't realize what had happened when he felt a rough scraping on the bottom of the skiff. Thinking the boat was about to capsize, he yelped and instinctively gripped the wet rope even tighter. It didn't sink in that they'd stopped until the sergeant pushed him onto the wet rocks of the island. He glanced back at the sergeant who gave him a contemptuous glare, making it obvious that even though he couldn't hear it, he knew Daniel had cried out. He pushed Daniel again and led the Waye off the boat. Gelnar climbed up to the tower and pulled down the lantern. He held it toward the shore and closed and opened the shutter twice before putting it back in place.

He climbed down and motioned for Daniel to follow him as everyone unlocked the metal rings and led the boat around the shore to the island's far side. The boat floated placidly in sheltered water as the sergeant led the Waye back on board and hobbled it. All men reclaimed their positions and Daniel's bowels turned to liquid as they set out once more.

He gripped the sopping line with numb fingers and pulled every time he heard Gelnar's extortion. Soon they reached the second island then the third. While they moved faster than the other boats since they had only one animal to load and unload, time ceased to have relevance for Daniel. He was locked in a morass of pulling with numb fingers and searching for sure footing on a wet deck. Each time he released his grip he was sure he'd die, and each time he found partial purchase on the line he felt a surge of relief before he had to release his aching grip again. His shoulders burned, and he gripped the rope so tightly he wore blisters onto his hands. By the time they left the third island, the rope was wet not only with water, but also blood as the blisters burst.

At last their boat ground to a halt and he looked up with dead eyes to see that they'd reached the far shore. He forced his wounded hands to open as he stepped off the boat and finally his footing failed him. His feet slipped out from under him, and since he no longer had either hand on the rope, there was nothing to stop him from slipping into the cold water. The panic that had been riding him the entire crossing broke loose as he thrashed his arms and legs, adrenaline pumping into veins and a scream escaping his lips.

He felt a strong hand close around his collar and pull him from the water, and he looked into Gelnar's sneering face. "You're on shore! The water is barely moving, Cunny! Calm down!"

Gelnar dropped him onto the rocks and Daniel looked back to see that the water was indeed very calm where it was sheltered by the shoreline. His face burned as he trudged up the coast. The relief of finally being on dry land was tempered by his cowardly outburst, and when he crested a ridge to find a dry grassy slope, he dropped to the ground. He lay on his back and rested his right arm over his face, trying to fight back tears of both relief and shame.

After a time the sergeant prodded him with his boot. He was still grinning smugly but he said nothing, instead motioning farther inland. Daniel saw fires blazing within camp, which was already set up. He got to his feet with a groan. His entire body was seizing up from the tension of the crossing, and he woodenly trudged along after the soldier.

Blue Belle hadn't been ferried across yet and his bedroll was not available, so instead of going to his tent, the sergeant allowed Daniel to sit by one of the fires. He watched the glowing embers with dull eyes as he considered his journey, and miserably wondered again why he was here. Fifteen men had died so far, how many more would follow? The fire dried his clothing and after what seemed like hours, the sergeant nudged him with his bedroll. He took it without comment and trudged to his tent where he collapsed and was lost to the oblivion of sleep within minutes.

~ * ~

Daniel woke several hours later, the ever-present roar of the Spirit Calling still pounding away at his eardrums. He blinked and stretched, feeling twinges of pain from the overworked muscles in his arms and hands. He rubbed his hands over his face, wincing as broken blisters grated across stubble. Looking at the damage to his hands brought back the horror of the crossing and he shivered. He looked around his brightly lit tent, and for the first time realized something was different. He had grown accustomed to waking early and setting out before the sun had fully risen, but today that hadn't happened. Based on how bright it was in his tent, he guessed it to be at least midday.

He crawled over to the tent flaps and poked his head out. One of the men guarding him looked down before nudging the other guard with his elbow. The second glanced back and sneered before walking away as the first moved to block the entrance. Daniel shrugged and hunkered down on his haunches with the tent flaps blanketing his shoulders. Soon the first guard returned with the sergeant who glared at Daniel before motioning the men out of the way so he could stand.

He led Daniel to the mess tent where they were greeted by the mouth-watering smell of roasted meat. Daniel's stomach gave a hungry lurch and only the roaring falls kept everyone from hearing his own roar. Set up along the side of the mess tent was a spit holding the roasted carcass of a wild boar, its fire-blackened tusks still visible. The pork was delicious, and after so many days of dried rations, Daniel and the sergeant both ate it ravenously, heedless of the greasy juices running down their chins. They ate their fill and then the sergeant led Daniel back to the lake.

Daniel looked to the great falls and saw that the wind had died away and misty fog enveloped them once more. His gaze wandered across the water until it landed on the closest island. He frowned when he realized he'd missed the first two, and he retraced his line of sight until finally he located them. They were barely visible against the gray of the mist and the clear water that lapped at their shores. From each a thin line of smoke rose, marking where the towers once stood. Squinting into the mist, Daniel could just make out smoke rising from where the lean-to had been as well. Evidently the last to cross the lake had set the building and towers on fire as they went.

Daniel briefly wondered how they'd anchored the ropes if the towers were on fire when he sensed the sergeant leering at him. He leaned in close and yelled over the noise, "Yer friends won' be followin' us now!" Partially-chewed pork hung from broken teeth as he sneered.

He shook his head and started to say he had no idea who followed them when activity near the shore caught his eye. Three men walked to the water's edge and pulled back longbows, stretching them to the limits of their strength. Each had flaming pitch smeared on the end of his arrow, and as Daniel watched, each released their shot in succession. The missiles arced over the water, trailing tails of smoke. Two hit their mark on the wooden spires of the last tower, and it immediately went up in flames. The wood must have been soaked in oil to burn so quickly, and soon the entire structure was a blazing inferno, collapsing in on itself as it was engulfed. Before long there was nothing but ash and a thin column of smoke rising skyward to indicate that anything had been on that island as well.

Daniel turned back to the sergeant, but he'd abandoned him and returned to camp. He felt a stab of excitement and briefly considered fleeing into the nearby timber. Almost immediately the feeling was replaced by a sense of hopelessness though. He had no idea where he was or how to survive in the dense forest. He shivered as he thought of the great cat that had attacked them before, and knew his death would likely be quick and horrible if he chose that road.

As his spirits sank, he realized why the sergeant let his guard down and left him alone. *Where would I go?* Distantly, he believed that in his past life there was no need for survival skills, but that glaring hole in his abilities seemed careless in the extreme now. He was disgusted by his predicament. Gelnar's angry words when he tried to explain that he was a pharmacist came back to him: *"Then what good are you?"* What good, indeed. He was trapped with cruel soldiers, and he feared what horrors they would show him next.

Chapter Five

Daniel was surrounded by darkness, silence, peace. *Please, not the Valley again.* Even as the thought came, he didn't know what it meant. He closed his eyes. Open or closed, it made no difference; the darkness was all-encompassing. As if from another place entirely a thought came unbidden and incomprehensible: *I'm sorry, Carmody.* The thought might as well have been from another person, for all it meant to him.

More thoughts came, but none had any significance. Daniel wished they would stop so he could be left alone in the darkness. He wanted to wrap the peace and solitude around him like a blanket and forget everything. Then a thought emerged that did catch his attention. *I love you, Baby.* It was unbidden like the others, but for a moment he was overwhelmed by an upwelling of emotion and loss. That one almost broke through the darkness. He froze, his right hand extended, reaching for the answer like a man that couldn't swim, finding himself in deep water and reaching for the shore. The peaceful darkness was forgotten as Daniel willed himself back to the thought. What did it mean?

Suddenly, the darkness ruptured and blinding white light poured in. With it came a true memory, not just a thought that was submerged in his subconscious. "I love you, Daddy." The little girl's voice was as clear as a bell, and tears rolled down Daniel's cheeks. The blinding light forced him to close his eyes and look away, but he knew that if he could see past the light, all would be revealed. If he could see the face of that child, everything would fall into place, and he'd remember who he was.

The light vanished as suddenly as it came and Daniel grunted in pain as he was prodded. He opened his eyes and the soldier that poked him yelled, "Git up! Time ta' go." Even though he yelled, his voice barely carried over the Spirit Calling.

Daniel nodded and the guard let the tent flap close. He rubbed his face, the tender skin of broken blisters crying out when they met his whiskers. He ignored the stab of pain but did pull his hands away when he felt something wet. They were damp from tears. Perplexed, he looked at them and tried to remember what he had been dreaming, but it was already drifting off, fading. He wiped his cheek and the words tumbled from his mouth before he realized he was speaking, "I'm a Daddy. I have a daughter." He rolled the idea over in his mind and for some reason it seemed to fit. He repeated, "I'm a Daddy," making it more a question than a statement, trying to assure himself of its validity.

Finally, he nodded to himself as a smile crept over his face. Something had come back, hopefully more would follow. He cherished the fragment of a memory, holding it close to his heart. It would be his shield; it would protect him from the indifference he knew he'd face from the men.

With that idea bolstering him, Daniel left his tent and greeted the predawn with confidence and renewed determination.

~ * ~

The company was on the road before the sun crested the mountains to the east, and the wondrous falls fell steadily behind them as they traveled ever northward. The going was easier on this side of the lake, and by midday the roar of the falls was no more than a distant hum, allowing comfortable conversation for the first time in days. The way was flat but wilder, and their path was a game trail that wound through a deep forest. Massive trees towered over them, the land choked with deadfalls and brush. Huge white-veined leaves blocked out much of the sunlight, leaving the path in semidarkness and giving what light that did make it through a green and mottled hue.

The men traveled cautiously and quietly. They were surrounded by the raucous cries of forest creatures, which would inevitably fall silent as the men approached, but resume their excited song once the interlopers passed. A couple times they heard a great cat roar, which silenced even the fearless raptors that swooped through the trees. The fearsome scream made Daniel jump every time, and the men gripped their weapons more tightly. The cat never appeared, though, so their resolve was never tested.

The morning's easy going was gone by late afternoon. Frequently, they had to stop and clear brush from the trail, a problem that persisted for several days. Since they lost most of their provisions during the lake crossing, they also had to stop earlier each night to hunt for food. Usually the hunters came back with deer or boar, but sometimes they returned empty-handed and the men had to content themselves with hardtack bread.

For the next three days there were no guerilla attacks, and Daniel began to believe the sergeant was right: Maybe their attackers *were* stuck on the far side of the lake. Eventually, the men let their guard down, and even roars from the forest's predators weren't noticed. They kept a wary eye on the darkness, but it was not with the fatalistic fervor they had prior to the crossing.

As the troops relaxed, conversation flowed, but not to Daniel. He was a pariah, more often than not ignored entirely. The isolation didn't bother him though, because the cherished memory kept his spirits up and the silence gave him time to think. Unfortunately, most of that time was spent wheeling in frustration. He started with what he knew and tried everything he could think of to work around the blind spots in his memory, but to no avail.

When he wasn't puzzling over his past, Daniel wrestled with feelings of uselessness. His lack of survival skills trapped him with the soldiers just as surely as if he were being dragged along in chains. Forget for a moment the implied threat of punishment. Even if the soldiers had no weapons and no evil intent, Daniel would still be completely dependent on them. *Hell,* he thought with disgust, *I can't make it out here alone. I'd either starve or be eaten, but either way I'd be dead.*

Daniel's helplessness made him wonder where he fit into the scheme of things in his old life. He did have a sense of usually being in control in that distant place, but reflecting on how little control he had now, he wondered how much of that feeling was true and how much was illusion. He inevitably wheeled back with renewed fury on the barriers in his mind, trying to batter them down so he could see what was so important that he didn't prepare. The walls always proved too much, though, and loathing lowered his self-esteem even more.

As he entered the darkest days of his journey, Daniel became an automaton that stopped functioning beyond the minimum the soldiers required of him. The darkness swallowed him, and even though he was surrounded by people, he truly traveled alone.

~ * ~

Four days after the lake crossing the land changed again. The once impenetrable forest was punctuated by large meadows and through the thinning trees, pastures and farmland could be seen in the distance. The soldiers relaxed, and security within camp and on the trail became more lax as well. The double watches stopped, while Daniel's passive demeanor convinced Gelnar there was no need to guard his tent. Daniel took his meals alone and then either sat by the fire or went to his bed, never attempting to interact with anyone. The sergeant still periodically checked on him, but even that became less consistent as the placid days passed. The isolation didn't bother Daniel, though, because he retreated so far into himself he was barely aware of anything around him.

And so they continued on their way, blissfully unaware of the enemies that were pacing them. As they moved along that morning, they broke from the forest into a large clearing, and the organized line of mounted soldiers branched out. Elbow-room was sorely missed while they trekked along narrow paths, so when they came to the clearing the men meandered across the meadow, all organization braking down.

Daniel's mouth was dry, his eyes itchy. He tried to swallow, but his throat was dry too. A distant part of his mind cried out for water, but he was so self-involved that he ignored it and left Blue Belle to choose her own course. She followed the rider before her, who moved far to the right of the line, staying in the shadow of the wood on that side of the clearing.

Daniel was just thinking how much cooler it was in the shade when his wandering eyes landed on the large yellow horn that hung under the left arm of the soldier in front of him. It looked like a horn from a mountain goat, or possibly a Quarenian Waye, with a brass mouthpiece fitted over the tapered end. Though Daniel had never seen it, he knew he'd heard the horn many times. Its owner was Gelnar's lieutenant, and he blew it to signal the men during their marches.

Daniel watched, mesmerized, as a drop of sweat beaded up on the end of the lieutenant's curly brown hair. It grew full and round before it plummeted to splatter on the side of the horn, adding to its shiny luster. As the drop fell, it appeared to Daniel as if it'd slowed to a fraction of normal speed. He fancied he could see his own inverted reflection on its surface. It hit the horn and made a deep sound of its own as it shattered into hundreds of tiny diamond-like pieces that reflected bright sunlight everywhere. The inward focus Daniel had maintained for days dissolved as he stared at the horn. *This has to be a hallucination*, he thought distantly. The realization didn't deter him, though, as he disjointedly thought, *I wonder if I could blow that h--*

The thought was cut off as four men charged from the trees. Two carried long spears and one held a great sword aloft in brawny arms. The fourth held both a short sword and a strange weapon that Daniel had never seen before. It was shaped like a capital letter "A", but the slanted sides were honed to a razor's edge, and the crosspiece was wrapped in leather, which was where the man gripped it. The two razor sides came to a point five inches in front of the man's fist, and the sides extended back to his mid-forearm. Daniel's parched and grasping mind latched onto the name A-blade at that moment, and he considered the weapon that ever after.

All four men wore hardened leather armor and trousers which had been dyed various shades of black, brown, gray, and green. They had long dark hair that was pulled back and tied at the base of their necks in intricate plaits, and dark tattoos of geometric shapes and swirls covered their bare arms. Crescent-shaped tattoos covered the face of the man with the A-blade, and they had the effect of intensifying his dark piercing stare. They reminded Daniel of patterns he'd seen before and his mind immediately suggested they were tribal pacific islander tattoos, though he had no idea what that meant.

The man with the A-blade rushed the lieutenant and stabbed up with his short sword, angling toward his ribs. The surprised lieutenant gasped and slumped to that side as his breastplate deflected the attack wide. He pulled his sword free while attempting to right himself, but the man sliced the A-blade across his face, blinding him on the right side. As the punch reached past the man's head, the attacker reversed direction and slammed his elbow into the soldier's helmet, knocking him to the ground. The lieutenant rolled with the blow and spun to his feet, a grimace of pain and hatred further marring his ruined face.

He thrust his sword straight at the man's chest, but at the last minute the man turned so the blade passed by harmlessly. Using the momentum of the turn, he continued his spin and swung his short sword back-handed at the lieutenant's face. Simultaneously, he reached across his body and punched the lieutenant's armpit with the A-blade, bypassing his protective armor. The lieutenant stared in shock with his one good eye as his life's blood spilled onto the ground. His arms dropped, and as the man pulled the A-blade free, he yanked it back, cutting the leather strap that held the horn in place. As it fell to the ground, the man with the great sword, who had already dispatched another soldier, swung his mighty blade and shattered it.

The other two men knocked another soldier from his mount with their spears and were bearing down on him when an arrow sailed in and hit one of them in the bicep. He sucked in a breath as his hand dropped to his side, fingers losing their grip on the spear. He caught it with his other hand and stabbed it into the face of the fallen man, leaving it to quiver as the soldier groaned his last.

Daniel reflexively pulled back on Blue Belle's reigns when the men attacked. Within seconds their opponents were down and they turned to him. Blue Belle reared as they approached, back pedaling several feet away from them. The lieutenant's blood dripped from the face of the man with the A-blade as he looked intently at Daniel before turning at the noise of galloping hooves. Troops were converging on the carnage, and soon he would be vastly out-numbered. With a final piercing stare at Daniel, he and his men melted into the darkness and disappeared as Gelnar rushed to the edge of the clearing, roaring and waving his massive sword overhead.

The men arrived to find three more of their number killed, but still no enemy dead to accompany them to the next life. Gelnar turned from the woods and saw his slain lieutenant, the shattered horn lying beside him. He gritted his teeth as he turned a glare on Daniel. "Sergeant! You will *watch* him! He does *not* leave your side!"

The sergeant forced his steed up beside Blue Belle and nodded. In a quiet voice he said, "Aye, Cap'n."

Gelnar mounted up and the depleted company fell in behind him as he set off across the center of the clearing, as far from the forest as possible. The sergeant turned a hate-filled glare on Daniel. "C'mon!" Daniel joined the line of troops, the sergeant riding so close to him that their knees banged together the rest of the morning.

~ * ~

The attack pulled Daniel out of his inward focus. He needed to concentrate, and to do that he needed hydration. He motioned to the sergeant's water skin, but the man only glared for a moment before relenting and handing it over. Daniel drank deeply of the sun-warmed liquid until his stomach cramped and he sputtered and coughed. He handed back the bag with thanks, but was already analyzing the attack in his mind and didn't hear the foul words the sergeant growled at him.

The men attacked with speed and skill, unseating and killing the men with ease. Daniel was sure they were the same men as before, and he wasn't surprised none had been caught previously. His mind flashed back to the first attack: the man whose throat had been cut so deeply that Daniel could see vertebrae. *A punch from that A-blade could do that.* Then he thought of Carmody's death, how his body was nearly cut in two after he'd been run through. *That guy with the huge sword could've killed him.* There was no doubt in Daniel's mind: They were the same men that'd stalked them since they left the army, a time that seemed like months ago even though in reality it had only been about two weeks.

He replayed the attack in his mind again and realized something interesting: *he* was their target. They hadn't attacked until he was at the far end of the line, close enough to the forest's edge that he could be taken quickly. When they attacked, they killed all the soldiers around him but left Daniel unscathed. They even lowered their weapons as they approached Blue Belle before reinforcements forced them to flee. Then Daniel thought about the assault's aftermath and realized Gelnar must have come to the same conclusion. After all, he singled Daniel out and ordered the sergeant to watch him more closely.

Daniel felt a real sense of hope blossom in his chest for the first time. He knew Gelnar hated him and wanted him dead. Only the captain's orders kept him alive. These new men fought from the cover over darkness, making lightning strikes against an enemy with greater numbers. Aside from that, Daniel knew nothing of them, but he'd seen enough of the Empire to know that they couldn't possibly be much worse. If the opportunity to flee came again, he would take it and hope they'd help him. *And if not, well, at least I'll be away from these guys.* He looked around and saw that not only was the sergeant riding on his hip, but several others had formed up around him as well. Daniel gritted his teeth and held tight to his hope, promising himself, *If I get the chance.*

~ * ~

After the attack, they paused only briefly for water and to allow the men to get their shields from the pack animals before continuing. Those shields were now held tightly in place, steely gazes thrown into the foliage, but by then the clearings became continuous enough that they could for the most part avoid the dark woods entirely.

They didn't stop for a midday meal until several hours later than usual that day, riding on until horses and men alike were lathered in sweat. When they finally did stop, they were at the top of a hill that marked the end of the forest. The hill descended into small farms and grazing land that stretched as far into the distance as Daniel's weak eyes could see. The horses and men noisily lapped water from a small stream as Gelnar stood with his new second in command not far off. "We stop there." He pointed down the hill as he spoke, and the lieutenant nodded.

Cool water sloshed around in Daniel's stomach and made it cramp as he pulled himself to his feet. He looked in the direction Gelnar had pointed and saw a small farm that was set apart from the others, closer to the forest's dark edge. His full stomach cramped again when he looked at the small house. They'd avoided people this entire trip, why stop at a farm now? Daniel didn't have the answer, but the angry glint in Gelnar's eyes worried him. He passed on food and rubbed down Blue Belle while the soldiers finished their meal. Through the rest of the day Daniel's eyes kept coming back to the small farm. He prayed no one was home.

By dusk they were less than a mile from the house, and Daniel's hopes that it was abandoned were dashed. He saw a man in a field guiding a horse-drawn plow and a woman feeding chickens and sheep in a nearby pen. The woman caught sight of them and ran to the man. When he also saw them, they turned and ran for the house. With a whoop, Gelnar whipped his Waye into a gallop and raced toward the farm, his men forming a ragged line of speeding horses behind him. Daniel was still boxed in by the other soldiers and was forced to keep pace as they ran, even though he could feel his gorge rising.

The farmers almost made it to the house when Gelnar and his men wheeled in and cut them off. The man pulled his young wife behind him, shielding her from the men with his body as Gelnar jumped from the saddle and strode toward the two, his eyes narrowed to slits. The man's dusky tan didn't hide his pallor, his eyes big as saucers as he returned Gelnar's stare.

The captain stopped two feet from them and allowed their fear to build. When the farmer's eyes dropped to the ground, he asked, "Have you seen men come through here?"

The man shook his head and stammered, "N...n..." Finally he gave up and shook his head once more.

Gelnar gave a grim smile. "But I haven't even described them to you. How can you be sure?" The man stood silent, his chin quivering along with his hands. Gelnar watched him squirm for a few more minutes, silently letting the tension build until he finally spoke, his voice like ice. "We were attacked by rebels today. Living this close to the forest you must have seen them. You *know* what happens to those who defy the Empire, so I will ask you once more. Have you seen any men?"

The young woman started to weep as one of his hands slipped back and found hers. He gave it a firm squeeze and then let go. He raised his chin and stared straight ahead, not to Gelnar but at Daniel, and firmly shook his head a final time. With a roar Gelnar sprang forward, moving faster than Daniel would have thought possible. Out came his great sword and it swung down and around, slicing the man's head cleanly off his shoulders. His headless body fell to the side, and his wife screamed as the head bounced on the ground. She dropped to her knees and grabbed it, cradling the head in her arms. She wiped blood from the cheeks as her body wrenched with silent sobs.

Gelnar wiped his blade clean on the man's breeches as he calmly looked around the farm. When he was done, he turned to his men and said, "Take her." The men gave a loud cheer and bounded from their saddles as the sergeant rushed forward and kicked the head from the woman's hands. He forced her to her feet as she finally realized what was going to happen. She screamed and tried to pull away.

Daniel felt hot fear in the pit of his stomach, but overriding that was an even hotter rage that he didn't know he possessed. He jumped from Blue Belle and pushed his way through the men, throwing his shoulder into the unsuspecting sergeant and knocking him to the ground. He looked into the woman's face and didn't realize until later that despite the horror surrounding her, she recognized him. He spun and pushed her behind him as her husband had done, looking at the hate-filled faces of the men.

Gelnar watched Daniel's charge with a slight smile on his face, and he laid a restraining hand on the sergeant's shoulder as he lurched to his feet. Daniel locked eyes with him and said, "Don't do this. You *know* it's wrong."

Gelnar's eyes narrowed and his jaws clenched before he finally chuckled and turned to the men. "Well now, the cunny's found his voice! And I thought he only had eyes for the goatherd." The insult thrown at Carmody was met with silence as everyone kept steely gazes on Daniel, murder in their eyes. Gelnar turned back to him and continued, "You presume much, but I am a...forgiving captain. You may have a turn with her, but you've hardly earned the Right of Firsts. I will allow you time...before she's done."

Daniel returned Gelnar's glare and shook his head. "*Don't* do this."

Gelnar's lip curled as he released the sergeant. "Remove him." The soldier roared and rushed forward, and Daniel crumpled as his full weight crushed into his side, tackling him to the grass. He immediately tried to buck the man off, but three more soldiers rushed forward. The sergeant grabbed one arm and twisted it behind Daniel's back while another soldier did the same on the other side.

The other two grabbed his legs, and the four picked him up off the ground. He gasped as his arms were twisted even tighter, but he let the rage take over and as they carried him, he bucked and fought their grasp. He could hear the woman screaming, and it only intensified his struggle.

As soon as they were beyond Gelnar's line of sight, the sergeant kicked Daniel in the side of the head with his knee. Daniel went limp as they carried him to a nearby tree and tied him in a kneeling position to the trunk with leather rope. He started to come to as they finished. Already the cruel lines were biting into his flesh, making his arms and legs go numb. The sergeant forced a dirty rag in his mouth before grabbing his hair and punching him in the face. "Don' worry," he growled. "I'll give 'er a little somethin' extra fer ya'." As the men turned and walked back to the farmhouse, the woman screamed again. Tears of horror and rage ran down Daniel's face.

~ * ~

The woman screamed through most of the night. Her home was burned to the ground and her livestock were slaughtered. What the men wanted they took, and what they wanted most they took from her until finally her cries stopped near morning. If Daniel thought the Valley of Death was the worst he'd find in his dreams, he was wrong. He felt each scream tear into his heart as he knelt on his knees, bent back awkwardly and lashed to the rough bark of the tree. His arms and lower legs were numb except for the hot jolts that lanced up his thighs when he tried to shift his weight. He ignored the pain, though, and focused on her cries. Daniel didn't try to block them out; rather he pulled them in, even though they sundered his soul. With each scream he repeated, *I will resist...I will resist...I will resist.*

Finally dawn came to the cruel world, and with it came the sergeant. He hunkered down beside Daniel and growled, "I carved my name in 'er back. Anyone what finds 'er'll know who she b'longs to!" Daniel stared at him dully as he pulled out a hunting knife and held it up so he could see the fresh blood smeared on it. "Hol' still," he breathed. "Wouldna' wanna hurtcha!" With a rough yank he cut Daniel's bonds and let him fall to the ground.

Daniel bit back a cry of pain as he landed. Blood flowed back into his limbs, and with it came agonizing fire. The sergeant sneered down at him until the fire relented, lapsing into prickly pins and needles. Daniel struggled to his feet and glared at the soldier. He tried to speak, but only a croak came out, and as he coughed, the sergeant leaned in to hear what Daniel had to say. In a hoarse whisper he asked, "You can read?"

The sergeant's smug brutality was replaced by confusion until his face turned purple as the insult sank in. He balled his fists and pulled one back to knock Daniel to the ground when Gelnar shouted from the dooryard. "Mount up! We ride!" He glanced over his shoulder as his hand dropped, but before leaving to get his horse, he gave Daniel a glare that promised blood.

Daniel staggered to Blue Belle and somehow managed to pull himself into the saddle. He stared down at his hands, not wanting to see what they did to the woman or her home. As the men formed ranks, Gelnar rode to the base of the hill that rose to the dark forest. He glared into its depths and roared, "Let this be a lesson! All who would defy the Empire witness and tremble!" He spit on the ground and turned to lead the men away as smoke rose from the ruins.

~ * ~

The trek north led into rich farmland. By midday even the hilltop that marked the forest's boundary was lost from view. Daniel's mantra of resistance still burned in his mind, but as he was surrounded by neatly tended fields, he didn't see any way to resist. He also didn't see how the guerillas could attack without being seen, so he contented himself with biding his time.

The troops avoided farmhouses and the occasional village, instead cutting through recently plowed fields and pastureland. The few times they passed near villagers, the peasants bowed down in fear, holding their shaking pose until they moved on. A couple of times, though, Daniel noticed a villager see him and do a double take before cowering. As they passed the peasants, the troops closed ranks even more tightly around Daniel, ostensibly to shield him, but really just so they could offer horrid hints of what they'd done to the woman.

They stopped at midday in a large field filled with wild grass and alfalfa. The swaying blades reached nearly to their knees as they sat in their saddles, and looking around it was as if they were rising from the waves of a sea of grass. Nothing could be seen for a mile in every direction beyond the swaying heads that would be feed for livestock by autumn, so Gelnar ordered a quick meal. The men passed around haunches of roasted mutton, cutting off portions and sending on the remainder. Daniel's stomach growled at first, but chasing the hunger was the realization that the meat came from the desecrated farm. He shook his head when the sergeant offered him a juicy strip and instead drank deeply from a water skin.

When he finished his meal the sergeant slid from his saddle, mumbling something about having to stretch the snake. He motioned other soldiers to guard Daniel and walked into the wild grass, loosening his belt as he went. He wasn't gone long before Daniel heard a high-pitched scream. The men pulled their swords and forced their horses into a defensive ring facing outward, with Daniel and Gelnar in the middle. The grass rustled as the sergeant stumbled back into view. He was bent over nearly double, his only remark a wheezing whimper.

One of the soldiers grabbed his shoulder and forced him upright before cursing and pulling his hand away. The sergeant's trousers were scarlet, the back of his hand sprouting black feather fletching. His hand covered his groin, and the arrow effectively nailed the hand to the offending organ beneath. He gave a final high pitched groan as another arrow lanced through his throat and he fell to the ground, his bare ass to the sky as his life's blood pumped onto the field.

The stunned men stared in silence for a moment until arrows flew into their midst from all sides. One caught a soldier in the eye and he fell from the circle. Another man had taken off his breast plate for some fresh air, and he now paid for his carelessness as three arrows thumped into his chest. Yet another man was hit in the thigh. He grasped at

the wound as blood drenched his horse and soon he fell to
. the earth also.

Three more men were hit but not mortally
wounded, and just as quickly as it began the assault was
over. Gelnar spun his Waye in a circle, looking at his ever-
shrinking force. "Watch for the rebels!" he roared. The
troops ignored the cries of their dying friends and obeyed,
looking for any bending of the grass that would give away
their enemies' presence. After seeing none, Gelnar ordered
three men to guard Daniel while he led the rest in a wide
circle through the grass searching for the attackers, but to
no avail.

When they finally returned, Gelnar shook with rage.
After a moment's hesitation, he looked to Daniel and
growled, "You're with me now." He ordered the men to
form a defensive ring around the two of them, and they set
off through the field. Daniel smothered a grin as he
followed alongside the captain, envisioning his challenge on
the hillside by the burned-out farm. *I guess the rebels gave a
challenge of their own*, he thought, biting off a chuckle before it
could come out.

Chapter Six

The company stopped earlier than usual that night when they reached a tall hill that rose above the surrounding fields like a miniature mountain. Daniel was closely watched by two soldiers as he stood at the crest of the hill, but he ignored them as a sense of peace and longing flowed over him. Puzzled, he considered where the feelings came from, as his adventures lately had been anything but peaceful. Searching within, he found no answers, so he sought inspiration from the patchwork of pastures and plowed fields.

The loamy smell of earth wafted to him on a light breeze, accompanied by the sharp tang of manure. "The smell of money," Daniel whispered, not really knowing what he meant. He heaved a great sigh and took in the farmhouses and barns built at irregular intervals, dirt tracks leading from one to the next. At the very limit of his vision, Daniel saw where the dirt tracks merged into a wider road a few miles to the north. *Feels like home.* The thought was unbidden, but he knew it was right.

He lifted his face and closed his eyes, breathing in the commingled scents of summer on a farm. Daniel hoped the aromas would unlock more memories, but he was stymied. Gelnar stalked over and growled, "Come with me." He turned and left without waiting for a reply. Daniel glared at his massive back, wanting to refuse, but he was afraid Gelnar would punish innocents if he did. He heard the farmer's wife scream again, and a shiver ran through him. The two soldiers stepped close, but Daniel hurried after Gelnar before they could force him along.

Daniel caught up in time to pass through a ring of hastily-constructed defensive earthworks. He glanced to the base of the hill and saw hunters returning, a deer lashed to a pole carried on their shoulders. They walked alongside five men carrying buckets of water for the horses, which were being picketed within the defensive wall. Gelnar led Daniel and the guards to his own tent where he motioned for the three to enter first.

Once Daniel's eyes adjusted to the dim interior, he saw that the tent was divided into two rooms. The larger of the two took up three quarters of the whole and included the entryway. There were few decorations in the tent aside from a large ornate chest and a sturdy cot with a thick mattress set in the corner. Gelnar entered and pointed to the smaller room. "You sleep there. Food will be brought." As Daniel glanced toward the second room, he continued, "One guard will accompany you at all times. I can assure you, you will be very…safe under my personal protection."

Daniel shrugged and moved to the second room which was empty. He turned and saw one guard already blocking the doorway. "What about my blankets?"

Gelnar glanced past the guard and shrugged. "It's warm…I don't think you'll need any."

The guard chuckled and shoved Daniel back into the room. He staggered backward and sat down hard on the floor, his teeth clicking together. With a wince he eased himself to his back and was surprised to find that the floor really wasn't so bad with the soft grass under the tent. He sighed as he stared at the ceiling and let exhaustion flow over him.

He hadn't slept the night before (*Don't think about last night,* he desperately told himself), but he couldn't relax. He closed his eyes and tried to regain the peace he'd felt outside, but the smells of canvass, leather, and sweat surrounded him, confounding the effort. *Oh well.* No meal was brought, but he wouldn't have noticed anyway. He was already drifting off to sleep even as he tried in vain to find peace.

~ * ~

Darkness enveloped Daniel. He was assailed with disjointed memories and voices that didn't mean anything. The images and sounds moved passed his consciousness like a collage with no cohesion, nothing to help him pull the disparate pieces together and make sense of the whole. At one point he heard the agonized screams of a woman, and while it was just as foreign as the rest, he cringed away from the sound.

The broken stream flowed past Daniel for what could have been minutes or hours, but he felt no connection to any of the fragments until finally a smell brought him around. It was a light, musky scent and it immediately aroused an interwoven jumble of feelings. The first was wild sexual desire, but it was quickly overridden by a love so deep and fulfilling that he could never want for more. That was also quickly replaced by a sense of loss so profound that he could feel his heart breaking. He reached his hands out, wanting to pull that phantom scent to him and hold it close.

Without realizing what he was saying, he whispered, "Ashley." He folded his arms over the nothingness, trying to capture that one memory in the multitude that flew by. As his arms closed, the scent broke up and drifted away from him, and he cried out in anguish. Suddenly, he gasped and opened his eyes wide. *The light!*

As if on cue, the darkness tore asunder and a light so bright he couldn't look directly into it shined on him. Though the light was blinding, he did not turn away, because he was finally wide awake, and he remembered why he was there. He squinted and held up his hands to block the glare, only to see the light shine just as brightly through his hands, as if they were translucent. Even his mostly closed eyelids didn't block it.

He stared at the outline of his hand and thought, *I'm not really here.* And with that one thought, a light of understanding dawned within him that nearly outshone the glare in his eyes. *I'm not really here*, he repeated. *This isn't really happening outside my body...it's in my mind. And if it's in my mind, then the light is* also *in me! If I'm making it somehow, I should be able to turn it off!*

The epiphany shook him but not as much as the voice that sounded from beyond the light. Had Daniel really been standing, he would have been knocked to his knees by the sound. It was a young boy's voice, full of love and with a slight hiccup as if he had just been laughing hard. "You're my best friend, Daddy."

A name surfaced to go with the voice, and he gasped, the heartache too much to bear. "Nate! Oh God, I miss you so much!" Tears flowed down his cheeks as he reached toward the light again, yearning to hold his boy. His vision was blurred by tears, but even with that he could see his arms more clearly through the light, and then he realized the voice and light together were fading. "No!" he cried as the light dimmed and was replaced once more by the all-encompassing darkness. He fiercely shook the tears from his eyes and focused all his willpower on one thought: *Remember this! Nate, Ashley. Remember!*

Daniel grunted. He opened his eyes on the wall of Gelnar's tent before rolling over to see a guard standing over him, reaching out with a halberd staff to poke him again. Seeing Daniel's eyes, he lowered the pole and hissed, "Shut it! Ye're gonna wake th' Cap'n!"

Daniel blinked several times and nodded to the soldier, who snorted as he turned and sat down in the doorway. He rolled back toward the wall and pillowed his head on his arm, shivering in the cool night air. He was just starting to drift back to sleep when an urgent thought came to the forefront of his mind. *Nate, Ashley. Remember!* His groggy mind asked, *Nate? Ashley?* with no recollection. He was at the dark precipice of sleep when the names struck him and his eyes flew open with a gasp. *I have a son named Nate! I have a daughter too…is she Ashley?*

The new facts didn't draw other memories from beyond the wall, but they warmed him just the same. He was gleaning more, bit by bit. He closed his eyes and breathed a deep sigh. *I have a family. More will come.* He was desperately hopeful the statement would be proven true after he remembered his daughter, but now he was sure. *More will come.* That assurance was his last conscious thought as he drifted off to sleep again.

~ * ~

Daniel slept the rest of the night through without interruption, and his dreams were neither revelations nor nightmares. He didn't awaken until he was again prodded in the back. "Ow!" he mumbled, rolling away.

"Git *up*!" growled the soldier as he leaned over and jabbed Daniel in the kidney. The sharp pain made him cry out, and he scooted away from the soldier, bumping into the wall. He sat up, completely disoriented, his hair floating in corkscrews around his head.

It took him a second to remember where he was, and a full minute more to completely shake the cloudiness from his mind. After not sleeping for more than twenty-four hours, he fell hard and slept deeply all night long. He felt something crusty on his cheek and brushed the back of his hand over his mouth. When he yawned, he could still feel something stiff on his cheek so he traced the salty line with his fingertips to below his eyes.

The soldier left the room when he sat up but returned when Daniel didn't follow. His glare was enough to get him to his feet. "C'mon. Breakfas'." He allowed Daniel to leave the room before falling in behind him and directing him out into the half light of predawn.

Daniel smelled roasted deer meat before he saw it, his stomach giving a great growl. When the reached the cook fire, he grabbed a skewer of meat that was leaning out over the fire and sat down to enjoy his breakfast. Two nearby soldiers gave him dark looks, but with Gelnar's tightened security, they couldn't get up and leave him in peace.

They ignored him completely, but after a few minutes the silence that followed Daniel through camp was broken as one soldier turned to the other. "Couldna sleep half th' nigh'." He motioned toward Daniel without looking in his direction. "'E kep' cryin' all nigh' abou' Na'." His voice rose to a high falsetto as he wailed, "Na', 'member Na'! I tell ya', it was enough fer me ta wanna be staked out than listen ta anymore, sos I wen' inta th' room and thumped 'im see? Tol him ta shut it."

The other soldier chuckled, passing a contemptuous look over Daniel. He was at a loss until he did vaguely recall being awakened at one point in the night. It seemed he was trying to remember something when he drifted back to sleep, but he couldn't remember what. *Na'*, he thought, *what the Hell does that mean?* He took another bite of the steaming meat and was slowly chewing when it all fell into place. He remembered thinking he had a son, and his name was...*Nate! Not Na', but Nate!* The soldier's accent stumped him for a minute, but now he couldn't believe he missed it.

He smiled as he chewed. He had both a daughter and a son. *There was more. Another name...what was it?* It completely eluded him, but he was grateful for what came back. He turned to the soldier. "Thanks." The man was so surprised he looked Daniel full in the face. "I'd forgotten," he explained. The veteran paled, a look of fear flashing across his eyes when he realized he might have inadvertently helped Daniel. He looked around to see if anyone was listening before finishing his meal in a hurry. He and his friend left without comment, leaving Daniel to savor the small victory.

The name alone didn't bring back other memories, nor could he conjure an image of what Nate looked like, but he was happy to have that piece of the puzzle just the same. *Nate,* he thought, mulling the name over in his mind. *It's a good name. Nate, I'm going to find out more about you. And your sister.* Daniel felt buoyed up by the promise, as if articulating it would guarantee that more would come. Now he remembered the vow as well, and he repeated it: *More will come.*

A strong breeze blew across the hilltop, bringing with it the scents of summer farmland. Daniel breathed in deeply, closing his eyes and tilting back his head, savoring the hint of a home he couldn't remember. He looked to the eastern horizon where the mountains had receded and were a barely visible silhouette against the rosy dawn. He nodded as he looked to the rising sun. *It's going to be a good day. More will come.*

~ * ~

The ragged remnant of the company moved off the hilltop and marched straight across fields, abandoning the northerly course they'd followed since starting their journey. They headed almost due west, toward the point that Daniel had taken to be a road the night before. Most of the farmers they passed saw them coming long before they arrived and fled before them. Perhaps they'd heard of the couple living nearest the forest, or maybe they merely feared the Empire enough to be prudent. Whatever the reason, the company still traveled alone, even though they now passed through civilized lands.

Gelnar didn't care about the locals, but his men became edgy and quiet again, just as they had when the attacks first started. The few peasants that didn't run were cowed by the men as they glared and rattled swords, silently promising pain. The captain raised his chin and marched on, ignoring both the frightened faces and his men's tension.

Daniel rode alongside Gelnar, and as the day stretched out, he got his first close look at the Quarenian Waye since their adventures began. The animal had suffered greatly. All of the fur was rubbed away along the sides of its face and neck where the reigns lay, leaving weeping sores. The Waye's green eyes didn't glow anymore, either. They looked out at the world listlessly. Occasionally, it would growl quietly, but the sound was more like a whimper than anything else. Gelnar had attached garish streamers in the colors of the Blood Guard to its curved horns, and the bits of blue, black, and red lace blocked its peripheral vision. Consequently, it couldn't see obstacles when Gelnar hauled hard on the reigns, and it frequently stumbled. When it did, Gelnar had a cruel riding crop at the ready, and bloody streaks marred the sides of its dull, once shiny coat.

Gelnar sensed his attention and turned an angry glare on him. "What bothers you, Stranger?" he asked with a sneer.

Daniel nodded toward the Waye. "Your animal doesn't look so good."

Gelnar glanced at the beast before turning back to Daniel, the sneer still in place. "What would you know of it?" he asked quietly, dangerously.

Daniel had enough. He refused to be bullied by Gelnar anymore. He narrowed his eyes, his voice dropping an octave into what would have been considered his "authority voice" in another life. "It's a Quarenian Waye...very rare and very valuable. It deserves better treatment."

Gelnar's mouth dropped open, shocked that anyone would scold him. He quickly recovered, though, and his brows furrowed. He glared at Daniel, waiting for his nerve to break, but he was done playing games and simply returned the stare. Finally, Gelnar broke the standoff himself, looking in the direction the troops were going. He returned his glare to Daniel and growled, "You may be beyond my reach now, but that could change. When it does, *you--will--howl.*" He punctuated each of the last three words with a swat on the Waye's flank with the riding crop. The animal jigged to the side and wailed as fresh blood oozed.

He flinched and Gelnar smiled, satisfied that he'd put Daniel in his place. In reality he'd done nothing of the sort. Daniel flinched for the animal's pain, not from fear of Gelnar. His anger increased, but he realized anything he did to resist would only lead to more lessons. As if to emphasize the point, Gelnar pointed at one of the farmhouses they were passing. "Should I set my men loose?" Daniel looked down and shook his head fiercely.

Gelnar offered an evil smile. "Then I trust I will have no more...problems with you."

Daniel looked at the rivulets of blood trailing down the Waye's flanks and shook his head again. The evil of these men cut to his very soul, and his blood ran cold just thinking about what more they were capable of. He felt tears of frustration and fear welling up, but he forced them down. He would not give Gelnar the satisfaction of seeing how much his words and actions hurt. The captain snorted and turned his attention to their progress while Daniel silently seethed and cast around for ways to resist. Coming up with nothing he rode on in silence, trying to ignore the pain-filled whimpers coming from the Waye.

The company pushed on until they reached the road, which was a wide stretch of dirt so compacted it resembled solid rock. Their speed picked up considerably, but the increased speed did not lighten the moods of the men. Daniel felt the tension rising as they gripped their weapons tightly and closed ranks, riding almost knee to knee. Despite his efforts to appear nonchalant, Gelnar also felt the tension and seemed gripped by the same fear that compelled his men. He ordered them to continue beyond midday, not even allowing them to water their steeds.

All of the tension was for naught though. There were no attacks, and while they met more people on the road, the peasants hurried out of the way and let the soldiers pass without incident. Most looked down or hid their faces as the troops passed, but those that did not almost universally wore a look of amazed recognition when they saw Daniel. He was just as mystified by their reaction as he'd ever been, but he'd gotten used to it. He no longer did a double take when they stared, and if he caught their eye, he nodded curtly and looked away.

As the day waned, Gelnar led the men off the path and toward a barn set a mile back from the road. Several people bolted from the building and ran, prompting a soldier to point at them with his sword and shout, "Cap'n, look! What're yer orders?"

Daniel's heart jumped in his throat. He could hear the hunger in the soldier's voice, and he sensed the building excitement in the other men as they waited for the command. The captain looked intently at Daniel for a moment, making clear that *his* will ruled the day. Daniel refused to lock stares with Gelnar, though, and instead kept his eyes on the fleeing peasants. Finally he said, "Let them go. We've come for the barn."

The soldiers stifled their displeasure, but the man that spotted the peasants let a small groan escape his lips. Gelnar smiled. "Cheer up, Squirrel. Maybe they left you a goat." The soldier reddened but didn't respond as the men laughed half-heartedly.

When they reached the barn they found the owners had indeed left a small flock of sheep behind, penned in a paddock alongside the building. Gelnar ordered his men to halt and rode out between them and the barnyard, stopping and standing in his stirrups. He shouted loudly to the countryside, "I am Captain Gelnar of the Elite Imperial Guard. I claim this barn and its contents for the Empire! Any who own it shall relinquish that claim now!"

Five men dismounted and searched the barn while the rest set up a perimeter. They started a large fire with a stack of neatly chopped wood and soon had two of the sheep roasting. The men that searched the barn returned to report it empty, but there was feed for the horses and rooms that could be used for the night. Gelnar nodded and ordered Daniel inside.

The dark interior was a potpourri of the commingled scents of hay, corn, livestock, and manure, giving Daniel another pang of homesickness. Unfortunately, the feeling didn't bring any new memories with it, so Daniel had to content himself with the sweet pain. He was led to a small room with tack hanging on the walls and hay scattered on the floor. The door was made of widely spaced warped boards and hung slightly askew on leather hinges. The men shut and locked it as best they could before taking up positions on either side.

After a time two wooden bowls were brought to him, one containing steaming mutton and the other water. Daniel wolfed it all down and lay back, drifting off to sleep. The last thought he had was, *Please, let more come tonight.* His plea was not answered, but he did dream.

Daniel watched from above. A man held the farmer's wife behind his back, staring down all the soldiers as lust burned in their eyes. He couldn't see his face; only thinning salt and pepper hair and a sunburned neck. The man was telling them to stop, but faster than his eye could follow, Gelnar swooped in, his blade drawn. Daniel saw the gleam of steel for only a second before the man's head fell from his shoulders. The woman cried out and lunged for the head, cradling it in her hands. As she turned the face skyward, Daniel could see it for the first time. His own eyes stared sightlessly back at him. As the woman sobbed, she gently traced the scar on Daniel's cheek with her finger, rocking back and forth in her grief. With a crow of delight, a soldier charged forward and kicked the head from her hands. Then the screaming started.

Daniel started awake, crying out, "No!"

A muffled curse came from outside the tack room then a voice whispered, "Quiet!" The smells of the barn flooded into Daniel's consciousness, replacing the imagined smells of blood and sex, and Daniel realized where he was. He gave a great ragged sigh and backed up into the corner of the room, shivering and huddling against the cool night air. He slept no more that night, longing for the dawn.

~ * ~

The next day the soldiers remained tense and dispirited as they traveled in tight formation down the road, forcing farmers and merchants to the side until they passed. Once again, those that didn't avert their gaze stared in shocked amazement at Daniel. After several men in a particularly large merchant caravan studied Daniel with interest, he raised his left hand and felt the scar that blossomed on his cheek. The mild pain he felt when he awoke on the battlefield was gone, replaced by numbness. *Must have severed some nerves*, he thought distantly. Of course he didn't know what that meant, but by then he was so accustomed to his mind offering mysterious information that he didn't even try to decipher it.

He ignored the unhelpful tidbit and thought, *I wonder if this is why everyone recognizes me.* He probed the scar some more, deep in thought, and decided to conduct an experiment. Daniel turned his face away from the next few groups they passed so they couldn't see the left side of his face. He stole sidelong glances at those that didn't cower and saw no recognition. After an hour, he stopped hiding his scar and the braver peasants again immediately recognized him. *That must be it. But why would they care if I have a scar? What does it mean?*

He looked into the face of an old man and again saw recognition, but too late realized Gelnar was watching too. Daniel looked away in time to see the captain raise a fist, halting the company. His stomach shriveled in fear as Gelnar rode to the old man and stared down at him from the saddle. The man stared at his boots and began shaking when Gelnar finally leaned forward. "Why do you watch us? See something you like?" His voice was low and dangerous.

The old man slowly shook his head, his eyes large as saucers. "N--no sir. I was just watchin' ya s'all." His voice shook as badly as his body, and it died away to little more than a whisper near the end.

Gelnar basked in his terror before looking back toward Daniel, whose heart was racing. He chuckled at the fear in Daniel's eyes and asked, "No? You don't like what you see?" The old man's eyes grew even bigger and his chin started to quiver as he shook his head again. Before he could speak Gelnar continued. "You don't like the Empire? Are you a sympathizer?"

The man's voice raised an octave. "No sir! No! I d--d--do like th' Empire!" Tears spilled from the corners of his eyes, seeping into a nest of deep wrinkles. Daniel could hear his heart beating in his ears as the man broke into hysterics. He tried to spur Blue Belle forward, but the soldiers on either side grabbed his reins and held her in place, their excitement palpable.

Gelnar leaned further forward, bringing his face to within inches of the old man's. "I don't believe you." The man stepped back as he cried and shook his head, but before he could take another step, Gelnar's foot shot out and caught him under the chin. He flew through the air and landed on his back with a grunt. Gelnar jumped from the saddle and stomped a foot onto his chest, knocking the breath from him. "Squirrel!"

Squirrel trotted forward, his body practically thrumming with excitement. "Yar Capn'?"

"Teach this fool not to look upon his betters."

Squirrel jumped out of the saddle and pulled a dagger from his belt as he rushed forward and kneeled beside the old man. Gelnar removed his foot and turned, walking away in disinterest as the old man screamed. Daniel could only see Squirrel's back as his arm pistoned up and down, and the old man's feet kicked weakly with every wail. He felt his gorge rise but forced it down and barely held his own cries of hysteria in check. The old man's screams died away to sobs as Squirrel stood up and turned back to his horse, a fine mist of blood covering his flushed face. Behind him the man laid in a scarlet pool, his eyes a bloody ruin.

Daniel looked on in horror as Gelnar sidled up beside him. "You may not want to look at the peasants anymore," he said in his deadly voice. "Your gaze seems to cause them great pain." Daniel looked him in the eye, and Gelnar gave a wild laugh as he trotted ahead.

The company set off again but Daniel hid his face whenever they met anyone, fearing the same or worse if they recognized him. He forced away the compulsion to touch his scar as he thought, *Why is this so important?*

~ * ~

If anything, Gelnar's lesson with the old man made the men even more edgy. Some rode with bare blades resting in their laps. After a time, one of them brusquely said, "Turtle up," and with grumbling agreement, the men closed ranks until they were shoulder to shoulder. The outermost men held their shields high, creating a wall that protected them from prying eyes and ranged attacks.

The unfortunate consequence of "turtling up" was that even the slightest breeze was blocked out, making the already hot day even more stifling. The flanking men tired quickly from the weight of their shields, and they had to be rotated out frequently. The defensive stance slowed their progress, which led to much growling and cursing from Gelnar, but even he was unwilling to part with the protection, so they plodded along as the day ticked by. They continued without stopping until about mid-afternoon when Gelnar looked into the exhausted faces of his men and acquiesced. "We have gone far enough."

The men gave a tired cheer as they left the main road and made for a barn surrounded by a small orchard. This time no one ran from the structure as they approached, but Gelnar still loudly proclaimed the barn and its contents the property of the Empire. Daniel sat astride Blue Belle and watched as the troops prepared camp, luxuriating in the slight breeze that cooled his sweat-drenched body.

Four men opened a large door on the barn to search it, but as it swung open, one fell to the dirt and lay still. Time seemed to stop as he studied the man, perplexed. *Why doesn't he get up?* The other men jumped back and yelped in surprise as two men burst from the interior. Daniel immediately recognized them as the two that attacked before, and blood already dripped from the great sword the tall one was carrying. The other had his A-blade and short sword drawn and was in a low crouch.

Daniel looked around, seeing that the exhausted troops hadn't yet noticed the attackers. Still stuck in a horrible sense of slow motion, he turned back to the barn, his mind urging his body to rush forward and escape. Though his mind was willing his tired body was not, and while he couldn't urge Blue Belle on, the warriors were too busy to come to him. The man with the A-blade launched a complicated routine at one man, who immediately rocked back on his heels and was barely able to mount a defense. The man with the large sword deflected two attacks deftly and brought his blade up between himself and his opponents, swinging it around wide and to the side and at the same time spinning toward the two surprised men. At the end of the spin he thrust out with his elbow, catching one man in the throat, then reversing direction and driving the sword through the other man's side, dropping him in his tracks.

The ringing of blade on blade brought the other soldiers around, and with a mighty roar Gelnar charged past Daniel, his own massive blade bared as he closed on the larger man. The shorter man lunged wide, deflecting the defenses of his opponent before thrusting his short sword straight in and up, slicing through the sinews of the man's left arm and knocking him from the fight. The taller man blocked Gelnar's downswing as the other swung in close and punched out with the A-blade, puncturing the Waye's unprotected chest. Rather than pulling the blade straight out, he swung his arm wide, cutting a huge hole through the animal's breast and shoulder. It whimpered and toppled on its side, dumping the surprised Gelnar unceremoniously in the dirt.

The man with the A-blade spared a quick glance at Daniel before he and his companion slipped into the dark recesses of the barn. Gelnar roared and lurched to his feet, charging forward, but four arrows whizzed out of the darkness and stopped him at the door. One lodged in his breastplate as the others planted themselves with soft thuds around his feet. He glanced down and knocked the arrow from his armor, grinding his teeth in frustration as a ruby glinted in the sunlight, falling from the intricate plate with the spent arrow.

Twice the troops charged the barn, only to be turned by a hail of arrows each time. The second time a man cried out as he fell with an arrow in his calf. Gelnar ordered the men to surround the barn and set it ablaze when a dull roar and a large cloud of dust came from within. He led several men forward and cautiously advanced on the entrance once more. When no arrows greeted them, they broke into a run, screaming battle cries as they rushed the darkness. Their cries faltered and finally stopped, and soon Gelnar came back out, arming sweat from his face.

One of the men rushed to him and asked, "Wha's happen'd, Capn?" Gelnar sent an annoyed look his way before glaring at Daniel and storming off.

The soldier repeated his question as the other men left the barn until one finally answered. "Tunnel...they's c'lapsed it."

Daniel felt a crazy desire to laugh, but he forced himself to hold it in. He still sat in the saddle, and for once was unnoticed by the soldiers. He dismounted and as he walked toward the fallen men, he looked to the Quarenian Waye. Daniel was glad to see its suffering was finally over. He reached the barn doors and saw that the first to fall was laying face down in a muddy puddle of his own blood. Next to him lay the soldier that had been stabbed in the side. He lay on his wound, his head almost resting on his shoulder, a look of astonishment on his face. Daniel barely looked at him, though, as he knelt beside the other. He wasn't surprised in the least when he rolled him over to see Squirrel staring stupidly at the sky, a look of surprise permanently etched on his face.

Daniel stood and took a quick tally. Twenty-four men had died, nearly half of the total that set out. Twenty-four men that would not see their families or friends or homes again. Daniel felt a momentary pang of pity for them, but on its heels his mind shot back a bitter response: *Twenty-four men that won't rape or murder again.*

The old man, the farmer's wife, the countless victims in the Valley of Death came to Daniel's mind, and he reflected that maybe the deaths of these men were not so great a tragedy. Rather than tragedy, their deaths felt like...justice. Daniel nodded and his lips stretched into more of a grimace than a smile. *Yes, justice sounds right.* But even as he came to that conclusion, Daniel was filled with regret. The men should have been stopped long before things had gone so far. Justice was delayed, and many suffered horribly because of it. And even if their deaths were just, is taking one's life ever justifiable? *Yes!* Daniel snarled. His stomach turned as he forced himself to relive the abuses he'd seen.

Then he thought about Carmody, a farm boy that had little in common with the hardened veterans. Was his death justified as well? Momentary doubt set in and Daniel closed his eyes, running a hand over his face. As he thought about it he remembered discussing the battle with Carmody. Daniel could hear his voice again as he explained that he didn't ride with the Elite. *"I wa' jus' cleanup. Ya know, finishin' thems that wernt done in."* He murdered helpless men after the battle was won, and he showed no regret or shame for what he'd done.

With that damning evidence, Daniel resigned himself to the belief that yes, these men deserved what they got. Though the Empire forced their actions in some part and the punishment for not going along was severe, it would be preferable to committing such horrible atrocities. Daniel looked down at Squirrel one last time and nodded again. Justice had been served.

~ * ~

They slept in tents that night, the scent of wood smoke blowing through camp. Gelnar ordered the barn burned until only glowing embers remained, and then they ate left-over mutton and sour apples from the orchard. Daniel slept fitfully, followed into the darkness by the screams of the old man and the farmer's wife. Once he even dreamed of Carmody. Blood poured from his side as he looked at Daniel and asked, "Am I kilt?" He looked so sad. Daniel had never known him to look more like an innocent sixteen-year-old than he did then, as the light left his eyes.

Eventually, the sky began to lighten and he was collected by the guard standing watch. As the men mounted up, Gelnar walked to the front of the line, anger etched in every line of his face. He climbed into his saddle and was lost from view. Daniel was so used to seeing Gelnar tower over him that it took him a moment to remember the death of the Waye. There were no other animals at the farm, so Gelnar was forced to ride a dead man's shaggy pony.

As they set out, Gelnar drifted back until he was riding beside Daniel, and he nearly laughed out loud when he saw him. The poor horse clearly was not meant to carry as large a man as Gelnar, and it staggered under his weight with every step. His feet nearly touched the ground and the reigns were too short for him. As a result, he had to hold his arms down at an odd angle to control the overburdened animal.

The company rode for nearly two hours until they met a merchant caravan, where they stopped and Gelnar bartered with the head merchant. Soon they were off again, a large draft horse that had been pulling the merchant wagon unhitched and replaced with the shaggy pony. The small horse had no chance of pulling such a heavy load, and the merchant watched them go, anger simmering below the surface as Gelnar led the company on the stolen horse.

They rode for several more hours until a small village came into view on the horizon. A man near Daniel nudged his friend and motioned toward the town. "Standing Stone," he said quietly. "Got's a good inn…cold ale." The other man grunted before turning cautious eyes back to a small crowd that had been forced from the road as they passed.

Daniel watched the town grow as they approached it. With his poor eyesight, he could only make out a couple dozen wooden structures arrayed mostly along the axis of the road. *Standing Stone*, he thought, mulling the name over. As he studied it, he caught sight of Gelnar at the head of the column. He viciously drove the draft horse just as he had the Waye, taking his rage out on his mount. He glared ahead at the town and Daniel tried to swallow a large lump in his throat. *I hope this goes well.*

~ * ~

It was nearing dusk by the time they reached Standing Stone, and Daniel's initial impression of the town was largely proven accurate. It draped the road, its wood and stone buildings crowding each other and the thoroughfare that bisected them. It stretched for about a quarter mile, breaking only once near the center of town where a side street intersected the main road. Most of the two and three-story buildings were various businesses, with a few small homes built behind the shops, farther from the compact press of the town.

At the juncture of the streets two large stone monoliths jutted from the ground with a massive lintel resting overtop, giving the impression of a great doorway. The doorway was aligned with the main street, and looking through it one could see the road shrinking in the distance as it continued westerly into the setting sun. If seen from above, the last rays of daylight would shine through the monoliths, like the light from an open doorway shining into night's darkness. A large greensward surrounded the monoliths, providing an area for public gatherings. The whole looked like a green island in the center of the brown river that was the road, which bended around the park on its continual trek westward.

The company was still several miles distant when the townspeople spied them and cleared the road. The town was eerily quiet as they passed between the silent buildings and Daniel saw ghostly images of people watching from behind rippled glass. The imperfect panes rendered their images indistinct, but Daniel could feel their eyes on him, crawling over his scarred face. *Not again*, he thought with an anxious groan. There were too many people here for him to look away and hide his face; he just had to hope their reaction would not provoke Gelnar.

The troops continued to the greensward, where a large group of people had gathered and silently watched their approach. Some wore looks of fear and some looked on with hooded eyes, as if they were ready to defy Gelnar and the Empire. The men watched the villagers with their hands tightly wrapped around weapons, their eyes narrowed to slits, and jaws clenched in grim determination. The soldiers were in a state of hyper-vigilance, their gazes continually ranging over the people and buildings, looking for danger.

When the troops pulled even with the gathered throng, Gelnar raised his fist and they came to a halt in military precision. Total silence fell as the jingle of harness and armor died away in the still air. The men stared menacingly at the villagers and they in turn stared silently back. Gelnar passed his haughty gaze over the townspeople a final time before speaking. "Who leads here?"

The villagers darted concerned looks at one another, their gazes frequently landing on Daniel, but no one broke the silence. Finally, movement in the back caught Gelnar's eye and a young man with chiseled arms and a barrel chest made his way to the front of the group. Only a scarred leather apron covered his naked torso, and dark eyes peered calmly at the soldiers from beneath a mass of dark hair. Though not as tall as Gelnar, he was nearly as broad and well-muscled, and while he seemed unaware of the effect, his naked torso displayed his impressive physique quite well.

As the blacksmith stepped forward Gelnar recovered from his initial surprise and hungry eyes crawled over the young man, frightening Daniel. In a clear strong voice he said, "Our leader, Westragen by name, is ill. He rests in his bed."

Gelnar leaned forward in his saddle, transfixed by the young giant. He was unperturbed at first, but uncertainty crept into his face the longer Gelnar watched him. "Bring him to me," he said in a quiet, dangerous voice.

The young man blinked and slowly shook his head. "He is ill. He would have greeted you already if he were able, but..." He trailed off, uncertainty creeping into his voice as well.

Gelnar reached over his shoulder and repositioned the handle of the massive sword that was strapped across his back. His fingers caressed the leather-wrapped pommel before tracing down the back of his head and neck. "Bring him," he repeated.

The young blacksmith opened his mouth to reply, but closed it again, his teeth clicking together mutely. The calmness in his eyes was gone, replaced by fear as he nodded and walked through the crowd and down the intersecting street. Total silence enveloped the greensward as everyone waited. Blue Belle threw her head back and whinnied, and Daniel looked down to see that his shaking hands were pulling tightly on her reigns. He forced himself to loosen his grip, and she nickered quiet gratitude. Gelnar looked over, smiling cruelly when he saw the anxiety painted on Daniel's face.

Time seemed to stop while the men stared silently at the mute villagers, and after what felt like an hour but was probably only a few minutes, the young man returned. He walked slowly down the street, helping an old man wearing cream-colored robes that hobbled alongside him. The old man had snow white hair except at the apex of his scull where pink scalp showed through, and a long white beard hung down almost to his waist. They stopped several times along the way whenever the old man coughed weakly, bent over almost double. As they passed through the crowd, the villagers' fear was replaced by concern as their attention shifted from Gelnar to their elder.

They stopped in front of the captain, and the old man looked up with piercing eyes. The frailty of his body did not extend to the strength that was in those eyes as they bypassed Gelnar and stared intently at Daniel. After a few moments, he let his gaze wander back to Gelnar, whose jaw muscles were bulging. He spoke in a reedy voice, as if a tired wind were sighing through an old bamboo chime. "I am Westragen." He leaned into the solid support of the younger man as he raised a frail arm to gesture at the buildings along the main road. "I am elder here."

He may have continued, but Gelnar's rage could be withheld no longer as he stared murder at the old man. "You kept me waiting. My time is *precious*. If you don't respect my time, you don't respect *me*."

The young man quaked in fear, just as Daniel did, but Westragen was unfazed by the outburst. Daniel's voice shook as he said, "Please, Captain. The old man is sick, these people meant no disrespect." He hoped his words would mollify Gelnar, but they had the opposite effect. He glared at Daniel and sliced a hand through the air angrily, ordering him to silence.

Daniel wanted to continue but couldn't, fear quieting him as much as the gesture. Westragen looked keenly at him for a moment, sizing up the intervention before turning back to Gelnar. "Many apologi--" he began, but faster than Daniel's eyes could follow, Gelnar bounded from the saddle, landing right in front of the two. He launched a vicious punch that caught the young man in the solar plexus, knocking him back with a cry of pain and surprise. He lost the elder's arm, and the frail old man would have fallen had another villager not lunged forward to support him. Before the young man could regain his balance, Gelnar waded in and punched him twice more with mailed fists.

As he dropped to the ground, the captain turned toward Daniel, his chest heaving. "People?" he growled. His upper lip curled back to expose sharp white teeth. "You call this filth *people*? They're nothing more than curs that nip at our heels unless we put them in their place." Two soldiers jumped from their saddles and ran forward at a gesture. "These dogs need to remember who their masters are."

Gelnar turned back to his victim and ordered the men to stand him up. Daniel's bowels felt like water as he tried to nudge Blue Belle forward, but the troops on either side of him grabbed his arms and held him in place. The men grunted as they struggled to get the large man to his feet, succeeding only in getting him to his knees. One held him in a headlock and the other pulled his right arm out toward Gelnar. The captain pulled a small dagger from an ornate scabbard that Daniel had never noticed on his belt before. The weapon was made of a bright blue metal, its blade six inches long and tapering to a needle-like point.

"Stop this!" Westragen demanded, but Gelnar ignored him and closed on the helpless man. He grabbed his wrist, pulling his arm taught between himself and the men holding him, and rested the dagger's point against the center of the young man's forearm. He gasped and tried to pull away, but he was held fast. Gelnar slowly pushed the blade through the skin and on through thick muscle. The terrified man moaned as blood trickled down his forearm.

The captain stopped just short of pushing the blade completely through the blacksmith's arm and closed his eyes, lifting his face skyward. After nearly a minute, the young man's sobs took on a frantic tone as his arm started to change. The dusky tan faded to white, then gray as the bulging muscles thinned and sagged against the underlying bone. Within minutes, the once strong arm from the elbow down looked frailer than Westragen's, and the skin blackened, eventually looking like the desiccated hand of a mummy.

At last the transformation stopped and Gelnar pulled the blade from the man's maimed arm. He stepped away and his troops let the young man fall to the ground, where he sobbed and cradled his ruined arm. The men holding Daniel let go during the spectacle and paid for their lack of vigilance when he shrugged off their loose grips and jumped from Blue Belle. He dropped to his knees alongside the young man and looked helplessly at the horrible wound, unsure what to do. Up close it looked even worse, the skin almost petrified and the skeletal fingers half-closed in a rigor mortis-like grasp. With great effort, Westragen dropped to the grass as well and laid a helpless hand on the young man's shoulder.

His sad eyes turned from the victim to Daniel and the piercing fire returned. His reedy voice whispered, "My people *must* have justice. Help us, Stranger."

Daniel couldn't look away from his sharp gaze and gave a slight nod. From behind him, Gelnar spoke to his men. "The rebels are not here. Clear those buildings. We stay the night." He turned to the blacksmith, who was sobbing in Westragen's weak arms as villagers supported the two and Daniel kneeled helplessly beside them. He raised his voice, addressing the young man but speaking to all of the assembled villagers. "I am a...forgiving man. You will not die today for your misdeeds, but if you keep me waiting again, I will not be so gracious."

He grabbed Daniel by the shoulder and forced him to his feet. Looming over him, he breathed in his ear. "They won't forget their master again. Will you?" Daniel stared into his leering face and saw that something was different about him. Gelnar practically glowed, seemed somehow more vibrant. It was as if he was so full of life that his skin struggled to contain his very essence. Daniel was too shocked by the punishment and Gelnar's transformation to answer, so the captain shook him once for emphasis before letting him go. He walked to a building nearby where his troops were throwing villagers out of the open door.

Daniel turned back to the villagers, but the soldier that had been restraining him grabbed his shoulder and spun him around. He pulled Daniel's face to within an inch of his own and growled, "Try 'at agin, an' ye'll try nothin' ever more! Got it?" He too gave Daniel a shake for good measure before digging his strong hands into Daniel's upper arm and pulling him after Gelnar.

Behind them the villagers gathered around their fallen friend, fear in their faces and tears rolling down their cheeks. They fashioned a stretcher and carried him down the intersecting street, Westragen grimly leading the way.

Chapter Seven

Daniel was hustled through the door of what had to be an inn. The main floor was dominated by a massive stone fireplace that jutted from the back wall and was surrounded by a maze of small tables. A burnished oak bar ran the length of the room, and behind it was a large pass-though that led to a kitchen. Beside the pass-through were two large wooden casks and wooden tankards lined shelves nearby. The room practically glowed, from the highly polished wood to the spotless furnishings, and Daniel was sure that ordinarily it was probably a very cheery place. Currently, however, the place was filled to the rafters with tension.

About ten soldiers ransacked the common room, upending tables and stacking chairs to provide cover if the inn was overrun. They spoke in clipped, quiet tones, eyeing the door and windows warily. Off to the side Gelnar stomped down a large curving staircase that led to the rooms above. He held a terrified boy by the scruff of the neck at arm's length, ignoring both his whimpers and weak struggles. The boy looked to be about ten, his face pale and lips quivering as he tried to hold back tears. The captain surveyed the room until he found one of the soldiers that had stopped moving furniture. He also had turned pale and snapped to attention when Gelnar stalked to him, shaking the boy in his face and growling, "You missed one."

He stammered, "S--sorry sir!" His voice lowered as he added, "I was…was savin' 'im…fer later." The man flushed but remained at attention as Gelnar smirked.

He stormed to the door and threw the boy outside where he sprawled in the dust before scampering away. Gelnar came back to the soldier and in a deadly, quiet voice said, "Keep it in your pants. I'm sure we could destroy this whole damn town, but we have a mission to complete. We don't have time to waste." The soldier's Adam's apple bobbed as he saluted. Gelnar smirked as he turned back to Daniel. His humor evaporated as he leaned in close and said, "If you try anything, anything at all, these people will burn."

Menace rolled off him and crashed over Daniel in waves. "All right," he mumbled. His eyes dropped to the small dagger in Gelnar's belt. The blue of the metal matched the blue in Gelnar's uniform, making it practically invisible unless you knew what to look for.

Gelnar saw where his eyes landed and chuckled. He patted the small blade and said, "Perhaps you'll get to see it again sometime. If you do, pray it's the last thing you ever see."

Daniel's eyes dropped to the floor. The blue blade frightened him badly, even more than the big man's brutality. However his adventure was to end, he hoped it wasn't at the point of that evil dagger. Without raising his eyes, he murmured something unintelligible which Gelnar ignored. He turned to the guard that still had Daniel's arm in a vice-like grip and motioned to the stairs. "Put him in the room at the end of the hall and stand guard."

With his free arm the soldier saluted. "Yessir." He marched Daniel upstairs to the second floor, which contained a long hallway lined with closed doors. He opened a door at the end of the hall to find a small room with only a bed and desk. He shoved Daniel inside and slammed the door, leaving him in semi-darkness punctuated only by a shaft of dim light that shone through the crack at the bottom of the door.

Daniel stood still until his eyes adjusted then he sat down on the bed and let out a long breath. The darkness was warm and inviting, the bed soft. He laid back and as he started to drift off, he cast his mind over his adventures. He was almost asleep when he realized that this was the first time in what felt like an eternity that he'd been in a proper bed. He sighed again, and the darkness claimed him, pulling him into deep sleep.

~ * ~

Daniel was once again within the dark void, surrounded by peace and quiet. For a long time there was only blissful silence, and he wasn't even aware of himself, so to speak. All that existed was darkness, and in that darkness one could retreat and hide from chaos. Gradually some level of awareness penetrated the cocoon of darkness, and Daniel realized that his eyes were closed. Not sure that he wanted to, but feeling he must, he hesitantly opened them. The darkness surrounding him was so profound that opening his eyes made no difference. With a great sigh he closed them again, hoping to find his way back into the cocoon, to stay there forever. *Better this than the alternative.* He was just drifting away when the thought sunk in, and his eyes snapped open again. *What alternative? What am I hiding from?*

As soon as the questions were asked, the stream of incoherent images and sounds began. Each had a voice of its own and clamored for him to pay it heed. The whole was such a jarring contrast to the silence that Daniel threw his hands to his ears, trying in vain to block out the cacophony. He began to wail in despair for silence when it occurred to him that this had happened before. He listened more closely to the voices as they swept by. While most were still too jumbled or fleeting for him to catch, a few were decipherable.

He distinctly heard a man's quiet, threatening voice say, *"They won't forget their master again. Will you?"* He flinched away from the voice and continued to scan the stream, trying to pick out coherent strands. The next one was a woman screaming, and his blood froze. A cold sweat broke out on his forehead, and he very nearly bolted for the darkness again. With great effort, he forced himself to turn back to the stream and was almost immediately rewarded. He distinctly heard his own voice say, *"I love you."* There was a brief pause, one filled with remembered anxiety, before a female voice replied, *"I love you too."*

Daniel's heart jumped into his throat, and his eyes opened wide. With the two voices came a certainty: that was the first time. The first time he'd told…Ashley! His wife was Ashley, and that was the first time he told her he loved her. Daniel knew what was coming next, and he closed his eyes and turned his head as a great rent sundered the fabric of the darkness, allowing blinding light to spill through. He knew what he had to do. Closing his eyes as tightly as he could, Daniel turned to face the light, but it burned through his closed eyelids, blinding despite his effort to hold it out. With a gasp he threw back his head, his arms and legs flung out wide as he opened his eyes, staring directly into the light.

It was overpowering, uncontrollable. Daniel couldn't stand against it, nor could he peer through it to see what he needed. It burned into him, cauterizing his mind with the intensity of what it contained. It was so close Daniel could feel it, could almost reach out and touch what was missing, what kept him from being whole. In frustration he staggered back and felt his footing give way under him. The unseen floor he stood on tilted, and he went with it, falling away from the light and back into the darkness. As he plummeted, Daniel howled. He remembered his wife's name, and he could remember the love he felt for Ashley, but there was still that damnable wall blocking him from embracing her.

The darkness was no longer inviting, the cocoon not a comfort. It was really a prison, holding Daniel back from himself, and he hated it. In his rage and misery he struck at the darkness. Though there was nothing there, once he started he couldn't stop. Before he knew it, he was punching and kicking and screaming with all his might.

Suddenly there *was* something there, as one of his punches connected with a soft mass. In surprise he twisted his arm and pulled back, but the hidden thing captured him and held him fast. Daniel twisted and bucked as he tried to pull free, his rage giving way to panic when he couldn't. He lost all coherent thought and gave a mighty tug that, while not freeing his hand, did make him teeter over. He was once more in free fall and whatever held him fell with him.

With a great jolt Daniel landed on the floor and cried out as his arm twisted behind him. He rolled to his side and pulled his arm out to see that bedding had somehow wrapped around it while he slept. He gently removed the coverings and flexed his hand a few times, wincing in pain. As he worked his hand, he looked around the room and in the dim light could make out a tray lying before the closed door. It held cold meat and bread, as well as a tankard of water, and his stomach growled hungrily as he devoured it all.

When the tray was empty, he turned back to the bed and a feeling of love washed over him. It was so heartbreakingly intense that he stopped in his tracks with a gasp. Seconds later, he whispered the name into the dark room. "Ashley." As he staggered to the bed, his legs gave out and he fell onto it. He sat up and rested his elbows on his knees, leaning forward and holding his head, his palms over his temples.

He had a new piece to the puzzle, and he incorporated it into what he already knew, repeating it several times to commit it to memory. "Ashley...Nate...my daughter...Ashley...Nate...my daughter." More had come. He knew eventually he'd have enough that the walls would come tumbling down. Until then he had to be patient. He sat in the darkness, repeating his mantra until a new day dawned.

~ * ~

Daniel's door opened and a soldier with purple bags under blood-shot eyes entered. His tunic was twisted askew under a hardened leather breastplate and it looked as though he'd slept in his armor. He glared through weary eyes as he stood in the doorway and growled, "Git movin'." Downstairs the troops had gathered for a morning meal, but most stood by the windows, watching the brightening sky with hooded eyes as they gripped weapons.

Daniel was handed a steaming plate of fried potatoes and escorted to a table, but as soon as he settled in, the front door banged opened. "Hurry up!" Gelnar yelled. "We ride in thirty!"

Men shoveled in their meals with gusto while others gathered equipment and prepared to evacuate, none taking their eyes from the windows for long. *Evacuation is the right word,* Daniel thought. *These guys are scared.* Part of him wanted the villagers to attack, wanted the men to fall even if it meant that he himself may die. But just as he considered the assault, Daniel remembered Gelnar saying they could wipe out the village if they had time. That may have been bravado, but even Daniel, who was untrained in the arts of war, saw how green the villagers were. Twenty-six men probably wouldn't be enough to completely wipe out the village before being overrun, but casualties would be horrendous.

Daniel's escort stopped eating long enough to glare at him. "'Urry up! Ah aint waitin' fer ya!" Bits of potato flew from his mouth, flecking the once spotless table as he tucked in, racing to finish. The wet shreds dangling from his beard took Daniel's appetite away and he just picked at his plate until the soldier was done. The two pushed away from the table together and prepared to leave.

~ * ~

The day was cloudy and blustery, the intense heat of the last few weeks but a memory. The company had stormed from the inn only to find the streets deserted. They mounted up and sped from town at a near gallop until they came upon a small stream where they stopped only briefly to water the horses. The frequent attacks and the town's empty streets spooked everyone, and even the brooding captain was anxious to put Standing Stone far behind them.

The horses watered and somewhat rested, they continued their hectic pace as the sky darkened and the wind picked up. When the storm came, its abruptness caught them all by surprise. Sporadic drops were quickly replaced by driving sheets of rain as the sky turned almost as dark as night, the black veil pierced by blinding flashes of lightning. The horses staggered in surprise with each flash and explosion of thunder, and the torrential rain slowed the column to a near standstill. When the wind and rain punched down so hard they couldn't even see in front of their mounts, Gelnar finally relinquished the road.

They found shelter in a copse of trees, huddling under interlaced boughs. Daniel had nothing to protect him from the onslaught as the men around him huddled in small groups under soaked blankets. Surrounded but ignored by the men, Daniel stood with his head bowed and his arms crossed, leaning against Blue Belle and trying in vain to ward off the chill. The storm raged for several hours and left everyone drenched, cold, and surly, but as quickly as they came, the clouds broke up and the warm sun beat down once more. Daniel still huddled against Blue Belle, and steam rose from their backs when he heard a curse and knew another had fallen.

He wandered to the edge of the copse where several men had clustered together. In the middle of their loose ring was an unmoving lump on the ground, smoke rising from bare flesh laced with fine burns. Daniel's mouth dropped open as he looked at the man's back where the clothing had burned off. He looked to the side and saw a thin wisp of smoke rising from the ground ten feet away. There on the ground lay the man's halberd, the once spotless metal blackened, pockmarked, and brittle, as if it had aged greatly during the storm. Where the weapon butted to the ground there was a large circle of blackened grass, and when Daniel probed it with his fingers, he found a hard mass in its center. He dug into the soft ground and exposed the jagged course the lightning followed as it turned the soil to glass.

Massive hooves pawed the ground beside him, and Daniel looked up to see Gelnar's jaws clenched. "Mount up." Daniel looked back to the spot where the unfortunate guard had died before woodenly getting back in the saddle. He and the twenty-five survivors returned to the road in silence and continued west.

~ * ~

The rest of the day passed without incident, though the men remained surly and quiet. The intense heat returned the following day, making the fierce storm and the life it took seem distant memories. Near mid-morning they came to the crest of a gradually rising hill only to see a large shadow stretch across the road about five miles distant. The dark spot was like a stain, stretching from the far side of the valley up to crest the opposite hill where it disappeared beyond.

As the men reached the top of the hill, around Daniel some gasped and cursed their luck. Mystified, he looked questioningly at them, but their eyes were fixed on the road ahead. Gelnar leaned toward his second in command and said, "Lieutenant, what do you see?"

The lieutenant shaded his eyes with his hand as he surveyed the distant horizon, squinting at the black line. Finally, he replied, "Hard to tell, sir. Could be our boys."

Gelnar studied the dark line for a moment before grunting his agreement. He turned to the survivors. "We are the Elite. We never back down from anything." He paused and gauged the strength in the troops' faces. "Those are probably our boys, come from Stonefall. But if they're not…well, we don't back down." The men gripped their weapons more tightly and nodded, taking strength from their captain's confidence. At a word from Gelnar they trotted down the road to meet the dark line of troops.

About an hour later, one of the younger men with sharp eyes gave a great shout. "They've got th' blue!" he yelled, thumbing his navy jerkin. Soon others could make out the same, and tension melted from the men. They laughed and told jokes again, slapping backs as they closed the distance, and soon the rhythmic thump of booted feet marching in unison could be heard over the intervening distance.

As the company's spirits rose, Daniel's fell. His eyes were glued to the edges of the sparse forests, hoping against hope that the rebels would burst forth and rescue him before the two forces met. His hopes were in vain, though, and by midday deafening silence replaced the sound of marching feet as the new army came to a halt. Most of the front ranks facing the company wore intricate breastplates of hardened leather armor, similar to the veterans surrounding Daniel. Farther down the line, however, he could see men wearing simple tabards like Carmody had worn.

At the head of the army was a middle-aged man with blond hair and a thick blonde beard, one eye covered by an ornately decorated patch. He wore armor that was richly detailed in royal blue and silver, and thrown back from his shoulders was a dark blue cape with silver piping. He sat ramrod straight upon a large black stallion, smiling warmly at Gelnar across the distance that separated their forces. "It is good to see you, Captain. We are at your disposal, if that is your pleasure, sir." He bowed his head and remained that way until Gelnar spoke.

The captain smiled and said, "Lieutenant Rangeford. We are well met. What have you brought me?"

The lieutenant raised his head and reported, "Two hundred Elite, sir, supported by two hundred Imperial regulars."

Gelnar took a deep breath and let it out slowly, studying the men before him. He nodded and replied,

"Good. Very good. We march to Stonefall, Lieutenant." He motioned to Daniel and continued, "I want this man surrounded by the Elite. He is to be guarded by twenty men at all times, no exceptions. He is your personal responsibility."

Rangeford's eyes darted to Daniel momentarily, gave an uncaring appraisal, and then immediately returned to Gelnar. "Yes, Captain."

Gelnar's steed nickered as he pulled the reigns hard to the side and led the horse from the road. Speaking over his shoulder as he sauntered into a clearing, he said, "Bivouac here for the midday. Bring me my meal. And I want a bottle of wine."

Raising his voice to be heard, Rangeford replied, "Yes, sir." He motioned the first three ranks of Elite troops to close around Daniel. Without so much as a glance at him, he rode past and clenched forearms with the lieutenant that rode with the veterans. Daniel looked into the disinterested faces of his new guards and sighed. Clearly there would be no escape now. One of the men took Blue Belle's reigns and led Daniel from the road to a small hillock in the clearing. A meal was brought to him which he ate dispiritedly before returning to the road with the joined forces.

The next three days were a blur of monotony as they continued unimpeded toward the Naphthalian capital. Daniel didn't see Gelnar or any of the survivors of the company during those three days, which was a bit of a blessing. He was confined to the middle of the army, surrounded by his own retinue of guards, while Gelnar and the survivors rode in the army's front ranks.

As they neared their destination Daniel became steadily more on edge, afraid of meeting the Emperor that ruled such a ruthless force. He caught snippets of conversation and knew as he went to his tent on the third night that they would arrive in Stonefall the next day. His stomach was in knots, and he didn't know if he would be able to sleep, knowing that his fate would soon be determined. He lay down and laced his fingers behind his head, and as he stared at the peaked canvas ceiling, he was surprised to feel himself drifting off. He closed his eyes with a sigh and was almost immediately pulled into a dark dream.

Daniel lay down in his tent and sighed deeply as he closed his eyes and started to drift off. He was nearly asleep when he heard Gelnar's voice, seeming to whisper in his ear. *"We do take pride in our work."* His eyes flickered open and he looked up to see, not the roof of his tent, but blue sky, the sun shining painfully in his face. He tried to lift an arm to block the glare but couldn't.

Trying to hold panic at bay, Daniel forced himself to blow out a heavy breath. Deep down, he already knew what he would see when he looked over his head, but he strained back his neck as far as possible to look anyway. As expected, his bare arms were lashed tightly to stakes that were hammered into the ground. His heart racing, Daniel raised his head until his chin brushed his chest. He was stripped naked, his legs spread-eagle and staked to the ground as well. Panic broke loose and overwhelmed him as he pulled with all his might on the bonds to no avail.

His head dropped back to the dusty ground and for the first time Daniel registered silent sobbing next to him. He didn't want to look. He *begged* himself not to, but he couldn't resist as his head turned in that direction. Staked next to him was the farmer's wife, also stripped naked. She had been horribly beaten, and she locked the one eye that wasn't swollen shut on his. Blood dripped from her face, pooling under her cheek. It broke Daniel's heart to see her broken body, but the worst was her mutilated chest. "Ashley" was carved across the tops of her breasts in jaunty scarlet letters.

Tears ran down his cheeks, mimicking the trails of blood left on hers, and Daniel could take no more. He turned his burning eyes away and saw that he was at the crest of a hill that sank down into a shallow valley…but not just any valley, *the* valley, the Valley of Death. He looked to his left and saw a massive cat closing on him, its eyes glowing green even in the midday sun.

His heart skipped a beat when the beast met his gaze, and he heaved against his bonds again, panic racing through him once more. The cat prowled up to him and sniffed gently at his side. He could feel first its whiskers tracing his heaving ribcage and then the sandpaper of its tongue as it licked him. He whimpered one last time before unbelievable pain arced through his body as the cat settled in for a meal. He tried to scream as the cat fed, but no sound emerged, and the last thing he heard was Carmody's voice saying solemnly, *"Ya' don't never defy th' Emperor's will."*

He woke with a start, his chest heaving, covered in sweat. He ran shaking fingers over his ribcage, wincing at remembered pain as his fevered mind kept repeating, *It was only a dream, it was only a dream.* He wished he could believe that. Finally he calmed down, but Daniel knew there would be no more sleep that night. He pulled himself into a sitting position and huddled in his blanket until dawn.

Chapter Eight

By midday rolling hills and sparse farms gave way to large walled estates, country homes for the capital's wealthy. As the buildings changed, so too did the road. What was at times little more than a packed dirt path had become a wide stone-cobbled avenue, lined with tall trees. Traffic also increased considerably, but the sheer size of the army forced all others to the side and prevented anyone from slowing them down or getting a good look at Daniel. The road continued generally westward until it met a wide river, which bent it to the northwest. While meandering along the river, Daniel got his first glimpse of Stonefall.

The massive city rested on a flat plane that covered nearly three miles of open space set back from the river. It was surrounded by a thick stone wall that soared to a height of forty feet, and was perforated by even taller watch towers. The wall enclosed the city proper, but outside the wall a district of shanties and warehouses hugged the riverbanks. Crammed before the warehouses and stretching out into the slow-moving water was a wharf used for shipping and fishing.

Three gates bored through the thirty foot thickness of the wall, one roughly directed to each of the compasses points, north, west, and south. To the east there was a dense forest that grew to within a quarter mile of the stout walls, blocking travel from that direction. The road the army traveled parted ways with the river about a mile from Stonefall and approached the western gate, which stood open at midday. A steel portcullis glinted in the sunlight at the top of the arched entryway, and the cavernous portal was pock-marked with murder holes and backed by massive steel doors that could be swung shut from the inside.

A large plateau that rose thirty feet higher than the outer walls occupied the center of Stonefall, backed up against the eastern wall. Nearly the entire surface of the plateau was covered by a fortress built of gleaming white stone that shined brightly in the midday sun. The square fortress had large towers rising from each of the four corners as well as from the center of the keep. The towers were at least one hundred fifty feet above the city below, and each was capped by a navy and black pennant bearing the mailed fist. The fortress was accessed by a wide gently sloping ramp that curved half-way around the plateau as it rose to its top. At three points along the ramp, watch towers defied gravity by hanging over the edge, seemingly suspended in thin air over the city far below.

They came to a halt before the gate where huge sheets of navy and black fabric hanging from the towers at either side bore the silver-fisted emblem of the Empire. The commanding officer spoke with Gelnar, and soon the troops guarding the entrance moved out of the way and saluted as the whole of the army marched inside. They moved from cool darkness of the stone tunnel into bright light of the interior, and most of the army pealed away toward barracks that were built along the inside wall. Gelnar led eighty of the Elite Imperial Guard, including Daniel's twenty shepherds and most of the survivors, into the city.

The broad avenue continued westward toward the fortress, periodically intersecting with narrower streets that ran deeper into the city. At the city's center a large square ringed by tall official-looking buildings was dissected by the merging of the main roads from the north, south, and west. The new, even wider boulevard continued to the base of the ramp that led to the fortress. The men paused only briefly in the courtyard to allow people to move out of the way before continuing to the ramp.

At the first tower they were ordered to halt as the commander of the watch walked out to inspect them. He was still chewing a mouthful of midday meal when he rounded the corner of the tower and grumbled without even looking up. "State yer bus'ness, an' it'd better be importan'." His petulant tone turned pinched at the end as he glanced up at Gelnar and blanched. His mouth fell open and the last bits of food dropped onto a sizable belly that hung low under his armor.

Gelnar glared at the man as he leaned forward and hissed, "I am Captain Gelnar, Commander of the Elite Imperial Guard, and my *business* is my own. Move or die where you stand."

The commander fell over himself as he backpedaled, slamming into the tower's wall. Gelnar and his officers rode past, but when Daniel reached the tower, he recovered some of his gravitas. He spotted a young soldier and shouted, "Run ahead, Fool! Announce the great man!"

The soldier broke into a sprint and passed Gelnar, who had stopped in his tracks. He glared back at the commander as he motioned to Rangeford. In his low, dangerous voice he said, "Lieutenant, the fat man has failed in his duty."

Rangeford nodded and turned back toward the gate, pulling his sword free. The fat officer saw him coming and his bowels let go as he shook his head, multiple chins wagging. A low moan escaped him as his bloated hands waved before him. Rangeford ignored the moan as he jumped from his saddle, pulling back his sword and giving a roundhouse swing. He grunted as his blade sliced cleanly through the pleading arm and deep into the man's neck. He wrenched it free as the commander toppled and a geyser of blood sprayed from his throat. Rangeford sidestepped the crimson tide and wiped his sword clean on the dying man's cloak before returning to his mount.

Gelnar and his men watched the punishment, Daniel included. His stomach turned at the blow, but after traveling with Gelnar for so long, he was not surprised by the brutality. Briefly, he wondered if he was becoming desensitized to the horrible violence, but his reflections were cut short when Gelnar shouted. "Your Emperor is among you! Everyone *must* remain vigilant!" He motioned to the still body, blood and feces staining the stone pathway. "This fat fool's fate would have been much worse if I had more time. Take care that you do not follow his path."

He glared into the pale faces of each guard in turn, resting at last on a young sergeant. "You're in command here now. Do not fail the Empire." The man gulped and nodded, his face becoming even paler than before. Gelnar started to turn but looked back a final time and said, "Put that carcass where the crows will find it."

There were no more lax soldiers as they passed the last two towers. The guards glanced fearfully at Gelnar as he approached, but their gazes darted straight ahead and they silently stood at attention as the retinue passed. *The runner did his job well,* thought Daniel as the men refused to make eye contact with him.

When they reached the top of the plateau, Daniel saw that the fortress was actually set back two hundred feet from the edge. The intervening space was covered with a tiled courtyard, surrounded by a three-foot-tall railing that ran along the very edge of the precipice. At the back of the courtyard white stone steps rose to the front entrance of the keep, which was also equipped with a steel portcullis.

In the center of the courtyard stood a thin balding man in intricate silver armor embossed with the fist, and behind him was an honor guard in silver decorative plate. The troops came to a halt, and Gelnar stared down at the older man. He would have dwarfed him if he were standing, but mounted on a huge draft horse he positively towered over the official. Rather than being intimidated by the display, the older man was only annoyed. Gelnar held his saddle just long enough to further nettle the man before dismounting and standing before him. The official silently surveyed the troop, his eyes resting on Daniel the longest. His gaze returned to Gelnar and he spoke in a deep, dry voice. "Captain Gelnar. You have arrived."

Gelnar chuckled. "Yes, Governor DePlaynes, you have cut to the truth of it."

The governor ignored his tone and surveyed the line of troops again. "Are these your men? All that traveled with you?"

"No." Gelnar frowned at DePlaynes's incredulous reaction.

After a moment's silence, he prompted, "What happened? And who is the prisoner?" His eyes returned briefly to Daniel, flicking over his scarred face.

Gelnar's voice dropped to his soft, dangerous tone. "I answer to the Emperor, not you."

The older man raised his head and looked down an angular nose at Gelnar as he theatrically wiped his hands, as if washing himself of the captain. If he hadn't been so much shorter than Gelnar, it would have looked like he were berating an underling, but the height difference between the men, and the complete lack of contrition by Gelnar made the move comical. "Well," he said in a snobbish tone, "by all means, report to His Grace."

Gelnar chuckled and shook his head as he walked past the man. Behind him his men dismounted and followed, handing their reigns to stable boys that ran out to retrieve them. Gelnar had just reached the steps when Governor DePlaynes called out one final time, his voice filled with rage. "Hope that you are never put under my charge, Captain."

Gelnar stopped and turned, an evil grin stretching his scarred cheeks. "You do the same, Governor." He stared menacingly at DePlaynes for a moment then turned and led Daniel into Stonefall Castle.

~ * ~

The castle was brighter than Daniel expected. Large windows let in natural light that illuminated a long door-lined hallway almost as wide as the ramp that curled around the plateau. The perimeter of the vast open space was punctuated by white columns, but the center was open and the ceiling soared four stories overhead. Daniel craned back his neck and saw that each of the upper floors had a railed balcony that encircled the great entrance hall, and each railing was draped in rich fabric, alternating by floor between navy and silver. In the center of the hall was a massive statue of a fist rising from the floor. The fist was gilded in silver, and within its grasp was a white cloth that almost draped to the floor on each side. The white marble was so cunningly carved that Daniel expected the stone fabric to sway in a wayward breeze.

Here and there throughout the great hall were soldiers, courtesans, merchants, and musicians, going about their business or chatting quietly with one another. Some doors leading to side chambers were open. Officials within periodically called for those waiting outside, who hurried in to finish their business. Whether it was the austere presentation of the great hall or the august presence of the Emperor, all who entered kept their voices muted, their downcast eyes throwing furtive glances around them.

The men stood in the entrance of the great hall for several minutes, awed and dwarfed by the sheer size of the place. Even Gelnar, who always looked larger-than-life, appeared smaller when compared to the hall, a fact that he was painfully aware of. He impatiently cast around until he found a desk sitting in the near corner. A tall middle-aged man sat behind the desk, decked in rich robes of deep navy with a matching velvet hat. He was working his way through a large stack of vellum sheets, writing missives and sealing them with blue wax before motioning to several young boys dressed in navy tabards and silver hose. They dashed off with the letters as three advisors stood to the side of the man, ready to offer assistance.

Gelnar marched toward the man, who was so engrossed in his writings that he didn't notice the soldiers approaching until they were almost on top of him. He frowned in annoyance as an advisor cleared his throat, but when he saw Gelnar, his expression changed to one of polite interest. Remaining seated, he laid his quill on an unfinished letter and in a liltingly soft voice said, "Ah, Captain Gelnar! Welcome back. How were your travels?"

Gelnar smiled. "Hello, Quarren. My travels were long and tiring. I would like to report to His Grace at the earliest convenience."

A wrinkle creased Quarren's smooth forehead and his neatly trimmed gray mustache twitched as he looked down at the mounds of papers covering his desk. "The Emperor is quite busy today, Captain. It may be a long…" He let the sentence die away, making his opinion clear. Compared to running the Empire, a simple report could wait.

Undeterred and unfazed, Gelnar continued politely. "I'm afraid it is quite urgent, Chancellor. We will wait as long as necessary." Daniel looked at Gelnar in amazement.

Could this be the same impatient brute he'd known on the road?

Chancellor Quarren made a show of shuffling papers, clearly wanting to get back to the unfinished letter. Finally he said, "Oh, very well. I will fit you in as soon as possible. You may wait in the lounge." He motioned to a door to his right before bending over his desk and picking up his quill, dismissing the captain. He put the quill to ink and wrote four more words before his attendant cleared his throat again. With an annoyed sigh he looked up to see Gelnar still standing before his desk. His frown was much deeper as he asked, "Yes? Was there something else, Captain?"

Gelnar inclined his head. "My men traveled long and hard in the name of the Emperor. They deserve recognition. I would like to have their names entered into the public record and a song of their feats prepared." He motioned to Lieutenant Rangeford and added, "I would also like to promote Lieutenant Rangeford to second in command of the Elite Guard. And I need orders to…recruit…new Elite members."

Daniel scowled at Gelnar, thinking, *Deeds? Which deeds were worthy of song? Rape? Torture?*

The chancellor stared intently at Gelnar for a moment, his eyes darting to Rangeford and Daniel. Satisfied with what he saw, in the same polite voice he said, "Yes, of course. Give the names to my assistant, and we will send a minstrel to the barracks. You will have your orders, as well. For the good of the Empire, anything is yours, Captain, as always."

Gelnar dipped a short bow. "Many thanks, Chancellor." One of Quarren's attendants produced quill and parchment, and Gelnar motioned the survivors toward him. The captain, Rangeford, and Daniel headed to the lounge with Daniel's guards in tow. Gelnar walked across the sumptuously appointed room to the far corner, where a window looked out over the city far below.

Rangeford came in last and, after making sure his men were appropriately stationed around Daniel, joined the captain, his face glowing with pleasure. "You honor me, Captain," he said, his voice filled with pride.

Gelnar smiled and gripped the lieutenant's arm briefly in a rough embrace. "You deserve it. You control the men well, they respond to your leadership." His smile faded as he got down to business. "Your first order is to return the Guard to full strength. Only the very best will do. Look everywhere."

Rangeford gave a quick nod. "Thank you, sir. I shall begin on the morrow." His smile slipped, replaced by an inquisitive look. "How did you know the Chancellor would allow you an audience?"

Gelnar chuckled. "Quarren is not so difficult to maneuver! But never underestimate him. He wields...too much power, for one not acquainted with the sword. Still, he can be a great ally or a great hindrance, depending on how he is persuaded."

Rangeford's forehead creased, deep in thought. "So you knew if you persisted he'd capitulate?"

Gelnar shook his head. "He and I have parlayed much over the years. Quarren knows I never persist unless it's important." He glanced at Daniel before continuing with a derisive chuckle. "Whether that weak cunny is important or not doesn't matter. If the Emperor is not pleased, the fault lies with General Ignatius. If he is, the glory is mine for succeeding in a difficult mission."

Rangeford nodded as they continued their discussion, and Daniel shook his head in wonder. He was amazed by Gelnar's political savvy. Clearly there was much more to the man than he had seen on their journey. The officers discussed various subordinates and generals, and soon Daniel was lost completely. He sighed and surveyed the large room, which was empty except for them. There were many overstuffed chairs and couches, and along one wall was a large table laden with fresh fruit, juicy cuts of meat, and numerous delicacies Daniel had never seen before.

The officers left the window and moved to the table, loading silver platters with food. Daniel's stomach growled, but just the thought of seeing the Emperor killed his appetite. Minutes turned into hours, and the room began to darken as the sun descended toward dusk. Finally, Daniel could ignore his stomach no longer, and so he went to the table and loaded a tray.

It was even better than it looked, and he groaned in pleasure when he bit into a sugary pastry. He closed his eyes and chewed slowly. *Was the food this good at home?* He savored the flavor a little longer before a vague feeling came to mind and served as an answer. *Yeah, I think sometimes it was.* He washed the food down with wine that was sweet and tart, and almost immediately felt effects from the alcohol. A small smile crept onto his face as he felt his inhibitions go.

He looked across the room at Gelnar and Rangeford and thought, *I should go tell that bastard what I think of him.*

He leaned forward, meaning to stand from the couch and do just that when the chancellor's attendant entered. "His Great Eminence, the Eternal Emperor and Keeper of the Realm, will see you now." The loud proclamation hit Daniel like a bucket of ice water. The wine-induced euphoria left in an instant, and anxiety rolled over him like a wave. His knees weakened and he dropped back to his seat, sinking into the couch's cushions.

Gelnar and Rangeford stood and Daniel's guards frowned when he refused to move. The captain pushed between two of the guards and looked down at Daniel, disdain in his eyes. "Where's your courage, Stranger?" The voice of the politically savvy confidant was gone, replaced by the quiet, deadly killer Daniel knew.

He closed his eyes and exhaled, sweat breaking out on his forehead. When he opened them, he glanced at Gelnar before forcing shaky legs to support him. The officers gave him one last look of contempt before they marched to the exit, the guards falling in around Daniel as he followed. When they came into the great hall, the attendant shook his head. "Only Captain Gelnar and the prisoner may enter His presence."

Gelnar stared briefly at the man before nodding to Rangeford. "Return to the barracks. Report to me in the morning."

Rangeford saluted. "Yes, Captain." He left the great hall, Daniel's guards falling in step behind him.

Daniel watched them go and took in the great hall. The crowds had largely dispersed, though there were still small groups of courtiers here and there, and Chancellor Quarren still sat at his desk, writing diligently. Gelnar's vice-like grip closed around his upper arm and lifted him slightly off the floor. "Come," he growled. He spun Daniel around before allowing his feet to touch the floor, and they followed the chancellor's attendant to the far end of the great hall.

Groups of courtiers turned to watch them, mostly because Gelnar's great size caught their attention. When they weren't recognized, most of the haughty nobles turned away with their noses in the air, but some did a double-take when their eyes darted to Daniel's face. Those few covered their involuntary reaction with a sneeze or cough and found a reason to excuse themselves. Daniel glanced at Gelnar and realized he must have seen the same thing, based on his clenched jaws. Unlike on the road, however, he was powerless to prevent the nobles from staring.

Daniel looked ahead and the nobles were forgotten as they approached four sets of ornate double doors that lined the end of the great hall. His heart hammered so hard all he could hear was his pulse beating in his ears, and his knees felt like jelly. He realized he could no longer feel his legs and stumbled slightly. It was only by a supreme effort of will that he was able to right himself and continue toward his doom.

A guard stood to either side of each of the four double doors. All were dressed identically in black, and each wore a silver breastplate similar to Gelnar's, engraved with an axe and sword crossed behind the mailed fist. Bright rubies glittered along the lengths of the engraved blades, resembling fresh blood. Each man stood with their feet widely spaced, and in each pair one had a large broadsword resting tip-down on the marble floor. The other had a long-handled axe, the haft of which rested between his feet. All stared directly ahead, their stoic faces unreadable.

They stopped before a set of doors and the attendant opened one, announcing their arrival. "Captain Gelnar of the Elite Imperial Guard and a prisoner, Your Grace." He stepped back so the two could enter, and as Daniel looked inside, he froze. His bowels felt like they'd turned to water, and he couldn't force himself to move. Gelnar obliged him with a shove from behind, and when he stumbled into the room, the captain followed. The attendant shut the door behind them with a soft thud.

The throne room was smaller than the great hall, but it was much more richly appointed. A white stone ceiling soared two stories overhead, its entire surface intricately carved into a magnificent mural. It appeared to depict the history of a people; in the first section they populated the land, then they explored and traded, then there was a great battle, and finally the crowning of a king. Daniel only briefly glanced at the mural, but in the section devoted to exploration, a massive waterfall that could only be the Spirit Calling jumped out at him.

Gold candelabras stood before each white marble column that supported the intricate ceiling, making the room glow in their soft light. Stained glass windows looked down on a marble floor that was covered with thick blue carpet, and a runner of silver ran up the middle of the room to a raised dais at the far end. The dais was made of silver, and at the top rested a huge throne inlaid with polished wood and gold. Behind the throne was a large blue flag fringed in silver, and on its navy field was a mailed fist in platinum. Guards dressed in black and wearing ruby-encrusted breastplates stood behind each column in shadows cast by the candelabras.

Seated on the throne was a middle-aged man with long golden hair plaited down his back and a neatly trimmed golden beard. On his unlined brow was a circlet of platinum that was inscribed with the raised fist. He was wearing a short-sleeved royal blue robe that hung to his feet, pulled tight at his waist with a wide silver belt. A circular pendant, also inscribed with the raised fist, was suspended from his neck by a thick gold chain. His bare arms were deeply tanned, and corded muscles were partially concealed by wide leather bracers, each of which was embedded with a flawless diamond over the inner arm.

A wave of disorientation washed over Daniel as the Emperor's ice-blue eyes pierced him. It felt like the Emperor was looking within him, rather than just at him, but the feeling quickly passed as he turned his gaze on Gelnar. The captain's face went pale beneath his dusky tan, and his eyes bulged from their sockets. As Daniel saw his Adam's apple wobble, surprise temporarily overrode his fear of the Emperor. *He's scared!* A cold feeling spread in the pit of his stomach as he considered what could make a fearless man so frightened.

Gelnar brushed by Daniel as he took two quick strides into the throne room and dropped to one knee, his head lowered. The Emperor held him there as he studied the top of his head for several minutes. Finally, he spoke in a deep, resonant voice, tinged with anger. "Captain Gelnar. You have returned."

They were the same words used by Governor DePlaynes, but Gelnar's reaction couldn't have been more different. His arms broke out in goose bumps and a shiver ran through him. His eyes never left the floor as he responded in a quavering voice. "Yes, your Grace."

The Emperor frowned. "And your men? How have you come?" His tone indicated he already knew the answer.

Gelnar was silent for a moment, not wanting to interrupt his master, and while he waited, Daniel remembered him asking Chancellor Quarren for a song to be written about the survivors. The *survivors*. If Daniel hadn't been so frightened, he would have smiled at the irony. Gelnar had let slip vital information, news that could have harsh repercussions for him. As it was, Daniel's legs shook so badly he could barely stand, and he just concentrated on not making a sound.

Gelnar's voice was small and timid when he spoke. "M--my men? We had...difficulties, your Grace." He paused, but the Emperor's silence compelled him on. "Twenty-five fell, sire."

Silence stretched out agonizingly until the Emperor spoke, ice in his voice. "Twenty-five. How did they fall?"

Daniel could hear Gelnar's throat click as he tried to swallow. Sweat soaked through the back of his cloak, and his bent knee started to shake. Seeing his terror, Daniel pitied Gelnar in spite of himself. The captain finally swallowed and replied, "S--six fell to nature, your Grace. The rest were killed...by rebel ambush." The last came out in a breathless whisper.

The Emperor's eyes narrowed to slits. "Rebels," he spat. "And how many of these *rebels* did you slay?"

If Daniel had been the man kneeling, he was sure his bladder would have let go at that point, but Gelnar held on to the last of his dignity. Barely above a whisper, he replied, "None, sire."

The Emperor sighed and thrummed his fingers on the arm of his throne. "How many did you capture?"

With a whimper Gelnar croaked, "None, sire."

A growl rolled across the quiet room. "None!" barked the Emperor, making Daniel and Gelnar jump. "You are the captain of my Elite Guard, and you allow this pathetic excuse of a people humiliate you! And if they humiliate you, they humble the Empire, and *I am the Empire!*" The last four words were nearly screamed, each punctuated by a heavy fist slamming into the arm of the Emperor's throne. Gelnar's body jumped with each loud bang, as if he himself were being struck. The first two knocked him to all fours, and the last two flattened him on the floor.

Gelnar laid there, his body wracked by silent sobs, and Daniel stood stalk still, afraid to even breathe. Eventually Gelnar pulled himself back to a kneeling position, never raising his eyes from the floor. His body heaved great gasps as he forced out, "M--my life is...is yours, my Lord."

The Emperor glared down at him, his cheeks flushed. For a second Daniel could have sworn he saw a green mist swirl over his eyes. He consciously made himself blink and when he looked back, the Emperor had regained control of himself. His high color was receding, and his icy stare had lost its intense hatred. "You may go," he said, his voice calm. "Replenish your forces."

Gelnar gave a ragged sigh. "Thank you, your Grace." He stumbled to his feet and backed toward the door, never raising his eyes from the floor. He reached back and grasped the doorknob when the Emperor called to him once more, surprise making him look his master in the eye.

"Gelnar, do not fail me again."

The captain blanched as he shook his head wildly. "Never, your Grace!" The Emperor stared into his eyes before he dipped his head in a slight nod. With that Gelnar pushed open the door and rushed out, leaving Daniel behind.

The Emperor seemed to forget Daniel was even there, he was so lost in his own thoughts. Seeing the mighty Gelnar crumble before him, Daniel was too terrified to even move. Without realizing it, he'd slowly slipped back, distancing himself from the captain, and now his buttocks and back were pressed against the marble wall next to the ornate doors. He was trapped, and so he took shallow breaths through his mouth, afraid that even breathing might give him away.

The Emperor stared into the distance to Daniel's right, slowly stroking his golden beard. After what felt like hours, he dropped his hand to the armrest which made Daniel cringe in expected pain that didn't come. Slowly he wheeled his attention around to Daniel, and a terrified whimper escaped his throat. When their eyes locked, the disconcerting feeling washed over Daniel again until the Emperor smiled broadly. The smile struck Daniel as if he had been a plant wasting in darkness until suddenly it was awash in bright sunlight. He was overwhelmed with a sense of warm well being and peace. All his worries and fears were forgotten as he basked in the warm glow, and all he wanted was to stay in that spotlight for the rest of his life.

When the Emperor spoke, his resonant voice was filled with love, like that of an affectionate father speaking to his favored son. "Welcome, Daniel. I hope your travels weren't too taxing?"

A part of Daniel's mind that was so distant it could have been back at the Spirit Calling screamed at him. It tried to insert the horrible cries of the farmer's wife and the blood running from the old man's ruined eyes, but all Daniel could say was, "No, they were fine." He spoke in a dreamlike daze, his voice light and airy.

The Emperor nodded in understanding. "I'm happy to hear that." He paused for a moment then looked coyly at Daniel. "You know, Daniel, you really should be kneeling before me."

Daniel's face burned with embarrassment as he dropped immediately to his knees, his joints making a hollow thud as they met the hard floor, made no less unyielding by the thick carpet that covered it. The same distant part of his mind that cried out before howled with pain, but the rest of him was beyond feeling anything, as long as he pleased the great man. "I--I'm sorry," he stammered.

The Emperor patted the air as if to say it was all right. He smiled again, and Daniel's rising anxiety was lost in a wave of gratitude. "Tell me how you came to be here."

His eyes never leaving the Emperor's, Daniel motioned to the door. "The captain brought me."

The Emperor smiled again and said with a chuckle, "Yes, of course he did. But how did you get to Naphthali?"

A grateful smile slipped from Daniel's face as he tried to remember, and his anxiety rose again. There was no fear of pain or punishment accompanying the knot in his stomach, just an overriding concern that the affection might be taken away if he couldn't answer. Finally, though it pained him, he said, "I don't know...I--I can't remember."

He wanted to go on, to say that he couldn't remember much of anything, but the glamour slipped as the Emperor's gaze became sharper and his eyes narrowed. He again felt like his mind was being searched, and there was no peace or contentment, only terror. The sensation faded as the Emperor smiled and euphoric stupor returned. "I understand," he said. "Do you remember anything?"

A humble part of his mind spoke up, insisting that he not bother the great man with the trifle scraps of memory he'd gleaned. "Not much," he admitted with a sad shake of his head.

The Emperor's face was filled with compassion. "I see. Now tell me this, Daniel. Are you the Stranger?"

Daniel frowned in genuine confusion. Mystified, he shook his head. "I'm sorry, I don't know what you mean."

"I understand." He continued to smile, but his focus drifted inward, and Daniel could sense that he was weighing what had been said. Daniel still felt the warm glow of his attention, but the euphoria did not seem as intense as it was before, and that distant part of his mind screamed at him to look away. He easily ignored it, basking in the gaze and waiting with longing for the Emperor's full attention to return.

After several minutes, he focused once more on Daniel and said, "I want to help you, Daniel. I have a...a friend that may be able to open your mind, help you to remember. Would you like that?"

Daniel nodded vigorously. He'd agree to anything the Emperor wanted. "Oh yes! Will...will you be with me?" he asked tentatively.

The Emperor smiled again. "Yes, I will be by your side." Daniel sighed as the Emperor continued, "He is far away, and it will take him several days to arrive. You may explore the fortress while you wait, but you mustn't venture beyond the gates. These are dangerous times, and I may not be able to protect you if you leave."

It was ludicrous to even consider leaving the Emperor's side, and Daniel nodded his understanding. At the same time, a dim sense of unease filled him when the Emperor mentioned danger. He grinned at Daniel again, but the look was more of the kind a wolf gives a plump lamb than a doting father gives his favorite child. Daniel's unease increased, and a frown creased his forehead. "You may go now. Two of my guards will accompany you and will see to it that you receive anything you need." With that he looked away and nodded to the sides of the throne room where the two guards closest to Daniel separated from the shadows and closed on him.

Panic swelled in Daniel's chest as the light of the Emperor's attention receded. "I--I can't stay?"

A look of irritation crossed the Emperor's face, and true panic raced through Daniel as Gelnar's questioning came rushing back. But the fear was washed away by one final loving look. "No, Daniel. I am sorry, but I'm very busy. I have tarried too long already." After a moment's consideration, the Emperor continued, "We will have a feast in your honor, tomorrow night. Until then I really must return to my work."

His hopes deflated, but buoyed by the prospect of seeing the Emperor again, Daniel nodded. "Oh...I understand. Thank you."

Daniel looked down as he pushed himself up from the floor when the Emperor called out a final time. "You may call me Master, if you like." He was smiling kindly at Daniel again, and the light of that love filled him with gratitude.

"Thank you, Master!" His voice was filled with such love and devotion that it made the Emperor laugh. In his euphoria, Daniel didn't realize that it was a derisive laugh, nor did he notice the strange green mist swirling over the Emperor's eyes again. He nodded to the guards as they helped Daniel to his feet and led him from the throne room. The Emperor's laughter followed him until the ornate doors closed.

~ * ~

Daniel stretched and slowly opened his eyes. Bright light streaming in the open balcony made him squint and the odors wafting in on a light breeze made his nose wrinkle. It was an eye-watering blend of smoke, cooking meat, livestock, human waste and a dozen other scents. In short, the odors of a city rose on warm thermals to his balcony in the eastern tower of the great fortress.

He stumbled out of bed and yawned, scratching his bare buttocks as he looked around the room. It was dominated by a large bed covered with a down mattress;

sheer heaven after more than a month of sleeping on the ground. As he looked at the bed, he realized how easy it was to get used to the pleasures of civilization. Even now thoughts of the long trek were fading, and after a long night's sleep the hard ground and cold nights felt like a distant memory. It was almost as if someone else had made the journey, for how distant the memories seemed, especially the darkest ones. As if they were waiting to pounce, those memories rushed to the fore of his mind, but with speed borne of panic, Daniel pushed them away. He blew the air from his lungs in a heavy sigh and shook his head, determined to find something else to occupy his attention.

A silver tray holding a decanter and goblets rested on a table to the right of the bed, and to the left was an open area where a food-laden table and four stuffed chairs sat on a dark blue rug. Just past the foot of the bed was the doorway that led to the balcony, little more than a railed ledge that jutted out a few feet from the tower's wall. Past the balcony doorway was a large stone fireplace and on the adjacent wall was a closed wooden door and a small oak bureau.

Daniel's crumpled traveling clothes lay in a heap on the floor before the fireplace. He vaguely remembered being led to the room last night where he stripped and fell into bed and a dreamless sleep. He looked to the tray of food then self-consciously down at his nakedness. He glanced with a grimace at the filthy clothes lying on the floor and shook his head. Wrapped in a blue cotton robe and slippers from the bureau, Daniel sat down for breakfast.

The food was delicious. Daniel's favorite was a fried bread that he smothered with fruit preserves and wolfed down until he thought he'd burst. He chewed the last bite slowly, savoring the bread's saltiness, a nice counterpoint to the sweetness of the preserves. He closed his eyes and swallowed and said to the empty room, "Frog bellies." He'd grown accustomed to odd bits of information coming to him, but that one made him raise an eyebrow. *Frog bellies? What the heck are frog bellies?* He looked at the last piece of lumpy bread on the tray and everything from its smell to its off-white color convinced him the name was right. *Hmm…what an odd name.*

At the sound of his voice the door opened silently and a guard glanced inside. When he saw Daniel was awake, he entered and stood loosely at attention before the table. He was in his twenties, his head shaved bald and glistening with a slight layer of sweat. Dark brown eyes looked sternly, though not unkindly, at Daniel and his jaw was covered with a close-cropped brown beard. He was dressed in black, highlighted by a breastplate inset with red rubies. In a brusque voice he said, "Good afternoon, sir. His Highest and Most Honored Majesty has commanded that you be given every comfort. When you are ready, I will arrange for a bath, and a tailor will measure you for attire."

"Uh, yeah, that'd be great," Daniel replied, glancing down at the nearly empty tray and the crumbs covering his robe. "I guess I'm ready." The guard gave a crisp nod and turned to leave, but just as he reached for the door, Daniel spoke again. "Um…I'm sorry, but can I ask, what's your name?"

The guard turned back, surprised by the simple courtesy. "I am Sergeant Stinton. I and Sergeant Dunn have been assigned to you."

"I see." With a dip of his head Daniel added, "Thank you, Sergeant Stinton."

Stinton looked at him uncertainly for a moment before saying, "I will notify the servants." When Daniel nodded, he left, closing the door quietly behind him.

Daniel sighed deeply. Obviously his initial impression of the Empire was mistaken. He was no one, just a stranger without even his memory, and yet he was staying in a beautiful suite with attentive guards and servants. And the Emperor...what a great man! Just thinking of him made Daniel want to be near him, to have his attention. Daniel considered his audience with the Emperor and realized he must've been more tired than he thought. Even now he couldn't remember large portions of it. He knew Gelnar was questioned but couldn't remember anything of substance, and he remembered the Emperor looking on him with kind understanding. He didn't think he helped much, and yet the great man offered to help *him* recover his memory!

Daniel's stomach did a somersault at the prospect of remembering. Under his breath, he whispered his mantra, "Ashley...Nate...my daughter...Ashley...Nate...my daughter." He'd yearned for more for so long, and now that longing was about to be realized, thanks to the Emperor. No doubt about it, he was wrong about the Empire. How could he have ever gotten the idea that it was bad? That same persistent part of his mind that spoke up the night before replied, *But what about all that...stuff? That happened on the way here?* It troubled Daniel to think of those dark times, but now he frowned and focused on them, to see if the thought had merit.

As he puzzled through his memories, he found that in hindsight, the actions were pretty...understandable. Sure it wasn't the best of circumstances, and certainly Gelnar got a little short with Daniel a few times. But who wouldn't be edgy if they were being attacked by madmen hiding in the forest? As he thought back over the long difficult journey, he wondered if maybe he'd judged Gelnar too harshly. He did, after all, get him safely to the Emperor, even though it cost him half his force. Daniel's face burned as he thought about how he'd treated the good captain.

The bothersome part of his brain spoke up again, hesitantly asking, *But what about the farmer's wife? What about the old man?* Daniel's hand came up and stroked his coarse beard. There was something there about a farmer's wife, but he couldn't remember what, and he didn't remember an old man at all. Unless it was the belligerent old fart that ran the village they came through. He refused to meet with Gelnar, and while his reasons seemed understandable at the time, in hindsight they only seemed rude. Daniel's mind returned with shame to Gelnar, the honorable and humble soldier that he'd treated so unfairly.

He sighed as his gaze wandered aimlessly across the room, coming to rest on the open balcony. He stood and walked into bright sunshine, leaning over and resting his forearms on the ledge that ringed the small veranda. Vertigo gripped him for a moment, but when it passed, he leaned his head back and looked to the top of the tower, feeling a crazy sense that he was tipping over the railing's edge as he did so. His heart beating hard, he lowered his gaze and took in the forest outside Stonefall's eastern wall. His room was nearly a hundred feet above the city, and from that vantage point he could easily see over the city's stone wall. A vast field of green stretched for miles, and while most of the trees topped out around fifty feet, throughout the canopy there were giants that stretched at least as high as his window.

Daniel looked directly down and fought another stab of vertigo as he took in the seedy district that sprawled below. Most of the buildings were no more than two or three stories tall, and all had a ramshackle appearance to them. The gray brick was dingy, with thatched roofs that were thin and poorly maintained. Vagrants dressed in little more than rags begged on the streets, and peasants dressed marginally better hurried from chore to chore. As Daniel's gaze wandered over the dregs of society, a man stumbling aimlessly down a street was dragged into a dark alley by three men.

He flinched and leaned out over the railing, trying in vain to get a better view as several people passed the black maw, giving it a wide berth. Daniel leaned out farther, his belly resting on the railing, and with a start felt his feet slip from the floor. His hands locked on the railing as he pitched forward and cried out, but strength borne of panic caught him half-way over he wall. He leaned back and pushed off the railing, propelling himself into the room at the same time as a guard charged through the door. The man had dark skin and hair, a pointed goatee jutting from his angular chin like an accusing finger. He frowned as a hand rested on his sword hilt, his wiry body thrumming like an over-wound spring. He scanned the room and then turned to Daniel who was lying on the floor, his robe falling open. "Is everything all right, sir?"

Daniel's face burned as he simultaneously pulled his robe closed and lurched to his feet. He motioned to the balcony and said, "Come quick! Someone was just attacked!" Daniel dashed to the balcony and pointed. "There! A man was just pulled into that alley!"

The guard looked impassively at the alley. When he turned to Daniel all he offered was, "I see."

Daniel motioned to the alley. "There might still be time to help if we hurry!"

The guard looked uncertainly at Daniel and finally motioned to his robe. "Sir, you are not dressed. And besides, the city is unsafe. We must stay here."

The Emperor's words echoed in his mind with the same admonishment: *These are dangerous times, and I may not be able to protect you if you leave.* He helplessly motioned to the alley again. "Well, we have to do something!"

The guard looked out at the city a final time and sighed. "The Captain of the Militia can investigate."

Daniel's head bobbed up and down. "Yes, thank you!" The man wordlessly marched to the door with Daniel on his heels. "Are you Sergeant Dunn?" The soldier nodded as Daniel added, "Thank you, Sergeant."

Dunn opened the door and threw up a muscled forearm to stop Daniel from following him out. He motioned to Daniel's bathrobe and said, "I must insist you remain within."

Daniel's face burned as he looked down and stammered, "Oh. Yes, thank y--" but the door clicked shut before he could finish. He rushed back to the balcony and watched for the promised troops. After nearly an hour, five soldiers marched down the street and into the alley. They returned a few minutes later empty-handed and marched back from whence they came. Daniel sighed with regret but continued his lonely vigil for another hour. A knock brought him back inside as Sergeant Stinton entered and stood aside as several sweating servants carried in a large copper tub.

He looked at Daniel. "Water is being heated." When Daniel opened his mouth to reply, he added, "The militia reported they found nothing in the alley."

"Yes, I saw them. Please thank Sergeant Dunn for notifying them."

Stinton nodded as another servant entered. He was a middle-aged man wearing a clean blue tabard belted at the waist with a wide strip of white cloth slung over his shoulder. Sergeant Stinton motioned to him and said, "This is the tailor."

The servant bowed, his eyes lingering on Daniel's face. He opened a small bag hanging from his belt and took out a piece of charcoal. Under Stinton's close supervision he measured Daniel, making marks on the white cloth. When he was finished, he murmured, "Your clothing will be ready by eve, Milord."

Daniel offered thanks as the man bowed and backed from the room. Soon servants returned with buckets of steaming water. When the tub was full, one of the men bowed and held out a small clay jar. The servant jumped when Stinton grabbed his arm and ripped the jar away. The man eyed the soldier nervously as he pried the lid off the jar and poked at the fine sand within. When he was satisfied, he nodded and handed the jar to Daniel, dismissing the servants and closing the door on his way out.

Daniel studied the sand for a moment, hesitantly lifting it to his nose and detecting a hint of lemon. He shrugged and dropped his robe to the floor. With a gasp he climbed in the hot water, easing himself in and sighing as stiff muscles relaxed. After soaking for a few minutes he scooped out some sand and scrubbed his body with it then his hair and beard. Feeling refreshed, he laid his head back against the top of the basin and closed his eyes. Without realizing it, he drifted off to sleep, small beads of perspiration forming on the bristles of his beard. He came back to himself when he heard a firm knock at the door and Stinton allowed the tailor in. Daniel raised his head and dropped his arms into the now cool water as goose flesh rose across his back.

The tailor ignored Daniel's efforts to cover his nakedness as he stopped in front of the tub and bowed low. "Your garments are prepared, Milord." He carried a large bundle wrapped in white cloth and tied shut with a blue ribbon, which he held out before him as he stood silently at the foot of the tub.

"Oh," Daniel said, his cheeks burning. "Thank you. Please leave them on the bed."

The servant hesitated, his eyes almost rising to Daniel's when he asked, "Would you not like to try them on, sir?"

Doing his best not shiver in the cool water, Daniel shook his head. "No. I--I'm sure they're fine. Thank you."

He hesitated a moment longer before gently laying the package on the bed. As he stepped away, his gaze shifted to Daniel's face, giving him a meaningful stare before his eyes fell to the floor. He bowed low once more and murmured, "May they please you, Lord." He backed toward the door in a half-bow, passing stoic Sergeant Stinton who followed him out and closed the door.

As soon as the door thumped against the jam, Daniel started shivering. He pulled his cold arms out of the water and stumbled from the tub, falling face-first onto the foot of the bed. Pins and needles ran the length of his numb legs as he rolled over and laid half on the bed and half splayed on the floor, trying to stifle groans of pain. He wiggled his toes, but he may as well have been moving pieces of dead meat for how much he could feel them. Out of the blue the rebellious part of his mind suddenly insisted, *it was like this the morning after.*

The thought caught his attention and the burning pain lost its intensity. He frowned. *The morning after what?* Even as he asked, he knew he didn't want the answer. It was as if there was a large flashing sign in his head, screaming in bright neon letters DANGER! GO NO FURTHER! He tried to pull himself away from the abyss, but before he had retreated completely, the answer came. *The farmer's wife.*

He shook his head violently, banging his numb feet against the stone floor in an attempt to distract himself. *No!* he screamed hysterically, grasping and twisting great handfuls of hair at his temples. *There is nothing there. The journey was bad, but nothing that bad. The Empire is good!* With the final thought, images of his time with the Emperor came rushing back and he relaxed, letting out a shuddering sigh. The Emperor's benevolence was a soothing balm on his mind, helping him to remain calm.

He nodded to himself, repeating, *The Empire is good*, and for once the rebellious part of his mind had no rejoinder. He became distantly aware that the throbbing from his legs had lessened, and so he delicately flexed his calves. He unclenched his hands, grimacing as hair came out at the roots, and stretched out his arms, dropping them onto the bed. Daniel didn't hear the door closing, nor had he seen Dunn's cold eyes watching him.

~ * ~

Daniel gave a low whistle as he held up the intricately sewn vest. An image of the Spirit Calling falls roaring down its course was preserved in thread across the back of the dark blue coat. Over the falls soared the peaks of mountains, crowned by a cloudless sky. Water crashed over the massive stone abutment that rested at its base, sending spray and foam in all directions. The image was so uncannily life-like that for a moment Daniel could hear the deafening roar. He turned the vest over, meaning to lay it on the bed, when he noticed something in the center of the image. Hidden within the crashing waves made of white thread was a silver star. Small lines radiated out from it, as if it's light were illuminating the water.

Daniel lightly traced the star, pondering its meaning. Unless one looked at the vest at an angle, the star was practically invisible. The front of the vest was not as elaborate. A silver fist was embroidered over the left lapel, and three silver buttons, all embossed with the same upraised fist, ran down the front. He slipped on the vest to top off his outfit, consisting of a white blouse with billowing sleeves, black cotton trousers, and black leather boots. Daniel tugged down the hem of the vest as he studied the other gifts that were in the tailor's bundle. Arranged on his bed was a light cotton gown, presumably to sleep in, two more pairs of leggings, and another shirt that was cream-colored. The clothing was made of fine cloth that was very soft to the touch and undoubtedly expensive, but clearly the vest was the treasure of the lot.

He absently ran his fingers over the vest as his eyes wandered across the room and landed on his filthy traveling clothes, still lying on the floor. Daniel could see the dirt (*blood,* the bothersome part of his mind cried, *It's blood!*) ground into the seams and cringed. He looked back to the new clothes and a sharp knock came at the door. Sergeant Dunn walked in and stood at attention. "The feast is prepared, sir."

Daniel was taken aback for a moment until he remembered the Emperor promising a feast in his honor. He shook his head, jaw slack. *The Emperor has already done too much!* When he didn't answer, Sergeant Stinton also entered the room and stared intently at Daniel. He finally found his voice and shook his head again. "I'm speechless. The Emperor is too great!"

Stinton smiled and nodded, but the warmth never made it to his eyes. "Yes, sir," he said. "But we must go. You are expected."

Daniel nodded, beaming. "Yes, yes of course. I don't want to keep His Majesty waiting." Stinton nodded and shared a momentary look with Dunn before the three left the room, Daniel flanked by the two sergeants.

At the great hall Dunn opened a side door to usher Daniel in. Soothing music played by a string quartet wafted out, carrying over the low-key roar of many simultaneous conversations. As the three entered the crowded hall, the guards backed away, though they paced Daniel as he wandered through the throng. The hall was packed with elegantly dressed men and women, and even the side chambers were open and filled with party-goers. Daniel scanned the room and spotted Gelnar, dressed immaculately in polished armor and a royal blue cloak. He made for the giant, but the crowd closed around him. While he tried to make his way through, Gelnar saw him coming and moved off. Losing sight of him, he gave up fighting the crowd and went with the flow.

Soon Daniel was disgorged by the crowd and stood against the far wall. He was virtually ignored by the other revelers, so Daniel turned his attention to the hall itself and was surprised by the change in its austere surroundings. The bare walls from earlier were now hung with vibrant works of art attesting to the greatness of the Empire. Everywhere Daniel looked he saw images in paintings, tapestries, sculptures, and metalwork that bore the mark of the mailed fist. All were continuations on a theme: the Emperor helping his subjects, his armies defeating enemies, or colorful parades in his honor.

He walked slowly along the wall, inspecting each work. He nodded politely to the few revelers that glanced his way but didn't stop to share in their conversations. Daniel was so engrossed in the artwork he didn't even notice that the revelers' glances were cool, fueled by either suspicion or disdain. Eventually he reached the front of the great hall where a final item stood in a dimly-lit corner. Curious as to why it wasn't displayed as prominently as the rest, Daniel walked over for a closer look.

On a polished wooden stand was a magnificent suit of plate armor. The center of the breastplate was embossed with a rose entwined around the pommel of a sword that pointed downward. The pauldrons were covered with large gold discs engraved with an intricate image of the Spirit Calling falls, and the steel vambraces and gauntlets were overlaid with gold roses. The silver-plated helm was topped by a golden crown studded with rubies, emeralds, sapphires, and diamonds.

Daniel stared at it in wonder. Though he couldn't put his finger on it, the armor seemed out of place somehow. Finally it hit him that it was the only decoration in the hall that didn't include the mailed fist. As that realization sunk in, he noticed something else different about the armor: it had several imperfections. It was riddled with small holes, a little larger than the diameter of a pencil. Also the right side of the breastplate and the helm had been dented in, though the latter was partially hidden by the crown.

Daniel ran a hand over the small holes in one pauldron, considering them when a man spoke behind him. "Ah, Marten." Daniel pulled his hand away and turned to see the unsmiling face of Governor DePlaynes, the man's bald pate shining in the candlelight. "Welcome to my city."

Daniel dipped his head. "Thank you. I'm sorry, but I don't remember your name."

DePlaynes' upper lip twitched. "Yes, of course. Captain Gelnar neglected to introduce us." He spat out Gelnar's name as if it were a curse, his lip curling in disdain. "I am Governor DePlaynes, ruling adjunct for his Glorious Majesty in the Eastern Provinces." With a shrug he added, "Stonefall is my provincial capital."

Daniel nodded, eager to move past the governor's apparent dislike of Gelnar. "Oh, of course. Please forgive me. You have a beautiful city. I would love to explore it sometime."

DePlaynes gave Daniel a thin-lipped smile. "It serves me nicely. However, it can be…rough at times. It would be best for you to stay within Stonefall Castle."

Daniel nodded. "I know what you mean. From my balcony I saw a man attacked earlier. The militia came, but they were too late to help."

DePlaynes frowned. "Yes, I heard about your involvement. We do as best we can to maintain order, but these Naphthalians are barbaric animals. We offer them the hand of friendship, and they push it away." He clenched his fist as he said the last, his dark eyes smoldering. His anger startled Daniel, but he didn't want to offend his host, so he nodded and hoped the look on his face would be taken for thoughtful understanding. At a loss of what to say, his gaze wandered back to the armor. DePlaynes saw his glance and asked, "Do you like the art of the Empire?"

Daniel nodded. "They are very nice." He motioned with his hand to the armor and asked, "I was curious about this one. Where did it come from?"

DePlaynes glanced at the armor and his face lit with grim satisfaction. "Ah, the armor of Begnauld the Fool. I must say, it is one of my favorites." He chuckled and glanced around the room before turning back to Daniel. When he saw his confused look, he asked, "Surely you've heard of Begnauld?"

Daniel shook his head. "I'm not from around here," he murmured, his face flushing.

DePlaynes studied Daniel for a minute before saying, "Well, I guess you could say Begnauld is the reason I'm here. Naphthali recently joined the Empire, you see. Before that Begnauld was their king."

Daniel frowned. "Oh really?"

The governor nodded. "The Empire had always…respected the Naphthalian desire for independence. We did not interfere with their internal practices, no matter how barbaric. Five years ago, their hierarchy was weakening, and so His Grace the Emperor personally offered friendship to Begnauld. The great fool refused, and was soon assassinated by his own countrymen."

Daniel looked back at the holes and dents in the armor. Now he could see arrows filling it like a pin cushion. "So the Empire stepped in?"

"Not at first. When His Grace heard of his friend's death, he sent envoys to broker a peace between the disjointed clans that divide this backward country. When the ambassadors where attacked, the Empire had no choice but to step in. It we hadn't, it could have destabilized the entire region."

Daniel nodded understanding. Still, the way DePlaynes referred to the Naphthalians bothered him. The annoying part of his mind screamed at him, but he ignored it. At that moment the musicians stopped playing and a silver bell rang out. Conversations died as everyone turned toward the front of the hall, to the right of where Daniel and DePlaynes stood. The four sets of double doors were thrown open, and out marched Chancellor Quarren, flanked by his attendants. Unlike the revelers, Quarren had not bothered to dress elegantly. In fact, he looked like he was wearing the same robes Daniel had seen the day before.

He raised his hands for silence, even though it had already fallen. In a pleasant, quiet voice that carried over the crowd he said, "Welcome to this evening's festivities. Many apologies, but His Great Eminence will not be able to attend. He asks that you enjoy yourselves, and please forgive his absence." He raised his hands again, smiling politely. "Thank you."

He retreated into the throne room, and the music started again, soon followed by the buzz of conversation. The doors remained open, and Daniel turned to excuse himself form DePlaynes but the governor had already disappeared into the crowd. Daniel shrugged and moved to the closest of the doors, following courtiers that entered the throne room where servants were preparing a feast. Quarren sat next to the empty throne, smiling as Daniel entered. "Welcome, Daniel Marten. I trust everything in your quarters was to your liking."

Daniel nodded. "Yes, thank you, Chancellor."

"That is good." His gaze moved on, silently dismissing Daniel, but when he didn't step away, his dark eyes came back. "Was there something else?"

Daniel flushed. "Well...I just, I wondered if I...I could see the Emperor." He felt the heat in his face, but he couldn't help himself. He *had* to see that great man again!

Quarren smiled again but shook his head. "Many apologies, Daniel. His Grace is a very busy man; he has been pulled away on important business. He commanded me to share with you his regrets. He assures me that he will meet you when Lord Malthion arrives."

Crestfallen, Daniel nodded. "Oh, sure, I understand. I just...I look forward to seeing him again."

The chancellor smiled one last time. "Of course. His majesty has that effect on many who meet him." His attendant held a scroll for Quarren to sign and his gaze returned to Daniel afterwards. "Please, enjoy the evening. If there is anything you need, send me word."

Feeling awkward, Daniel bowed and said, "Thank you, you are very kind." The chancellor nodded, but his attention had already returned to his work. Daniel sighed and walked to tables laden with food. He wasn't hungry but didn't know what else to do.

~ * ~

As he stepped away, Quarren's sharp gaze snapped back to Daniel. With a flick of his wrist, he dismissed the attendants. His intense gaze rarely missed anything, and that evening was no exception. He saw the image on the back of Daniel's vest, and more importantly, the image hidden *within* the image. His eyes narrowed as he considered it before motioning for the Blood Guard.

Within twenty minutes the guard moved unseen down a darkened hall dedicated to servant's quarters. When he found his mark, he silently cracked open a door and glanced inside. He took a deep breath and held it, closing his eyes. When he opened them, he exploded into action, throwing the door open and charging in.

In another twenty minutes, the tailor was forced down a stone stairway into darkness. His eyes were wide with terror and his thin hair was askew as blood ran from the corner of his mouth. Along with him came his wife and their teenage son. Next was his sister, her husband and their three children, the youngest a five year old girl. Finally, his elderly mother and father were led down the stairs. The Rule of Ten applied and was enforced ruthlessly. The tailor's family entered the dungeons of Stonefall Castle and was never seen again. The Emperor's will be done. Long live that great man.

Chapter Nine

Daniel picked at a meal of exquisite delicacies before wandering the hall a while longer. Captain Gelnar and Governor DePlaynes were nowhere to be found and the other guests continued to ignore him, so he soon cut back toward the side door where he'd entered. As he approached, Stinton and Dunn materialized out of the crowd and Dunn stepped forward. "Did you need anything, sir?"

Daniel shook his head. "No, Sergeant. I think I'm ready to return to my room."

Dunn opened the door, Stinton darting out into the corridor. Daniel and Dunn joined him and the three men retraced their steps up several flights of stairs. When they finally reached Daniel's floor, he was breathing heavily. His face was pink from the exertion, and perspiration beaded on his forehead. In contrast, the two guards weren't taxed in the slightest. They shared a quick look of contempt when Daniel bent over and rested his hands on his knees, wheezing. When he regained his breath and the alarming color faded from his cheeks, they led him to his room.

Dim light shone down the hall from widely-spaced torches hanging in sconces, and as they approached, Daniel could see light shining underneath the door of his apartment. He glanced at the doors they passed and saw that all of the rooms were dark within except for his. Had he not been so addled by the Emperor, Daniel would have found his isolation disconcerting, but as it was, he just thought, *Everyone's still at the party.*

When Stinton finished searching his room, Daniel wished the men goodnight and shut the door quietly. The copper tub and soiled clothing were gone, and a small fire was burning briskly, looking out of place in the huge hearth. The flames lit the room in muted yellows and oranges, making the blue carpet appear black. Daniel shuddered as he looked at the inky darkness and his rebellious mind whispered, *It's blood.* He mentally skipped away from the thought, turning to his wardrobe. He took out the light cotton gown and ran the fabric through his hands. Feeling foolish, he stripped out of the fine new clothes and slipped the gown over his head.

The light cloth felt really quite comfortable, even though he couldn't shake the feeling that the gown looked too effeminate. He shrugged and climbed into the soft bed, sighing as he relaxed into the plush mattress. *I'm ready for a good night's sleep.* Soon Daniel drifted off, but he didn't find the restful sleep he'd hoped for.

~ * ~

From Daniel's perspective, it wasn't so much that he'd drifted off as that he'd blinked. His eyelids descended, blocking his view of the stone ceiling, and when he opened them again, he was squinting into bright lights. He felt a brief stab of elation and immediately yearned to look through the brightness, but his elation faded when he realized that he *could* see through them. It was a cluster of four circular white lights, and they weren't really pointed at him, but rather off to his side. Daniel squinted a little more and could see the four lights were interconnected on a stainless steel bracket.

Then all thought fled as his left hand was crushed and a feral scream rent the air. He cringed away and at the same time tore his gaze around to see where the noise was coming from. Ashley lay on a table beside him. She was wearing a blue hospital gown, her dark blonde hair looking almost black it was so soaked with sweat. Her bare legs were in stirrups and a doctor knelt between her open thighs. She had Daniel's left hand in a death grip, and his right hand was behind her right knee, supporting her.

The doctor looked up and said, "Okay, Ashley, one more time. Now push!"

Ashley bore down and Daniel gave her leg a gentle pull toward her shoulder, willing his strength into her petite body as she pushed with all her might. Tears rolled from the corners of her closed eyes, and her lips pulled back from white teeth in a grimace. She held her breath as she pushed, her face turning purple and small veins standing out on her smooth forehead. Daniel felt a stab of pain and then wetness as Ashley's fingernails cut into his left hand. She pushed more, her head tilting back and veins standing out on her neck as well. Again came the feral cry. "Aaaahhh!"

Daniel felt as if his soul was being torn apart, watching the woman he loved in so much pain and not being able to help. Tears coursed down his cheeks as he cooed, "Good, Baby, now breathe, breathe."

The doctor overrode him, saying, "That's it! We're past the shoulders! Now just one more push, Ashley, and we're done!"

She moaned as she hitched in a couple of breaths and bore down one final time. Even Daniel could sense how effortlessly the baby slid out. Ashley's gasp of relief was drowned out by the newborn's cry, sounding more like the chirps of a little bird than the lusty cries that the baby would soon offer. "Congratulations, Mom and Dad. It's a boy!" The doctor held up the tiny baby and a goofy grin split Daniel's face. The floodgates opened, and all the stress and fear of the past few hours rushed out, coursing down his cheeks.

He couldn't speak. All he could do was smile at his son and turn to look at his wife's exhausted face. She smiled tiredly back and said in a weak voice, "Another boy?"

Daniel nodded, tears still flowing. Finally he was able to force words past the knot in his throat. "I love you."

He couldn't hear her, but Daniel could see Ashley's lips move as she said, "I love you too."

At the same time the doctor asked, "Dad do you want to cut th--"

Through the entire sentence, the doctor's voice steadily faded away until it was completely gone. Daniel was so focused on Ashley's face that he didn't notice everything fading to white until even her lovely features started to fade. Startled, he whipped his head around and saw nothing but thick white fog. Panic clawing inside him; he looked back to Ashley, and only her blue eyes were visible, looking at him with such love and exhaustion that it broke his heart. "No," he groaned. He closed his fingers, meaning to hold onto hers, but his hand was empty. He glanced down and when he looked back up, even her eyes were gone. He stood alone in the white light…the *blinding* white light. Tears coursed down his face again, only they were tears of frustration and anger. "No!" His voice was a growl rather than a groan.

He knew where he was, and he needed to get beyond the light. *He* was beyond that light. Everything that meant anything to him was hiding within the brilliance. If he could only part it…

Even as he thought it, the light started to fade, steadily dimming to black. Daniel roared in rage, "No! Let me *through*!" The blackness was complete and Daniel opened his eyes to see the stone ceiling. He was in his bed, the first rays of morning sun shining in the open balcony door. Again his door quietly snicked shut, Sergeant Stinton retreating into the hall unnoticed.

He looked down at his mostly naked body and thought, *Stupid gown!* He'd tossed and turned in his sleep, and the night gown had shimmied up his body and was bunched around his neck. He stood up and pushed it down; his mind was still in the delivery room. The dream had not been like the others. It wasn't flashes of memory that slowly came back to him upon waking. He was there, fully immersed as if he were watching a television in his mind. He lifted his left hand and saw a small white scar on the inside of his little finger where Ashley's nails gouged him. "Ashley," he murmured. "We had two boys. Nate, and…another. A girl and two boys."

As usual no other memories came back, even though the new one was the most intense and complete of any he'd had so far. His wife's image was fixed in his mind, but it didn't bring back any other insights into her personality, or their history together. Still he cherished the new piece of his past. He replayed the memory over and over again, holding it close to his heart as if it were the baby boy that his wife had just brought into the world. *But what world? Certainly not this one. The...hospital...wasn't like anything I've seen here.*

He thought of the Emperor's promise. He'd see him again when his assistant arrived, a man Chancellor Quarren named Lord Malthion. The Emperor said perhaps this Malthion could help Daniel recover his memory. He again saw the delivery in his mind and memorized every detail. He grimly nodded to himself. He would do *anything* to remember Ashley and his children. And he'd do *anything* to get back to them. His conscience quailed with foreboding at his intensity, but Daniel didn't care. No price was too high. He would remember them, and he would return to them.

~ * ~

Daniel dressed and sauntered onto the balcony, surveying the city in the light of a new day. The citizens greeted one another as they went about their business, many going out of their way to speak with neighbors. A baker left his shop carrying three large baskets of fresh bread. As he reached back to shut the door, a basket tipped and would surely have spilled had a passer-by not stabilized it. The man helped him carry the baskets to his street-side stand and when the baker offered him a loaf, he smiled and shook his head, continuing down the street.

Governor DePlaynes' words echoed in Daniel's mind. *They don't look like animals to me.* Thinking of the arrogant governor made him frown and wonder why the Emperor would tolerate such a man. Then he remembered the rebels that attacked Gelnar's troops as they peacefully made their way to Stonefall. He again heard the screams of the dying men and the woman, and he shuddered.

The hair on the back of his neck stood on end. *Screaming woman? There were no women in our group.* Even as the thought formed he knew it didn't sound right. He felt like he was just on the cusp of some greater understanding, and it made his blood run cold. He shook his head and retreated from the thought. *There were no women. I don't know what I was thinking.* He raised a goblet of water to his lips and saw his hand was shaking. Something like panic was rising inside him, and his eyes swam with tears as he looked without seeing into the blue sky. He kneeled and rested the cup on the balcony floor. He took a deep breath and held it before slowly letting it out, and finally the racing, clamoring, *clawing* feeling in his chest subsided.

Daniel shuffled back into the room and dropped heavily into a stuffed chair. He hid his face in his hands and breathed deeply. Unbidden, the governor's words returned to him, and he thought about the horrors he'd witnessed on the road, carefully keeping his mind vague on the particulars. Then he thought of the old man that was dragged into the alley. He gave a tight nod. *Governor DePlaynes is right. Some of them* are *barbarians.* Now he understood. The Emperor probably didn't particularly like the governor, but he needed his skills and understanding of the populace to bring peace. Sometimes we do what we must, and we use the tools at hand, even if we don't like them.

Daniel's new clarity helped calm him and reminded him that he had some unfinished business as well. He walked across the room and opened the door to find Sergeant Stinton, his bald pate gleaming in the sunlight. Daniel nodded and said, "Good morning, Sergeant. I would like some breakfast. Then I'd like to speak with Captain Gelnar, if possible." He was long overdue in apologizing for how he'd treated the wise captain during their travels, but he meant to rectify that.

Stinton looked at him warily. "The captain is a busy man. He may not have time today."

Daniel was crestfallen but not completely daunted. "Oh, yes, of course he is. Well, could you see if it would be possible? I really need to speak with him."

Stinton studied him for another minute and finally shrugged. "I will see what I can do." Daniel blew out a heavy sigh and smiled, while it was all Stinton could do to keep from snorting in his face. With great effort he controlled himself and asked, "Is there anything else, sir?"

The stupid smile still plastered on his face, Daniel replied, "Oh, no, Sergeant. That'd be great." Stinton nodded and reached in to pull the door shut when Daniel added, "Thank you." He nodded once more, barely maintaining an impassive façade as the door shut with a soft thud.

Within minutes Stinton opened the door and a servant entered carrying a tray of food and cider. She walked to the table and curtsied, her eyes never leaving the floor. "Milord," she murmured, her lower lip trembling.

Daniel could tell she was frightened as she sat down the tray and retreated. He was so surprised by her demeanor that she was at the door before he remembered his manners. "Thank you." She froze, her eyes opening wider. When Daniel said nothing more, she curtsied and backed out of the room, Stinton following her with hungry eyes as he pulled the door closed. Daniel felt the hair rise on his neck again. With a great effort he forced the girl's terrified face from his mind, but his appetite was gone.

Minutes later there was a sharp knock, and Dunn entered before Daniel could invite him in. "Captain Gelnar sends his apologies. He will be unavailable today, sir."

Daniel nodded, disappointed. "I understand. Thank you, Sergeant. Would it be possible to walk around the castle? I'd like to see more."

Dunn gave a brisk nod. "Yes, sir. When Sergeant Stinton returns, we may venture out if you wish." He left the room and the door thudded shut once more.

Soon there was a brief knock and the two sergeants entered with a servant. Stinton stepped forward and said, "This man will guide you."

Daniel nodded and looked over the young man. He was no more than fourteen years old, with just the ghost of stubble on his cheeks. Like the other servants, he did not raise his eyes from the floor. He stood practically shoulder-to-shoulder with Dunn, but even so he leaned slightly in the opposite direction, as if he feared getting too close to the sergeant. His hands shook as he tried to stand motionless.

Daniel smiled and said, "Hello."

His eyes glued to the floor, the boy stammered, "M--milord."

Thinking of the violence he'd seen on the streets, Daniel smiled and leaned in. In a quiet voice he said, "It's all right. You're safe here."

Daniel intended to calm him, but his words had the opposite effect. The boy flinched and bobbed his head. "Y--yes, m--mil--l--lord." Both his hands and voice shook more than ever, and his face had gone very pale.

Mystified but determined to keep trying, Daniel infused his voice with kindness again. "What is your name?"

The boy stammered, "M--my name is...is G--G--Gor, Lord."

The boy never raised his head and wouldn't see the gesture, but Daniel nodded encouragingly anyway. "Gor, it's nice to meet you. I'm Daniel. Can you show me around the castle? I would like to see more of it."

Gor swallowed, his Adam's apple jittering. "Y--y--yes, L--l--lord".

Daniel saw Stinton sneer at the boy. When he noticed Daniel watching him, his face took on a blank look as impassive as the one Dunn usually offered. He looked back to Gor and said, "Very good, Gor. Let's go."

The four men spent the next several hours passing through a maze of levels and rooms, seeing the best Stonefall Castle had to offer. Finally they came to a large oak door that opened onto one of the castle's perimeter towers. Gor turned and stammered, "Ob--ob--observation t--t--t--tow--tower."

"Sounds nice," Daniel said with forced cheer, already dreading the stairs that waited on the other side of the door. He needn't have bothered. The tower's interior was hollow, the expected stone staircase winding around the wall, receding in the darkness far above. What brought Daniel up short, though, was the center of the tower, which was completely filled by a complex network of wooden beams and ropes. In the midst of the vast construction was a wooden platform with a rope rail ringing its perimeter. The platform could easily hold ten men. At one corner a thin rope descended from above.

Gor gingerly stepped onto the platform, the guards following without hesitation. Daniel saw the look on Gor's face, though, and stopped short. "What's that?"

When Dunn saw that Daniel hadn't followed them, he immediately stepped off himself. "It is a lift, sir. It will spare us a long climb." The words were spoken in the same impassive voice the sergeant always used, but Daniel sensed contempt in his tone. The climb would not faze the soldiers, but they knew how much it would tax him.

Daniel nodded slowly, his cheeks burning. He swallowed his fear and stepped into the compartment. Stinton pulled on the thin rope hanging overhead and high above a tinkling bell could barely be heard. Within moments the lift lurched upward and Gor whimpered, but soon the ascent smoothed out and they rose quickly to the top of the tower, where a hole was cut in the floor that fit the size of the platform. They passed through the hole and came to a halt.

To one side was a massive cog wheel wrapped with thick rope that had spokes jutting from it. Men stood between the spokes, resting after turning the wheel to raise the lift. The other side of the room was filled with a large wooden table that had detailed maps painted on its surface. As the men walked past the table, Daniel saw an intricate drawing near the center of the map that closely resembled the fortress. Around the base of the fortress was a banner that read in flowing script "Stonefall." Daniel would have loved to examine the map more carefully, but the other men continued toward double doors on the opposite wall, so he hurried to keep up. Gor held a door open as bright sunlight bathed the room. Daniel walked through the door, and the view took his breath away.

A wide stone terrace ringed the top of the tower, hedged in by a waist-high stone wall. Daniel walked to the wall and let out a low whistle. As far as the eye could see were green pastures, the darker green of forests, and the occasional black squares of tilled fields. The most prominent features nearby where the wide blue ribbon of the river and the massive shantytown that stretched along its flood plane. Daniel recognized the western road as it stretched out before him, eventually being lost in the distance. The great Cloudspeak Mountains were only a purple shadow on the horizon; unless one knew what to look for they could be mistaken for dark clouds.

Seeing the smudges brought home for Daniel just how far he had traveled. He was uncertain of much of his journey, but he distinctly remembered traveling at the base of the Cloudspeaks, and how they'd towered over him. To see them reduced to something so inconsequential awed Daniel. "I've come a *great* distance," he murmured.

Dunn stepped forward. "What was that, sir?"

Daniel glanced at the sergeant and murmured, "Nothing...it was nothing." He walked slowly around the veranda that ringed the tower, enjoying the views of the city and the countryside. To the east he looked directly into the fortress itself. Rising up before him was the central tower with its massive imperial flag flapping in the breeze. Behind that was the East Tower, and beyond that Daniel could see the vast forest that stretched away from the city. He could tell that in the distance the forest ended, but his vision was not good enough to see what might lie beyond.

Eventually he reached the double doors and returned to the interior. He moved to the detailed map and saw that much of Naphthali was the rolling green hills and prairies he saw from outside. Due east, beyond the vast forest, was more of the same until it tapered into rocky coastland. Written in white scrolling letters across the deep blue was "The Azure Ocean". He lingered at the map for quite awhile, and when he finally had his fill of its intricate details and fine craftsmanship, he joined Gor and his guards. "This is amazing! Thank you for bringing me here."

Gor dipped a deep bow and murmured, "M--m--milord."

Stinton asked, "Would you like to see more, sir?"

Daniel stifled a yawn and shook his head. "No, I've seen all I can for one day."

Stinton nodded. "Very well. We will return to your quarters." He turned to Gor and said, "You are dismissed." His hard tone held nothing of the usual deference he offered Daniel, and he'd already turned and was walking to the lift as Gor bowed and stuttered an acknowledgement. Daniel glanced uncomfortably at Gor, feeling badly for how brusquely he was dismissed. Stinton and Dunn were waiting, though, so he dropped his gaze and followed them, leaving the young man still bowing at the top of the winding staircase.

It took nearly an hour for the three to return to the East Tower. Daniel had a painful stitch in his side as he dropped heavily into a chair, clutching his flank until the wheezing subsided. Food was already on the table and a fire crackled in the huge fireplace once more. The walls of the suite were reflected in hues of reds and oranges by both the flames and the setting sun as Daniel ate his supper. Soon he'd dressed in his gown and crawled into bed, hoping for a more restful night's sleep. It proved to be better than the one before, but restfulness still eluded him.

~ * ~

The next two nights were a continual flow of disconnected memories. Piece by painful piece, he slowly broke down that damnable wall within his mind and reclaimed his history. He now knew that his family lived on a farm, and that his daughter went away to learn every day. Where she went was on the tip of his tongue, but like so much it refused to come, though a large yellow vehicle of some sort was associated with it.

He also had disjointed memories of his parents. He could see his mother standing at a stove, cooking the "frog bellies", and he had a brief image of his parents in hushed conversation, not realizing their children were listening. Their faces were pinched with worry, and with the scene came a sense of foreboding. The word STRIKE floated on his consciousness, only in his mind's eye the word was fire engine red and in letters ten feet tall. He didn't like to think about it, but at the same time he was so hungry for more that he obsessed over it, exploring to see if it led to anything else.

During the days Daniel toured more of the fortress, but nothing captivated him as much as the Observation Tower. The truth was that although it was all very impressive, after awhile it tended to blend together. He reflected on his nights rather than paying attention to the latest wonder and finally he told Stinton he'd seen enough. That didn't mean he stopped calling on his guards though. Daniel still felt eaten up by guilt about how he'd treated Gelnar. Each morning he asked for an audience, and each afternoon was denied. He also requested updates on Lord Malthion's progress, and if he could see Governor DePlaynes or Chancellor Quarren, but all queries were refused.

Daniel was slipping into boredom, and even watching the city from his balcony ceased to hold his attention by the third day. He paced his room, endlessly rolling over the memories he'd recovered, like a treasure hunter carefully examining the clues that would lead to the mother lode. His efforts were always in vain, but it didn't stop him from trying to ferret out new gems.

While the relative inactivity had given his body time to recover from the near exhaustion of traveling, the long dream-filled nights had taken a toll on him. Dark wells grew under blood-shot eyes, and his ruddy tan quickly faded. The overall effect of his obsession was that he started to take on the look of a haunted man. His focus frequently drifted, and a glassy-eyed stare greeted the sergeants when they silently opened his door to check on him. He stopped eating more than a few mouthfuls of the food they brought, and his rooms began to take on the sour tang of sweat and single-minded focus.

On the dawn of the fourth day the news he'd been waiting for finally came. Lord Malthion would arrive later that day. When the Emperor and the Lord would make time for him was still unsure, but definitely his wait was nearing an end. When Sergeant Dunn told him, it was like a bucket of cold water thrown in Daniel's face. He snapped fully awake for the first time in days and thrummed with excitement. "I would like to take another bath, please."

"Of course, sir," Dunn replied, unconsciously wrinkling his nose at the smell.

Daniel was oblivious to Dunn's reaction as he nearly bounced in place, unable to contain himself. He bobbed his head and said, "This is great news. Thank you!"

~ * ~

Dunn nodded and exited the room to order the bath. After the orders were given and he and Stinton were alone in the empty hallway, he allowed himself a moment of undisguised derision. As a member of the Blood Guard, personal body guard for the Emperor, Dunn had delivered the news that Lord Malthion was coming to many people. This was without a doubt the first time anyone was excited. The fool would learn soon enough.

~ * ~

As the day waned, Daniel marked off time by watching shadows march up the wall of his suite. He was scrubbed clean and dressed in the same outfit he'd worn to the dinner, seemingly so long ago. He sat at the table and unconsciously tugged on the fine vest to smooth out wrinkles that set in from wearing it all day. He rested his arm on the table and bumped an untouched tray of food. He was too excited to eat and the tray sat unnoticed all day long, the freshly cut fruit turning brown and soft cheese melting into a stiff puddle. When servants came for his bath and again with food, Daniel's heart jumped to his throat. "Any news?" he asked the sergeants, but both times they shook their heads and closed the door behind them when the servants left. Daniel sighed and tried to control his impatience. *What is taking so long?*

As the room began to darken, Daniel lost hope. He sighed deeply yet again and drummed his fingers on the tabletop, obliviously nearly catching the edge of a silver tray and flipping food in the air. Dusk arrived and the room darkened further. When a knock came, he assumed it was a servant coming to light the fire, and he couldn't even muster the energy to look toward the door when it opened. He was lost in thought when he finally realized no servants had entered. He looked over and saw Dunn and Stinton standing in the doorway, looking back at him. He returned their gaze uncertainly for a moment before he realized what it meant. "Is it time?" he asked, a ghost of a smile lifting the corners of his mouth.

Stinton nodded. "His Grace the Emperor will see you now."

Daniel sprang across the room, his heart welling in his chest. Radiant joy shined from his face making him look ten years younger as he skidded to a halt in front of his guards. "Yes!" he crowed, pumping a fist in the air. "I'm ready."

The sergeants shared a look before Stinton said, "Come with us." Daniel bobbed his head, and they led him out of the East Tower and through the maze of halls. Finally, they came to a door guarded by two more of the Blood Guard. They nodded to Dunn and opened it, allowing them into the back corner of the throne room. Dunn and Stinton flanked Daniel just inside the door and grabbed his arms, stopping him from going further. He frowned at them and tried to pull away, but they stared straight ahead and held him tightly.

The first blossom of doubt bloomed in his chest, but Daniel stamped it out and looked around the room. To his left were the double doors that led to the great hall, but his view of the dais was blocked by a line of columns. The beautiful candelabras that stood at each column were gone, the room looking darker and more sinister without their warm light. Torches giving off a foul odor and greenish smoke replaced them, fastened to plain iron sconces.

Daniel's unease continued to build as the center set of double doors opened and Gelnar marched in, followed by two more of the Blood Guard. His polished armor reflected the torches' green light as he took two steps forward and dropped to one knee, lowering his head. Echoes of his footfalls died away as he continued to kneel and silence fell over the room.

Finally, a gravelly voice commanded, "Come." The voice was thin and reedy, but its tone spoke of unfathomable power, unspeakable malice. It froze Daniel's blood, and as the sergeants stepped forward, he couldn't make himself follow. Unfazed, they dragged him two steps into the room before he was able to make his legs respond. When they cleared the columns, Daniel saw the Emperor seated in his throne, glaring down at him. At the base of the dais stood Chancellor Quarren, and a few steps before him was the man that had spoken: Lord Malthion. Even the presence of the Emperor was not enough for Daniel to take his eyes off the man. His knees shook as he was led into the center of the throne room and stopped.

The sergeants let go of his arms, and Daniel swayed slightly as they drifted two steps back and off to either side. He heard ringing footfalls as Gelnar closed directly behind him, stopping about even with Dunn and Stinton. Panic was building in Daniel, and even though he'd misjudged Gelnar, his back felt particularly exposed as the captain advanced, heard but unseen. He tried to swallow but his throat was bone dry. All that came out was a clicking sound.

Malthion was a tall thin man, so thin he looked emaciated, but an aura of power surrounded him and negated any impression of frailty. He wore a full-length blood red robe, a black mantle hanging down from his shoulders and ending in a peaked hood that rested on his thin back. His head was shaved bald, but his whole scalp was covered with intricate arcane tattoos that terminated in an artificial widow's peak over pencil-thin brows. His cheeks were covered with a thin gray beard, and the flesh under his eyes was pierced by a series of gold and platinum rings. The thin eyebrows and lines of piercings framed his burning black eyes, looking like twin windows into Hell. Thin, papery white skin covered his face and skeletal hands.

Malthion pulled Daniel in with a burning gaze that rooted him to the spot, and it seemed that he was not just looking into Daniel's eyes, but rather through them, just as the Emperor had. Finally, he croaked, "Your mind is blocked." His thin lips parted with the words to reveal black stubs of ancient teeth that had seen far better days.

Daniel wanted to look away but couldn't. He whimpered as the Emperor coldly asked, "Can you remove it? I would read him."

Daniel whimpered again, unable even to cringe as Malthion closed on him. A skeletal hand as cold as the grave rested on his forehead. Malthion pressed upward with his thumb, opening Daniel's right eye wider. "I believe I can." A single tear tracked down his cheek as the sorcerer released him.

Malthion stepped back and pushed his voluminous sleeves up, revealing scrawny arms covered in arcane tattoos. He raised his arms at the elbow, fingers splayed out and palms facing him. His eyes rolled up in his skull as he chanted under his breath. The chanting came faster and faster, and the middle three fingers of each hand slowly closed, leaving only his thumbs and little fingers extended. His forearms crossed over his chest, the extended thumbs touching, as the chanting reached a fevered pitch. A ball of light formed in front of Malthion's forearms and as the chanting reached a crescendo, he threw his arms wide, his eyes focusing on Daniel. The ball shot out and exploded blinding light over Daniel, rocking him back.

He would have screamed if he could, but he was still frozen in place by Malthion's will. His mind was on fire. He could feel Malthion's consciousness within his skull, pawing carelessly through the memories he'd recovered. Desperate to stop the pain, he tried to force the alien presence out and close his eyes, but to no avail. Finally, Daniel felt a terrible rending, as if he had been mentally torn in two. Pain the likes of which he'd never imagined descended over him. Through the roaring pain he dimly heard Malthion whisper, "Ah. I am through, My Lord."

He could hear the Emperor's voice, as if from a great distance. "Show me." The pain reached new heights, and even Malthion's will was not enough to keep Daniel in place as an even greater alien consciousness entered his mind. He fainted, collapsing in a heap on the stone floor.

~ * ~

Daniel was lost in a black void. There was no thought, no sentience or understanding, just all-encompassing darkness. He had no idea how long the darkness lasted, but eventually it did lift, and when it did there was no fade to white, it was instantaneous. One second there was nothing, and the next a thought raced through his abused mind, *I forgot. Ashley wanted me to get a gallon of milk.* When the thought registered, his eyes popped open and without realizing it he gasped, "Ashley!"

He expected to be in his SUV, but instead he saw the floor of the throne room in Stonefall Castle, and everything came rushing back. *Everything.* All of his past fell neatly into place, and he could remember every important event and mundane moment from his entire life. He knew his children were Elizabeth, Nate, and Ethan, and that Ashley was worried about him making it home in the storm. He remembered the storm, and the crash. He remembered cutting his face, and the blood and the numbing cold. There was a black void, but then he remembered waking in the field.

He remembered *everything*. He knew how the journey to Stonefall really happened, and the atrocities Gelnar committed. He remembered the farmer's wife, and the blinding of the old man. Worst of all he remembered the terror of having that cold presence in his mind, leafing through his thoughts as if it were flipping carelessly through the pages of a book. The alien consciousness had exposed him to the very core of his being, and he felt corrupted, he felt *violated*. The mental assault was as violent and shattering as rape. Daniel almost wished he could forget everything again, if it meant he could escape that feeling. The…*thing*, creeping with cold fingers through ideas and thoughts it had no right to even see, let alone experience as it had.

Every precious memory was tainted by the sorcerer's presence. It was almost as if he could see him lurking in the background of every birthday party, every intimate moment, and every laugh and tear he'd shared with Ashley and the kids. He trembled with rage, but also with fear. If Malthion could do this, what else could he do?

All of this flashed through Daniel's mind in seconds, and much of it he didn't actually consider and analyze until later. The incredible depth of his hurt wouldn't become evident until afterward, but for now he only knew that his memory had returned, that the effort had cost him greatly. And that a monster awaited him.

Daniel stared blankly down at the stone floor, and as he came back to himself, he raised his head to see that Stinton and Dunn were holding him by the arms. Dunn saw him raise his head, and they roughly pulled on Daniel's arms, hoisting him to his feet. The throne room's furnishings had been changed while he was unconscious. A large stone basin sat in the middle of the floor, a few feet in front of him. The Emperor stood on the near side looking at him while Malthion rested his thin arms on its far edge. His bald head was lowered as he studied whatever was within.

Hatred and fear welled up within Daniel as he looked at the Emperor, but when their eyes locked, a sense of calm washed over him. He smiled as green mist rolled over his blue eyes and said, "It's good that you've come back to us, Daniel. Many apologies for Malthion's…techniques, but I trust you understand it had to be done."

The vitriol that Daniel wanted to spew dried up under the Emperor's gaze, and he only managed a slight nod. His smile broadened, engulfing his entire face except the ice blue eyes, which still coldly studied Daniel through the green mist. "That is good," he murmured. "I do still want to help you, you know. My servant was able to use what he learned to open a window." He beckoned toward the stone basin and said, "Come."

The sergeants released Daniel's arms as he walked to the edge of the basin and looked down. It was filled with a silvery liquid that swirled continuously. Within the ripples there appeared to be shreds of images, stretched thin and pulled apart as they traveled the currents and eddies within the stone pool. Before Daniel's eyes the liquid stopped undulating and the surface turned completely black. A light began to grow from within until it finally resolved itself into a large image that made Daniel gasp. Ashley stood in the kitchen of their farmhouse, wearing an old pair of jeans and a work shirt, her hair disheveled. Boxes stood on the countertops around her, and behind her Daniel could see through the door into the completely empty living room. Tears floated on the surface of her puffy eyes, and as he watched, she lowered her head and covered her face in her hands, sobbing silently.

Tears traced down Daniel's face as well. His heart ached to hold her. She seemed so close he could almost reach out and touch her. The Emperor's voice was a quiet, lulling whisper in Daniel's ear. "You've been gone a long time. They never found a body, so the life insurance wouldn't pay. Ashley couldn't run the pharmacy herself, and she couldn't find a buyer. She mortgaged the house to get enough collateral to entice a new pharmacist to manage it. She lost the store, the house, everything. All because you came here."

Daniel's eyes grew wide as he spoke, and he slowly shook his head, as if his denial could make what the Emperor was saying untrue. A hand rose to his mouth, covering his lips like a child holding back a scream while watching a scary movie. It was scary alright, but it was no movie. The Emperor paused to savor Daniel's pain while the image in the basin faded and the silvery liquid churned once more.

He continued, but his voice took on a persuasive, suggestive tone. "You could go back." Daniel's eyes darted to the Emperor. "You may be able to salvage some of your life if you return now. At the very least, you could hold your dear Ashley, and the children. You could find another job...give the American dream another go."

Unable to believe what he was hearing, Daniel finally found his voice. "You--you can take me back?"

The Emperor nodded. "Yes. As I said, I want to help you. I have the power to return you to your world...if that is what you want." He paused for a moment before asking, "*Is* that what you want, Daniel?"

Daniel dared to hope against hope, gratitude welling within him again. He nodded vigorously. "Yes! Yes, that *is* what I want!" He practically shouted it, forgetting for the moment all the pain the Emperor had caused him and the people of Naphthali.

He chuckled and patted the air, as if to calm Daniel. "Very well, Daniel. We can return you...but you'll have to do something for me first."

Around the edges of his exuberance, Daniel felt a stab of disquiet at the words, but he pushed it aside. "Anything!"

The Emperor's eyes bored into him for a moment, and Daniel's euphoria started to evaporate until he smiled once more. "It is really such a small thing. Nothing to bother with, actually...forget I said it."

Daniel shook his head. "No, what is it? I'll do anything, just tell me!"

The Emperor looked coquettishly to the side and drawled out his response. "Well…there is one--little--thing you could do for me."

Daniel didn't realize until then that the Emperor had been holding his left hand behind his back. He motioned with his right for Daniel to turn. Gelnar stood at the back of the throne room. Three terrified children stood before him, tears coursing down their cheeks. All had light brown hair and fair features. The oldest was a girl. The older boy looked to be three years younger than her, while the youngest was barely more than a toddler. They didn't look like his children, but perhaps it was their ages that made Daniel think of them. In his ear again, the sweetly encouraging voice of the Emperor. "They look like your children, don't they? Your kids need you now more than ever, Ashley needs you. You *must* return to them!"

The words reverberated within Daniel, as if the Emperor were thrumming his heartstring. *Yes! I have to get back to them! Now!* He didn't realize his head was bobbing, or that the Emperor's left hand had finally come out and was pressing something hard into Daniel's. He looked at the children and saw his own, and he knew that they needed him. *Nothing* would stop him from getting back to them!

The Emperor gave him a nudge toward the children and said, "Do it now! Only after the deed can you be free!"

Not understanding, Daniel nodded and stumbled toward the children. They quaked and tried to back away, but were stopped by the grinning Gelnar. Seeing his evil face light up was what finally got Daniel to stop and think. He looked down at his hand and saw that the Emperor had pressed a long dagger into it. He looked back at his wolfish

Ron Hartman

face, knew what was expected, but also knew he could never do it. He closed his eyes and took a deep breath. As he held it, the image from the basin came to him, and he looked into Ashley's crying face a final time. *I'm sorry, Baby.*

He opened his eyes and his hand at the same time. The dagger fell with a loud clang on the stone floor, jarring the Emperor out of his blissful anticipation. The smile evaporated from his face, and he looked at Daniel with barely contained rage. "No," Daniel said quietly, looking into the handsome face that was now ugly with rage, green mist swirling before the eyes. "I can't do that."

"You can't!" the Emperor roared. He raised his hands and slammed them together. Magical force threw the children violently into each other. Their heads crashed into one another, the horrible sound of splintering bone rending the air. The three fell lifeless to the floor as the Emperor roared, "You *can't!* I will tell you what to do, and you...will...do it!" Each word got louder and more unhinged as spittle flew from his mouth. Daniel cowered where he stood, looking in shocked horror at the children.

The Emperor panted and glared at Daniel for a moment before his eyes snapped on Gelnar. "Kill him." Stinton and Dunn moved forward and latched vice-like grips on Daniel's arms, dragging him toward the smiling Gelnar. As he was pulled past the small crumpled bodies, the Emperor roared, "Do it now, in the public square! These *vermin* will know there is no Messiah!"

Gelnar bowed. "Yes, Your Grace!" Daniel was hustled out the double doors, and as they closed, Gelnar walked up to Stinton and Dunn, who still held Daniel, his head bowed. He grabbed a fistful of hair and forced

Daniel's head back so he could stare into his eyes. He gave a feral grin before spitting in his face. "Now you pay, Cunny."

~ * ~

Daniel was dragged along the great hall and thrown down the steps to the front courtyard. His left forearm hit the leading edge of one of the steps and he heard a dull snap as bones gave way. He cried out in pain, but Dunn and Stinton ignored him and dragged him to his feet. Moaning in pain and terror, his feet barely touched the ground as he was hustled down the ramp wrapping around the plateau. At the ramp's base the sergeants threw him down, and Daniel screamed when his left arm hit the stone street. Gelnar wheeled and launched a vicious kick at Daniel's midsection, knocking the wind and the scream from him. He nodded to the guards as they picked Daniel up again, pulling him on.

They didn't stop until they reached the large greensward that was at the convergence of the three main roads. The park was dotted with white stone benches and as they came to a halt, two beggars that were near the park's edge darted farther into the darkness offered by benches and trees. One beggar that seemed particularly small followed his comrade, but then turned back to watch with hungry eyes.

Daniel raised his head just in time to see Gelnar's fist sail in. It connected with his face, smashing his nose in a spray of blood and slicing his upper lip. He groaned and the sergeants dropped him to the ground again as Gelnar turned to the dark city. "Look at your Stranger! This is a lesson. No one challenges the Emperor!" Lamps brightened the windows of the official buildings lining the square as he turned back to Daniel and yanked the fine vest from his shoulders. He hawked and spat on the beautiful piece of art before ripping it in two and throwing it to the ground.

The captain grabbed a fistful of Daniel's hair and forced him up to his knees. Holding him in place by his hair, Gelnar rained punches down, closing an eye, reducing his nose to pulp, and fracturing a cheekbone. Daniel sucked so much blood down his throat he could barely pull in any breath at all, let alone cry out. Gelnar let him drop back to the ground as his chest heaved, excitement dancing in his eyes. He closed on him again when Stinton said, "Sir." As Gelnar stopped and stared at the sergeant, Daniel felt a ray of hope shine through the mist of pain. The hope crumbled when Stinton asked, "May we?"

Gelnar motioned to Daniel with a wicked grin and Dunn and Stinton exploded into action, stomping and kicking. Daniel felt ribs break and kidneys bruise, but he couldn't even pull in a breath as the beating continued. Another guard stepped up and kicked him in the groin, and then all six guards accompanying him were stomping on Daniel's legs and back. He curled into the fetal position, trying to find safety from the flying feet, and raised his hands in a placating gesture. Dunn pushed his right hand away, and when it fell to the ground, he stomped on that too.

Daniel's agony knew no time, but eventually the blows stopped. His left eye was swollen completely shut and his right eye could only open half way. What he saw from it was shrouded in a patina of blood from ruptured vessels.

His entire face was awash in blood from a dozen cuts, the worst being his ruined nose. Daniel pulled in ragged breaths that burned like fire, his expanding lungs causing further damage. While his legs weren't broken, they were covered with bruises and knots, and all Daniel knew was pain. All he could see, hear, taste, and feel was blood. He would've happily begged for death, if only to make the pain stop.

The blows to his head made his ears ring, so Daniel couldn't hear what Gelnar said as he was pulled up once more. He closed on him again, this time slowly, as if he were savoring the moment. He had something in his hand Daniel couldn't make out as two guards grabbed his right arm and pulled it out straight. The jolt made him whimper, and when he finally saw what Gelnar held, terror reflected in his bloody orb. He tried to speak past the blood rolling down his throat but was only able to say, "N--n--"

Gelnar stepped up to him and terror superseded the ringing in Daniel's ears as he clearly heard what the captain whispered. "You think you hurt now, Cunny, but it's just started. You will *know* what it means to test *me*. Hold him!" The command was unnecessary, because the Blood Guard was all that was keeping Daniel upright. He lifted the thin blue dagger and waggled it in front of Daniel's face before positioning it over his right forearm. With adrenaline pumping, Daniel threw all his weight into one desperate lunge and pushed away from Gelnar, but the guards easily pulled him back.

Gelnar sneered at him but then focused on the dagger as he pushed it through the center of Daniel's forearm. At first there was just burning as the razor-sharp blade punctured his skin and hot blood ran down his arm.

Then a dull ache like a deep muscle cramp came, followed by the draining. He could feel the dagger *pull* at his essence, siphoning it away. The ache deepened and spread along the length of his arm and then the sinews burned away, as if Gelnar was holding it in a fire.

Daniel's heart hammered in his chest, his pulse beating in every battered part of his body, but he only felt it peripherally as he moaned in agony. He watched in horror as his arm sank in on itself, as if there were no connective tissue or muscle to hold it up anymore. While his arm collapsed in on the bones, the skin that covered it tightened like a drum and blackened. It was as if his arm was petrifying before his very eyes, and all the while the draining continued until finally, mercifully, it stopped.

Gelnar threw his head back and closed his eyes, but when the damage was done he slowly lowered his chin and opened them. He looked at Daniel in astonishment and murmured, "Fascinating." He looked somehow overfull, as if his skin could barely contain him, just as he had in Standing Stone. "We must do that ag--" he started, but was cut off by Stinton's surprised cry.

He stumbled sideways and Daniel nearly fell before he was caught by Dunn and another guard. Gelnar's attention snapped to the sergeant as he dropped to all fours, his life's blood spilling out around an arrow in his neck. Within seconds four more arrows whistled from the night, wounding two more Blood Guardsmen and killing a third. Daniel was dropped to the ground as the men spun and pulled weapons. The little breath he had was knocked from him, and he barely had the energy to spit out a tooth. He used his left arm to cradle his maimed right, all the while silently sobbing bloody tears.

Gelnar roared and pulled the great sword from his back while at that same time four more arrows sailed in, all catching him in the chest. Two of the arrows lodged in his breast plate and were easily knocked away but the other two were another story. One sank deep into his shoulder, and the last punctured the base of his thick neck. He could feel blood running down inside his armor, and his nerveless left hand opened of its own volition, dropping the dagger to the pavement

He looked up just in time to see four assailants racing toward him, weapons bared. At the same moment four more men charged silently in from behind the guards, killing a wounded man. The attack was expertly timed, but the Blood Guard was the very best the Empire had to offer, and soon they met the attackers move for move. Dunn stepped up beside Gelnar to meet the four that charged from the front. Gelnar's eyes bulged when he recognized two of them: the man with the A-blade and the tall man that had stalked them on their journey. Those two closed on Dunn while the two newcomers attacked Gelnar.

The captain lunged to the right and feigned a stumble, drawing in one of the assailants who lost his head when Gelnar brought the blade soaring back. His sheer strength was too much for the other, who was nearly spun in a circle from the force of their colliding blades. Sparks and blood flew as Gelnar yanked their swords apart, the tip of his sword opening the man's arm from wrist to elbow. He dropped his weapon and also would have died if the tattooed leader hadn't pushed him aside at the last moment.

Gelnar growled as the shorter man circled, crouching low with the A-blade in his right hand and a short sword in his left. Though Gelnar's strength was great, he could feel himself weakening and knew he had to finish quickly. He feinted straight ahead, and with a roar brought the massive blade whistling down from the side. The rebel caught the blow on his crossed blades and used Gelnar's momentum to yank the weapons down low and spin a roundhouse kick to the captain's face.

Dunn gasped as the taller man cleaved his right arm off. He then followed with an overhead swipe that sliced through the sergeant's left collar bone and came to a halt past his sternum, nearly cutting him in two. Gelnar pulled in a ragged breath and lunged at the taller man, who easily parried. Spinning with his momentum, he sent the great blade flying for the shorter man, catching him unawares. He pulled back, but not quite fast enough, and the tip of Gelnar's blade sliced through his hard leather armor and nicked the skin beneath. The man with the wounded arm slipped behind Gelnar and came up with a dagger, but Gelnar saw him from the corner of his eye and spun, catching the assassin across the abdomen. His blade sank in deep and caught for a second on the dead man's spine, but a second's opening was all the two seasoned fighters needed.

The taller man sank his blade into Gelnar's side, just above his hip and Gelnar grunted as he spun, his sword falling from his hand. The wounded hip wouldn't hold him and as he stumbled to one knee, the tall man pulled back for a killing blow. At the last second Gelnar's numb left hand shot out and wrapped around the man's throat, his face locked in a rictus of rage. The shorter man leapt into the air and punched out with the A-blade, goring Gelnar's throat. He yanked it out sideways, spraying a jet of blood. The giant froze as the taller man pried his fingers from his throat and Gelnar fell face first, dead before he hit the ground.

Two rebels and one Blood Guard fell while Gelnar battled his last. When the two warriors joined with their allies, the last of the Emperor's finest was soon bleeding out on the ground, sure to be remembered only as failures. They gathered up their fallen comrades while the leader came to Daniel. He clenched his jaws when he saw Daniel's wounds, especially his ruined right arm. "We have to move," he said. Daniel tried to nod, but he was already fading out. Soon darkness overtook him and carried him far from pain.

BOOK TWO: FLIGHT

Chapter Ten

Sunlight filtered through thin curtains and cast a bright rectangle into the room. It stretched across the polished wood floor and up pine paneling on the far wall, illuminating a bed and small dresser. The rectangle grew as the day lengthened until it finally covered the entire bed, shining on the face of the sleeping man. He winced and attempted to roll to his side, but gasped in pain and fell back into the light.

Where am I? Daniel thought. His view was partially blocked by a large bandage that covered his nose, and when he tried to sit up, sharp pain shot through his abdomen. He gasped and a scab on his lip tore open, leaking a coppery taste into his mouth. Blood brought back the beating, and Daniel winced once more, feeling his lip tear farther. He raised his right arm to shade his face, only to be brought up short by a deep ache. In an instant, the blue dagger piercing (*draining*) him came back and he cringed in horror as he looked at his ruined arm.

The blackened skin wrapped tightly over the bones, more like leather stretched over a drum than human flesh. He couldn't move his fingers at all, and when he gently probed the area with his left hand, the skin felt cool and dry, the tissues numb. Even in the absence of sensation the dull ache persisted, lighting the arm with electric fire. The burning ache continued to build as he cradled the arm to his chest with his heavily bandaged left. Unfortunately the ache didn't go away. Instead it got worse, building in intensity until finally it reached a zenith and slowly faded back to a dull ache. Through it all Daniel was afraid to even move lest he rouse greater pain. Tears rolled from his bloodied eyes and traced down his bruised cheeks.

When the pain receded to a dull throb, he let out a shaky breath and gasped at the sharp stab in his side. Without thinking, he raised his right hand to rub away tears but caught himself when the ache intensified again. Daniel dropped it down as gently as he could, terrified the pain would come back. It was like having a sleeping monster beside him; if he moved too much it burst from its lair, slavering and screaming as it bore down on his raw nerve endings. Tears of frustration and fear coursed down his cheeks as he lay there, unable even to shimmy out of the sunlight. *What do I do now? I can barely move!*

As the sun continued its course through the heavens, eventually the rectangle of light shrank until it no longer blinded Daniel. Even after it receded, he kept his eyes screwed tightly shut, alternating between feeling sorry for himself and for his family. Burned into his mind was the image of Ashley in the basin. "What have I done?" he wailed as he saw her weeping once more.

The door creaked open, but Daniel barely registered the sound over his soul's agony. An old man with stooped shoulders and balding pate shuffled in and stopped at Daniel's bedside, pulling him from his painful reverie. He had a full white beard that hung down over a thin belly, his piercing blue eyes almost lost in a nest of wrinkles. He jumped in surprise when he saw that Daniel was awake, and Daniel started as well when he recognized him. The old man smiled and in a quiet voice said, "Ah, Stranger, you are awake. My name is Westragen. I am a healer. Welcome to my home." He paused and looked over Daniel's body before finishing with a rueful chuckle, "Though I wish you had come in better condition."

The last time he'd seen those compassionate eyes they were filled with grief, and he'd demanded that Daniel help him. He tried to speak, but only then realized how dry his throat was. "I--I kn" was all he managed before the coughing started, and with it came a searing pain in his side.

Westragen patted the air, grave concern in his eyes. "Easy, Stranger. You mustn't overtax yourself; your ribs are just starting to mend." He pulled loose a poultice dressing that was wrapped around Daniel's ribcage and nodded to himself when he saw the yellowing bruises. Next he looked deeply into Daniel's eyes, gently opening them wider with his thumbs. Daniel shuddered involuntarily, remembering Malthion's touch as a cold sweat covered his brow. The healer was gentle, though, and his inspection was done with care, not the sorcerer's horrible violation.

After checking all of Daniel's other wounds, he finally came to his right arm. Westragen's expression became very grave, but at the same time Daniel saw recognition in his eyes. He gently prodded the tissue then leaned down and gave a delicate sniff. Daniel winced but pushed away the ache when Westragen straightened as much as his old frame would allow. "Well..." he said, drawing out the word and leaving it to hang on the still air. "You are mending. Soon you will walk again." Westragen nodded, no doubt meaning it as a reassuring gesture, but Daniel caught him shooting a dark look at his arm and dread settled in his stomach. He opened his mouth, but the man shook his head. "Do not speak now. Yes, you have many questions, and I will answer them, but now you must rest." He glanced once more to Daniel's arm and added, "And heal."

Westragen shuffled from the room but soon returned with a steaming cup. He sat on the edge of the bed and ignored Daniel's groan as he raised his head enough to drink. Hot tea nearly scalded Daniel's mouth but soothed as it rolled down his raw throat. Westragen helped him drink the entire cup, taking small sips and resting once half-way through. When all that remained were small leafy dregs, the old man nodded and stood. He offered Daniel a brief smile and said, "Rest well, Stranger."

He turned and had nearly reached the door when Daniel decided to give his voice another try. "Wait," he barked in a hoarse cough. Westragen turned, his eyebrows raised politely. "Thank you."

He smiled and shook his head. "No thanks are necessary." He hesitated for a moment and added, "It is an honor." With a final smile he left the room, closing the door quietly behind him. Daniel only had time to glance up at the thatch roof before the tea took effect and his eyelids slid closed. As he slipped away, he thought of Ashley sobbing in the kitchen, and his heart broke once more before darkness claimed him.

~ * ~

Daniel awoke the next morning feeling somewhat better. He probed his body with his left hand and winced when he brushed against the poultice and mending ribs beneath. He bypassed the bandage on his nose, figuring it was good that he could breathe through it, even if he was congested and wheezy. His left forearm itched terribly, and it was all he could do to prevent himself from ripping the splint off and gnawing at the knitting skin.

An image of a dog wearing a lampshade collar came to mind, and an unexpected chuckle escaped him. *That might help!* The chuckle made him stop, and he realized it was the first time he'd found anything funny since meeting Malthion. Just thinking the foul name didn't fill him with anxiety and dread anymore either. The laughter, muted though it was, had a cleansing effect. It helped him to let go some of his grief and pain, and he realized he'd survive. Daniel relaxed and felt the scabs on his lips pull tight as he smiled.

The newfound serenity didn't mean that he'd forgotten the pain. Nor did it lessen the horror of those poor children being murdered. A part of him burned to confront the evil men, but an even larger part quailed at the mere thought of Malthion and the Emperor. He hastily pushed the thoughts away. All that could come later. For now he had to rest and heal, just as Westragen counseled.

With a quiet knock the door opened to admit Westragen and the tattooed man that saved Daniel. He wore a molded leather breastplate with the A-blade strapped across his chest. Its sheath was angled down and to the right, so that he could easily reach up with his right hand and pull it free. A short sword hung on his narrow hips and his legs were covered with brown leather britches, augmenting the camouflage of his cloak of mottled greens and browns. Long dark hair hung down his back and his clean-shaven face showed many tattoos that swirled around his eyes and cheeks. He was only an inch taller than Daniel's five-foot-nine, but he carried himself with such power and poise that he seemed like a much larger man.

The warrior sat two stools down before Daniel's bed as Westragen came forward. "Good morning, Stranger." He made a cursory inspection of Daniel's injuries and murmured, "Good, good." When he was finished, he lowered himself with a groan onto one of the stools. Daniel tried to speak but only a croak came out of his raw throat and Westragen nodded. "Easy, friend. You are still mending." He motioned to the warrior and said, "This is Captain Soren, leader of the Naphthalian Resistance."

The man bowed low and said, "It is an honor, Stranger. Many apologies for your wounds. Our spies didn't indicate the Emperor would see you that night." As he apologized his eyes wandered over Daniel's injuries, stopping on the blackened right arm. He gritted his teeth and his dark eyes flashed, the black tattoos ringing them making them look like pits of fire.

Daniel nodded, trying to convey that he understood. Westragen turned to Soren and said, "There will be time for talk when the Stranger is more comfortable. Captain, please fetch water." He nodded and left, returning with a tray containing a clay pitcher and mug. He poured a cup of water and gently helped Daniel raise enough to drink.

When Daniel had his fill, he laid back and croaked, "Thank you. And thank you for saving me."

Soren glanced at his injuries and said, "I wish I could have done more, Stranger."

Daniel looked at the two men and asked, "Why do you call me that?" He thought for a moment and added, "The general that found me...*he* asked if I was the Stranger too. So did the Emperor."

Westragen stammered, "You--you don't know of the Stranger, and the Prophecy?" Daniel's bewilderment spoke for itself as the healer's eyebrows shot up. "And the Burning Sea...you don't know of that either." The last was more a statement than a question. Daniel could hear the bitter disappointment in Westragen's voice.

He was taken aback by his change in attitude and Soren studied him closely for a moment. Finally, he nudged the old man's arm. "Tell him, Wes."

Westragen gave Soren a look of despair, tears swimming in his eyes. With a great effort he pulled himself together and nodded. When he turned to Daniel, his demeanor was different. The deference and hospitality that was in his eyes before was gone, replaced by a cool politeness. "There...is a prophecy." He sighed deeply, as if didn't have the heart to continue. "There are various versions...some call the savior The One, others The Stranger."

He paused, lost in thought, and Daniel felt a stab of uncertainty. *The savior?*

Soren silently nudged him again and when he continued his voice was deeper, as if he were intoning words of deep meaning. "The Starburst Stranger will cross the Burning Sea and bring the Light to set the people free."

His voice died away and Daniel looked blankly at the two men. Soren stared intently back and Westragen's gaze wandered to the room's corner as he stroked his beard with a palsied hand. When Daniel could take the silence no longer, he said, "I don't get it." The only thing he was coming up with for a starburst was a fruity candy.

Westragen stopped stroking his beard and looked at Daniel. "It is believed that the Stranger will bear the mark of the starburst."

Daniel frowned as Soren stood and left the room. He returned with chalk and a slat of wood and drew a quick sketch. He handed it to Daniel, who saw an admirable representation of himself. Soren pointed at the scar on his left cheek, which had been intentionally highlighted. "The starburst, do you see?" He pointed to the spider web-like projections that stretched across his face. "They radiate, or burst, from the star!"

Daniel couldn't believe what he was hearing. He slowly shook his head and asked, "You think I'm this...this Stranger?" Westragen looked away, and Soren continued to stare intently at Daniel, but neither said anything. He shook his head again and said, "None of this makes any sense." He motioned to his face. "This was from an accident." Silence stretched out. "I'm sorry," he mumbled, his ears burning.

Westragen repeated, "An accident." He lifted a hand and tapped his chin for a moment then stood and shuffled from the room without looking back.

Soren watched him go before turning back to Daniel. He smiled and said, "It's alright. We still have much to discuss, but you must rest. We will continue later." He paused for a moment, staring into Daniel's eyes. "What shall I call you?"

Daniel's cheeks burned again when he realized he hadn't introduced himself. "M--my name is Daniel Marten."

Soren nodded. "Very well then, Daniel Marten. I am Soren." He started to lift his right arm, but flushed before dropping it and offering his left instead. Daniel raised his left and Soren gently took it, grasping his forearm and allowing Daniel to do the same. He looked into his eyes again and said, "It is an honor."

Daniel's eyes dropped and his voice cracked into a hoarse whisper as he mumbled, "Daniel, please just call me Daniel. And thank you."

Soren nodded and gave Daniel's arm one gentle shake. He stood and motioned to the water pitcher questioningly, but Daniel shook his head. Moving toward the door he said, "Until later then, Daniel. Rest well."

He closed the door and Daniel rested back on his pillow. *The Stranger?* The idea of him as some sort of savior was preposterous! He closed his eyes, hoping sleep would come, but the prophecy kept burning through his mind. He rolled it over continuously, trying to make sense of it.

~ * ~

Westragen came to check on Daniel three more times that day. His compassion returned, but he was still more reserved than he had been when Daniel first woke. He didn't speak of the Prophecy again and mainly kept his comments focused on Daniel's overall improving health. He was encouraged by how quickly Daniel was recovering, and Daniel was astonished to learn he'd been unconscious for nearly a week. He knew Westragen's town was where Gelnar used the blue dagger on the boy, and its name finally came back to him while the healer checked his wounds. "Am I in Standing Stone?" When Westragen nodded he asked, "How did I get here?"

"Soren and Thosten carried you on a litter."

Daniel's jaw dropped. "All the way?"

The healer nodded again. "The roads are dangerous; the Imperialists are looking everywhere. They traveled at night. When they could, they used hidden tunnels."

Daniel nodded, remembering the ambush and the collapsed tunnel inside the barn on the trek to Stonefall. In his mind's eye he again saw Soren and a taller man lash out from the barn. "Is Thosten a tall man, with a large sword?"

Westragen nodded. "Thosten is Soren's greatest friend and closest advisor. Together they are very formidable."

He had that right. Daniel remembered how quickly they dispatched so many men. Their attacks were so coordinated they appeared almost as a single entity rather than two distinct men. "Is he here? I would like to thank him."

Westragen shook his head. "Thosten left as soon as you arrived. He went back to guard the trail, to make sure that the Empire wasn't closing on us." Daniel shuddered to think about what the Emperor and Malthion would do to the warrior if they caught him. Seeing his reaction, Westragen said, "You needn't worry about Thosten! It would take more than the Emperor's got to finish him. Do not fear, Str--Daniel--he will be back soon."

His ears turned scarlet and his eyes dropped to the floor with his slip. Daniel's cheeks burned as well. He couldn't pretend he was the Stranger they were looking for, and he couldn't think of anything to say that would reassure Westragen, so the moment slipped away in uncomfortable silence. Finally, he raised his right arm and studied it grimly. "Do you think this will heal?" he asked, thinking he already knew the answer.

Westragen latched onto the change of subject and immediately joined Daniel in inspecting the arm. His countenance grew almost as grim as Daniel's as he gently said, "I am afraid this...dark sorcery...is beyond me. Nothing helps." His lined face became even grimmer as he stared into the distance. "I've seen another afflicted with this...wound. Would that I could take it upon myself, give back what was lost. But I cannot."

Daniel knew he wasn't talking about him. "I would never ask another to carry my burden. I'm sure he feels the same."

Tears swam in Westragen's eyes when he looked back to Daniel. He gave a slight nod and blinked. "Many thanks for your kind words, Daniel. My grandson is strong, and I know he will survive. However, life is much more difficult for him now." The words died away at the end, his reedy voice getting husky. His chin quavered as he tried to smile at Daniel. When that failed, he reached forward and patted him gently on the left shoulder as he stood and shuffled from the room.

As the door closed Daniel thought, *His grandson! My God!* The dull ache in his arm increased as the nerves screamed at him. Soon he could tolerate it no longer and had to lay the arm at his side. He gritted his teeth as the electric fire built to a crescendo before receding.

~ * ~

Daniel woke early the next morning feeling much better. He pulled in a deep breath and was delighted that there was no pain. His left arm didn't itch as badly and even his nose seemed to be healing quickly. He patted his ribs and decided Westragen's tea must speed healing faster than the poultices alone. He was just finishing a cup when Soren knocked and entered. "Good morning, Daniel. How are you feeling?"

Daniel smiled back. "Much better." He held up the empty mug. "Whatever's in this tea works wonders!"

Soren chuckled. "Wes brought me back from the brink a few times with that brew. We're fortunate to have him." He offered Daniel more tea before settling on a stool, becoming serious. "We have much to discuss. The Emperor searches for you. You're safe for now, but eventually his gaze will turn this way. You will need to know what to do when that time comes. Now, to help you I need to know your tale...how you came here."

Daniel's heart skipped a beat when Soren mentioned the Emperor, but he steeled himself for the interrogation and nodded. Soren grunted. "You must have many questions for me. Well, sooner begun, sooner done. You are my guest and as such, I invite you to go first. Ask anything, I will answer true." To Daniel's surprise he dipped his head and extended his hands as if to say *after you.*

Daniel forced himself to relax. He didn't realize until that moment how nervous he was. He appreciated the captain's willingness to share first. Silence stretched out as he gathered his thoughts until finally he sighed and said, "Tell me about Naphthali."

Soren's face lit up. "Ah, my home and heart. What would you like to know?"

Daniel motioned around the room. "Everything! I don't know…well, anything, really."

"Very well." Soren's focus drifted for a moment before he began. "Naphthali stretches from the Cloudspeak Mountains in the east to the Azure Ocean in the west. The impassible Cloudspeaks surround our borders, enveloping and protecting us from much of what happens on the rest of Enialé." When Daniel frowned he added, "Enialé is the continent Naphthali shares with the Empire, as well as a few other countries. Where the Cloudspeaks end we are further protected. In the north is the Great Northern Swamp. The Darjeen Desert straddles our southern border. Both can be deadly, in fact the only safe ways to travel from Naphthali are by sea or through the great mountains.

"In most areas, the Cloudspeaks are too tall and treacherous to cross, but there are a few places where it can be done. Most are little more than goat trails that lead through mountain valleys…they can still kill a man if he's not prepared. Excluding those, there are only two safe passes: the Iron Gate and the Pass of Perfundi.

"The Iron Gate is in the south-central portion of the range. It is by far the widest and most commonly used. It's a highway of commerce that opens our borders to the rest of the world. We send out wonders from across the seas, as well as magnificent works of art and weapons from our artisans. Returning are other wonders, rare and beautiful, such as the fantastic Quarenian Waye you traveled with for a time. Many mundane items travel the highway as well, such as food, clothing, and a thousand other items.

"The Gate was a wide and inviting door, but in the past our leaders saw that some day we may have to close that door. Keeping that in mind, they built a massive fortress that straddles the pass. It stood solidly for many years and safeguarded both the border and the people that entered our land." Soren's gaze hardened as his voice died away until he let out a heavy sigh.

"The Pass of Perfundi is to the north. It is much less accessible, as it opens into the Great Northern Swamp. The journey to reach it is very...formidable. There are many dangers, and the land is only sparsely inhabited. In fact, the only time large caravans can attempt the Pass is in the winter, when the Swamp recedes slightly.

"Our natural barriers have afforded Naphthali great isolation from the rest of Enialé. They have protected us from the Empire for many years. In fact, isolation has allowed the history of Naphthali to be largely unhindered by outsiders. Most deemed the dangerous trek to our rich lands not worth the effort."

Soren saw Daniel frown and paused. "So how did your ancestors get here?"

The captain shrugged. "The original settlers were explorers from the sea. They arrived in great ships, but no one knows for sure where they came from. Our sailors and merchants have traveled the breadth and depth of the Azure Ocean, but we've never come across a people that claim kinship with us. Those first warriors settled near the shore and migrated inland until all of Naphthali was theirs."

Soren shook his head. "But I get ahead of myself. Wherever they came from, the original settlers did not come in a single tide. There were four different migrations, each bringing a different clan of the same fierce and proud people. The different migrations landed at different points along the coast, and each clan controlled the territory around its settlements. The four are the Colegi, Quai, Durmeer, and the Harshorn.

"At first, my forebears lived together peacefully. They helped one another when in need and slowly increased their holdings as they stretched inland. But eventually they reached the natural borders and couldn't expand anymore. When that happened, they turned eyes on their neighbors, and the Clan Wars began.

"The descendents of those original fierce warriors hadn't lost their bloodlust, even though many were now farmers and artisans. They turned on one another, and anyone not from their clan was massacred. Family lineage and status within the clan became everything. People died for disparaging a family or for falsifying their lineage to move up the ranks. Honor was prided above all else; there was no greater honor than to die for one's clan."

Soren raised his eyebrows. "If the Wars hadn't stopped, all my people may well have battled to extinction, or at least would've been easy pickings for the Empire. But that was not to be. After many years of bloodshed, one man rose through the ranks of the Colegi Clan, eventually ruling their entire holdings. His name was Wolfbane. Some say he wasn't Naphthalian at all, but rather a Stranger, come to save us." Soren paused for only a second, not stating the obvious similarities to Daniel and the Prophecy.

"He saw the road the clans were traveling and knew it only led to despair. Determined to change course, he sent missives to all of the clan warlords, offering free travel through Colegi territories for missions of trade and mercy. To ensure his words would be heeded, he personally vouched for every person of any clan that entered his lands. He gave his *word* that none would harm them."

Soren drifted off at the end. The words were murmured in a low voice, as if he were no longer speaking to Daniel, but rather to himself. He drained the last of his tea and swirled the dregs, deep in thought. Finally, he sighed and looked up. "Wolfbane was a great man. To any *true* Naphthalian, your word is your bond...none would give it lightly. I wish I could say his road was an easy one, but as with most that stride against the current, his journey was arduous. Many of his closest friends died defending him and his beliefs, and he himself nearly died too many times to count. However, he won over those that stood against him when a horrible storm came to shore, killing thousands from every clan. It laid waste to miles of shoreline and he nearly drained the Colegi coffers as he helped his fellow Naphthalians.

"Near the end of his days he achieved what he'd always hoped for. He united the country under one rule for the benefit of all. He was crowned the first king of Naphthali, Wolfbane the Wise. He continued his reforms for a few years, melding the country together and reducing clan influence."

"So he ended the clans?" Daniel asked.

Soren shook his head. "People still look to their clans with pride, but they no longer hold sway as they had before. The country as a whole progressed quickly as a nation. One of Wolfbane's favorite sayings was 'Iron is strong and can be fearsome in its own right. But when combined with charcoal, steel is stronger by far. Only by combining all of our talents, may *we* become steel.'

"Legend says Wolfbane looked at all he'd accomplished and knew he'd done well. He went for a final ride in the countryside of his beloved land and…disappeared."

Daniel raised an eyebrow. "Disappeared?"

Soren nodded and shrugged. "He was never seen again. Those that say he was not of Naphthali claim he returned to his own lands. Whatever the case, there is no more mention of him in the histories."

Soren allowed the words to sink in until Daniel motioned for him to continue. "His son followed in King Wolfbane's footsteps, and so started a long line of strong kings that looked to the well-being of the country as a whole. We were blessed with many great rulers, and all were needed to prepare for the dark threat that rose in the west. It was Wolfbane's son that began constructing Iron Gate, but his grandson saw it finished. The great fortress, named for the pass it protects, was manned with the best warriors of every clan. It proved to be an impregnable defense for many years."

A spasm of pain crossed Soren's face and he fell silent. He tried to keep his voice even and dispassionate, but Daniel could hear his heart breaking when he quietly added, "Until the deception…until the Fall."

He pulled in a ragged breath. "I don't know how long the Empire has been growing, but I believe it has been for quite some time…*much* longer than any one man's life. And yet the Emperor has always led it. Now it covers nearly all of Enialé." Daniel saw the concern in Soren's dark eyes, and his thoughts returned to the Emperor killing the children. To think of him as immortal made him shiver uncontrollably.

"When the Emperor's eye turned to Naphthali, he threw all his might into capturing us." Soren smiled bitterly. "We proved to be more of a challenge than he expected. He sent a massive army to take Iron Gate, one that was so vast it outnumbered the Gate's defenders at least ten to one. They failed and were rewarded with death." Soren drifted off again, fierce fires blazing in his eyes.

Daniel quietly asked, "How did they hold out?"

Soren's eyes snapped to Daniel's and the fire burned on for a moment until he remembered his tale. "You see, the beauty of Iron Gate is that it spans the entire pass, rim to rim. His army was huge, but the narrow pass choked them down. Only a few could engage us at once. Wave after wave came until the pass was drenched in blood. Our walls were never breached, and they had to accept defeat when the piles of their own dead were too high to climb over.

"I was a young recruit then. I thought the screams of the dying were bad, but they were *nothing* compared to the living... On the far side of Iron Gate, the mountains recede and open into a valley of sorts." Soren paled and Daniel's stomach clenched. He was pretty sure what was coming. "The screams from that valley continued for *days*. Finally when the cries of carrion birds replaced them, we sent out our scouts. The entire army was lashed to crosspieces and flayed alive."

"The Valley of Death," Daniel murmured, his chin quivering.

Soren looked blankly at him. "Yes, I suppose that is a good description." He wiped away a tear with the heel of his hand and continued. "The Emperor didn't try his luck again, and we were naïve enough to think we'd won. We celebrated and we boasted, and as time passed we forgot the evil deeds that were done in that valley."

Soren's face became stony, his tone clipped as he plowed ahead. "For five years we enjoyed peace and prosperity. Then one day assassins from the Elite Imperial Guard...they ambushed and murdered our last king, Begnauld the Wanderer. We...lost ourselves...when that happened. Unity was forgotten, people turned from an allied Naphthali to the time-honored clans. Soon in-fighting started, old prejudices and jealousies resurfacing.

"We were so consumed with ourselves we stopped looking outward...and *he* was ready. Troops bled away from Iron Gate as remnants of the government tried in vain to stop clan violence. Consequently none saw the approach of an army even larger than before. I believe they still wouldn't have breached the walls, but as it turned out they didn't have to.

"A traitor, driven by clan hatred, opened the gates in the dead of night and allowed the Imperial Guard in. Their first act was to kill the gullible fool." Soren chuckled mirthlessly. "I guess you could call it a reward. At least his pain was over quickly. By the time the alarm sounded, it was too late. The Imperialists decimated the few troops within, and the gates were thrown wide, allowing the army to march through. We had no chance, what with the in-fighting and division. They swept across Naphthali like a plague, enslaving us all."

Soren's cheeks flushed and his nostrils flared. His brow knitted as fires burned brightly in the pits of his eyes. He looked toward Daniel, but really he was no longer in the room. His mind had taken him back to the atrocities that started that night, his hands opening and closing spasmodically.

Westragen knocked and entered. He looked from Soren to Daniel and said, "It is time for food. Then our guest needs rest, Captain."

Westragen's voice snapped Soren out of his reverie. He looked to the healer and the fires died away. "Yes, of course, Wes." He stood, stony-faced and pale and excused himself.

Daniel tried to rehash all he'd been told, but his mind stuck on the image of the Emperor sacrificing his own army. If a man could do that, what would it take to stop him? He looked down at his half-empty mug, the tea gone cold while he listened to Soren. "How're you feeling?" Westragen asked with a kind smile.

Daniel handed him the cup and said, "Better. Your tea is amazing."

Westragen smiled as he checked Daniel's wounds. "You're recovering well. You should be able to leave this bed in a day or two." He removed the bandages from Daniel's nose, and after some gentle prodding, grunted. He left the bandages off and Daniel gently touched his nose as well, wincing at the light pressure. "The break is healing," he murmured. "It will be sore for a few days, but you don't need the bandages anymore."

When he finished his examination, Daniel asked, "What clan are you from?"

Westragen glared at him, an angry crease bisecting his forehead. "Soren told you our history. Surely you must realize clan allegiance is what got us in this trouble to begin with. I am *Naphthalian*. For me there is no clan."

Daniel lowered his eyes, chagrined. "I--I'm sorry. I meant no offense."

Westragen sighed. "You are not from here. You don't understand the pain we've endured. Outdated prejudices may still kill us all." He looked sternly at Daniel for another minute before returning to business. "Now, I will bring you some broth, and you must rest. The tea will not work if you push yourself too far too fast."

Daniel mumbled, "Thank you, Westragen."

The gruff healer relented and a trace of a smile crossed his face. "Call me Wes." His satisfied gaze slipped over Daniel one last time, but it grew grim when it came to rest on his petrified arm. He shuffled from the room and returned with a steaming bowl of broth. Daniel's nose wrinkled at the smell, and he didn't think he could keep any down. He started to shake his head, but the healer raised a warning finger. "Ah. You need to do what I say if you want to heal. Now open up." His shaky hands lifted a spoonful of the thick broth to Daniel's lips, spilling a few drops on his chest in the process.

Daniel cringed but obediently opened his mouth and was surprised to find it really wasn't too bad once he got past the smell. He emptied the bowl in no time and Westragen grunted his approval. He patted Daniel's left hand as he stood, but the herbs were already working. Daniel was asleep before the door closed behind him.

~ * ~

Daniel stirred. He was being stalked by an unseen enemy. While the intruder made no sound, Daniel knew he was closing. Soon he'd have to flee or risk capture. And capture meant a painful death. His heart sprinted in his chest as he sensed the inevitable ending. He shot furtive glances into the gray mist that surrounded him as hackles raised on his neck, uncertain where to turn. Footsteps echoed through the mist and he froze in terror, unable even to breathe, let alone flee. A skeletal hand dropped on his shoulder and a dead voice chuckled in his ear. He recognized the voice, thrumming with power. Malthion had him and there was no escape. He screamed, "No!" and jerked out of the grasp.

His eyes shot open and pain spiked through his torso as he twisted. He instinctively reached out with his right hand and latched onto the bed frame to keep from tumbling from the mattress. More pain shot through him as the blackened limb slammed like so much dead weight into the frame. He hissed in pain as the door flew open and Soren launched into the room, A-blade in hand. When he saw there were no intruders, he sheathed it. "Are you all right?"

Daniel's jaws were locked shut, holding in a moan that wanted to escape. He closed his eyes and gave a terse nod as he lay back, trying to control his hitching breath. Westragen followed the soldier in, albeit a bit slower. He shuffled to the bed with a concerned look on his face and rested a cool hand on Daniel's sweaty brow. "Was it a dream?"

"Y--" Daniel choked on his reply as the electric fires buzzed in his arm. He forced himself to pull in a slow breath and gritted his teeth. Eventually the pain cycled down and returned to a dull throb. When he was able to open his eyes, he looked into the men's anxious faces. "Yes, it was...a dream. I guess I zigged when I should have zagged." He gave a pained smile, but the two shared a confused look and shrugged. Daniel shook his head. "Doesn't matter. Can I have some tea?" Westragen nodded as Soren retrieved the tea and helped Daniel sit up enough to drink. The soothing herbs helped him relax, and he nodded his appreciation.

The two men turned to leave, but when they reached the door, Daniel said, "Wait. I want to hear more, Soren."

Soren looked doubtfully from Daniel to Westragen. "Perhaps tomorrow. You had quite a shock. You shouldn't push yourself too hard."

Daniel still felt the cold hand on his shoulder. He shook his head. "No, I'm fine. I think…I think we don't have much time. You better tell me what you can."

Soren frowned. "What--"

Westragen cut him short. "He's right. You mustn't tarry long." He looked at the captain and added, "I'll get something to eat." He left the room, closing the door quietly behind him.

Soren stared at Daniel before sighing. "Very well. Ask away."

He gathered his thoughts and considered his journey before speaking. "I saw you on the journey, before Standing Stone. How'd you find us?"

Soren shrugged. "We have spies throughout the country…beyond our borders as well. We even have some in Prosperity."

Daniel frowned. "Prosperity?"

"It's the Emperor's capital, where he reigns from a golden palace." Daniel's sense of urgency effected Soren as well and he added, "But that's not important now; I'll stay on point, lest time gets away from us. Our spies within General Ignatius's camp sent word about you. Thosten and I were in the area, supporting Clan Durmeer's rebellion."

"I thought you said clan allegiances brought about the Fall." Soren dipped his head. "Then why did you stand with only one clan in such a large battle?"

Soren sighed. "Naphthali is a torn country, Daniel. The distrust that came before the Emperor and the hardship that followed made many turn their backs on neighbors. Believe me, I'd have rather united the clans against Ignatius, but the battle was in Durmeer holdings,

and their warriors were all we had." As his mind returned to
the battle, his face darkened. "The attack was a desperate
gamble, and it failed terribly. Most of the Bloody Hoard was
killed." He answered Daniel's confused look by adding,
"Durmeerian warriors. They paint themselves scarlet before
battle." He shook his head and added, "We didn't expect the
Elite Imperial Guard. We made them pay, but we were
outmatched…and lost so many."

Daniel remembered the red-clad men that were
surrounded and butchered on the battlefield. He looked
into Soren's eyes and saw the same desperation he'd seen on
the faces of the fallen that day. "The Empire is too many,"
he said quietly. "I fear we may all be running out of time."

Daniel felt a chill at his words, but before he could
respond, Soren picked up the tale again. "Thosten and I
barely escaped. We were hiding nearby when we received
word about you. We tried to close quickly, but Naphthalian
steeds are known for their stamina. It wasn't until Gelnar
reached the foothills that we finally caught up. Our intent
was to thin Gelnar's numbers so we could rescue you before
they could be reinforced."

Daniel nodded. Not sure he wanted to hear the
answer, he asked, "What about Carmody? Why did you kill
him?"

Soren's face softened. "I know you'd grown close to
him, Daniel, but the boy was the only one that watched you.
If we'd the chance to take you quickly, we would have. And
he would've prevented us. Many apologies for your pain,
but we had no choice."

Did they have no choice? Really? Carmody was just
a boy! Why did he have to die? Then he remembered the

way Carmody worshiped Gelnar and he understood. He *would* have tried to stop them, even if it meant his death. He blinked away tears and thought, *how many will die because of me?* "I…understand." He thought about the trek again and asked, "How did you make it past the river, by the waterfall?"

Soren snorted. "It wasn't too hard to figure out Gelnar's heading. Once you were in the gorges, your horses were more hindrance than help so we outpaced you. We crossed the lake the day before and watched from the forest. We would've rescued you then, but in the darkness and confusion we lost sight of you."

Daniel grunted. He sat by the bonfire rather than going directly to his tent. If his routine had held firm, so much pain could have been spared. Others would still be alive. With that thought, his stomach did a somersault and he considered another victim. Afraid of knowing but having to ask anyway, he whispered, "And the farmers?"

Soren's ears burned, but his eyes were cold and dead. "We did stay with them two nights before their deaths… If we had the numbers, we would've killed them all that night. If not for Thosten, I'd have gone alone, doomed to fail." His voice dropped lower and he added, "I still hear her screams."

"Me too." Daniel's voice was little more than a sigh.

Soren blinked back tears. "I'd have given my life to save her, Daniel. But it would have made no difference. Fewer would have…*hurt* her, but there were just too many." He gritted his teeth. "I will not rest until this *evil* is purged from my home! *No more* of my people will be hurt like this! I swear it, Daniel."

Blinking back tears of his own Daniel said, "I'm glad to hear it."

Soren gave him an uncertain look before nodding. He studied the corner of the room as Daniel wiped his nose. After a moment's silence, almost to himself he said, "We almost had you in the clearing, another minute and you would've been safe." Daniel remembered when the lieutenant died. "Once they left the forest and fields, we lost the advantage of surprise. We lost all hope when Gelnar met the army, but we continued to follow."

Soren's voice drifted off and Daniel murmured, "And here I am."

Soren smiled. "Yes, here you are. Many apologies, Daniel. This has been difficult for you. If you'd come at another time, my people would welcome you with open arms. But, of course, that could not be…"

Daniel frowned, uncertain what he meant until finally realization sunk in: the Prophecy. He suppressed a groan and changed subject. "Tell me about your king."

"King Begnauld the Wanderer. I had the privilege of serving him for many years. He was…an unusual man. He did many great things for Naphthali."

Daniel raised his eyebrows. "Unusual?"

Soren nodded. "He was forever possessed with wanderlust. Nearly every summer the king embarked on voyages, visiting distant lands, finding friends and new trade routes. He increased the comfort of every Naphthalian more than any king before him, what with the goods that flowed into our country." Soren's smile slowly faded. "But he could also be reckless. At times he would leave m--his guards--behind and take unnecessary risks…"

Soren's voice faded away as the pain of memories became too great for him. After nearly two minutes of silence, Daniel was desperate to break the tension and blurted out the fist thing that came to mind, although he wanted to kick himself immediately after saying it. "Governor DePlaynes called him Begnauld the Fool. He said he was killed by his own people."

Soren's face darkened before he relaxed again and said, "Well, history is written by the victors, isn't it? Clan allegiance is strong now, but when the Kings ruled, nothing was greater than national unity. That was embodied by King Begnauld. He loved Naphthali, all his countrymen loved him. *No one* wished him ill."

The door opened and Westragen shuffled in. Daniel glanced out the window and was surprised to see it was getting dark. The afternoon evaporated like rain in a desert, and its passage made Daniel uneasy for some reason. Westragen said, "You must rest, Daniel. Your wounds are still raw…you mustn't push too hard."

Daniel shook his head. "I understand, Wes. But I feel like I don't have much time. We better continue. Please, stay."

The healer opened his mouth to reply, but with another look at the anxious sincerity in Daniel's eyes, he shrugged. He shuffled to an open stool, grabbing the teapot and Daniel's mug as he passed the dresser. He handed the tea to Daniel and said, "Very well. But you must drink more tea."

Daniel gave the cup a suspicious glance. He was afraid of drifting off again if he drank more, but he saw Wes's determination and nodded. Soren glanced at the healer before turning back to Daniel. "Ask what you will. I will answer true."

He shook his head. "No. You've been more than fair answering my questions. Now I'll answer yours. Ask and…and I'll answer true." The strange phrase felt awkward on his tongue but he could see it pleased Soren.

The warrior leaned forward, resting his elbows on his knees. "Tell me how you came here."

Daniel breathed in until he felt a twinge of pain and slowly let the breath out. He talked through the night, starting slow and uncertain, but gaining speed as he went. He told them his entire tale, offering not only what happened, but also what he was thinking and how he tried to rationalize everything. They listened silently, only offering words of comfort or asking for clarification when Daniel stumbled, or when the memories were too harsh to share.

Soren only stopped him once, when he told them about his dreams. "They started near the waterfall?"

He thought back and nodded. The first dream came shortly after the lake crossing, when the falls were still loud in his ears. The listeners shared a look and Westragen breathed, "The Spirit Calling."

Daniel frowned until Soren said, "The Spirit Calling is a holy place, visited by many pilgrims in…happier times. The mighty falls overpower one's senses, isolate a person from all outside distractions. It forces him to contemplate the calling of the spirit within. *Your* spirit was calling to you, Daniel, helping you to remember." His voice dropped and he added, "King Wolfbane saw a unified Naphthali when he visited the falls. Later he visited Spirit Calling often to ponder his path."

Silence stretched out until Daniel murmured, "A beautiful vest was made for me when I was in Stonefall. The Spirit Calling was embroidered on the back." He frowned and his voice quavered as he added, "Gelnar tore it off me when he...you know." He fought for control and finally added, "I saw it on murals in the throne room, too."

Westragen nodded. "The Spirit Calling is a national symbol. Many associate it with Naphthali, and by that I mean Naphthali as a whole, not this fractured remnant you've seen." He searched Daniel's face and when he continued, his voice was even more reedy than usual. "Was there anything else on the vest?"

"Yeah, there was a--a star--hidden in the falls." Soren and Westragen shared another look, this time filled with sorrow. "What?" Daniel asked.

With a final troubled glance at Soren, Westragen said, "The star is a symbol of the Prophecy...'the Starburst Stranger'. When it's hidden within other images, it is a secret message of hope...for the One." Daniel blanched, but it was missed when Westragen turned to Soren. "I was afraid of this."

Soren nodded and answered Daniel's questioning look. "We had a spy within the castle, a tailor that worked for the Governor. He disappeared shortly after you arrived in Stonefall." He looked at Westragen. "Now I share Daniel's sense of urgency. We must assume the worst and prepare to escape."

A jolt of anxiety shot through Daniel's stomach as Westragen studied him. "How do you feel, Daniel?"

He considered the question before shrugging. "I haven't been out of this bed yet. I feel quite a bit better, but I don't know how strong I am."

Soren cut in. "We will do what we have to *when* we have to. Now we need to hear you out, Daniel, for there is still much to discuss. Please continue."

Daniel kept the rest of his story as brief as possible. The only other interruption came when he forced himself to relate the murder of the children. Soren slammed his fists together and swore, bouncing to his feet and pacing the room. When he regained control, he sat back down and nodded to Daniel to continue. He finished with what he could remember of the beating, but tears rolled down his cheeks and words failed him.

Westragen rested a comforting hand on his shoulder. "Thank you, Daniel. I know this was hard."

Daniel was speechless as tears welled. He stared at the dead right hand that lay in his lap until remembered grief and terror passed. Finally, he looked to the two men and asked, "Do--do you think he really could've sent me home?" He felt bad asking, considering all the pain they'd been through, but he couldn't help himself.

Westragen raised his eyebrows and shook his head. "Magic is beyond my ken...but my heart tells me no. For one thing, if he could why force you to kill the children first? Second, above all else the Emperor is cruel. It would be unlikely he'd show kindness and send you home."

Soren nodded. "My guess is he'd rather Ignatius killed you on first sight, not parade you half-way across the country. By then the damage was done and he only had a few options." He counted them off on his fingers. "See you willingly join the Empire, discredit you, or kill you.

"If you'd joined him, you would've been a powerful tool in shaking the Resistance's faith. But a simple review of your actions on the march proved your character was too…too good…to accept his darkness." His voice dropped, and Daniel saw the anger in his dark eyes. "You see, I saw you at the farm as well. It took great courage to stand up to Gelnar and his men, alone and unarmed as you were."

Daniel heard the woman's screams again and shivered. "I couldn't just stand aside and watch them. I *couldn't.*"

The fires in his eyes smoldered as Soren nodded. "Since you couldn't be swayed, they tried to trick you into killing the children. If you'd done that, you and the Prophecy would have been discredited. Then you're just as powerful a weapon against us as if you'd openly joined the Emperor. He probably would have kept you alive but imprisoned. Whenever he needed to show people the folly of standing against him you'd appear."

Soren smiled grimly. "But you proved greater than that challenge, as well. All the Emperor had left was to execute you, publicly, so all would know the Prophecy died with you." Triumph glowed in his eyes when he added, "He failed there, as well."

Daniel looked into the fires of Soren's eyes as long as he could, but then had to turn away. He wasn't a messiah, and Soren's intensity frightened him. What did he expect him to do? He probably couldn't even stand on his own, let alone fight the Empire. He cleared his throat and asked, "So what do we do now?"

The intensity still shone in Soren's eyes as he said, "You tell me. I've answered your questions and you mine. What do you wish, Daniel?"

Daniel closed his eyes and sighed. He considered his options, but in truth it didn't take long because he didn't have many to consider. He looked in the corner of the room as he quietly said, "I'll not stand with the Empire...but I don't know how to fight either. What I want--what I *need* is to get home..." He let out another long sigh and turned to Soren, shaking his head. "I'm *not* your Stranger. I *can't* help you." An image of the Valley of Death flashed through his mind. "If I stay, the Emperor will find me...and everyone will die. I don't have any choice but to leave."

Tears welled in Daniel's eyes. These people offered him so much, and there was nothing he could do to repay them. He knew he had to leave to protect them, but he was terrified of being alone in this strange land. He thought about Ashley and the kids, and despair threatened to overwhelm him. Soren cleared his throat, but Daniel couldn't bring himself to look into those eyes, so filled with a hope he couldn't provide.

Quietly, Soren said, "I will stand with you, Daniel." He was so lost in his misery that at first he thought he misunderstood. He raised his eyes to see a grim smile on Soren's face. "You're right. We must flee soon, or we endanger all of Standing Stone. When we leave, we face what comes together."

Tears flowed unchecked as gratitude overwhelmed Daniel. He tried to speak, but no words would come. Soren looked out the window, his mind racing. Finally, he said, "For now, you need rest. I'll gather men and supplies. We must decide where we go from here." He leaned forward and clasped Daniel's left shoulder. "Sleep well, my friend."

Daniel mutely nodded as the two stood to leave. When they reached the door, Westragen stepped out but Soren hesitated. He looked back to Daniel and said, "It's alright that you don't believe, Daniel. For now, it is enough that *we* believe in *you*." He gave a firm nod and left, closing the door quietly behind him. Daniel was left in the silence to wonder what was worse: despair at the prospect of going it alone or fear of failing the people that refused to abandon him.

Chapter Eleven

Daniel closed his eyes and felt his body relax. He sought the darkness in his sleep, the comforting void that was safe and familiar. His mind fled the corporeal confines of his body and he considered how inviting nothingness could be. Here he was truly free. Free from reacting to the forces acting on him, from accepting the expectations of others. *No pain can reach me here.* He luxuriated in the void, moving his hands (*my whole hands!*) around him in a slow dance, as if he were treading water.

He sensed something approaching, but in his bliss he ignored the instinctual urge for caution. Daniel was still moving in a slow dance when the newcomer reached him. The voice was quiet and indistinct, as if it came from a lifetime away, but he recognized it just the same. How could he not? He knew that voice almost as well as he knew his own. "I love you, Dan."

Daniel's eyes were still closed as he nodded and smiled. *Yes. Yes, Ashley. I love you too.* The scent of Ashley's perfume filled his nostrils, and the feel of her skin rippled over his fingertips, fingers that still traced nothing in the still air. He wanted to reach out and pull her to him. She would rest her cheek on the hollow at the nape of his neck, and he'd lose himself in her embrace.

Almost as quickly as it came, her presence dissipated away. He could barely make out her words when Ashley said, "I need y--". Her voice faded, and so did the scent and feel of her. Daniel's smile evaporated and his forehead creased in concern.

No, wait! His arms finally stopped their slow dance and reached out longingly to grasp the love that was slipping away. But before they could wrap around her imaginary form, Daniel sensed another presence in the darkness, one that was far more comfortable there than he was. It was reaching out for him, searching for him, ready to receive the embrace he offered. Hackles rose on his neck and he froze, his eyes flying open. He was not alone, and the void was not the comforting cocoon he mistook it for. It was actually a cleverly devised trap, intended to snare him. Daniel didn't even breathe as he cast about, trying in vain to locate the hunter.

After an immeasurable time, the alien presence dissipated just as Ashley's voice had, and Daniel started to relax. He heaved a deep sigh of relief, and that simple act triggered unseen tripwires. The hunter roared back and finally Daniel knew who it was. The cold presence had been in his mind before, ripping down walls and carelessly thumbing through cherished memories. *Malthion!* He cowered in the nothingness as if he could hide from the sorcerer. Powerful evil flowed into the darkness, and as it materialized, Daniel's terror soared to new heights.

He sensed the sorcerer come fully into being and felt unseen air currents rush past his shoulders as Malthion closed on his unprotected back. He thought his heart would burst from fear as a skeletal hand fell toward his shoulder. One thought penetrated his terror: if Malthion reached him here, there would be no escape. He heard the whisper of fabric as Malthion's robes moved over ancient skin. A dry chuckle drifted toward him, promising unimaginable pain before death. His own skin rippled in gooseflesh as the hand inexorably fell toward him, but at the last second another voice spoke. The voice didn't actually speak, but rather boomed through the void, making Daniel wince at the pressure change in his ears. FLEE!

The voice could not be denied. Daniel lunged forward, and as he did so he felt ice prick the back of his neck where one long fingernail grazed him. He fell forward out of bed and landed on the wooden floor. At the last second he threw his arms out to break the fall, and his body impacting onto his right arm caused an explosion of pain. The burning he experienced before was nothing compared to the hot fire searing through his nerve endings. Later Daniel would reflect on how bitterly ironic it was that his arm was lifeless except for when it caused him pain. For now, though, it was all he could do to roll off the screaming hand and sit on the floor cradling it to his chest while he sobbed quietly.

The roaring fire continued to build until Daniel thought it would drive him insane, but eventually it did recede. When he was capable of conscious thought, Daniel considered the dream. The hair on his neck stood on end again when he thought about how Malthion had so easily lured him in with a false memory of Ashley. He reached with his left hand and winced when he touched the back of his neck. The flesh was raised in a welt shaped like a long scratch. He didn't understand how, but he knew it was much more than a dream. By some magic he'd nearly died, if not for…what? There had been something there; for just an instant it commanded him to react, but what was it? Who was it?

Daniel forced himself to his knees, being careful not to jostle the wounded arm. His legs shook with the strain of bearing his weight, but with steely determination he shimmied into bed as best he could. By the time he was back in place, sweat rolled off his forehead and he was breathing heavily. He laid his head back and drifted in and out of consciousness the rest of the night. He never allowed himself to fully succumb to sleep, though, afraid of what might follow him there. Time dragged on slowly until daylight finally brightened the room. The night's long siege was finally over.

~ * ~

Daniel looked dully at the door when Westragen opened it and entered the room. His smile faltered when he saw Daniel's face. "Daniel, are you alright?" He sat the tray he carried on the dresser and shuffled to the bed, frowning as he laid his hand on Daniel's forehead. After a moment's silence, he repeated the question. Daniel shook his head and told Westragen about the dream. When he finished, Westragen stared at him silently for a moment. "Perhaps it was just a dream." Daniel could tell by his tone he was trying to convince them both of that, but he was failing in the effort.

Daniel leaned forward with a wince. He rested his chin on his chest and murmured, "Does this look like it was only a dream?"

Westragen sucked in a breath and after a moment's hesitation he gently prodded the injured flesh. When he pulled his hands away, Daniel leaned back and stared at the elder. His face was pale, his hand shaking when he raised it to absently scratch a hairy cheek. "Well," he murmured, "that could be a problem."

Daniel gave a desolate chuckle. "You think so?"

He nodded, lost in thought. Finally he said, "We'll have to tell Soren of this when he returns." In response to Daniel's frown he explained, "He's gone to find Thosten. The Empire still hunts you, but there have been no reports near here."

Daniel felt a cold knot in his stomach. Soren was gone and he was alone. It took him a few tries to swallow his fear before he could ask, "What do I do now?"

Westragen's eyes roamed over Daniel's body before he answered. "Now? Now we get you ready to move. You need to get up, get strength back in your legs...at least, as much as you are able." The last he mumbled to himself as he prodded Daniel's wounds, most of which were nearly healed. When he was done he said, "But first, you need to eat. You'll need all your strength, and sooner than I would like."

Eating was the last thing Daniel wanted to do, but he nodded as Westragen retrieved the tray. Once he started, though, it was as if there was a hole in the middle of him that he couldn't fill. He cleaned the tray in no time, pausing only to ask, "What did Soren do before the invasion? I heard you call him Captain. Was he still in the army?"

Westragen turned a surprised look on Daniel. "He didn't tell you?" More to himself he added, "No, I don't suppose he would." He cleared his throat and answered, "He was Captain of the King's Guard." Daniel raised his eyebrows, nearly choking on a mouthful of broth. "Soren holds himself personally responsible for the King's death. And by extension, the Fall."

Daniel swallowed and said, "But that can't be. Surely there were other reasons for the invasion…the…the Fall."

Westragen nodded again. "As we all have told him, repeatedly. But he won't listen. He will not rest until he finds a way to save Naphthali. That is the only way he can redeem his honor."

The implications of Wes's words dawned on Daniel. "So he thinks I'm the--the One. And he hopes I can help him save Naphthali? That's why he'll help me?"

Westragen's solemn expression hardened as he shook his head. "You misunderstand. Soren is a good man, an honorable man. He would *never* abandon anyone he's sworn to protect. Even if the true Stra--if another were to come along tomorrow, Soren wouldn't leave you to face the Empire alone." His cheeks flushed at the slip, but he ignored them and continued. "You *must* understand this, Daniel. Fight or flee, Soren will stand with you. To not acknowledge that would be a disservice to his aid."

"I…understand." Daniel sighed. "I don't deserve this. You've risked so much already by helping me…" His voice drifted off as emotion overcame him. Without these men, he'd be dead already. He had no way to repay their kindness, and it seemed likely that he would have to ask for more.

A smile played across Westragen's lips, but Daniel could see in his eyes that he agreed with him. They *were* risking too much by harboring him. But what he said was, "That's alright. 'An enemy of your enemy is a friend'...we may yet help each other." He looked down at the empty tray and said, "Ah, you are finished, good. We must get moving. Sooner begun, sooner done." He carried the tray to the dresser and took something out of a drawer. He returned to Daniel, holding a mass of leather straps in his hand. "You'll need this."

Daniel took it from him and examined what looked like some sort of harness with a deep pocket for his elbow. Westragen murmured, "Greggor--my grandson--found this helped...after..." Daniel looked up, but before he could say anything, Westragen continued. "Any movement appears to make the pain worse. If you keep your arm close to your body, the pain is minimized."

He helped Daniel slide the sling over his head and gently nestle his right arm in the pocket. A leather strap wrapped around his right bicep then across his chest and back, immobilizing his upper arm. Another strap wrapped over the end of the pocket and fitted into a belt that wrapped around his waist. Daniel experimented moving and saw that while his left arm was free, his right was so secured it was as if it wasn't even there anymore. He winced at the slight burning that just putting on the sling caused and thought, *It would be better if it wasn't there. Then there wouldn't be the damn pain!*

Westragen stepped back and eyed him critically. In an apologetic tone he muttered, "Well, Greggor *is* bigger than you." Daniel was so absorbed in his pain and bitterness that he didn't really pay attention to the harness until then. When he looked down, he couldn't help but chuckle. It looked like a small child trying on his father's shirt for how well it fit him. The loose ends of the straps nearly dragged the floor, and the sling's pocket was so large his entire arm disappeared in it. Only blackened fingertips protruded from the end, adding to the impression that his arm was no longer there. The healer misunderstood his reaction and said, "A new one will be made today."

Daniel smiled and waved away the offer. "No, this is perfect." He bent at the waist to see the straps hanging to the floor. "Maybe we could trim it back though."

Seeing the smile on Daniel's face lightened Westragen's mood as well, and he allowed himself a reedy chuckle. "A good point." He found a sharp hunting knife and cut back the straps before asking, "Shall we go out?" Daniel's heart lurched in apprehension at the thought of leaving the room, his weakened leg muscles cringing at the prospect. He looked uncertainly at Westragen who assured him, "We won't go far. There are many places to rest if need be. Come."

Westragen turned and stepped out of sight, leaving the way clear for him to follow. Daniel heaved a great sigh and decided that since his only other option was to cower in his room, he'd go along. Outside was a short hallway with a flag pinned to the opposite wall. It was divided into four quadrants colored red, blue, green, and white, and at its center, where the four met, was a golden rose. Daniel stopped and studied the flag, not realizing Westragen was waiting for him at the far end of the hall. "The sovereign flag of Naphthali," he offered.

Daniel glanced at him before looking back to the flag. "What do the colors represent?"

"The founding clans. Each clan contributes equally to the well-being and prosperity of Naphthali. But the important part is the rose. It is the greatness we can achieve when we come together and work as one."

The rose's stem started about halfway up the flag, between the red and green fields. It branched into two leaves at the axis of all four quadrants, and the petals opened full between the white and blue. "I saw that rose on a suit of armor, in the castle," Daniel murmured.

Westragen grunted. "King Begnauld's armor...I'm told it still bears the marks of his attackers." Daniel remembered the arrow holes and nodded. "They say it's one of the governor's prized possessions." After a moment he gently prodded Daniel from his reverie. "Let's go." He threw open the door at the end of the hall, letting bright sunlight shine in, along with an unexpected silence.

~ * ~

The glare off the polished wood floor dazzled Daniel and he turned away. When the spots in his vision faded, he walked to Westragen, and it wasn't until he was practically to the door that he realized something was amiss. Standing Stone was a small but vibrant community when he last passed through with Gelnar. Even though the townspeople were terrified by the Elite that day, there was still the background noise of any town. The people may have been silenced, but dogs still barked, sheep lowed, horses whinnied. Wind whipped through clothing drying on lines and any of a hundred other mundane noises added to the din.

But not now. Daniel didn't hear *any* noise at all. He froze as he crossed the door jam, one foot already extended to take him outside. His instincts screamed at him to stop, but it was too late. He looked outside with a heightened sense of danger and saw about forty men standing in a loose semi-circle around Westragen's dooryard. All stared intently back at him. Hairs on Daniel's neck stood on end, and he started leaning back just when Westragen's reedy voice spoke in his ear. "It's alright, Daniel." The old man rested a hand on Daniel's shoulder and gave a light push. Daniel was still standing with one foot raised over the threshold, and the slight pressure was enough to carry him outside.

His heart hammered in his chest, and his already weak knees felt like they were going to collapse. As one the forty men dropped to their knees and lowered their heads. Daniel's heart pounded loudly in his ears as he looked at them in confusion and Westragen said something. "What's that?" he asked.

Westragen's voice was low but insistent, pulling Daniel back from his panic and confusion. "They believe you're the One. I told them you're not, but they wouldn't listen." He allowed the point to sink in before adding, "Please, talk to them."

Wes's words were like a bucket of ice water thrown in Daniel's face. His fear lifted and he was able to think clearly. He cleared his throat and said, "Please, stand up.

You honor me, but I'm not what you think I am. I'm Daniel...just Daniel. Sorry." The last was an afterthought, and he knew how lame it must sound to these people that were investing so much in him. The men raised their heads and searched Daniel's face, as if the answers to their questions were written there. They looked to one another and stood.

One man came forward and held out his right hand. He hesitated before dropping it and raising his left instead. He was in his forties, slightly taller than Daniel. He wore a leather apron and leather breeches, and a bristly salt-and-pepper beard covered his chest. A mace was tied to his belt, a shield strapped to his back. His face was a mass of careworn wrinkles, and faded blue eyes studied Daniel grimly as they roamed over his scars. "Welcome, Stranger. I am Regnar. I am--was--a leader of this town."

Daniel reached out and his hand was engulfed by Regnar's calloused paw. He felt the man's strength in his tight grip as he shook his head. "Thank you, Regnar. But I'm not the Stranger..."

He would have continued if he could, but the bearded man was already nodding. As soon as his voice trailed off Regnar answered, "I understand. Yours is a difficult road. We will aid you as we may." He dipped a short bow and backed away, cutting off anything else Daniel would have said.

They're not gonna take no for an answer, Daniel thought in exasperation. He scanned the small group and noticed that to the far right there was one man that didn't rise with the rest. His left arm rested on bent knee, his head bowed. Daniel could tell from his blocky shoulders and thick arms that the man was huge. His mop of curly dark blonde hair seemed somehow familiar. With a gasp he realized who it was. He staggered over and stopped before him. "Greggor," he murmured in a husky voice. Westragen's grandson raised his head, tears streaming down his cheeks. Daniel was shocked but not surprised by the changes he saw in the young man. His face had aged dramatically, and his enormous bulk already showed signs of softening.

He opened his mouth to reply, but Daniel stopped him by grabbing a fistful of his jerkin and pulling him up. He was too weak to move the man on his own, but Greggor stood at his urging and was pulled into a rough embrace. Daniel only came to Greggor's chest, but he held the young man as best he could while both wept, Greggor resting his head on Daniel's shoulder.

"I'm so sorry," Daniel mumbled, his words barely understandable. Racking sobs coursed through Greggor, and Daniel's arm trembled as he held the young man tight. Eventually Greggor's tears lessened, and he pulled away from Daniel. His right arm was in a sling identical to Daniel's, a blackened hand protruding from the pocket. Both men wiped away tears with their good hands while Westragen looked on, tears standing in his own eyes as well.

"Come," the healer said as the two men turned to him. Daniel stumbled, his legs giving out, but Greggor caught him with his left arm and helped him to a bench. The three sat down and Westragen murmured, "Rest for a moment, Daniel. I suspect you have more questions for me."

Daniel looked around Westragen's dooryard as the men milled about, speaking to one another and sending furtive glances his way. Their voices broke the unusual silence somewhat, but it lingered over everything, almost as if the silence itself were roaring to be heard. Greggor cleared his throat and said, "I'll get water." Westragen nodded and after a shy smile at Daniel, he lumbered toward the door.

Daniel turned to Westragen. "What happened? Where is everyone?"

The healer studied the men before answering. "They're gone."

"What do you mean 'gone'?" Daniel asked, trying to keep the fear from his voice.

Westragen refused to make eye contact. His gaze wandered over the road as he said, "It is not safe here. We'll follow the rest when you're well enough to travel." His voice trailed off. When he continued, there were undertones of bitterness and sadness. "We were...fortunate...when you came the first time. Only one paid." Daniel felt ashamed for Greggor's injury. Granted, he had no power to stop Gelnar or any control over the course that brought them through Standing Stone. Nevertheless, he would always feel guilty for what happened.

His eyes dropped to the ground as Westragen continued. "It is different now. I believe the Emperor will not stop until you're found. If he learned you were harbored here, he'd torture us all until everything was revealed. The Resistance was based here, and so too much was at risk." He let out a desolate sigh. "Standing Stone is a ghost town. Only we few remain to flee when we're able."

Daniel hung his head in shame. Not only had he caused so much pain to Greggor, but the entire town was dying just because of association with him. They paid so much, and yet they wouldn't abandon him. They protected him, though it cost them everything. Daniel's misery beat him down, but with a great effort he lifted his head and saw Regnar dispersing the men. He was afraid the answer would only bring more blame, but Daniel couldn't help asking, "What's Regnar's story?"

Westragen glanced in his direction and sighed. "Sometimes it seems all Naphthali has left to offer is grief...in that we have plenty to go around." His voice dropped and as if he were quoting something he added, "'When it comes to grief, she pays in full.'"

He fell silent for several minutes. Just when Daniel thought he wouldn't continue, he said, "In happier times, he was a carpenter." His eyes momentarily lost their focus as he remembered how things were. A slight smile lifted the corners of his lined mouth as he said, "His two sons could be heard before they were seen, roaring with laughter as they raced around town. And his wife, now, she was the most beautiful woman in all the land. I don't mean physical beauty, though she shown brightly there as well. She had such a pure...spirit. Any man would have been honored to call her wife. Many would have vied for her hand if not for Regnar. He was a blessed man, and he knew it...he cherished what he had."

His smile faded, Westragen's voice growing so lonely and forlorn it broke Daniel's heart to hear it. "She died giving birth to their third. The baby...well, I couldn't save her." He absently wiped a tear from his cheek and his voice grew quieter still, so that Daniel could barely make out the words. "Then came the Fall, and his sons were killed at

Iron Gate. Grief took Regnar, it broke him…*changed* him. When he came out the other side, he wasn't the same man. He joined the Resistance seeking vengeance. He found what he sought." As an afterthought Westragen added, "He was with Soren and Thosten when you last came."

Westragen paused as Greggor returned with a tray balanced on his good arm. He took a pitcher and poured mugs of water for all three before adding, "Regnar is a good man, a good leader. We're lucky to have him."

"Hmm," Greggor murmured as he took a long pull on his mug. "He's helped me much, since…"

He glanced at his right arm and his eyes dropped to the ground. An awkward silence stretched out until finally Westragen asked, "Are you ready to walk?"

Not sure he was, Daniel nodded and pulled himself to his feet. The three made slow progress down the street, frequently stopping to allow Daniel rest. They were shadowed by Regnar and three men, all loosely holding weapons, and whenever they passed another of the men, they gave Daniel a slight bow. The men murmured, "Stranger," or "One," and Daniel's face flushed as he nodded in return.

By mid-afternoon they made it to the greensward in Standing Stone's center. They rested near the ancient stone lintel while one of Regnar's men brought them a light meal. Daniel was light-headed and bathed in sweat from so much exercise after nearly two weeks of inactivity. Each breath came in a harsh rasp, and a stitch in his side hurt almost as badly as his broken ribs had. Greggor finished his lunch and sauntered off to relieve himself, flinching when his maimed arm bumped the ground as he stood. Daniel mutely watched him go, a frown on his face. "It still pains him."

He turned and saw that Westragen also watched his grandson with concern. "Has it improved at all?" Daniel felt selfish asking, but he couldn't stop, nor could he hide the desperation in his voice.

Westragen's eyes lingered on Greggor for another minute before he shook his head. "His arm is the same as it was a month ago, when that bastard came. It's dead to everything but pain…almost as if the dark magic has cursed him to…to eternal torment."

Daniel looked at his own arm and despair weighed him down. In a small voice he asked, "Nothing helps?"

Westragen murmured, "I am sorry, Daniel. Any movement worsens the pain, but even when the arm is strapped to his side, there is always the dull ache." As an afterthought he added, "The sling helps some."

Daniel nodded. Even with his arm immobilized, the pain had been steadily building all morning. He could feel the fire smoldering as they sat in the shadow of the lintel. Daniel looked up at the massive stones and asked, "Where did they come from?"

Westragen glanced up and shrugged. "They have been here since time out of memory. Our oldest tales tell of a ring of stones that filled the whole commons. Over the years they've fallen. This is all that remains."

Mystified, Daniel imagined an entire ring of behemoths closing in the town's center. "What were they for?"

The old man shook his head, but then shrugged. "No one knows." He searched the ground beneath the stones until he finally grunted in satisfaction and plucked a small plant. It looked to Daniel like clover, with small rounded green leaves, a short stalk, and a white root that pulled easily from the soil. "This is Valor Root. Crushed leaves will stop bleeding; chewing the leaves helps with pain…or it can be brewed into a potent tea." He answered Daniel's look with a nod. "Yes, *your* tea. Valor Root grows in many places, but I've never seen any as potent as this. The stones seem to power it."

Daniel's pharmacy training taught him of the many curative properties of plants. After all, plants are the basis of some of the most successful drugs. But did Westragen really expect him to believe magic increased their potency? He started to shake his head, but then looked down at his wounded arm and stopped. He had to admit that with his newfound understanding of magic, anything was possible. "Hmm," he chewed his lip as he shaded his eyes with his left hand and took in the stones. He could just make out worn symbols carved along the lintel. "What do those mean?"

Westragen shrugged again. "No one knows."

Greggor returned. "Do you need more Root, Grandfather?"

Westragen smiled and rested his hand on the boy's shoulder. "No, not now, son. You're a good boy." Greggor smiled, but it never quite reached his eyes. Daniel saw the haze of pain there and shivered as he considered the dull roar in his own arm.

Regnar walked up and asked, "Should we start back, Wes?" As he gave Daniel a side-long glance, he was suddenly aware of how shaky his legs felt, just from standing by the stones for a few minutes.

Westragen nodded. "Yes, let's. Ready, Daniel?"

Daniel shrugged. "I guess." He could hear the exhaustion and shakiness in his own voice. Based on their concerned looks, the others could hear it as well. He tried for a reassuring smile but failed.

~ * ~

Dusk was darkening to full night by the time they arrived back at Westragen's home. Daniel needed more and more rests until finally his shaky legs could carry him no farther. He slumped on the steps before an abandoned house, gasping for air. Regnar joined them and quietly said, "I'll fetch a stretcher."

Greggor sat beside Daniel, offering quiet company until Regnar spoke. He looked up and said, "No need, Regnar. I can carry him."

Daniel looked to him and said, "No, Greggor, I can't ask you to do that."

Before he'd finished the boy was shaking his head. "It's alright, Daniel. I want to help."

Daniel looked into his earnest eyes and saw a need to please shining through the clouds of pain. He glanced at Regnar and Westragen, but both shrugged and stepped away. Westragen looked back over his shoulder and frowned, but when Daniel turned to Greggor he couldn't deny his eager hope. "Very well, if it's not too much for you."

Greggor's face lit up with a lopsided grin. He practically bounced in place as he said, "No, no problem at all."

Daniel sighed inwardly and pushed to his feet. The effort nearly ended before it began as the two disabled men considered how to proceed. Since both lost their right arms, Daniel couldn't simply sling his arm over Greggor's shoulders. They tried several different positions without success until finally Greggor kneeled down. He effortlessly hoisted Daniel onto his hip and carried him as a mother would a toddler. Daniel's face burned as Greggor straightened and walked in a loping stride down the street. He definitely wanted the relative dignity of the stretcher now, but was powerless before Greggor's joy. The boy was finally able to help again, and so Daniel stoically bore the indignity until they reached Westragen's doorstep.

Greggor gently sat him down on a bench and grinned at him. Daniel's face was still burning but he smiled anyway. "Thanks, Greggor, I appreciate it." After a momentary silence he added, "You are very strong."

Greggor shrugged. "I'm happy to help you, Str--I mean, Daniel."

Westragen shuffled to Daniel's side and smiled warmly at them both. Daniel saw the gratitude in his eyes, but all he said was, "Come, Daniel. You must rest." He nodded in appreciation to Greggor one final time before standing unsteadily and shuffling into the house. He lowered himself with a sigh onto his bed while Westragen brought him a cup of tea and stayed until he finished it. Too tired to talk, Daniel handed him the cup and the healer shuffled toward the door. With his hand on the knob, he turned back and said, "You did well today, Daniel. You are recovering faster than I'd hoped." He hesitated, clearly wanting to say more but finally turned and opened the door. As it closed, Daniel heard him murmur, "Good night."

~ * ~

Daniel shut his eyes and thought, *Please, God, let me sleep undisturbed tonight.* His prayer was answered, at least in part. He wasn't visited again by Malthion, nor did he have any nightmares, but still he didn't sleep well. It felt like he'd just closed his eyes when someone was gently shaking him.

"Wake up, Daniel. We have to go, now!"

He groggily opened his eyes and saw a shadowy figure leaning over him. "Whosit?" he mumbled. The person stepped away and uncovered a lit lamp. The bright light made Daniel wince. As he tried to shield his eyes, his right arm screamed at him. The cycle of burning pain started anew as Daniel gently dropped the arm to his side with a groan. He squinted past the light to see Soren standing before him. A wild look in the captain's eyes sent a jolt of fear through Daniel as his grogginess evaporated. "What's wrong, Soren? What happened?"

Soren's jaw worked frantically. His eyes were alight with a mixture of desperation and anger. "They've found us." He rushed to the dresser and searched through the drawers, throwing useful items in a leather backpack. "We have to flee now, or die." The news was like a double-fisted punch to the gut. Daniel couldn't pull in a breath, and at the same time his heart raced. He threw his legs from the bed and sat up, fumbling with the sling. He ignored the burning in his dead arm as he cinched it in place and stood on shaky legs.

As Soren turned, Daniel forced down his fear and asked, "How?"

With a wild look Soren shrugged. "I backtracked until I found Thosten. As we greeted one another they came marching into view, not two miles distant! We've been running for hours, using every shortcut and tunnel we know to get here first." He glanced in the pack a final time before slinging it over his shoulder. "This is cutting it too close."

Soren turned to the door and Daniel followed on numb legs. His heart roared in his ears so loudly that he could barely hear the noise of other rooms being ransacked. He hobbled along behind Soren as he darted out the exit and into a scene of fevered chaos. Men raced to and fro, gathering supplies. All had frightened but determined looks on their faces, but none spoke as they rushed to complete their tasks. Soren kneeled by a pile of supplies as Daniel realized that only a fraction of the men he'd met earlier were there. "Where'd everyone go?"

Without looking up Soren said, "Twenty-five of Regnar's men doubled back to slow the Imperialists." He looked up and Daniel could see that the concern on his face mirrored what he heard in his voice. "There had to be at least two hundred of them."

Daniel's mouth dropped open. Quietly he asked, "What about the men?"

Soren turned back to the supplies. He sighed and said, "They go to their deaths to buy us time. If we don't leave now, their sacrifice will be for nothing."

Daniel swallowed a lump in his throat. He turned at a noise behind him and saw a tall muscular man exit the house, followed by Westragen and Greggor. The healer had on traveling clothes and carried a walking stick, and a bulging pack was thrown over Greggor's left shoulder. Daniel recognized Thosten and returned his grim nod as he moved off to organize the supplies.

Soon everything that could be carried was loaded in packs and the remaining men stood loosely around Daniel and Soren. Regnar and Thosten were there, along with about fifteen men. Westragen stepped forward and handed a small pack to Daniel. "Valor Root tea and fresh leaves," he explained. "There are also bandages and other supplies for injuries. I fear you will need them, and far too soon."

Daniel nodded numbly and slung the pack over his left shoulder. "Are you coming with us?"

Westragen's grim frown softened as he smiled kindly. "No, Daniel. An old man would only slow you down now. Greggor and I will go into hiding with the rest of the townsfolk. We must all flee Standing Stone."

Daniel opened his mouth to thank Westragen but was interrupted by Greggor. "No, Grandfather!" he said angrily. Everyone turned to him, and he blushed before pressing on. "I won't run anymore! I can help Daniel, I know I can." He glared defiantly at his grandfather as his voice died away.

Before Westragen could speak, Soren shook his head. "You cannot come with us, Greggor." The boy turned pleading eyes on Soren, but the warrior continued firmly, "No. I am sorry, but we need to move quickly." His cheeks flushed as he motioned to Greggor's arm. "You might slow us down." He couldn't look the boy in the eyes as he finished.

Westragen murmured, "You have to come with me, Son."

Tears stood in Greggor's eyes. "*No!* I won't go with you! I may be…injured, Soren, but I *won't* slow you down." He looked around the circle of grim faces for support and stopped at Regnar. "Tell him I'm right, Regnar! You know me!"

The carpenter lowered his gaze and considered quietly for a moment. When he looked back up he said, "The boy is right, Soren. He's the hardest worker I know. He hasn't let the arm slow him…he'll be no burden."

Greggor looked back to Soren victoriously. The captain ran a hand through his hair and looked to Daniel. "What say you, Daniel?"

Daniel was caught off guard. He wasn't expecting to have any say in the argument, and besides, he had no idea what *to* say. He saw hope in Greggor's eyes, as well as fear in Westragen's. He glanced down at Greggor's arm, a twin to his own, and thought, *No one knows his pain better than me.* He sighed and said, "Let him come."

Greggor bounded over and pounded him on the back, nearly knocking Daniel from his feet. "Thank you, Daniel, thank you!"

Daniel winced and murmured, "Don't thank me yet." He glanced at Westragen and saw the hurt reproach in his eyes. He had to look away.

Soren nodded to Daniel and said, "Very well, it's settled. We have no time to lose." He pointed to men as he spoke. "Thosten, Greggor, Regnar, nine of Regnar's men, and I will go with you, Daniel. The remaining six will accompany Wes." Westragen opened his mouth but Soren raised his hand. "We've no time to argue, Wes. We have to leave, *now*." The healer's ears burned at the dismissal as Soren turned to Regnar. "Choose the men to come with us." In a quiet undertone, he added, "Those with families should go with Wes."

Regnar nodded and divided the men. Those going with Westragen gathered their packs and started off. As the old healer turned to follow, his shoulders slumped, his head bowed. Daniel cried out, "Wait!" He couldn't leave the man like that, not after everything he'd done for him. Westragen slowly turned to him, a dark look on his face. Knowing it wasn't enough, Daniel said, "Thank you, for everything, Wes. Without you I would be lost." Not knowing why he said it, he added, "Go in peace."

Westragen studied him for a moment before turning to Soren. "Protect my boy, Soren. Bring him back to me." Soren just stared at the healer as Westragen motioned to Greggor. He walked to his grandfather and Wes gave him a rough hug before turning and shuffling off in silence with his guards.

It hurt Daniel to watch him go, but fortunately he didn't have time to dwell on it. As soon as they rounded the corner, Soren said, "Alright. Time to run." He asked Daniel, "How are you holding up?"

His legs felt stronger than the day before, but he could already feel them shaking. "I can go for awhile," he offered with a shrug.

Soren nodded. "Thosten has a stretcher. Likely we'll have to use it."

Greggor shook his head and started to say, "I can car--", but Regnar cut him off.

"No, Greggor. Focus on yourself." The young man looked crestfallen until Regnar added, "You'll have time to prove yourself."

Soren looked around at the faces turned toward him. "Thosten and I lead." He motioned to Regnar's men. "Surround Daniel and Greggor. Bring up the rear, Regnar." When everyone nodded, he added, "Let's go. Double time."

The men jogged down the street and north out of Standing Stone. Daniel ran road races throughout college, so he was familiar with the need to pace himself. But college was a long time ago, and the stakes were a lot higher than in a road race. Soon he was breathing heavily, and he knew before long he'd need the stretcher. He pushed the thought away and ignored the stitch in side, loping along as best he could.

Daniel and his protectors fled. The hunt was on.

Chapter Twelve

They ran through the night and continued into the dawn. Always northward, through farms and green pastures. The men took turns carrying Daniel on his stretcher until they could go no farther. Then they traded off and ran on. It was a bitterly miserable night for Daniel, carried like a helpless babe, exhausting the men that risked everything for him. Unbidden, Gelnar's words came back to him: *"Then what good are you?"* What good indeed? Once again he was at the mercy of those around him, carried along by their whim.

Added to Daniel's misery was the electric fire that burned in his arm. The men were careful not to jostle him, but even the slightest bump sent hot charges shooting up aggravated nerve endings. He bit back the pain, refusing to cry out for fear it would slow the men that carried him. Slowing down meant their lives; Daniel knew it as well as anyone, so he bit his lip until it bled and remained silent.

By mid-morning he could hear the men wheezing while the raging fire had almost reached his shoulder. He knew none of them could take much more. He closed his eyes, falling into the cadence of ragged breathing and loping stride. That tempo and the building crescendo of pain was all he knew. He was so absorbed that he didn't immediately realize a new sound was building until it drowned out everything else. It finally penetrated his pain-filled mind when they came to a halt and he was gently lowered to the ground. Sweating men freed him from the stretcher before collapsing on the ground, drawing in ragged breaths.

Daniel sat up and saw they were along the banks of a swiftly flowing river. Soren and Thosten stood nearby, scanning the water. The captain nodded to him as he walked over on shaky legs. "We'll rest for a short while," he said. "Hopefully our friends bought us time. If not, it soon won't matter; we'll all be too exhausted to fight."

Daniel ignored his screaming arm and asked, "Do you think we've lost them?"

Soren snorted and shrugged. "Anything's possible. They were marching on Standing Stone, not really following a trail, so they may not have picked ours up." He didn't sound very hopeful. "But we weren't really trying to hide our passing, so it should be fairly easy to find..." His eyes wandered back to the river.

After a time he turned a chagrined gaze on Daniel. "Many apologies, Daniel." He motioned to Thosten and said, "This is my greatest friend and closest ally, Thosten. He and I have been through much." The tall muscular man had dark shoulder-length hair held back by a red headband. Like Soren, he wore molded leather armor and a mottled green cloak. A great sword was sheathed on his back.

Daniel offered a weak smile and lifted his left hand. "Hello, Thosten. It's good to meet you. Soren and Westragen have told me much about you."

Thosten glared at him for a moment before snorting and walking away. Daniel looked uncertainly at Soren, only to see shocked surprise on his face as well. His gaze followed his friend as he said, "Please pay him no mind...that was not like Thosten."

Daniel let his hand fall. "That's okay. It's been a tough day for everyone."

Soren frowned, his eyes still following Thosten. "You are right, of course." He sighed and looked back to the river. "This is the Gleneden River, small but swiftly flowing. It travels from the Cloudspeaks all the way to the Azure Ocean. This is the only place it can be safely forded for miles. From here it's a three day march to the nearest bridge."

He was lost in thought again until Daniel said, "So, we cross here."

Soren looked to him. "Hmm? Oh, yes. But safety is relative. It's still a dangerous crossing, what with the wet spring we've had. And the Gleneden is known to be cold and deep. Men could be lost if we're not careful, especially with the river as swollen as it is." He considered the river for a few more minutes before sighing. "We'll rest a couple hours. Allow the men to eat and regain their strength. Thosten and I will back-track, try to hide our trail."

Soren told the men the plan, patting Daniel on the shoulder as he passed. He tried not to show it, but even the friendly pat stirred the angry monster nesting in his arm. Daniel sat down at the outskirts of the impromptu camp and opened the pack Westragen gave him. He thumbed past the bandages until he found several small waxed parchment packages and a large bundle of fresh leaves. He opened one of the packets to see dried Valor Root: the promised tea. Greggor walked over and sat beside him, his face pinched with high color in his cheeks. Daniel could tell by the way he lowered himself that he was also in considerable pain. "You alright?"

Greggor turned haunted eyes on him, wincing as he raised his right shoulder, indicating his arm. He tried speaking several times before he was finally able to say, "It always hurts." Daniel nodded, still feeling electric jolts shoot up his own arm. He offered him a packet of tea, but the young man grunted and shook his head. "Doesn't work." Daniel hesitated before dropping the packet, but Greggor stopped him before he could close his pack. "No, you need your strength. You drink it."

Daniel shrugged. "I don't know."

Greggor gave a brusque nod. "Grandfather wouldn't have given you the tea if he didn't think you needed it. Besides," he added as he looked around, lowering his voice, "the sooner you get your strength back, the faster we can move."

Daniel felt a stab of guilt and lowered his head in shame. He got a water skin and cup from another man and mixed the tea. It tasted terrible cold and the crushed leaves clumped together, forming a scummy film over the water. He grimaced but forced himself to drink the whole cup before settling in beside Greggor. He was determined not to move his arm any more than necessary for the rest of the break. Food was passed around and the men ate listlessly, keeping one ear open for the sound of approaching troops. When he finished eating, Daniel laid back as delicately as he could, careful not to jostle his arm. Greggor looked at him with understanding. "It's better if you don't move."

Daniel forced a grim smile. "Lucky for us we don't have anything to do this afternoon."

Greggor forced a dry chuckle. "Indeed."

Daniel closed his eyes and focused on the sound of the rushing water. He remembered the breathing techniques from Ashley's birthing classes and decided to give them a try. He slowly breathed in through his nose and out through his mouth, holding each breath for ten seconds. After a few repetitions he felt more relaxed, but his arm still burned. Daniel considered the original purpose of the exercises and thought, *How the Hell is this supposed to help with labor? It's only my arm that hurts, and it's still driving me crazy.* He nearly chuckled as his respect for Ashley grew, but even that slight movement sent shockwaves up his arm. He gritted his teeth, relaxation and humor gone. Eventually the pain cycled back down to a dull throbbing he associated with "normal" and he relaxed.

Soren and Thosten returned three hours later and after quickly eating, Soren announced it was time to cross. The sun had already passed its zenith and he felt they were pushing their luck if they tarried longer. He took a long coil of rope from his pack and had all the men tie themselves together, with Daniel between him and Regnar. He led the way into the river, the rope paying out to Daniel and the rest of the men behind him. Daniel lowered his left foot into the water and it was pulled by the current before it even got to the bottom, nearly throwing him off balance at the very beginning.

He looked farther out, where Soren was already in up to his chest. *Oh man.* He plunged his right foot to the bottom, resisting the current's tug. Daniel trudged farther out and was almost immediately inundated with cold water. Initially it felt good on his hot skin, but soon that feeling gave way to numbness, making his unsure footing on the rocky bottom even less certain. He thought the cold water might soothe the fire in his arm, but when it was submerged, it only replaced white-hot pain with an icy cold one instead. The cold was almost worse than the fire; after all, he'd almost grown accustomed to the heat. He gritted his teeth and pushed on.

The river hadn't seemed so wide from the shore. But with his legs feeling shaky again and the cold water rising past his hips, it looked like the far side was miles distant. His chin quaked as he shivered uncontrollably. Daniel was so absorbed in his misery that he didn't realize the rope in front of him was bending back to his left until it started to tug at his waist. Alarmed, he looked up and saw that the current had pulled him downstream from Soren, the rope pulled tight between them. When Soren frowned back at him, Daniel motioned he was okay as he turned his body more directly into the current to make up lost ground. The going was even more difficult than before, and Daniel could feel all of the strength draining from his legs.

Panic started to set in when he looked up to see how much farther the shore was. At that moment his numb foot slipped off a slime-coated rock and he went down. As his head went under, Daniel sucked in a surprised breath, bringing the cold fire into his lungs as well as his right arm. He popped up, coughing and sputtering, his numb feet foundering for a purchase that wasn't there. His feet slid out from under him again and he was taken by the current, the rope around his waist pulling tight. As he struggled against the tether, his right side slammed into a submerged boulder. Even though he was underwater he couldn't help but open his mouth and scream. Bubbles rose past his head, pulled away by the strong current, and more water rushed into his lungs.

He thrashed violently, trying to stand and pull himself from the water, but by then he was so far gone into panic that he couldn't tell which way was up. He didn't realize his kicking was actually pushing him toward the bottom. Daniel felt his legs slowing, and his mind started to fog out as he slipped away. Dimly, he saw bubbles rising up from a pair of feet running through the water toward him. The last thought he had before losing consciousness was, *Dear God...*

~ * ~

When the line pulled tight, Soren turned a questioning eye on Daniel. He motioned that all was fine and the captain barely turned back around when he heard the splash. He spun and yelled, "Daniel!" Regnar was knee-deep when he went under. Without hesitation, he pulled a dagger from his belt and cut the rope behind him. He clamped the blade in his teeth and ran against the current, feet slipping on rocks all the while, as Soren did the same from the opposite direction.

Regnar arrived first and found Daniel pressed against the side of a boulder under the surface. Acting on instinct, he grabbed a fistful of Daniel's hair and pulled him from the water, gripping him in a bear hug until Soren reached them. The two carried Daniel to the far shore and Regnar used his dagger to cut the ties that held Daniel's sling against his belly. He rolled him to his back as Soren leaned over Daniel's blue-tinged face, his ear hovering just over Daniel's mouth. "He isn't breathing." The carpenter nodded as he wiped water from his face and rushed to Daniel's feet. He picked his legs up by the backs of his knees and pumped them toward his stomach as if he were a bellows.

Soren turned Daniel's face to the side. After a few repetitions Daniel coughed raggedly as water ran from the corner of his mouth. His eyes flew open and he tried to suck in another breath, only to vomit out more water. The two men grabbed his hands and pulled him to a sitting position. Soren patted his back as the last of the water came up and he was able to take in a shaky breath. As soon as he was up and supported by Soren, Regnar gasped and dropped Daniel's right hand. He fell to his knees, and after a few more ragged breaths asked, "Are you alright, Stranger?"

~ * ~

Daniel barely heard Regnar over the screaming pain that burned through his right arm and shoulder. He opened his mouth but all that came out was a moan. It turned into a wracking cough that shook his whole frame, wounding the arm even more. He closed his eyes and delicately grasped his right wrist. With a whimper he cradled the dead arm in his lap. The two men shared a concerned look before Soren murmured, "Daniel?"

Daniel leaned forward and hunched to the right, favoring his wounded arm. His jaw muscles working furiously as his legs rubbed against one another. He pulled out great tufts of grass with his left hand as he fought the pain. Soren glanced up as the first of the troops came out of the water. He motioned to the river and said to Regnar, "Go help them. I'll stay here."

Regnar pulled his gaze from Daniel and nodded. Everyone else crossed the river without incident, but the near loss of Daniel shook them all. As they reached dry ground, they circled around Soren and Daniel, looking at their great hope with fear and uncertainty. Finally the pain scaled down and Daniel took a great ragged breath.

Soren glanced at the men before he murmured, "Daniel? Many apologies, Daniel, but we have to keep moving."

Daniel cracked his eyes open and peered at the captain before nodding. In a hoarse voice he said, "The stretcher."

He bit back a groan as he was strapped down and the men picked him up to continue on their way. They traveled west, parallel with the river for several miles before cutting back to the north again, leaving the Gleneden behind them for good. Thosten led while Soren and Regnar brought up the rear, erasing their trail as best they could. The men were exhausted and moved with exaggerated care as they stoically bore Daniel.

Two hours after nightfall they crested a small hill and Thosten called a halt. The men dropped to the ground where they stood, too tired to talk. The inky sky was painted with strange constellations and a light breeze blew over the hill, carrying with it the perfumed scent of flowers. The music of a summer night filled the air as birds and insects sang. Suddenly a tremendous explosion roared across the land, silencing all of nature.

Exhaustion fell from the men as they jumped to their feet. They looked to one another, then back to the south where the sound originated, even as its pealing echoes rolled over them. The night was not so dark on the southern horizon, where it was tinged orange and red. After a minute Daniel broke the silence. "What the Hell was that?"

No one answered for a time, but finally one of the men spoke in a hoarse whisper. "It's Standing Stone. They're burning Home." The shocking certainty of the statement washed over the men as they stared in open-mouthed despair. They grieved together, watching the orange glow until long after the reverberating echoes died away.

Daniel couldn't help but feel responsible. The only place he'd had any peace since coming to Naphthali was in flames, his defenders homeless because of him. Soren cleared his throat. "We've gained much ground. We rest here tonight." One by one, the men turned away from the glow and started the business of setting up camp. Eventually only Daniel and Greggor remained, staring into the red-tinged darkness and wishing they could undo what had been done.

~ * ~

The next days were a study in torture and humiliation for Daniel. He slept fitfully, jolting himself awake whenever he started to dream, afraid of being trapped by Malthion. More often than not, when he woke he disturbed his right arm and the fires would be stoked. He'd grit his teeth until the pain subsided, only for the course to repeat itself a few hours later. To make matters worse, his sling didn't fit as well after Regnar cut the straps. The improvised leather ties they used either kept coming undone or tightened unbearably if they got wet. And getting wet became more of a problem as they continued north, the weather turning increasingly sultry, with powerful storms stirring up every afternoon.

The days took on a monotonous, tortuous routine as Daniel battled pain, weakness, and embarrassment in never ending cycles. He started every day by walking as long as he could, which was easier since they weren't pressing the pace as hard. Eventually his legs weakened and gave out, and he would be consigned to the stretcher. The men never complained, but soon Daniel couldn't bear to look any of them in the eye. He found excuses to be left alone during breaks, where he drank the horrible tea and prayed for his strength to return. All the while, the pain in his right arm cycled from dull throbbing to electric jolts of agony. Inevitably the damn sling would come undone just when it returned to a dull ache, sending him into paroxysms of pain once more.

Everything compounded Daniel's guilt and self-loathing. He'd always believed God didn't give anyone more than they could handle, but now that he was being tested so extremely, he wasn't so sure. Everyone has their own cross to bear, and the ability to bear it stoically was always something Daniel admired. He expected to find the same within himself, but as his pain and despair mounted, he was dismayed to find that he was losing faith as well as his stoicism.

He was so buried in his own misery that he didn't even realize he was getting stronger. The periods of exhausted weakness spent strapped to the stretcher were becoming fewer and farther between, and he was shocked one day when Thosten called a halt at midday. It was the first time since they'd fled Standing Stone that he walked the whole morning. He looked around wide-eyed, knowing smiles flashing back at him. Greggor patted him on the shoulder. "Your strength is back." It was a statement, not a question. Daniel nodded mutely and Greggor offered a smile of encouragement before grimacing as he repositioned his sling.

The words rolled over and over in Daniel's mind until finally he was able to voice them himself. "My strength *is* back." He never would have thought such a simple statement could be so uplifting, until he heard it coming from his own mouth and knew it to be true. The freedom to move on his own, not to mention the burden he lifted from his allies, filled Daniel with such joy that he momentarily forgot even the constant pain in his arm.

He closed his eyes and lifted his face to a sky that was rapidly clouding over. He sighed deeply and felt the tension melt from his shoulders as he repeated the line in his mind. *My strength is back!* He joined the men for the midday meal and felt their camaraderie, which in truth had been there all along, though he was too consumed by misery to see it.

When Soren said it was time to continue, Daniel joined the men in repacking their diminishing supplies. As they set out and rain started to fall, he could feel the pain returning in his arm. The leather strap bit painfully into his hip as it tightened, but the burden didn't seem so great anymore. He stoically grimaced as he kept pace with the men. As it turned out, for today at least, he could bear his burden after all.

Chapter Thirteen

Soren called a halt for the day shortly before dark. They made camp at the foot of a massive hill that topped out several hundred feet over the surrounding countryside. It first came into view when they crested a rise shortly after midday, and they'd been advancing on the behemoth ever since. It was truly enormous, stretching for miles at its base, covered by a forest so thick that it looked like a giant had laid a great piney coat over the mound. Nearby a shallow river, swollen by the latest daily deluge, gurgled along. Surrounding its banks were twisted trees with flowing branches that reminded Daniel of weeping willows.

He sighed as he sat on a fallen log and examined the massive hill. Its slope was gentle, but it continued upward for at least a mile. Looking at it Daniel knew he couldn't have made the top if he'd tried that day, but still he was happy with his efforts: he made it through the day without slowing them down or asking for help. His arm buzzed angrily at him, but he didn't let it get the better of him. Regnar ambled over and sat, greeting him with a nod. He motioned to the hill and said, "'Tis called Mount Dlanor. We'll need our strength tomorrow."

Daniel grunted. "Interesting name. Bit short for a mountain, though, don't you think?"

Regnar shrugged. "The tale of Dlanor is a warning for us all." His voice drifted off for a moment before he asked, "Would you like to hear it?"

Daniel nodded. "Please."

Silence stretched out as Regnar stared at the peak. Daniel decided he'd changed his mind when he gave a great sigh and began. "Long ago there was a clansman named Dlanor. He was very wealthy, very powerful. His lands stretched as far as he could see and all owed him fealty. First, he was humble, thankful for his blessings. But in time he changed. He began to think he *deserved* all that was his. He collected many things to show his greatness: tools, weapons, art…all the very best.

"His pride swelled like a carcass in the sun, and like a carcass it repulsed all those that once cherished him. His friends left as he focused on things rather than those that loved him. One night at a banquet he drank too much. He boasted that his land was the greatest of all, and nothing outshone what he possessed. One of the guests said, 'Surely, great Dlanor, the Cloudspeaks are a greater wonder than any that can be found here. There is nothing to compare in your land.'

"Old Dlanor was enraged by the man's audacity, and so then and there he swore he would create a mountain greater than the Cloudspeaks. He spent the rest of his life fashioning this hill, using the gadgets and trinkets he valued over friends and family. Over time his estate dwindled, sold off to pay for his obsession. Work on the bare dirt hill slowed to a crawl.

"As the unpaid workers abandoned him, Dlanor began to work the hill himself, building it ever higher. He grew embittered and angry as the work slowed, and eventually only his daughter openly showed love for the old man. It broke her heart to see how the mound broke his spirit, so one night she went out and crowned the hill with trees and flowers. She hoped her father would see the beauty he'd created and leave off his labors.

"Her heart was in the right place, but she didn't realize that *his* heart was lost to him, consumed by pride. When he saw what she'd done, he was thrown into a rage. He ordered her to leave his lands and never return. As she left in tears, he tore out the beauty she placed on his ugly mound. He continued alone, no one left to help him or care for him. Finally, one day he died on his damnable obsession, and none mourned the once-great man. He was reduced to nothing, all because of pride.

"A neighbor found his body, picked clean by carrion. The fool was buried on top of his hill, his great mountain. His former subjects came and planted trees and flowers, covering the whole mound. They hoped to blot out the ugliness…the ugly turn his life took." His voice drifted away and they studied the testament to foolish pride in silence.

After a time Daniel said, "That was a good tale. Thank you for sharing it." He turned back to the mound and the strap on his sling gave way. His right arm bumped the log and he sucked in a breath as he carefully repositioned it.

When he'd composed himself, Regnar said, "You did well today, Stranger."

Daniel forced a grin past the pain. "Thank you." After a short pause he added, "Please, call me Daniel."

Regnar took a long pull on a water skin and nodded as he passed it to Daniel. "Alright. Daniel, then." They passed a few more minutes in companionable silence before he said, "There's no doubt you've gone through some darkness. 'Tis good to see you coming out the other side." He motioned to the men that were setting up camp. "These are good men, every one. They will help you with anything. They'll give you everything."

Daniel nodded uncertainly. "Yes, I know. I am grateful."

Regnar waved away the appreciation. "We're not doing this for thanks...we *need* this." Daniel's face burned when he realized where Regnar was going. Before he could speak the carpenter raised a hand. "It doesn't matter if you're the One or not. What matters is we need something to believe in, something to *hope* for." He turned from the hill, his need burning in his eyes. "We--I--need to know your measure. Are you ruled by pride like Dlanor was? Or can we place our faith in you?"

Daniel's heart rose in his throat. He wanted to say he had no idea, that he was wandering, lost and alone. Don't look to him for guidance, he couldn't even guide himself. He wanted to tell Regnar about his fears and worthlessness, about how afraid he was that he would let them all down, if not get them killed. But the lump in his throat and the unabashed need in Regnar's eyes stopped him. After a long pause all he could offer was, "I don't know, Regnar. I...I hope so."

Regnar stared into Daniel's eyes, earnest need meeting earnest uncertainty. He turned back to the hill, wiping his eyes with a sleeve. After a moment asked, "Do you have kin?"

Daniel was surprised by the change of topic, and at first he thought he'd misheard until Regnar glanced at him. "Yes, I have a wife, three children." Just saying that much brought their faces fresh to Daniel's mind and tears to his eyes. His voice was thick when he added, "God, I miss them so much."

Regnar studied the hill until Daniel wiped away his tears. "You wish to go to them?"

Daniel nodded. "More than anything. They nee--" He caught himself halfway through, thinking how Regnar used the term. He hesitated for only a second before finishing, "They need me too…and I need them."

Regnar studied Daniel and nodded. "Family is important. When all is said and done, that's all a man has. 'Tis *everything*. Without that, he…well, he might not go on." Regnar's voice was thick with despair. Daniel laid his left hand on his shoulder, lending comfort in silence. At first he pulled away, but as his grief overcame him he leaned into Daniel, accepting the support. After a few minutes he gently pushed away as Greggor walked over, balancing two wooden plates on his good arm. Daniel's arm dropped to his side as Regnar stood. "You are a good man, Daniel. Our trust in you is well-placed."

Daniel looked up at him and all his fears came back, balanced on the tip of his tongue, dying to be let out. But again the hope burning in Regnar's eyes silenced him. Regnar gave a lop-sided smile, the first Daniel had seen from him. As he walked away, Greggor turned a quizzical look on Daniel and offered him a plate. "What was that about?"

Daniel couldn't speak. If he started, he wouldn't stop until his entire tale of worthlessness and woe was spilled at the young man's feet. He saw the same veneer of hope shining from Greggor's eyes, though, and knew he couldn't share his darkest secrets with him either. He shrugged and dug into the food. His gaze roamed around camp until he found Soren, who was sitting on the ground with a group of men. Greggor murmured, "He's a great man." He nodded toward Soren when Daniel looked at him and added, "We'd all be dead now, if not for him."

Daniel nodded whole-heartedly, knowing the personal truth of the statement. "He sure is driven." After a small pause he asked, "He really hates the Empire, doesn't he?"

Greggor grunted. "Yeah, well, you'd hate 'em too, wouldn't you? I mean, *you* have a family."

A pang of loneliness and guilt jolted through him but he pushed it away. "What do you mean?"

Greggor turned surprised eyes on Daniel. "Grandfather never told you?"

"Never told me what?" Greggor stared in shock until Daniel frowned. "What, Greggor?"

He darted a look around before leaning close and speaking in clipped tones. "Soren had a wife and daughter. When the Empire invaded, they took them. Before he knew they had them, Soren attacked the Imperialists, wiping out nearly an entire regiment." Greggor stopped for a moment and Daniel's heart skipped a beat. "The Empire didn't even tell him. They...they just gave them to...to the soldiers..."

Daniel laid his left hand on Greggor's knee. "That's enough," he moaned. "My God." Once more he heard the screams of the farmer's wife and he understood how truly horrible it must have been for Soren. Daniel could see him straining against Thosten, hate burning in his eyes.

The two sat silently for awhile until Daniel walked away to relieve himself. When he returned, Greggor was sitting in a circle with the other men not on guard duty. Daniel felt self-conscious and suddenly shy as he joined them, uncertain he'd be welcome. He needn't have bothered. They smiled and made room for him, filling Daniel with a rush of gratitude. They barely knew him, but they fled their homes and watched them destroyed because of him. Not only that, but he'd nearly cost them their lives by slowing them down. Daniel knew he didn't deserve their friendship, and so he was deeply touched that it was offered anyway.

One man on the far side of the circle lowered his head in a deep bow. He returned his gaze to Daniel and with a warm smile said, "Welcome, Stranger."

He looked at each man and saw Regnar's hope reflected in their faces. He sighed inwardly. *This can only end badly.* Quietly he said, "Please, call me Daniel."

The man lowered his head again. "Daniel. Welcome."

The man beside him leaned forward, studying his face closely. The speaker raised his eyebrows and returned the stare until he brushed at his friend's forehead. "You're gonna get dirt on your face if you keep that up, Clem."

Daniel's tension melted away as they laughed and returned to friendly banter. Occasionally they asked him questions, but to his relief they no longer looked at him in awed wonder.

Daniel sat with them until nearly dark, feeling the bonds of friendship. They spoke on many topics but never the Empire or Standing Stone, careful to avoid painful subjects. Eventually Daniel's exhaustion caught up with him, and Clem chuckled when he let out a jaw-popping yawn. "It's been a long day, Daniel. You should get some rest." With that he stood and stretched. "I'm to my bed too."

Another man laughed. "Bed? No wonder ya march slow, Clem! I didn't know ya packed a whole bed!"

He feigned irritation. "Very funny, Trumble." He waved as he stepped from the circle. "I'll take second watch. 'Night, gents."

Daniel yawned again and decided to follow Clem. When he stood the men stopped speaking and turned to him. He suddenly felt self-conscious as he murmured, "Goodnight." They smiled and offered him the same as he turned to the tents. He lay down and thought of Ashley and the kids and felt the familiar stab of loneliness. It was almost as constant and wearying as the pain in his arm, but that night it didn't seem as intense, knowing he was among friends. He drifted off and slept dreamlessly until dawn.

~ * ~

They broke camp early the next morning, eager to conquer Mount Dlanor. Daniel cinched the leather thongs on his sling and looked at the green peak with trepidation. It was, after all, only the day before that he finally went the whole day without needing help. Would the climb be too much for him? He hoped not, but fear gnawed at him. It had been with him ever since they left Standing Stone, a constant certainty that he'd let the men down. His conversation with Regnar didn't help, either. He was asking too much, they all were. He was just one flawed man, not some great Messiah. Daniel wished he could find a way to tell them, but every time he looked at the hope in their faces, the arguments died in his throat.

He sighed as Soren spoke to Regnar. The carpenter nodded and darted ahead of the main group while the captain spoke to Thosten, who dropped back as they set off. Less than a half hour into the hike Soren fell in alongside Daniel. He smiled and asked, "How are you doing today, Daniel?"

He tried in vain to cover his heavy breathing with a sigh and said, "So far so good." When Soren didn't reply, he glanced over and saw concern in his face. Daniel raised his left hand in a warding gesture. "I'm fine, Soren." Just thinking of the hated stretcher was enough to push him harder.

Soren watched him a few more minutes before shrugging. He took in the scraggly firs, thick willows, and gingkoes surrounding them and sighed. "Isn't this beautiful country?" he murmured, more to himself than Daniel.

Daniel grunted. His breath was coming in short gasps, and sweat ran down the sides of his face. "Kinda humid...but not bad."

Soren nodded. "I grew up near here. My brother and I would come to Dlanor and race to the top."

Daniel grunted again. "I bet it's...quite a view."

Soren smiled. "Yes, you can see for miles. On a clear day you can just make out the purple shadows of Dlanor's nemesis to the north."

Daniel cast a confused glance on Soren. "Dlanor's nemes--oh you mean the Cloudspeaks."

"You've heard the tale?" he asked, surprised.

"Regnar told me...yesterday."

Soren took in Daniel's flushed cheeks and just said, "Ah," letting the conversation die. They traveled in companionable silence for some time, Soren remembering the past and Daniel focusing on his footing.

After three hours Daniel's breathing was so harsh that all the men stole concerned glances at him. He didn't see the looks, though. He was completely absorbed by a constant litany that ran through his mind. *One more step...I miss you, Ashley...One more step...I love you...One more step.* He'd march to the end of the earth if it meant he could return to his family, but he didn't think that was where this road ended. The camaraderie he felt at the campfire slipped away as he fell into self-imposed solitude.

Soren pulled him from his thoughts when he grabbed his arm and made him stop. He looked up from the ground and saw the men standing around him, concern stamped on their faces. It took a minute before he realized the weird wheezing sound he heard was coming from his own lungs. Then he felt the stabbing stitch in his side, a pain he'd completely blocked out as he marched. "Are you alright?" Soren asked, still holding his left arm.

Daniel started to nod, but he was doubled over by a coughing fit. He wrenched his right arm and fireworks went off that nearly sent him to his knees. He groaned against the pain and nodded weakly with his eyes closed. Soren turned to the men. "We rest here. We'll go again in--well, we rest here for now."

The men murmured agreement as the reached for water skins and sat down wearily. Daniel felt rather than saw that Greggor had walked up to him. He stood by his side, ready to help. When the pain cycled down, he stood up straight and opened his eyes. Greggor stared at him in grave concern. "Let's sit down." With a nod Greggor supported Daniel as best he could and they shuffled to a sun-dappled spot. Greggor lowered him to the ground with a groan and sat beside him, offering Daniel a water skin.

Soon Soren hunkered down before the two. "You alright?" he asked quietly.

Daniel lowered the skin and gave a weak nod. "I think so...I pushed too hard."

Soren's intense eyes roamed over Daniel. "We can help you, with the stretch--"

Daniel cut him off. "No. I can make it on my own. Besides, I...I've been a burden long enough." His face burned as he looked away.

After a long pause Soren said, "Alright, but tell me if you need to rest." Still unable to make eye contact, Daniel nodded. After a few more seconds he walked away, leaving the two alone.

Daniel took a deep shaky breath and let it out slowly. He willed his guilt over endangering the men to flow out of him as well, and after a few breaths relaxed. When he stopped wheezing, Greggor clumsily patted his leg. "Don't worry, Daniel. It will be alright."

Daniel smiled weakly and Greggor beamed back. *I'm not so sure about that*, he thought, but he smiled at Greggor anyway. He could feel the burden of Greggor's hope and optimism, but it was precious to him. He wouldn't risk damaging it if he could help it, especially given the pain Greggor had already endured because of him. His eyes wandered to Greggor's arm, lying lifeless against his belly; a twin to his own pain. *I don't think anything will be alright.*

~ * ~

It was well past midday before Daniel said he was ready and they set out again. They traveled much more slowly, with Soren watching him carefully as they went. He could feel his legs burn, but he maintained the slower pace. After about an hour he motioned to Soren's A-blade and asked, "What do you call that?"

Soren glanced down at the blade, sheathed in its leather scabbard across his chest. "It's called a Katareen. It is a weapon that is favored in a land far from here, across the Azure Ocean. I found it on my travels with King Begnauld."

"Nice," Daniel offered.

"Yes, I am quite fond of it." Soren untied the thong that held it in place and pulled it from the sheath. It gleamed dully in the dim sunlight filtering through the forest canopy. "When you thrust out with it, like this," he said, extending his fist, "it can rend chain mail." He made several sweeping motions side-to-side. "Of course, it also works well for slashing." Daniel remembered seeing the weapon in action against Gelnar and his men. He paled and gave a quick nod. Soren sheathed the A-blade and looked away while Daniel regained his composure. After a pause he asked, "Are you familiar with any weapons?"

Daniel shook his head. "No, where I come from weapons like yours are considered outdated. Most of ours are called guns, which fire bullets--like small metal balls--that can kill from far away." Daniel thought about the hunters he allowed on his farm every winter and added, "Some people use bows and arrows though."

Soren frowned and asked, "So all combat is fought from a distance?"

"Most is…some do hand-to-hand combat, but mostly for sport."

A shadow crossed Soren's face. "How far away can these…guns…kill?"

Daniel shrugged. "I don't know…I'd say for most probably at least the length of a field."

Soren fell silent for awhile before he said, "Where is the honor in fighting your enemies from so far away?"

Daniel shook his head. "I don't know." He thought about the bloodshed he'd seen since coming to Naphthali and thought, *Where is the honor in any of it?*

Soren opened his mouth to ask another question when Clem shouted, "Regnar comes!"

Soren rushed ahead to meet the carpenter. Sweat flattened his bristly beard to his cheeks and his eyes were wild with fear. The two spoke briefly before Soren looked back to the group, his eyes burning in their tattoo-ringed pits. "We must pick up the pace! We're nearly to the top now." He looked to Daniel and asked, "Can you push harder?" Regnar's fear and Soren's steely fire made Daniel's stomach flip somersaults. He nodded woodenly. "Good." He looked back to Regnar and said, "Sooner begun, sooner done. Lead them on. I'll warn Thosten." He dashed back down the trail and was quickly lost from view.

Greggor filled the space at Daniel's side as Regnar got them moving, nearly jogging up the last of the incline to Mount Dlanor's summit. Trees still blocked their view, and if not for the leveling of the ground, Daniel wouldn't have realized they'd reached the top. He was wheezing again and his legs felt shaky. Regnar quietly said, "We wait here for Soren and Thosten." The men shared concerned looks, but no one spoke as they passed around water skins.

When Soren and Thosten arrived, the captain ordered the men to wait as he motioned for Daniel and Regnar to join him. Daniel's stomach did another flip as Soren led them off the path and into the woods. Ten minutes later they came to a clearing that was dominated by a circular stone platform. A stone staircase wound around it to the top, where it jutted above the surrounding trees. He turned to Daniel and said, "This is purported to be where Dlanor was buried. The watch tower was built to remind us of his tragic tale, but it also gives a good view of the countryside."

As Daniel followed him up the stairs a detached part of his mind thought about the mixed messages we all send. *So they build this to warn people, but at the same time glorify his accomplishment with the fine view it offers.* He was wheezing again when they reached the top, but even if he had breath, it would have been taken away by the view. To the north and east a stretch of savannah gradually gave way to The Great Northern Swamp, which was dotted with willows and magnolia trees. It stretched as far as the eye could see, and at the limit of Daniel's vision was a dark haze which he assumed was the Cloudspeak Mountains. It was really the view to the southwest, though, that hit Daniel the hardest. Several miles distant a dark smudge covered the farmland they'd crossed. He squinted toward it as Soren swore. Afraid he already knew the answer, Daniel asked, "What's that?"

Soren and Thosten shared a look before he answered. "They haven't lost our trail, after all." He studied their enemies awhile before adding, "They're no more than two days behind us."

Daniel's anxiety tilted toward full panic as he asked, "What will we do?"

Thosten gave Daniel a dark look. "We run."

Soren glanced back a final time. "We should be able to outpace them...we can move faster." He looked to the other three, the fires in his eyes burning bright. "But we have to go now. Back to the men." They ran down the tower and to the waiting troops. Adrenaline erased Daniel's exhaustion and the throbbing of his arm was a distant distraction. Soren explained the situation and they quickly set out down the trail, jogging after Thosten while the captain turned and ran back down the trail from whence they'd come.

Daniel allowed himself to be swept along by the men. He felt as though he was floating along currents of terror, not being carried so much of his own volition, as by the will of the dauntless townsmen-turned-warriors that surrounded him. Occasionally his fear receded enough for him to marvel at their composure. They did share looks of fear, but those glances were outweighed by determination. Even Greggor, who was easily the youngest of them, stared grimly ahead and pushed his unwhole body to keep up. He never slowed though he did seem to retreat into himself as they ran.

After nearly two hours (*two hours!* Daniel thought. *It took nearly all day to climb it!*), the ground leveled off and trees gave way to scraggly grassland. When they stopped, Daniel doubled over, his legs shaking uncontrollably as air wheezed from his lungs. Thosten surveyed the men, his gaze falling at last on Daniel. While he was still in thought, a frown creasing his brow, Regnar walked up to him. "The men need rest."

Thosten turned to Regnar and searched his face before looking to the men again. They were tired but not overly so. His gaze returned to Daniel and with a grimace he relented. "Alright, Regnar. We rest, but only briefly. We must gain ground."

He nodded and walked away to spread the word. The men settled down for a break but continually threw anxious glances up the slopes of Dlanor. Daniel felt their fear but exhaustion kept his own in check as he dropped to the grassy earth with a groan. His right arm roared at him and the remnants of the stitch in his side ached. He pushed his left elbow into the stitch while trying to hold his right arm as still as possible. The electric fire threatened to overwhelm him if he let it, but he grimly pulled together the tattered remains of his will power and forced the pain away. When it receded, Daniel was surprised to realize Greggor hadn't joined him. He cast around and found him sitting by himself, mutely gritting his teeth. The constant dark rings under his eyes seemed darker, and they stood out starkly against his pale skin.

Daniel's ears burned as he lurched to his feet. He took for granted that Greggor would comfort him, but never considered Greggor's needs. They commiserated together when they first met, but since then he hadn't tried comforting the young man, even though he alone truly understood his pain. As he stumbled across the camp, Regnar met him half way. He leaned in close and murmured in Daniel's ear, "Leave him be, Stranger. He needs time."

Daniel shook his head and shouldered past the carpenter, staggering to a halt before Greggor. He continued to stare straight ahead, oblivious to Daniel's presence as he dropped gingerly to his knees. "Hey, you okay?" he murmured.

At first Daniel didn't think he'd answer, but then he finally shook his head. A single tear welled up in his eye, over-spilled and trailed down his cheek. In a broken whisper he said, "I don't know how much more I can take."

Tears stung Daniel's eyes as he caressed Greggor's cheek with his left hand, wiping away the tear. His hand slipped to the nape of Greggor's neck and pulled him into an awkward embrace. No words came to mind; none that would help, at least, so he just quietly held the boy. Minutes later Regnar kneeled beside them. "We need to move out." He offered a careworn look to Greggor and asked, "Can you make it, son?" The young man pulled away from Daniel and both men saw the fear and despair, naked on his face. He tried a smile, but it quickly faded as he gave a minute nod. He gasped as he bent to pick up his pack. Regnar intercepted his reach and threw the pack over his shoulder, where it bounced off his own bulging bag. Greggor turned haunted eyes on him, and Regnar grunted, "I've got it."

Daniel patted his back and said, "Let's go." They joined the other men and Daniel turned to Regnar. "Slower now?"

The older man shrugged and then nodded. "I'll see what I can do." He walked away to join Thosten and soon the men marched out into the grasslands, leaving the cover of Mount Dlanor behind. Thankfully, their pace was slower than before. Daniel marched alongside Greggor, ready to share his friend's burden.

~ * ~

They continued through the night, falling into a monotonous routine of walking for two to three hours, then resting before going again. They never lit fires and the new moon provided little illumination as they marched through the waist-high grass. Each time they set out Daniel felt rested and strong, but when Thosten halted the line, his legs were quivering and on the verge of collapse. He and Greggor would drop to the ground and fight to stay awake until Thosten roused them to march on.

The sky lightened in the east and the grasslands took on color and texture. Daniel drank it in through an exhaustion-numbed mind and wondered dully if they'd ever stop running. Still they marched on until Regnar hissed a warning from the rear of the line. The men pulled weapons free as they dropped low in the grass. Daniel also dropped and listened with all his might, but adrenaline flooded his system and all he heard was his heart hammering. Regnar hefted his mace and drifted back into the grass. Silence stretched out and the tension built until finally he whispered, "All clear! It's Soren!"

The men let out a collective sigh as the captain joined them, covered in sweat and breathing heavily. He looked into the eyes of each man, taking a silent reckoning before moving on to the next. His gaze lingered longest on Daniel and Greggor, concern etched on his face. Greggor couldn't hold Soren's stare as his chin dipped to his chest. Daniel refused to let his friend stand alone, though. He took a step closer and gently rested his left arm on the young man's shoulder. Soren's gaze left the pair as he addressed the crowd. "Our enemy closes the gap. They near Mount Dlanor and will attempt it tomorrow. I say *attempt* only. Some surprises await them. Hopefully they'll buy us more time." He raised a water skin to his lips, drinking deeply.

As he lowered it Regnar asked, "What will we do?"

Soren considered a moment before answering. "We have two options." He pointed to the northeast. "We can make straight for the Great Swamp and lose them in the moors." The men shared dark looks at that suggestion, but none spoke as Soren continued, now pointing due north. "Or we can follow the grasslands toward the Cloudspeaks. The Swordgrass lies there, but we may be able to escape them for good."

Daniel saw that some of the men looked blankly at Soren, but others paled and their eyes grew round. Silence stretched out until he turned back and saw the captain looking directly at him. Suddenly self-conscious, he pointed in the opposite direction and asked, "Why can't we go that way?"

Soren shook his head. "To the south the Great Swamp widens into a vast delta before emptying into the ocean. We'd be trapped between the Empire and the sea." He pointed back toward the Cloudspeaks and said, "Our only hope is to make for the Pass of Perfundi. I have contacts outside Naphthali that can aid us."

Daniel saw a shadow flit across Thosten's face, but it was there and gone so quickly that afterwards he wasn't sure it happened at all. He considered the men's reaction and asked, "What if we chose the swamp?"

"You remember my description of Naphthali?" When Daniel nodded Soren continued. "The Pass of Perfundi usually should only be tested in the winter. The reason is because the swamp is very dangerous, especially in summer. Spring rains flood the moors, making paths impassible. One wrong step can sink a man to his death. Also, the smallest bite from an insect can kill, not to mention the great cats and dragons that call the swamps home."

The hair on Daniel's neck stood on end at the mention of cats, bringing to mind images of the beasts feeding in the Valley of Death. Soren's last words gave him the greatest chill, though. "Dragons?" His voice was little more than a whimper.

Soren nodded and several men gasped in spite of themselves. After a moment he added, "Eventually we will have to brave the swamp, whichever path we choose. But if we make for the Swordgrass, we can stave off that moment a while longer…and our trek through the swamp will be shorter." After a moment's silence, Soren asked, "What say you, Daniel?"

Daniel glanced around and saw that all looked to him to make the decision. Their confidence and insistence on his leadership humbled and frightened him. He wished Thosten or Soren, or even Regnar, would step forward and decide, but he knew none would. This was his road. Live or die, the decision was his. He swallowed his fear and said, "The Swordgrass, then. Let's do that."

Soren nodded his approval and Thosten grumbled under his breath before turning away. The captain's frown followed his friend for a moment before returning to the men. "Very well, our course is set. Whether my traps slow them or not, the Imperialists will soon have the high ground and may spot us. We travel by night." He paused for a minute and considered the tall golden grass. "The land will hide us during the day. Spread out and cut the grass, but don't take much from any single area."

The men dispersed and Soren walked to Daniel. "You chose well," he said with a grim smile

Daniel wasn't so sure. He opened his mouth to tell Soren that when Regnar joined them. "We're running low on supplies."

Soren nodded. "There is little for it. We may find some along the way, but for now we press on." He considered for a moment and added, "Three quarters rations." Regnar inclined his head and walked away to collect grass. Soren looked back to Daniel and said, "Come. Sooner begun, sooner done." He and Daniel walked away from their packs and pulled grass.

When everyone returned with armloads of the supple grass, Soren showed them how to loosely weave it into a net. When it was large enough to cover the camp area, he went back over it, adding tufts of grass to break any obvious straight lines. The result reminded Daniel of camouflage netting. Regnar produced short wooden staffs from his pack that screwed together into tent posts nearly four feet tall. It was midmorning by the time the project was done. The netting was not only indistinguishable from the surrounding grasslands, but underneath it was also nicely shaded, offering a cool respite from the heat of the treeless savannah. After a cold meal Greggor and Daniel dropped to the ground and fell head-long into sleep. The last image Daniel had as he drifted off was of the men looking to him for orders. His stomach turned at the certainty that he could only lead them to their doom.

~ * ~

The heat was stifling, even with the shade of the netting. Daniel slept fitfully and finally gave up the effort late in the afternoon. Near dusk he hunkered down for a brief meal and was joined by Soren and Greggor. The captain casually took in the two and asked, "How are you doing?"

Greggor turned listless eyes on him and shrugged. He was covered in sweat and shadows lay below his eyes like dark smudges. "We're doing," he grunted.

Soren studied him closely. "Tell me how you're holding up, Greggor. If you need help, you'll get it, but I have to know."

Greggor grunted again and his lips pulled tight in a humorless smile. "I have good moments and bad. Right now I'm fine."

Soren stared into Greggor's eyes, and the younger man refused to look away. Finally he said, "Can you keep pace?" He hesitated before nodding and Soren sighed. "Very well." He turned to Daniel. "And you?"

Daniel shrugged. "I'm OK." Before Soren could lock eyes with him as well, he laid a reassuring hand on his arm. "I can keep up." He let it drop and looked over the other men sitting in a loose circle. Thosten sat between Clem and Regnar on the other side of the ring, frowning as he picked at his rations. Daniel saw his gaze stop at his friend and asked, "Is he alright?"

He glanced at Daniel. "Thosten? Yes...I believe so." His tone wasn't very convincing as he resumed studying the man. "You and he have much in common, did you know that?" Daniel shook his head and Soren nodded. "He has three children, like you, and a wife he adores." A stab of loneliness left Daniel speechless, so he merely grunted. After a few minutes he asked, "Have you sons or daughters?"

Daniel's voice was thick with emotion when he answered. "Both. Our oldest is a girl, the other two are boys."

Soren didn't detect Daniel's sadness. He still watched Thosten when he nodded and a smile crossed his face. "It is the same for Thosten. His daughter, Isolde, is truly a vision. And the boys! They favor their mother in appearance, but both have their father's temperament." He chuckled. "Poor Daphelle. I'm sure she misses him."

Tears stung Daniel's eyes. "And I'm sure he misses them."

At last Soren heard the pain in Daniel's voice and turned to him. "Many apologies, Daniel. I did not wish to cause you pain."

Daniel blinked away the tears and murmured, "It's…it's alright."

Greggor leaned forward and pointedly asked, "How long till we reach the Swordgrass?"

Daniel silently thanked the young man before turning back to Soren. The captain nodded to himself and said, "It should take two nights…maybe three. There will be no moonlight." The sun set as they ate and the sky shifted from deepest navy to black as Soren glanced at it. "Speaking of which, we should get moving."

Their diminishing supplies were packed, and the netting was carefully rolled and strapped to Regnar's pack. Daniel glanced at the dark silhouette of Mount Dlanor rising over the horizon behind them. No campfires dotted its peak, so he hoped their enemies hadn't reached that far. He gave an involuntary shiver at the thought of them, and Greggor patted him on the shoulder. He forced a smile for the younger man and followed him through the tall grass.

~ * ~

While they marched through the night, Soren's words came back to Daniel as he studied Thosten. Were they really that similar? He'd been so distant since they'd met that Daniel had no real idea who the warrior was. During a brief break Daniel motioned to him as he spoke with Soren. "What do you know of him?" he asked Greggor.

Greggor gave him a disinterested glance. "Thosten? Not much. They say he's a southern noble. He and Soren met in the army." His face darkened and he added, "During the Fall, other nobles scrambled for position. Some missed the old clan ways so much they welcomed our enemies in! No better than the butchers, if you ask me. But not Thosten...he stood with Soren."

As they marched through the darkness, Daniel's mind returned to thoughts of his family. When he traveled those roads, his heart was torn afresh, but he welcomed it. The familiar pain was devastating in its intensity, but he wrapped himself in it, cherishing even that vestige of Ashley and the kids. He remembered how he desperately sought his lost memories when he woke in the battlefield. When a memory came back, he pushed for more, even though it caused pain, like a tongue prodding an infected tooth. That pain came from a need to know, but this was different. Daniel gritted his teeth and thought, *This is like...a death.* Happy memories brought only sadness, and despair welled up inside him.

The sharp intensity of the pain reminded him of another time long ago. He'd been very close to his grandmother, and there was nothing he'd rather do than spend long summer days at her house, playing cards or talking. They were so close that when Daniel was a teenager, he once made his friends stop at her house so they could meet her. It was an awkward introduction for his friends, but Daniel didn't care. He loved her so much...and he knew it pleased her to be included in his life, whether it was cool or not.

He was in college when she died. He still felt the soul-deep sadness when he realized he'd never hear her voice again. And so, with the sharp tang of loneliness, he replayed all their conversations, committing them to memory. He thought of her often, and wondered what she would think of how he'd turned out. But as we all do, over time his busy life pulled him away from those thoughts and didn't allow him to dwell on the sadness that he'd walled up inside. He still remembered the day he realized with dismay that he no longer heard Grandma's voice in his head. Even though he'd committed her to memory, eventually he still lost her.

The pain of losing his grandmother paled in comparison to losing his family. The thought that some day he wouldn't hear *their* voices anymore, that he would forget the feel of their skin or the smell of their hair, was more than he could take. He gritted his teeth and let the sadness and heartbreak wash over him anew, searing his soul. He held onto their faces, their voices, and the feel of his children's tiny hands in his own. He forced away the lump that rose in his throat and blinked away the tears, swearing for the hundredth--the thousandth--time that he would return to them. But even as he swore, despair refuted his claims. It laughed at his loss, mocked his resolve.

Thosten walked past him, not even sparing a glance. *"You and he have a lot in common. He has three children, like you, and a wife he adores."* Soren's words, making a comparison that Daniel didn't see. He considered the words again and realized Soren was right. If Thosten was a father, then he surely missed his children as poignantly as Daniel did.

An epiphany struck him as he realized the probable cause of Thosten's cold indifference. Both carried the pain, and so Daniel decided to reach out to Thosten, to foster a relationship that must be there. As he trekked through the night, the burning in his right arm was like nothing compared to the pain he inflicted on himself with memories of his family. And as he marched, he twined the pain with his resolution to help Thosten, if only by sharing their loss.

~ * ~

They stopped at first light. In the distance Daniel could see the dark outline of a massive tree, silhouetted against the advancing dawn. It was the first thing he'd seen that broke the continual plane of undulating grass, and his eye kept returning to it. Wide branches supported an inviting canopy, promising cool shade. Even in the half-light of predawn, sweat rolled down his back and the tree called to him. Soren broke his contemplation when he stepped up beside him and asked, "Can you go farther, Daniel? There is something you should see."

Daniel nodded. Warning jolts ran up his shoulder, but he thought that he could go a little longer before resting. He motioned to the men unfurling the camouflage netting and asked, "Are we camping here?"

"Yes, but we need supplies. Come." Soren joined a group of five men including Regnar and Trumble. Daniel hesitated and looked to Greggor, who waved him on with a wan smile. He shrugged and joined the group just as Soren began speaking. "We head for the great tree. It provides a good view of the savannah, so our concern will be cats. They may be nesting in its boughs." Hair stood up on Daniel's neck and his heart raced when he saw the men exchange frightened looks. Soren shook his head. "Do not be frightened. The savannah cats are smaller than those in the moors. They'd rather run than fight, but they will protect their young. We'll watch for them, avoid them if necessary."

Trumble wasn't comforted by his words. "What makes ya' think there'll be any at yonder tree?"

Soren shrugged. "I've seen their spoor. It's a likely spot for a lair." He chuckled and added, "Be at ease. I hunted savannah cats when I was a boy. I know their moods. If we avoid their nests and young, they will shy away from us." Trumble refused to be reassured, though, and cursed under his breath. Soren looked to the lightening sky and said, "Sooner begun, sooner done. Let's go."

He led them away from camp and at an angle that would skirt around the west side of the tree. They moved quietly, everyone watching the waving grass with trepidation. When they were even with the tree, the sky had brightened enough for Daniel to see that it was some sort of Banyan. Its canopy cast a large area into shadow, and many runners dropped from the branches to form additional roots. He didn't see any cats, but that hardly calmed his hammering heart.

Soren stopped and gathered the men together, his voice barely more than a whisper. "There should be a small cave nearby, blocked by a large stone. Spread out and look. If you find it, whistle. Do not call out." He paused and gave an example of the whistle before continuing. "Go no closer to the tree."

They spread out and walked slowly away from the tree, searching the ground. As Daniel walked he thought, *Wouldn't we be able to see the cave?* He could just see Trumble to his right, and Regnar was lost in the distance to his left. He searched for several minutes to no avail and looked around once more. The tree was steadily receding behind him when to the right he saw the top of Trumble's head, but the man suddenly disappeared with a muffled shout. Daniel froze, the hair on the back of his neck rising on end. He could imagine hungry cats pulling men down, one after another. His eyes were as large as saucers as he turned in a tight circle, hardly daring to breathe. He jumped when Trumble whistled, slapping a hand over his mouth to stifle a moan of terror. Then he heard something rustling through the grass behind him. He gasped and spun, raising his left fist to fight off a feline charge...only to see Regnar.

He offered a brief smile and said, "Ease, friend. I'll not attack you."

Daniel let out a shaky breath. "You scared the crap out of me!"

Regnar's smile broadened as he motioned toward Trumble. "Let's go."

Daniel followed Regnar until they found Trumble sitting on the ground, his feet resting in a shallow depression. He grinned up at them and whispered, "I fell in! 'Tis well hidden."

As the others joined them, Daniel inspected the hole. It was the same drab tan as the plain and blended in completely. It was little more than a natural ditch that ran about four feet and stopped against a slight rise. He studied the rise and was surprised to see that it was actually a large stone encrusted with dried grass. Loose soil had fallen in around it, finishing the deception.

Soren dropped into the ditch and walked to the stone. He studied it for a moment before motioning to Daniel. "This is what I wanted you to see."

Daniel looked blankly at it. "A rock?"

Soren smiled. "Look closer."

Daniel looked back to the stone, but after a moment he shook his head. "I don't see anyth--" He stopped in mid-sentence when a hint of straight line caught his eye. He pointed at it and said, "I do see something." It intersected another line at an angle not far off and then ended abruptly. "What is it?"

"A calling card," Soren replied. He hunkered down and pointed to another straight line at an angle to the other two, farther down the stone:

Daniel looked blankly at it until Soren leveled off the loose soil at the rock's base. He traced the same image in the dirt and said, "If you are ever separated from us and need help, look for this."

Daniel shrugged. "Okay. What does it mean?"

Soren turned back to his drawing and connected the lines to make a star.

He looked at Daniel and said quietly, "A sign of hope...a sign of Prophecy." Daniel's hand involuntarily rose to his cheek and touched the scars. Soren nodded. "This is the secret symbol of those that battle the Empire. If you see it, help is near." Daniel's hand dropped as Soren murmured, "Remember, Daniel."

He nodded mutely and stepped back as the men helped Soren pull the stone away. Behind it was not so much a cave as a vault. The interior was lined with carefully fitted bricks, creating a chamber three feet high and wide that stretched five feet into the hill. The front half was empty, but the back half was filled with large leather sacks.

Soren crawled in and pulled the closest sack out. He looked inside then handed the bag to Regnar with a smile. "We're back to full rations." Regnar took it from him and pulled out a wax-covered bundle. He sliced away the wax with his dagger to expose dried beef. The next bundle held dry bread. "The wax seals the food, keeping it from spoiling," Soren explained. "It's not the tastiest, but it will keep us alive."

Regnar turned to Trumble, the smallest man in the group. Without a word he nodded and crawled into the vault. "Leave a few for the next group to come this way," he murmured as Trumble shimmied inside. Soon their packs were bulging and they carefully put the stone back in place. Soren loosely mounded soil around it, recreating the illusion of a hillside. They walked back toward the tree until Soren held up his hand. Daniel followed where he pointed and could just make out a tawny colored cat, about the size of a mountain lion. It stared at them, its ears flat on its head. The breeze shifted and carried its growl to them. They slowly moved away and turned toward camp.

When they arrived, everyone enjoyed a meal of full provisions. Afterwards exhaustion finally caught up with Daniel, and so he settled in to sleep. He thought about the star-burst sign that would take him to friends in time of need. As he drifted off, he brushed his scarred cheek, as if he could wipe away the mark that drove everyone he met.

~ * ~

Dusk bathed the savannah in reddish hues that recast the tawny grass in sepia tones, giving the impression that it was covered in blood. Daniel stood just outside the netting, looking at the horizon and feeling a sense of dread fill him as he took in the view. There was no wind the unmoving grass adding to the impression of lifelessness. The air was also much more humid than the previous nights, and Daniel's clothing was already sticking to his sweaty body. He looked to the horizon, trying to take his mind off the sense of foreboding, and was surprised to see darkly-shadowed ridgelines rising to either side of their heading, no more than a mile distant.

As he squinted at the dark shapes, Soren stepped from the netting beside him. "The Harshorn Cliffs."

Daniel jumped and turned to look at the captain, his cheeks burning. "You--you move quietly. I didn't even hear you coming."

Soren smiled and inclined his head. "Many apologies. I didn't mean to startle you." He motioned toward the nearby ridges and continued. "They are the traditional border between the Quai and Harshorn clans. North of the cliffs are Quai holdings, which stretch all the way to Perfundi Pass." Soren paused before adding, "We should reach the Swordgrass this night." The playful smile faded from his face as he fell silent.

"What's Swordgrass?"

Soren glanced at him. "Swordgrass is a special plant...special and terrible. It's incredibly resilient and will overwhelm any other vegetation. It grows no taller than your waist, but plays a vital role in the history...and legal system...of my family clan, the Harshorn."

Daniel studied the cliffs as Soren spoke and didn't notice the change in timbre of his voice at the last. "How so?"

Soren gathered his thoughts before continuing. "Swordgrass is aptly named. It is rigid, the blades razor-sharp. For generations my ancestors used the blades for arrow and spear points. They also fitted them in simple wooden knives, called Hata."

Daniel grunted. "What did you say about the legal system?" His pause this time was much longer. Finally Daniel looked away from the horizon and into his face. He could see Soren's discomfort as he tried to keep from making eye contact. The uncharacteristic reaction had a confused Daniel back-pedaling. "Hey, that's okay. I shouldn't pry."

Soren shook his head. "No, Daniel, it's alright. It is I who must apologize. I should have told you the tale before asking you to choose our course."

Suddenly Daniel remembered the dark reactions some of the men had at the mention of Swordgrass. His stomach dropped as he stared at the captain and in a meek voice asked, "What?"

Soren sighed. "For the most heinous crimes Swordgrass was punishment. If a man took another's life, or took a woman against her will, or, well, many other things...he'd be taken to the Swordgrass field. He would be stripped and forced to walk into the field."

Daniel felt his pulse beating behind his eyes. When Soren stopped, he asked in the same meek voice, "How far?"

"Until he could go no farther."

He stared at the captain as the words sank in. In a whisper he said, "He walked to death." It was more statement than question, but Soren nodded anyway. Daniel blew out a low, shaky whistle. "And you want us to cross it?"

Still unwilling to make eye contact, Soren nodded. "There is a way. Sometimes, if a man's courage failed him and he refused to walk, he would...well he'd be dragged."

He saw Daniel's horrified look and raised his hands in a placating gesture. "Please don't get the wrong idea about my forebears. We are a brave and courageous people, strong warriors all. Honor and duty rule us, and the Swordgrass was only rarely used as punishment. The only reason I mention it is because the sleds used for the…the unwilling…are still there. We can use them to cross into Quai."

Images of screaming men dragging through grass that butchered them came unbidden to Daniel's mind. Was that any less gruesome than staking people to the ground? Daniel shook his head roughly, trying to dismiss the idea. *Soren is not like the Emperor!* When he found his voice he asked, "And the Empire can't follow?"

Soren was visibly relieved when Daniel spoke. He shook his head and said, "Not if we take all of the sleds with us."

Daniel looked to the horizon and asked, "Can't they just go around?"

"Not likely." He pointed to the right-hand cliffs and said, "The Great Swamp comes right up along the cliffs to the east. The way north is blocked with impassible moors and deadfalls." Daniel thought again about the humidity that drenched him and nodded. Soren pointed to the left and said, "The western cliffs stretch back to the south for miles, leaving nothing but sheer drop-offs, impossible to climb."

Daniel looked to the horizon for a long while. Finally he pointed straight ahead and said, "Ok…to the Swordgrass."

Soren smiled tentatively at Daniel and said, "If the Imperialists follow us there, they will be trapped. We could lose them once and for all."

Daniel was silent for a moment before saying, "You should have told me, Soren."

The warrior looked to the ground and nodded. Quietly he said, "Many apologies, Daniel. This is the fastest, safest path open to us." Daniel looked to the savannah grasses and again saw them lifeless and drenched in blood. He dearly hoped Soren was right, but the feeling in the pit of his stomach told him something else. He nodded and walked past his friend, returning to prepare for the night's march.

~ * ~

As they hiked through the night Daniel saw the rugged faces of the Harshorn Cliffs rising to either side of them. The first gray light of dawn arrived but Soren and Regnar continued to press forward, showing no signs of stopping. The sense of dread that had been with Daniel all night continued to build as they moved down the wide throat of stone. Daniel's arm screamed at him, and his gaze rarely left the ground once there was enough daylight to see any holes threatening to jar his wounded limb. He plodded on mindlessly for several hours, following where the man in front of him went, stepping gingerly and cringing until each foot reached solid ground. Always the sense of doom was with him, weighing him down as if it were a stone hanging from his neck.

Slowly the sense that something was amiss penetrated Daniel's fog of pain. He came out of his self-induced isolation and looked around. To his right Trumble walked gingerly, his wide eyes scanning the area around them. Daniel could tell by the tension in his every move that he felt the wrongness as well. He heard a quiet creak with each step, and after a moment's consideration realized it was the leather of his boots. He looked around in fear once more and thought, *I don't remember my boots creaking before.* That was when he finally realized what was wrong: the gorge was completely silent.

He'd grown accustomed to the sound of insects and birds as they traveled. Occasionally he'd catch some grassland animal scurrying through the swaying blades, and once even the screech of a savannah cat came to them on the breeze. But as they moved down the stone throat, there was no more wind, and as the wind went, so too did all life on the savannah. Daniel swallowed his trepidation in a mouth that had suddenly gone dry, and his sense of dread rose to a crescendo. They approached a low stone ridge that crossed the valley from one cliff to the other, reaching no more than six feet up the sides of the towering walls. As they approached it, Daniel realized it wasn't a natural projection, but rather a man-made stone wall. He could just make out a ramp that rose to its top when Soren called a halt.

The men gathered in a semi-circle around him and he studied the frightened faces that stared back at him. He motioned to the wall and said, "We've reached the Swordgrass. Beyond this wall is the field of blades that we must cross. But take courage! We will not be stopped." He squinted as he looked toward the far end of the wall where it butted into the sheer cliff. "In the shadow of the cliff there is a hidden cave. Come."

Soren led them to the end of the wall where it appeared a small avalanche had fallen. He examined the rocks for a moment, spit on his hand, and wiped saliva on one near the bottom of the pile. His spittle darkened its surface and washed away grit, exposing the symbol of the incomplete star. He looked to Daniel as he said, "Move the boulders." The men set to work and soon they were cleared away, revealing the mouth of a cave.

Soren led the way inside and soon they returned wheeling two narrow carts. Each was made of wood overlaid with steel on the undercarriage, sides, and long sloping front and back. Tall wooden spoked wheels were also overlaid with steel. A wooden pole rose up six feet from the center of each cart and was capped by a hinged clamp that could be closed into a circle. There was a narrow platform fore and aft of the pole, each large enough to hold only one man.

As they wheeled the carts to a stop, it was obvious they'd seen better days. The wood was warped, the steel covered in rust. Clem let go of the fender on one and a large portion flaked off and crumbled to dust in his hand. Soren studied both the carts and the men before saying, "We'll cross with these."

The normally stoic men couldn't hold back gasps and curses. "They be fallin' ta pieces!" one groaned.

Soren dipped his head. "Yes, they are in poor shape. But they're what we have to work with and we *will* work with them." For once his words and conviction didn't buoy the men, and silence stretched out until he growled, "Come on. Sooner begun, sooner done." He grabbed the lead cart and they hesitated for only a moment before joining him. He led them back to the ramp and up onto the stone wall. Daniel and Greggor followed behind the second cart, and as they reached the top of the wall, he felt dread rising in him like a hot wave threatening to engulf him.

From cliff to cliff and as far as the eye could see stretched a continuous expanse of dark green leaves that stood three to four feet tall. They looked like huge blades of grass, and were so dark green they were almost black. A breeze blew over the field and the rigid blades barely moved. There was no other vegetation, nor were there birds or any sign of animal life. Swordgrass was all that grew in the strange valley, right up to the base of the stone wall. It was ten feet wide, and on the far side another ramp descended into the field of blades. Just above the ramp was a rusty steel grommet that bolted into the end of a thick rusty chain. The chain stretched from the grommet down the ramp and into the deadly grass.

Soren and a few men positioned the first cart in front of the ramp. They moved the chain up over the cart and locked it into the clamp at the top of the pole. Daniel's dread broke into outright panic as he caught the gist of what they were doing. Visions of the lake crossing at the Spirit Calling returned to him and he whimpered, "No." Soren looked to him and he repeated, "No, I can't do this."

The captain stepped beside Daniel and rested a reassuring hand on his shoulder. "It will be fine, Daniel. I'll cross with you. Don't worry, you'll be safe." He cooed the words into Daniel's ear, but he continued to mutely shake his head, staring in horror at the rusty cart. Soren sighed. "Well, we shouldn't start with you at any rate." He thought for a moment and said, "Thosten and I will take four men across. Then you and Greggor, then the rest." He smiled at Daniel. "Get some food. We'll have you across in no time." Daniel hitched in a deep breath and nodded as Soren patted his arm and turned to two men. "You two first. Clem, you're with me."

Clem paled but swallowed his fear and nodded. He and Soren climbed in the cart with Soren in front of the pole and Clem in back. They took up the chain as several men pushed the cart to the lip of the ramp. It tipped and rolled down the ramp, its long steel-encased prow pushing the Swordgrass down before it. The rigid grass scratched along the steel underside of the cart, no doubt flaking off rust. When it came to a halt, Soren looked back at Clem and nodded. The two took up the chain and pulled, and the cart lurched away from the safety of the wall. As it moved, the grass that was bent under the cart sprang up as if it had never been disturbed. Soon their cart was lost from view and even the horrible scratching noise receded.

Thosten looked at his passenger and asked, "Are you ready?" The man gave a shaky sigh and nodded. The two climbed into their cart and were soon lost from view.

Daniel stared at the unmoving grass long after they were out of ear-shot until Greggor stepped up beside him. "You hungry?"

Daniel glanced at Greggor and was gratified to see the same fear he felt stamped on the young man's face. He swallowed past the lump in his throat and said, "No."

Greggor murmured, "Me either." He passed Daniel some dried bread anyway and the two sat on the wall to eat their rations without tasting them.

After a time Daniel whimpered, "This scares me."

Greggor grunted. "I heard they had to build the wall to keep the Swordgrass in. It would have overrun the whole grasslands if they hadn't." He paused and his own voice was shaky with fear when he added, "It doesn't suffer anything else to live."

Daniel felt his skin crawl. He thought of the Empire and realized the same could be said for it. They sat in silence for an hour until the scratching noise started to build again. The carts could evidently be attached together somehow, because when the blades bent they moved as one. Soren and Thosten had stripped to the waist and sweat poured from them as they pulled the cart to the ramp. Their hands were red from rust flaking off the chain. *Looks like blood*, Daniel thought with a shiver.

Soren pointed at Regnar and another man and said, "Now you two." They looked to each other and gingerly walked down the ramp. Once they were in place, all four men hauled on the chain and quickly pulled away. Again Daniel watched the grass. His fear started to build once more when he realized he was next. He looked at Greggor and saw that he must be having similar thoughts. He tried and failed to muster the courage to rest a comforting hand on his shoulder.

After nearly a half hour one of the men cursed loudly. Daniel looked up, expecting to see him looking in despair out over the Swordgrass, but instead he was staring back the way they'd come. With yet another stab of fear,

Daniel stood to see what caught the man's eye and cried out in spite of himself. Near the mouth of the valley was a black smudge that could only be Imperial troops. "How'd they get here so fast?" Trumble asked, despair and anger in his voice.

Panic overwhelmed Daniel as he whimpered, "What do we do?" He looked around but everyone was looking back at him for instructions. He had none to give. He held out his hand in a placating gesture and shook his head, unable to speak.

After a moment Trumble spat and walked up to Daniel, kneeling in the dust before him. He kept his head down for a minute, and when he looked up tears stood in his eyes. "Save my family, Stranger," he whispered, clasping his right fist to his breast.

Daniel stared at him in horror and shook his head. "No, don't."

Trumble looked up at him for a moment longer, his face filled with faith and courage. He nodded once and turned to the other men. "I'll try 'an hold 'em off." He looked back to the dark smudge and realized how foolish that sounded. "We *have* to buy time," he added quietly. Without looking back, he ran down the ramp and raced toward the army, angling toward the eastern cliff face.

Daniel shook his head again and moaned, "No!"

One by one, the remaining men knelt before him and said, "For you, One," or "Save us." Then they also turned and rushed from the wall, leaving only Greggor and Daniel. Tears ran down Daniel's cheeks as he watched the men recede. His left hand was held out to them as if he could make them come back. Within minutes, they heard battle cries and the clang of metal on metal. Soon the element of surprise was gone, and the roar of the Imperial troops echoed off the walls. Their quarry was cornered.

In images blurred by tears, Daniel saw navy-clad warriors running toward the wall. Daniel was so engrossed in their progress that he didn't realize Greggor was moving up behind him. He had removed his sling, and groaned in pain as he wrapped both arms around Daniel's midsection.

"What're you doing?" Daniel groaned as the Greggor's strong grip forced the air from his lungs.

He didn't answer, but with a quick lurch and another groan of pain, Greggor slung Daniel over his left shoulder. He saw stars momentarily as his own injured arm slammed into Greggor's shoulder and he cried out. Then Greggor turned and lumbered down the ramp. Realization sank in and Daniel screamed, "No, Greggor! Stop!" but the young man didn't listen. He ran into the Swordgrass, holding Daniel above the sharp blades. Greggor immediately cried out and stumbled, but then he regained his footing and ran again, ignoring the great bloody wheals that opened on his skin.

He ran for nearly thirty feet, sobbing with every breath, before he slowed. From above Daniel could see that Greggor was a mass of blood. He didn't know how the man was still on his feet. Daniel sobbed too, and cried, "Greggor! Oh, Greggor, *stop*!"

He shuffled a few more feet before finally stopping. Daniel felt his strong arms begin to shake, and he knew that soon he'd be on the ground beside his friend no matter what. Slowly he was lowering toward the deadly grass, Greggor whimpering and wheezing with every breath. Daniel whispered, "Put me down, Greggor. It's alright!"

But the brave young man refused. He gasped, "No," and with the last of his strength he leaned back and threw Daniel away from him, right into Thosten's cart. His back hit the pole at the cart's center and he heard it crack, but it didn't matter. He wept bitterly for Greggor's sacrifice, and didn't even feel it when his right arm slammed into Thosten's gauntlet as the warrior caught him. He passed Daniel to Soren, then slid down the metal-covered front of the cart and grabbed Greggor's bloody and ragged shirt.

The grass sliced right through his leather tunic and opened cuts on his arm, but he ignored them and pulled the young man into the cart. He rested Greggor's bloody body on the floor of the cart as best he could, and then he and Soren shared a look. They both scrambled over the fenders to Soren's cart and pulled with all their might. Daniel yanked his pack off and dumped the contents in the cart. Through tear-blurred vision, he could barely see what he was doing, but he finally found the Valor Root Westragen had given him. He tore open the packets and dumped the dried roots indiscriminately on Greggor's bloodied body.

Through hitching gasps he murmured, "Don't worry. It's gonna be okay, Buddy. I got ya'." When the root was gone, he reached for the bandages and unrolled them. His panic started to recede when he looked back to Greggor and realized his young friend was no longer breathing. He felt for a pulse in vain and closed his eyes. Raising his face to the heavens, he screamed out all of his rage and fear and despair. So many had died for Daniel. How could he ever justify their sacrifice?

Chapter Fourteen

The cart's platform was too small for Daniel to climb in with Greggor, so he leaned against the pole and wept. He wanted to cradle his young friend's face, smooth his sweaty hair and wipe away drops of blood that sprayed on his cheeks. But as the cart lurched along, his broken body slipped down to the floor and all Daniel could do was rest his hand on the top of his head. The mast partially broke when he hit it and with every lurch it creaked, threatening to tear away and throw Daniel from the cart, but he didn't care. He just leaned his good shoulder against the pole and wept for the horrible sacrifice Greggor and the all the men made.

The carts bumped into something solid and stopped. Daniel turned with disinterested eyes and saw they'd reached the ramp at the far end of the field. Clem stood on the wall and yelled something, but Daniel didn't hear him. Soon the other survivors appeared on the wall, Regnar's eyes big and round, his mouth a perfect "O". They were windows into his terror and loss, and Daniel saw his own pain reflected there. He focused on Regnar and didn't realize Soren had scrambled over the fenders until he grabbed Daniel's left arm. He tried to gently open Daniel's grasp, but he jerked away and growled, "No!" When he pulled away, the mast reached its limit and with a mighty crack broke and fell sideways into the Swordgrass. If Soren hadn't been there to grab Daniel's belt he would have followed it and his tale might have ended there.

As it was, they fell backward onto Daniel's platform, Soren's arms wrapped around Daniel's midsection. He immediately strained against the grip, but the captain held firm, whispering into his ear. "Shhh. It's alright now, Daniel. I've got you."

As he half-sat in the compartment, Daniel could see Greggor's still, pale face beyond the broken mast and tears flooded down his cheeks again. Soren held on tight, but Daniel raised his left arm and reached for Greggor longingly. "Daniel, we need to get Greggor out of the cart. You need to help us." He nodded mutely and stood. Thosten waited on the fender, and Regnar stood in the first cart behind him. They passed him from one sure grip to the next until he was out of the cart and Clem led him up the ramp.

The villager's face was a shocked mask. "What happened?"

Daniel opened his mouth but nothing came out. He closed his lips and shook his head as he moved away. The men carried Greggor's body up the ramp and gently laid him on the wall. Daniel dropped to his knees beside his friend, only vaguely aware that Regnar did the same on the other side. He took in the torn clothing and ravaged skin as sobs wracked his body. Eventually Regnar's quiet voice penetrated his grief and he looked up at the carpenter. Tears tracked down his weathered cheeks and into his bristly beard. His eyes roamed over the horrible wounds as he kept asking, "How? How?"

Seeing his pain reminded Daniel how close the two were. He deserved answers. Daniel swallowed the lump in his throat and said, "The...the army...caught us...on the other side."

He peripherally glimpsed Soren's angry shock and Thosten staring over the Swordgrass. "How is that possible?" Soren growled in barely contained his rage.

Daniel ignored him and stared at Regnar. "Th--the other men...they ran out and tried to stop them. And Greggor...Greggor...he p--picked me up...and ran..." His voice failed him so he raised his arm and pointed hopelessly back through the grass.

Clem gasped. "No! Damn!" He stormed away, wiping his eyes.

Anger smoldered in Soren's eyes as he pulled free the A-blade and turned to the ramp. He punched it through the chain near the grommet and wrenched his arm back and forth. Rusty flakes rained to the ground as Soren's attack increased in ferocity until the rusty loop finally gave way. He carried it down the ramp, unlocked the clamp on the pole of the lead cart, and threw the chain back into the deadly grass. Daniel saw hate burning in the pits of his dark eyes when he returned to the wall. His mind flashed back to the many men Gelnar lost, how he threw them away when they were of no more use. He glared at the captain and rested his hand on Greggor's chest. "We're burying him!"

Soren's anger melted away, replaced by surprise. "Yes, of course we will."

Daniel glared at him a moment longer before returning to his friend as a distant part of his mind insisted, *He's not the Emperor.* Regnar took bandages from his pack and wiped blood from Greggor's head and neck. He offered Daniel one and they silently wiped Greggor's body clean. The others left the wall and found a shady spot nearby where they dug a grave. When all was ready, they returned and helped Daniel and Regnar carry Greggor's body to its final resting place. They gently lowered him into the ground as Daniel stared at his right arm. It was as still and gray in death as it had been in life, but at least he was finally beyond the pain. As if the mere thought of pain was all his arm waited for, it roared to life but he refused to acknowledge it.

Regnar's voice was gruff as he said, "He was a good an' courageous boy. He reminded me of…of my sons." His voice cracked on the last and he fell silent.

Soren added, "He honors us with his sacrifice. He and all of the men died warriors' deaths. I've never known better."

Daniel cleared his throat and murmured, "He was my friend…my first since I came here." He glanced at Soren and thought, *I don't deserve this.* He looked at the grave and barely above a whisper added, "I'll miss you, Greggor."

They stood in silence in a loose ring around the grave. Finally Regnar scooped sandy soil onto the boy's face. Everyone joined in, and before long a mound of dirt marked where the maimed blacksmith rested. One by one, they moved away, setting up camp with the scant supplies they had left.

Daniel stayed until he was alone with Greggor. He leaned forward until his forehead rested on the warm, sandy soil and his tears dripped down, muddying the dirt. He felt like he may never stop weeping as the magnitude of the sacrifice weighed on him. He heard Trumble's final words: *"Save my family, Stranger."* How could he ever repay that debt? He wasn't their Messiah, but their sacrifice made his arguments insignificant. He scratched at the scar on his face and wished he could tear it off. Why did any of this have to happen? As thoughts of despair and grief circled, Daniel drifted off to sleep, his head resting on Greggor's grave.

~ * ~

When camp was set, Soren and Regnar walked to Greggor's grave. They gently lifted Daniel and carried him to camp. They laid him down and shared a look of concern. Regnar's eyes were still puffy and bloodshot while fires burned once more in Soren's tattooed pits. Regnar looked questioningly at him and Soren hesitated before shrugging.

Many hours later Daniel woke and looked up at twinkling stars. He was at a loss for what was different until the oddity of sleeping at night struck him. With it came the realization of what happened the previous day, and with that came the inevitable guilt and grief. He sat up and looked around the quiet camp. Four still bedrolls surrounded him, while two men stood watch. The band of fourteen that left Standing Stone was cut in half in one brief encounter with the Imperialists. How could they hope to escape? Daniel sighed and looked toward Greggor's grave. The eastern sky was just lightening toward dawn, but the gloom was still too dark to see where his friend lay.

From behind him Soren murmured, "Good morning, Daniel." He turned to see the captain hunkering down while watching the camp perimeter. Daniel nodded and accepted the water skin he offered. After he drank his fill, Soren led him north, away from camp. After a few minutes the captain stopped and Daniel was struck by how small and fragile their camp looked, surrounded by the menacing darkness of night. "This is far enough. They need their rest."

The two turned their attention away from camp, and as dawn approached the surrounding landscape became distinct. The rocky ravine they were in continued a ways before the walls gradually tapered to the northeast. After about a mile it veered far enough to the east that the walls blocked what lay beyond.

"What now?" Daniel asked in a husky voice as he stared at the valley.

Soren glanced at him before answering. "We follow the path before us. This ravine opens into the Great Swamp. We'll skirt its edge and reach the Pass."

Mention of the swamp caught Daniel's attention. "Will it be dangerous?"

Soren shrugged. "There is some danger, yes. But we're past the moors, so the worst is behind us...hopefully." Soren added the last under his breath.

"What about the insects and cats?" Daniel pressed. "What about the dragons?"

Daniel's frantic tone brought Soren's gaze back to him. "We may see them."

"Sounds risky."

"Yes, Daniel, there is risk," Soren replied. "But in everything there's risk, even leaving your bedroll to face the dawn." He looked back to the perimeter and added, "It's what we do with that risk that defines us. Do we acknowledge the risk, stand to face the challenges, or do we let the risks dominate us and cower from what might be?"

Daniel shook his head. "I can't risk more lives." His voice was tight with emotion.

Soren considered his words for a moment. "You have but one life, Daniel. There are no others for *you* to risk. Everyone knew the risks and accepted the consequences. *We* chose to stand and fight the Empire, no matter what." He fell silent for a moment before adding, "You are not to blame for Greggor's death." Daniel let out a ragged sigh and stared down the ravine, trying to hold back tears. "We cannot stay here, Daniel. Let us face our fears and raise our chins in defiance to the risks."

Daniel hesitated before nodding. As he raised his chin, the first light of dawn fell over the canyon's wall and shined on his weather-beaten features. *You're half right,* he thought. He would feel guilty for their deaths the rest of his life, but they must continue, regardless of the risk.

~ * ~

The men gathered what remained of their supplies and followed the valley through a series of switchbacks as its walls dwindled. While they advanced, the humidity continually rose, as if someone were throwing wet blankets over their shoulders. They rounded the last curve and the Great Swamp opened before them. A great gray-green expanse stretched as far as the eye could see. Bogs of brackish water were interspersed with dry hillocks that burst through the scummy mire, ringed by willows, dogwoods, and cypress trees.

Daniel looked at the fetid swamp and shuddered. Soren studied it for a moment before walking to the nearest pool where a bushy tree grew. It had blue-green leaves and dark green thorns nearly an inch long bristling from every limb. Soren carefully reached in among the thorns and plucked a small blue berry, no larger than a grape. "This is a Jomja berry. Its juice keeps the insects away." He squeezed the berry until it burst, spraying clear juice on his forearm. As he rubbed it in he pointed out several more Jomja berry trees along the pool's shoreline and said, "Get as many as you can, but be careful! The thorns cause a terrible wheal if you get stuck."

They carefully collected as many berries as they could, filling a small leather pouch Soren produced. Daniel grimaced as he popped the first berry and a horrible smell wafted from it. The sticky juice dripped onto his arm and he nearly gagged when he tried to rub it in. Soren smiled grimly and said, "You'll get used to it."

Daniel watched Soren pop another and spread the thick juice on the back of his neck. He blanched and said, "I don't know." Soren held out a berry and squeezed its juice into Daniel's hand. He made urping noises as he rubbed it on his neck, and when his stomach settled he asked, "How much do we have to apply?"

Soren shrugged. "Our arms and necks should be enough." He grimaced himself as he popped another berry. Daniel locked his jaw and held out his hand for more juice.

He gently covered his right arm and hand with it, biting down on a groan. Soon they were covered, and after Clem vomited, they set out northward, skirting deeper pools and staying to the spongy high ground as much as possible. By midday there were no landmarks and only Soren's sense of direction kept them from getting hopelessly lost.

They rested on a wide island and had a meal of cold rations. Swarms of insects moved steadily closer and to Daniel's great discomfort Soren made them reapply the juice. He nearly lost his lunch, which made him slightly luckier than Clem, who vomited again. Regnar offered him a water skin and Clem turned green, waving it away. They continued ever northeastward. By dusk they were exhausted and drenched in brackish water that smelled only slightly better than the juice.

They climbed one final island and found an open area where they made camp. After much cursing, Thosten was able to get a small fire going by dousing soaked wood with oil. The miniscule flames didn't warm the men, but the eye-watering smoke that poured from it did keep the insects at bay. Soren decided the juice wouldn't be needed overnight, which relieved Daniel but made Clem ecstatic. He wolfed down his rations and gave a loud belch. They settled in, but if they hoped for a restful night's sleep, they were disappointed.

The sun went down and the swamp came alive. The ever present hum of insects was punctuated by the roars and screams of unseen animals, waging battles of life and death. None came within the ring of the camp's meager firelight, but the constant noise kept everyone on edge. When dawn came, it was only greeted because it signaled an end to the night-long hunt. The men coated themselves with Jomja juice before dousing the fire. Clem grimly refused breakfast and his jaw muscles bulged as he tried to keep down his gorge. He was almost as gray as the swamp water when he was covered, but he did manage not to throw up.

The morning passed without incident, but shortly before midday their luck changed for the worse. They waded through a pool, making for a far-off hillock where they planned to break, when suddenly there was a shout of alarm and a large splash. Everyone spun to see Clem sink below the surface. Men jumped forward as he splashed, choking and wheezing, before being dragged down again. Thosten lunged and grabbed his hand. With all of his might, he yanked him far enough from the water for the other men to see a huge snake wrapping itself around his torso.

Weapons were pulled free and the gray water ran red from the snake's blood, but as Clem shed its body his freedom was short-lived. Even as he pulled in a ragged breath, a cloud of insects descended on him, hungry for blood now that the Jomja juice had washed away. He screamed as hundreds of needle-like bites riddled him. "Hold him up!" Soren shouted. He pulled a handful of Jomja berries from his pouch and smashed them over Clem's neck and back.

The swarm dispersed, but the damage was already done; red welts rose all over Clem's flesh. Even his eyelids were swelling shut. He gritted his teeth, trying to resist the pain and poison that pumped into his body. "Pick him up!" Thosten roared, and the men fell in, grabbing their friend and holding him out of the water. "To the high ground, quickly!" They thrashed through the shallows and gently lowered Clem to the ground as Thosten and Regnar collected wood. It was thrown in a pile beside him and Thosten poured most of his oil on it. Setting flint to steel, a fire roared to life and pushed the insect swarms back.

Daniel kneeled beside Clem and his stomach dropped when he saw how bad he looked. His skin was ashen and his breathing was ragged and uneven. He passed out as they carried him, and now he twitched uncontrollably. One of the men looked to Soren. "What d'we do?"

The captain looked from the man to Clem and slowly shook his head, his eyes wide with shock. "I don't know." His voice was soft and meek. If it was an enemy that could be met with blades, Soren would wade forward willingly, but when attacked by something as small as an insect, he was out of his element.

Daniel looked from the captain to Clem and ran his fingers through his hair. *Man, oh, man!* As panic rose he ripped off his pack and dumped the contents on the ground, looking for inspiration. Among the detritus were the last two packets of dried Valor Root leaves. Daniel latched onto the packets and said, "Give me some water!" He poured water into a steel bowl and carefully sat it on the fire. As soon as it was steaming he removed it with a hiss of pain and poured in one of the packets. He swirled the bowl and dipped a bandage in the water, using it to wash the bites.

The men gathered around, silently watching Daniel work, praying he'd be successful. Shortly after he finished, the swelling stopped and in about thirty minutes it started to go down. Daniel let out a great sigh, not realizing he'd been holding his breath. Regnar hunkered down and murmured, "Good work. Do you think he'll be alright?"

Daniel shook his head, hesitated, then shrugged. "I don't know. But we definitely don't want to move him."

Regnar nodded and looked to Soren. "We'd best gather wood."

The call to action snapped Soren out of his horror and helplessness. "Yes, you're right." He pointed to Thosten and Daniel. "You two stay with Clem. We'll get more wood." Before he turned to go, he looked with frightened eyes at Clem once more before marching off, coating his skin with more juice as he went.

Throughout the afternoon the men frequently came back with armloads of wood, and Thosten kept a pall of smoke covering the hill. Occasionally Daniel washed Clem's wounds, but the repeated washings didn't have the dramatic effect they did the first time. He could only stare at the man as his breathing continued in the same ragged and uneven rhythm.

As dusk settled, Soren walked up to Daniel. "How is he?"

"I don't know. He seems comfortable, but who knows?"

Soren nodded as he watched the man breathe. Finally, he looked back to Daniel and said, "You did well. You saved him."

Daniel shook his head. "I didn't do anything! I don't even know if the tea helped or if I'm just..." His voice trailed off. He was going to say, "prolonging the inevitable," but he couldn't make the words come.

Soren nodded and murmured, "Well, we'll see what the morning brings." Daniel looked at the wounded man and didn't hold out much hope for the dawn. He sighed and blinked away tears from the smoky cloud as he settled in for a long visage.

~ * ~

Dawn found them clustered around Clem's motionless body. They kept the fire stoked through the night, and all the men looked on with blood-shot eyes from the continual smoky haze. It not only burned Daniel's eyes, but also his throat, thickening his voice to a rough croak. He continually deflected questions about Clem's condition until his voice gave out, after which he merely grunted and shook his head. As the gray mists brightened, Soren asked once more, "What news?"

He grunted and shook his head for the hundredth time, but when Soren didn't leave, he croaked, "No news." He gently laid a hand on Clem's forehead. "He's got a fever now, but the bites haven't changed."

"What do you reckon? Will he improve?"

Daniel let out a bone-weary sigh. "I don't know, Soren...I don't have a lot to work with. And the washes don't seem to be helping anymore." He motioned to the last of the leaves, which had settled to the bottom of the bowl. Soren grunted and considered the man. After a moment Daniel said, "We can't leave him."

Soren glared at Daniel. "Of course we're not leaving him!" he snapped. He closed his eyes and took a deep breath. When he opened them, his anger was gone. "The

Empire *would* cast him aside…but we are not them. Clem is our brother, we stand by him."

Daniel's ears burned as he lowered his gaze. He was ashamed that he thought Soren capable of such an act.

"I have an idea." Both men turned and looked at Regnar as Soren motioned for him to continue. "When we were collecting wood, I saw smoke to the southeast. Maybe someone can help us."

Daniel's face lit up at the suggestion. "Yes! Let's go! We could put Clem on the stretcher."

But Soren was already shaking his head before he finished speaking. "We can't risk you, Daniel. If it's Imperialists, all our suffering would be for nothing."

Daniel's face darkened and his brows drew down in a sharp frown. "You're the one that said we should face our fears, disregard the risks! What the Hell are we waiting for…or was that just talk?" Anger flared as he hissed the words and a corresponding fire built in his right arm, but he didn't care.

Soren returned Daniel's dark look with one of his own before taking another calming breath. "Peace, Daniel. Yes, we must take the risk. Clem is counting on us." Daniel opened his mouth, but Soren held up a warning hand. "But we mustn't *all* take the risk." He turned and raised his voice to take in everyone. "Regnar and I will investigate. If help can be found, we'll return by dawn." His eyes fell on Thosten as he added, "If we don't return by the following morning, you *must* leave." He pointed to the northeast. "Continue in the direction we've been traveling. You should be free of the swamp within three--," he looked down at

Clem and amended, "four to five days at the most. Make for the Pass, safeguard each other."

Thosten nodded and Soren looked around at the others, approval shining in his eyes at their determined looks. He patted Daniel on the back and turned to Regnar. "I'm ready," the carpenter said with a grimace as he applied Jomja juice. The two waded into the brackish water and moved away without looking back. When they disappeared into the swamp's gray mists, Daniel turned to the three men that remained. Thosten refused to meet his gaze as he slathered on Jomja juice. The two villagers stared back at Daniel; equal parts hope and fear radiating from them. He couldn't face the need in those stares, so he looked back to Thosten questioningly.

The warrior slung a short bow over one shoulder and his great sword over the other. He glanced at the survivors and growled, "I'll hunt and gather wood." He looked at the soldiers and said, "Stay here. Keep the fire going…and your eyes open." With a final dark look at Daniel, he turned and trudged away.

What does he have against me? Daniel thought, but he didn't have time to dwell on it. He glanced to the southeast. *Hurry back, guys. Hurry back.* He turned back to Clem and washed his wounds once more with the tea.

~ * ~

The day wore on with agonizing slowness as Clem alternated between fever and chills. Daniel hoped it meant his body was fighting the poison, but he didn't say anything to needlessly raise the men's hopes. Thosten returned with a small deer at midday. He dressed it and placed some meat on spits over the fire. Daniel's mouth watered at the savory smell, and soon he and the three soldiers shared a hot meal for the first time since Mount Dlanor. The delicious food lifted everyone's spirits, and hopes rose that soon Soren and Regnar would return. Thosten retrieved several loads of wood after their meal and as the afternoon waned, so too did hopes that their friends would reappear. As night settled in with still no sign, hope gave way to despair.

Thosten grimly assembled the stretcher and studied the exhausted men. In a low voice he murmured, "If we must leave tomorrow, we need rest. I'll take first watch." His eyes skated over Daniel as he said, "I will wake you if Clem's condition changes." He didn't even wait for a reply before walking to the edge of the hillock where the smoke was less dense. Daniel saw the villagers share a concerned look before he bedded down alongside Clem. He feared for his friends that searched the swamp and he feared for them all if they had to leave without Soren and Regnar. Exhaustion and despair took him, and even the screams of swamp animals didn't stop him from slipping into blackness, not to be disturbed until morning.

~ * ~

Daniel blinked sleep from his eyes as he wiped Clem's wounds with the dregs of the last packet of Valor Root. The villager was still wracked by alternating fever and chills and his breathing had taken on an alarming wheeze that didn't bode well. Thosten stood behind Daniel and asked, "Is he improved?"

He jumped at the question and shrugged. "No, I don't think so." He was just about to ask the warrior what he thought they should do when he walked away.

One of the villagers put more wood on the fire, increasing the protective blanket of smoke. Daniel grimaced and wiped his eyes. When he lowered his hand, the man was hunkering down on the other side of Clem. He studied his friend's face before turning a frightened gaze on Daniel. "What do we do?"

Daniel didn't answer immediately, trying to think of something encouraging. Finally he shrugged and said, "I don't know." He looked down and could feel the man's eyes on him, but he couldn't meet those pleading orbs again. He kept his gaze on Clem until the soldier stood and walked away.

They spent the morning aimlessly wandering the hillock that had become their base for too long. Daniel never strayed far from Clem's side, but in truth he didn't think there was anything else he could do. Midday came and went and they ate more roasted deer meat. The afternoon waned and Thosten filled his pack with what little supplies they had left, intent on following Soren's orders. Daniel had just worked up the courage to confront him when one of the men hissed, "Someone comes!"

Thosten dropped the pack and pulled free his great sword. His eyes narrowed as he tried to look through the smoky haze. He glanced at Daniel and growled, "Get down!" Daniel dropped alongside Clem, his heart in his throat. He took a knife from Clem's belt, feeling clumsy holding it in his shaky left hand. He knew in his heart that if an attack came, he would be more apt to hurt himself than an attacker, but he held the knife tightly just the same. Thosten edged away, motioning for the two villagers to advance on either side of him. He was swallowed into the swirling smoke, and soon Daniel was alone with Clem, cowering on the spongy ground.

It was an eternity before Daniel heard anything, and then instead of the expected clash of weapons, he heard shouts and laughter. For a split second he was confused but then realized their friends had returned. He gave a great sigh as he sheathed the knife and stood. Soren and Regnar were accompanied by a small man in a dull brown jerkin and pants. He had a full gray beard and gray stringy hair that hung loosely down to his shoulders. His clothing had been repeatedly patched and they were so form-fitting they appeared to be a part of the man that wore them. Soren started to introduce him to Thosten, but he shouldered past the warrior and marched to Daniel.

His face was pinched in a scowl as he moved through the billowing smoke, but when he could see Daniel clearly, he stopped dead in his tracks and his eyes flew open wide. At the same time his mouth fell open to reveal four teeth in pink gums. Before Daniel could say anything, the man dropped to one knee and lowered his gaze to the ground. In a dull whisper he gasped, "Stranger!"

Soren strode up beside the older man as Daniel's cheeks burned. "Daniel," he said, part greeting and part introduction. He gestured toward the still kneeling newcomer and added, "This is Garn. He is a friend."

After a moment of silence, Garn raised his face to Daniel's, tears standing in his rheumy eyes. "Ye've come!"

he gasped in the same dull whisper, as if he were unaccustomed to using his voice. "At last!"

Feeling self-conscious, Daniel stepped forward and helped pull the man to his feet. "Please," he mumbled. "Call me Daniel."

Garn allowed Daniel to help him rise and then remained close for a moment, almost pressed against him as he intently studied the scars on Daniel's face. Finally he stepped back and glanced at Soren. "Ye've got th' right o' it, Blade!" His gaze returned to Daniel and he added, "Never did me think I'd be seein' th' One!"

Soren stepped up beside the older man and said, "Yes, Garn, as I said. Now to our injured friend..." He steered him to where Clem lay silently on the ground.

The hermit reluctantly pulled his gaze from Daniel and looked at Clem. He dropped to his knees and cursorily inspected the wounds before mumbling, "Damned bugs." He rested his hand on Clem's forehead before raising one eyelid and looking at the orb beneath. He noticed the metal bowl lying beside him and picked it up, sniffing at the leafy residue in the bottom. His tongue darted out and licked it before he turned to Soren. "Who did this?" Soren motioned to Daniel, and all too soon the hermit's wild gaze returned to him. He nodded and said, "Valor Root...hadn't thought o' that afore. Well done."

He stammered, "It--It didn't seem to help much--" before Garn cut him off.

"Well o' course not! Them bugs're stubborn!" He gave a wild cackle and returned to Clem.

"Can you help him?" Soren asked quietly.

Garn glanced at the captain. "Yar, but not here... Me home." He scanned the gray sky before giving Daniel a shy look. "Be me guest, Stranger." When Daniel realized it was an invitation, he gave a mute nod. Garn brightened and turned to the swamp.

"Wait!" Soren called out. "We need a moment."

Garn nodded as the men prepared to leave. He grimaced when Soren smashed Jomja berries and waved away the smell. "Whew! What're ye doin'?"

Soren looked at him blankly as the juice dripped from his palms. "To keep the insects away," he murmured.

Garn rolled his eyes and shook his head. "No, no, no!" he said in a sing-song voice. He reached into a pouch at his waist and poured a few drops of thick yellow oil from a small leather-clad bottle into his palm. He motioned for Daniel to lean forward and the hermit ran the oil-covered hand through his hair. He did the same for all the men and put the bottle away. "There. No bugs an' no stink!"

The oil weighed down Daniel's hair, but he was grateful that it was odorless. He smiled and said, "Thank you, Garn."

He dipped a bow before giving the sky another nervous glance. "Come, now. It'sa gettin' late." He led them to the southeast, away from the hill that was permeated with despair. Daniel's sense of doom stayed behind as well, his spirits buoyed by hope as he followed the hermit.

~ * ~

They followed Garn the rest of the afternoon, only occasionally stopping for brief rests. At every break Garn glanced at the darkening gray sky, all but tapping his foot with impatience. The later it got the more preoccupied he became, jumping at every sound from the encroaching darkness. Finally, with the last hint of daylight filtering through the swamp, they came to a tall island crowned with a wood cabin.

Along one side of the small cabin was a wide overhanging roof, two sides of which were covered by swamp moss hanging nearly to the ground. A small garden graced the other side, ringed by walls of tightly stacked firewood. A rock-lined fire pit topped by a metal spit sat before the house and beside it was a single hand-made wooden chair. The clearing as a whole was neat and orderly, offering a comfortable but solitary existence.

Garn gave a relieved sigh as they climbed the hill to his cabin. He turned to the others and with a gap-toothed smile said, "Me home. Be welcome."

Daniel took in the clearing and did a double-take when he saw the cabin's front door. The broken star was carved deeply into the wood. He felt a stab of self-consciousness and turned to see Garn staring at him, wonder stamped on his face. Soren stepped beside Daniel and said, "Many thanks for your help, Garn."

The hermit turned to Soren and waved his hand dismissively. "Bah! 'Tis me honor to help the One." Daniel flushed as he dipped a quick bow, but before he could respond, Garn turned to the men carrying Clem. "Take 'im to the house." He turned back to Daniel with a look of regret. "Me home is small...I can take yer friend, but the rest..." He spread his hands and both men nodded.

"Of course," Daniel said. "We'll be fine out here. We're just happy you can help Clem."

Garn glanced at Clem as he was carried inside. "Yar, he'll be good in a day er two." He looked to Soren. "Swamp's dangerous, 'specially at night. Keep atwixt the house and the fire. I reckon ye'll be alright."

"I understand."

Garn gave a distracted nod and hurried up to the cabin to help Clem. Soren watched him go and said to Daniel, "We were fortunate to find him." The cabin's door swung closed as Garn went inside, exposing the broken star. Soren motioned to it and said simply, "He's a friend."

Daniel leaned close and murmured, "I'm glad you came back." His eyes dropped to the ground, afraid the anxiety he felt over nearly losing Soren showed on his face.

The captain smiled. "Have faith, Daniel. We're not done yet!" The captain patted his shoulder as he walked over to build a fire in the pit. Soon it was crackling away and Thosten roasted some deer meat on the spit.

Everyone gathered around and enjoyed the warm meal, allowing themselves to relax in the safe haven. When they were finished, Garn and Thosten dug a shallow hole. They sealed the leftover meat in a leather sack and covered it over with the dirt. "Don't want critters comin'," the hermit murmured.

True night fell while Soren and Regnar told how they met Garn and convinced him to help. They frequently paused to allow him to interject, but he shyly looked away and refused to speak. When their tale was told and voices died away, cries of nocturnal hunters pierced the night. They sounded far away, but the keening howl still made the hair on Daniel's neck stand on end. Garn murmured, "Ye should be safe, but ye'll want a watch. An' don't leave the firelight!" He stood and mumbled, "Night," before heading for his door. The men set watches and settled in for the night, feeling safe in spite of the unseen dangers.

Daniel drifted off and almost immediately dreamt of Ashley. She wore a light blue sundress and sat in the clearing before Garn's cabin. Bright morning sunlight shone on her, setting her blond hair aglow. Her face was cast demurely down and the dress was carefully arrayed on the grass as if she were posing for a picture. Her white lace gloved hands were clasped in her lap.

Tears stung Daniel's eyes. "Ashley! Oh God, Ashley, it's you!" He was stumbling toward her when her eyes rose to his and stopped him in his tracks. They weren't Ashley's. His upwelling happiness came crashing down, replaced by heartache and caution. He looked more closely and saw several subtle clues that she was an imposter. No wedding ring bulged out from the glove on her left hand, her hair was parted on the wrong side, and there was a light spray of freckles across the bridge of her nose that shouldn't be there. "You're not Ashley, are you." Daniel's dead tone made it a statement, not a question.

The woman's smile faltered before widening. She remained in the posed posture as she gently said, "No, Daniel. I am not she."

He sighed and the last of his happiness flowed out of him. "Who are you?"

Her eyes looked left, then right, as if to say no without shaking her head. "There is no time for that. You are in danger." As she spoke the cabin faded from view and their surroundings were lost in darkness. With the darkness came a familiar presence that terrified Daniel. He felt like he'd been punched in the gut. He tried to breathe but couldn't, tried to turn toward Malthion but couldn't. In a panic, he looked back to the fake Ashley. She wasn't smiling anymore, but she was still frozen in the same pose. Her eyes bore into him. "Awaken, now, Daniel! Do not sleep this deeply again!"

He sensed Malthion running toward him and his bladder let go. Hiccups of hysteria overwhelmed him. His eyes pleaded with the woman as he whimpered, "How?"

He saw worry in her face, though she still hadn't moved. "Daniel!" she screamed. "Awaken! NOW!" The voice changed as she screamed. It no longer sounded feminine. It didn't even sound human. The final word thrummed with power and Daniel felt it burst over his eardrums like a sonic boom. The volume and the pressure change made him jump, and he rolled sideways, crashing into Soren.

The captain woke instantly and ripped the A-blade from its sheath. His eyes swept the camp, but when he saw no intruders he spun to Daniel. He was covered in sweat and each breath came as a whistle. "What is it, Daniel? Are you alright?"

After several minutes Daniel's breathing slowed, and he armed sweat from his face. He let out a deep sigh and murmured, "Yeah, I'm fine now."

Soren's gaze plainly said he wasn't convinced. "What happened?"

Daniel shivered and shrugged. "Nothing…just a bad dream."

Soren stared silently at him for another minute until Daniel calmed and finally lay back down. He shrugged and lay down as well. "All is well," he mumbled as he drifted back to sleep. Daniel stared at the stars that could be dimly seen through the swamp's mists. *I'm not so sure*, he thought. He let out a great sigh and relaxed as best he could, but with the taint of Malthion fresh in his mind he didn't sleep anymore.

~ * ~

As a new day dawned Soren studied Daniel. He wanted to ask about the dream, but could tell Daniel wasn't ready to share. He saw Soren's concern from the corner of his eye and decided, *Not yet*. He was still confused about who--or what--saved him from Malthion, but something about the commanding voice was familiar. He was still puzzling over it when Garn opened the cabin's door and proclaimed Clem fit to see visitors. The men entered two at a time, leaving Daniel and Soren as the last to see their friend. Clem was pale and weak, but he gave them a smile just the same. Daniel returned the smile and said, "It looks like there's some fight left in you."

Clem nodded as the smile faded and he grew serious. "You saved my life, Stranger. I'll not forget it."

Daniel's ears burned as he shook his head, but Garn grunted in agreement. "He'd never uh made it, if not fer yer actions, One."

Daniel's shoulders sagged. "Yeah, well, I'm glad you're pulling through."

He and Soren pressed themselves against the wall as Garn maneuvered past them to Clem's bedside. He carried a steaming pot filled with thick green liquid that he dipped bandages in before dabbing at the bites. Clem's face turned green and he groaned, "Ugh! That smells worse than the berries!"

Soren chuckled. "You may have spoken too soon. The cure may kill you!" Everyone but Clem laughed as the wounded man tried to keep his gorge down.

Within a minute the odor wafted to them, reminding Daniel of a cross between decomposing fish and a pig farm. He stopped chuckling and blanched. Glancing at Soren, he said, "Well, Clem, we gotta go. We'll check on you later." Clem held his breath as Garn wrapped a poultice around his head to cover bites over his left eye. He waved them away, and Soren and Daniel made a quick exit. When they reached fresh air, Daniel gasped, "Poor Clem. Maybe we should've let the snake get him."

Soren looked at him sharply, but when he saw Daniel's grin, he chuckled. "That might have been a kindness."

They spent the morning taking stock of their provisions while Thosten and Regnar hunted. They returned with another deer, which was roasted and shared with their host. Garn took most of the remainder, along with the buried meat from the previous night, and placed it in a barrel filled with brine for curing. When chores were done, he took Daniel and Soren on a tour of his island. He was proud of what he'd carved from the swamp's wilds and his desire to share outshone his natural shyness. At the far edge of the hill he pointed to a vine wrapped around a small pine tree. It had waxy yellow leaves and was covered with small blue flowers. "Tha' vine keeps 'em bugs away," he murmured.

He plucked an unusually thick leaf and squeezed it, collecting its yellow oil in the leather-clad bottle from his belt pouch. He held up the bottle and said, "A dab'll keep 'em off all day." He shook the bottle once before holding it out to Soren. "Here, Blade," he said gruffly. "Now don' use those stinkin' berries!" He cackled as Soren and Daniel smiled back.

He turned to lead them onward and Daniel whispered, "Blade?" Soren shrugged and pointed to the A-blade.

Day and night passed uneventfully, and by the second morning Clem greeted the men at the cabin's door as they rolled from their blankets. He was shaky but his color had returned, and Garn said he'd be ready to go the next day. Thosten decided to hunt for their benefactor a final time, and to his apparent displeasure Soren and Daniel offered to go along. They stalked quietly through the swamp, Thosten and Soren carrying bows with arrows laid along the strings. After nearly an hour, Thosten held up his hand and silently pointed ahead. A spotted doe nibbled at scruffy grass on a nearby hill.

He indicated he'd move to the right while Soren moved left. Daniel stood motionless, afraid to even breathe lest the deer catch wind of him and flee. Just as Soren and Thosten closed, the deer raised its head, looking around in sudden alarm. It sniffed the air as the hunters froze and Daniel cursed inwardly. It reared back to leap away when a massive shape burst out of the water, sending fetid liquid flying in a mist. The animal screamed as the water exploded and a gigantic alligator clamped its jaws on the deer's flank, dragging it under. Daniel's mouth dropped open as he stared at the huge monster. Its head was nearly four feet wide and its tail waved through the water an impossible distance behind the deadly jaws. It rolled violently, tearing limbs from the dead deer and swallowing pieces that floated on the bloody water.

"Move!" Soren hissed. "The dragon may not be done!" Daniel gave a numb nod and the three retreated as quietly as possible. As they returned empty-handed to Garn's cabin, they agreed it would be best not to tell the other men about the attack. "No point in needlessly worrying them," Soren said.

Daniel nodded, but he was distracted by every ripple in the murky water. *Yeah, why worry them? If one of those bastards comes at us, we're all dead.* They ate leftover deer at midday, but Daniel oddly lost his appetite when he looked at the torn flesh.

Regnar saw how pale Daniel was and asked, "You alright?"

He nodded and pushed the meat away. "I'm just not hungry."

Later Thosten and Soren prepared to hunt once more. The captain looked at Daniel and murmured, "Maybe you should stay."

Daniel glanced around before whispering, "You'll get no argument from me!" Soren smiled as he and Thosten trudged into the murky mists. It was close to evening before they returned with a covey of large birds. The men ate and bedded down, and by morning Clem was back to normal.

Ron Hartman

Garn inspected his disappearing bites and proclaimed him healed. The men collected their supplies and prepared to leave, also preparing to bid a fond farewell to their new friend. As they assembled, Garn dropped to a knee before Daniel, bowing his head. His ears burned as he helped the hermit climb back to his feet. "Thank you, Garn, for everything," he murmured.

The old hermit studied his scars a final time and said, "T'was me honor, One." His eyes sparked with fire as he growled, "Save us!"

Daniel was taken aback by the man's sudden change and stammered, "I--I'll do what I can."

Garn's anger quickly faded, tears standing in his eyes. "Me wife--an'--an' me--me daughter. Th' Imperialists--they…" His voice broke as the tears came. Daniel gave him an awkward hug as he sobbed bitterly, his small frame shaking as tears fell on Daniel's shoulder.

Daniel could well imagine what the Imperial troops did, and he could feel tears standing in his own eyes as well. "Yes, Garn," he murmured. "Yes, I'll fight them."

Eventually the hermit's tears played out, and he stepped back from Daniel. He nodded gratitude to Daniel before turning to Soren. "Mind th' One carefully, Blade!"

Soren nodded. "I will, Garn. Many thanks for your help." Garn nodded brusquely before turning and walking to his cabin without looking back. With a gentle shove he closed the door, exiting Daniel's tale. The dark blight of the Empire could be felt everywhere in Naphthali, even in the lonely home of a hermit. The happiness the men felt at Clem's recovery was blunted by Garn's reminder of the evil that hunted them. They left the island in silence, continuing ever northward.

Chapter Fifteen

For three days they marched, Daniel, Soren and Thosten on constant vigil for dragons. None appeared, but on the second day the men froze when they saw another inhabitant of the great swamp: a Moor Tiger. It had dingy brown fur and great green eyes that studied the men without fear. After a time it lost interest and stalked away, and Daniel gasped in spite of himself. It was nearly twice the size of a grown lion, easily dwarfing most horses. It clutched a giant snake in its jaws, similar to the one that nearly killed Clem.

On the third day after leaving Garn's cabin, the mists lightened and the ground became solid. Mossy bogs gradually gave way to grassy plains until they finally came to great steppes that stretched to the Cloudspeak Mountains, no more than ten miles distant. They set camp on the windy plain and the breezes proved too great for Thosten to safely build a fire. He feared he may set the entire steppe on fire if he succeeded, so they settled for the half-light of a waxing moon, enjoying the cool dry air. Easy conversation flowed from the men, and after answering nature's call, Daniel found himself sitting beside Thosten.

He remembered his vow to bond with the man, and so as the warrior stared off into the distance, he leaned in and asked, "Thinking about your family?" His eyes narrowed as he looked side-long at Daniel. "I think about mine all the time, too." Daniel swallowed his loneliness and pressed on. "Soren tells me you have a daughter and two sons. So do I! Ours are Elizabeth, Nate, and Ethan...how about you?" Thosten turned to face Daniel squarely, his jaws clenched. Daniel was dismayed by his rising anger as he rested a hand on Thosten's forearm. "I miss my family too. I know how you feel."

Thosten's cold stare smoldered, and Daniel snatched his hand away. The warrior jerked to his feet and all conversation died. His hands balled into fists as he glared down at Daniel and spat, "You know nothing!"

"I--I'm sorry," Daniel stammered.

"Stand down, Thosten!" Soren shouted, standing as well.

The large warrior glanced at Soren and then looked down at his closed fists. With a concerted effort he opened them and stormed off into the night. Daniel looked across the circle at Soren, his eyes wide in surprise. He answered the captain's unspoken question with a whimpered, "I don't know..."

Soren shrugged, a frown still creasing his brow. "Best to leave him for awhile." He sat back down and eventually the awkward silence gave way to subdued conversation, but Daniel no longer had the heart for talk.

After a few minutes he stood and silence reigned once more. "I...I'm going to sleep," he mumbled. He crawled under his blankets, but it was a long time before sleep came. He kept replaying the conversation in his mind, trying to find the comment that set Thosten off. Eventually he drifted into a fitful sleep as the winds blew across the steppe, cooling his brow but not the troubled thoughts within.

~ * ~

The next night they camped on the very doorstep of the Cloudspeaks. No matter how often Daniel took them in, his gaze kept returning to the massive peaks. He was in awe of how truly tall they were, and how insignificant he felt in comparison. They spoke the truth of how unimportant he was in the overall scheme of things, no matter the beliefs of his companions. His eyes wandered from them and fell on Thosten. They locked gazes and the warrior's jaws clenched once more as he moved away, setting a perimeter on the far side of camp.

Daniel sighed. Thosten had refused to speak to either him or Soren throughout the day, instead choosing solitude. It appeared he planned to spend the evening in the same manner. Soren left camp and joined his friend, the two speaking in hushed tones for several minutes. When they finished, they stood together and clasped forearms, Soren resting his free arm on Thosten's shoulder. They separated and Soren returned to camp as Thosten sat back down, studying the steppes far below their camp.

Soren came to Daniel as he returned to camp. He motioned to Thosten and asked, "Is he alright?"

The captain opened his mouth and closed it again. He raised his hands, fingers splayed wide, and shrugged. "I don't know. He won't tell me what ails him." Daniel sucked in a breath, but Soren raised his hand for silence. "I know, Daniel. You did nothing." He sighed and looked back toward Thosten. "He is my oldest and dearest friend. Whatever his demons, I *know* he stands with us."

Daniel gave a noncommittal nod. *He stands with* you, *at least.*

Near mid-afternoon of the next day they rested. Daniel sucked air into his burning lungs, trying not to jostle his angry right arm. The foothills gave way to mountains, and they'd already climbed more than a thousand feet. He glanced back the way they'd come and saw the steppe, a small patch of green impossibly far below. Then he turned and looked ahead, where the tallest peaks still towered over them. *If not for the road, we'd be screwed.*

Their route widened as they left the foothills, becoming a packed dirt road that rose ever higher into the peaks. The air became thinner and cooler, making everyone gasp for breath. Near evening the road's incline leveled off into a boulder-strewn valley which Soren proclaimed to be the Pass of Perfundi. Taller peaks soared to either side, but the darkening skies prevented Daniel's poor eyesight from making out the far end of the valley or what lay beyond.

They found a sheltered overhang of rock and set up camp, their breath puffing out in white clouds as they pulled blankets tightly around themselves. As night arrived and the temperature dropped, Daniel huddled close to the men around a small fire and considered his time in Naphthali. He realized he'd never been truly cold; in fact most of the time he was drenched in sweat. Now that he was leaving, he felt his first taste of cold weather, as if Naphthali had been warmly shielding him from the Empire's cold bite. His teeth chattered as he pulled the blankets close. He fervently hoped that idea was just his imagination and not a promise of hard times to come.

~ * ~

The sun rose over men huddled together, a fine layer of frost covering their blankets. Most didn't sleep as they fought for warmth and shivered through the night. It didn't take long for the thin air to warm under the sun's gaze, though, and they found the heart to let their blankets drop to the ground. Goose flesh rose over Daniel's bare arms as his own blanket fell and he lifted his chin, reveling in newfound warmth.

Soren smiled at them as frost melted from their hair. "Good morning, friends." He pointed to the far end of the rocky valley and said, "The border between Naphthali and the Empire. We leave our homeland, but soon we'll return...in victory!"

They raised their fists and returned the cry. "Victory!" They pumped the air two more times, repeating the refrain, each more loudly than the last. When their voices fell away, all eyes turned to Daniel. His ears burned and his gaze was locked on the ground. After a minute's silence he mumbled, "Well, let's go."

Soren nodded. "Yes. Sooner begun, sooner done. Gather the gear...we move out."

The Pass of Perfundi was longer than it looked. It took nearly four hours to reach the far end when Daniel finally glimpsed the world outside Naphthali. Green fields and pastures stretched as far as the eye could see, connected by narrow dirt roads and punctuated by farmhouses. Their path wound down from the Cloudspeaks and continued unhindered into the crosshatched mass, continuing to the horizon in the north. It wasn't until Daniel saw that the road was not guarded that he realized he'd been dreading the descent. He'd envisioned a massive garrison and an unbreachable wall blocking their way, but it looked like they would slip undetected into the Empire.

Daniel and the men enjoyed the view until Soren herded them down the pass which proved to be as easily accessible as the Naphthalian side. They let gravity do the work and made good time, reaching the base of the mountains by nightfall. The previous night's chill was forgotten as they armed sweat from their faces and stretched sore muscles. Daniel looked back at the imposing peaks as he caught his breath. The last rays of the setting sun shined on the mountainsides, the tops lost in the clouds their namesake suggested.

Regnar stood beside him and studied the peaks as well. "Glad I am we're quit of that." Daniel nodded and the carpenter was quiet for a moment before adding, "'Tis my first time outside Naphthali."

Daniel smiled, ready to say it was his first too. But his smile died when he saw the sadness in Regnar's eyes. "What's wrong?"

Regnar glanced at him before returning his gaze to the mountains. He sighed and said, "Nothing, One. I...I just wish my boys could see this." Tears swam in his eyes as he looked down at his hands. His voice was barely above a whisper when he said, "They've been gone so long, but it still seems they should be here when I turn 'round."

The man's heartache opened wounds in Daniel's that swallowed him. Through a throat made raw with emotion, he said, "Time flies, doesn't it?"

Regnar nodded slowly. "Aye. Like an arrow, leaving naught but destruction and grief in its wake." Time sometimes seems to slow when you are lost in despair. When another shares your pain, it can stop altogether. So it was for Daniel and Regnar until after minutes that felt like hours Soren called everyone to him. The carpenter offered Daniel the barest hint of a smile, though sadness reigned in his eyes. He motioned for Daniel to go ahead of him as they joined the others.

Soren didn't see their sadness in the growing shadows of dusk as he turned a grim eye on the men. "We are in the Empire…enemy lands. We *must not* bring attention to ourselves. We avoid people as we advance." He reached into his pack and pulled out a short linen robe made of a light airy material. It was off-white in color and had long sleeves and a deep hood. He gave Daniel an apologetic look as he held up the robe. "You can't be recognized."

Memories of the journey with Gelnar flashed through his mind, how he hid is face in terror of what Gelnar would do to people that recognized him. And now Soren asked him to do the same. "Oh…sure," he mumbled. He took the robe with shaking fingers, his left hand feeling as wooden and lifeless as his right.

From the side Thosten asked, "Where do we go?"

Soren stared at him for a moment and Daniel thought, *Is he questioning Soren? He's never questioned anything!*

After the briefest hesitation, the captain pointed west. "Namtrah. It's a city two days' travel from here. A contact there may help us."

In the silence that followed Daniel's anger flared. "*May?*" he blurted. "He *may* help? You don't know?" He thought of the men that had fallen to get them that far, all for what suddenly seemed but a whim. Greggor's face rose unbidden before him and guilt fueled his anger.

Regnar rested a hand on Daniel's chest as Soren's calm eyes returned Daniel's hot glare. "We had no other choice, Daniel."

He stared at Daniel. A minute slipped by and Daniel mutely glared back, his only companions the guilt in his heart and the pulse thrumming in his ears. That pulse screamed in his mind. *My fault! My fault! MY FAULT!*

Finally, Soren broke the standoff and looked to the other men. "No more fires. We must be as silent as the night, as elusive as the shadow. Now, set up camp. Sooner begun, sooner done."

Regnar patted Daniel's chest before walking away. Soren helped the men set up camp, also leaving Daniel alone with his rage and guilt. He looked down at the robe's deep cowl. *Why me?* After a few minutes the anger faded, but guilt remained. With a sigh he walked into camp. He felt the men's eyes on his back, their need weighing him down. He sat down and fingered the robes and a thought came unbidden to him. *This is my burden, I will bear it.* He sighed again and pulled the bedroll from his pack, settling in for the night.

~ * ~

In the morning Daniel pulled on the robe. The cloth was light, allowing a breeze to pass through the fabric and cool his skin. His right arm complained bitterly when he pulled it through the sleeve, but he pushed the pain away and repositioned it against his belly. Soren gave him an approving nod which Daniel ignored as he reached back for the hood. He started to pull it up but couldn't bring himself to hide within just yet. Instead, he let the fabric slip through his fingers and drop back to his shoulders as they set off.

The next two days were uneventful as they cut around the edges of fields and pastures, staying under cover whenever possible. On the third day they crested a hill and stopped short, surprised by the change in scenery. Farmland petered out over the next few miles, replaced by a sprawling city. A tall wall punctuated by towers and gates ringed it, and they could just make out men patrolling the fortifications. Daniel's stomach tied in knots when he knew it was time for him to hide. He pulled his hood up until it extended several inches past his face, casting his features in shadow.

"Namtrah," Soren murmured. "We will make for the main gate. If we're stopped, I do the talking. We're advance scouts for a merchant caravan, looking for safe passage. If anything is amiss, at my signal you *must* flee."

Regnar's jaws clenched, making his beard bristle. "What's the signal?"

Soren's brows knit together and the fire in his eyes kindled. "I kill the guards." The captain motioned to Regnar and Thosten. "If it comes to that, one of you stays with Daniel. Everyone else separate...spread any pursuit." When Soren paused, the silence was so complete Daniel couldn't even hear the others breathing. Soren looked at him and added, "Remember the sign. Find friends and hide."

Daniel dipped his head. He tried without success to answer until finally he mumbled, "Al--alright, Soren."

The captain stared into the shadows of his cowl, but Daniel could tell he wasn't looking at him so much as testing the concealment of the hood. "Very well. Sooner begun, sooner done. Let's go."

They made their way to the open front gates where several guards in navy tabards questioned a long line of peasants and merchants waiting to enter the city. Soren marched forward, head held high, ignoring soldiers and citizens alike. His stride said he had nothing to hide, but Daniel's legs shook with every step, his heart racing on the very edge of panic. Thosten walked calmly beside him, a look of disinterest on his face. His thumbs were casually hooked in his belt, resting on throwing knives that were hidden there. A hand closed on Daniel's left arm, nearly making him jump. Regnar's grip tightened for a second before he released it, murmuring, "Steady..." He too wore a look of boredom as his gaze wandered around the gatehouse.

Four guards accosted a group of peasants as Soren neared the front of the line. They wore vicious glares as they yanked away belongings and searched them, spilling bundles on the ground. In the middle of the group was a girl of about sixteen, her frightened eyes cast downward. The soldiers eyed her hungrily as they circled. "P--Please, sir," whimpered an old man at the front of the group. His hands were ringing an old leather coin purse. "W--we need supplies...fer the farm."

A guard growled, "Ho, supplies, eh? She could supply *me*!" The others snickered and their leader snorted when a tear rolled down the girl's cheek.

The old man's face darkened, his eyes wide with fear. "Please," he said again, holding out the purse in a trembling hand.

The chief guard glanced at Soren and his evil smile vanished. He ripped the purse from the old man's hands and growled, "Go on, then, all a ya!"

The old man offered a tentative smile, exposing toothless gums. "Many tanks, sir, many tanks!" He stepped aside and motioned for his group to hurry through the gates, keeping the girl in the middle. His head bobbed and he bowed repeatedly as they entered.

"Yeah, yeah," the guard grumbled, turning his attention to Soren. He tried to match the captain's angry glare but soon his eyes shifted away. "Goo' mornin', sirs!" he chimed. His evil smile was replaced by an oily, subservient one.

"Good morning to you, *Captain*." His voice was a low growl, the last word spit out as if it were an insult as the fire in his eyes roared to life. The guard paled when he couldn't meet his gaze, instead scanning over the rest of Soren's group. Daniel felt his stomach drop, sure they'd be found out, but it was clear the man wasn't registering what he was seeing. In the face of Soren's unspoken judgment he stopped truly doing his job and was just going through the motions.

After the briefest of glances he said, "Well, thank ye sirs. Enjoy 'ar fair ci'y. Goo' day!" He stepped aside and without another look Soren led them into the bustle of Namtrah.

They walked about a block before Soren stepped out of the press of people and glared back toward the gate. "Vile!" he growled. "Animals like that have no business in *any* army!"

Regnar rested a restraining hand on his shoulder. He leaned in close and murmured, "Easy, Captain."

Soren glanced at the carpenter before glaring back toward the gate. Regnar's hand remained on his shoulder until he closed his eyes and took a deep breath. He let it out slowly before opening them. "Many thanks." Regnar nodded and dropped his hand, glancing back toward the gate with a glare of his own.

Daniel glanced back as well and saw some guards looking their way. "We're attracting attention," he murmured.

Soren's head dipped and he grunted, "Let's move."

They merged with the flow of humanity entering the city and after several minutes Soren cut through a series of narrow alleys and wide avenues, occasionally even backtracking to lose potential pursuers. With every turn they continued deeper into Namtrah until finally Soren pulled up in a narrow alley. "Well done," he said, motioning in the general direction of the gates. "Many apologies...I endangered us all." His cheeks flushed and his eyes dropped to the ground.

Daniel looked around the tight circle of faces and saw the same outrage mirrored in all. No one would have responded better than Soren. He cleared his throat and said, "Yeah, well, we're in. Now what?"

The captain considered the question before answering. "We need shelter. The sooner we're off the streets, the better." He glanced at the alley's entrance and said, "Everyone stay here." He jogged down the alley and disappeared in the throngs of passersby. Daniel felt a stab of anxiety which only grew when he saw the same fear in the other men's faces. Time went by agonizingly slow until after nearly an hour Soren returned. "Let's go," he said, leading them from the alley. They ambled along, trying to blend in with the crowds of shoppers and townspeople.

After a time they passed through another gate which could be closed to separate different districts of the city. On the other side the buildings weren't as large or grand, but they were still neatly maintained. Soren continued for nearly thirty minutes until he called a halt before an inn. It was three stories tall and had a wooden placard hanging from a post over the door. A moderately talented artist had painted a large fish jumping from a mug, and below the illustration was written "The Kettle O' Fish"

Soren glanced around the street before walking along the edge of the building and disappearing down a narrow alley. It was so blocked by wooden crates and barrels that someone wouldn't even see it from the street unless they knew it was there. The alley ended at a small iron-bound door which Soren opened with a key and ushered the men through. They found themselves in a small storeroom that smelled like the inn's namesake. Three long tables were stacked high with crates of fresh fish, and along the walls were two doors. Soren re-locked the entry and cracked open the smaller of the two. After a moment's study, he opened the door and silently motioned for the men to follow him.

They moved down a short hallway and up two flights of stairs to the inn's third floor where he opened a door at the end of the hall. Inside was a fairly large room furnished with two beds, a table and chairs, and a small fireplace. Soren walked across the room and peered out the windows to the street below. He grunted and nodded to himself. "We should be safe for now." He pointed to the door. "I've another room across the hall, but we'll stay in here." He looked to Thosten and said, "A man on the window at all times."

As the large warrior nodded Daniel asked, "So what do we do now?"

Soren sighed. "Now...we find my contact." The words hung in the air and Daniel's unease grew.

"You don't know him?" Clem asked, trying to keep his voice even.

Soren shook his head. "He's been sending me information for years, but I've never met him. I know he has a shop in Namtrah...we just need to find it."

Daniel's heart lurched and in a weak voice he asked, "You've never met him?" Soren shook his head again. "Then how do you know he even exists? Who's to say he's not a mole, planted by the Empire?"

Soren frowned. "His information proves his intentions. He can be trusted."

Daniel couldn't believe what he was hearing. They'd come so far and lost so much, all on a plan that was sketchy at best. "But--" he started before Soren cut him off.

"Have faith, Daniel. He *can* be trusted." He closed his mouth and gave a numb nod as his fear continued to grow. Soren turned to the others. "Regnar and I will search for the shop. Everyone else stay in this room. Thosten, you're in charge."

The large warrior hesitated before saying, "Perhaps the search would go more quickly if I accompanied you...What is the name of the shop?"

Soren smiled and said, "No, my friend. I need you to stay here. Keep the others safe. Besides," he looked over his friend's frame before continuing with a grin, "you tend to stand out in a crowd."

Thosten hesitated again before sighing and nodding. Soren patted his shoulder and looked questioningly at Regnar. "I'm ready," the carpenter said as he dropped his pack to the floor.

The two stopped at the door and Soren turned. "Stay in the room. Do not open this door for anyone. When we return we'll use the phrase 'Dragon's Tooth'. If we say *anything* else, assume we're coerced. Then you must flee." He looked around at the men one last time, his eyes landing lastly on Daniel. "Stay safe." The two left the room and the others shared a look of concern as their friends wandered into the foreign city.

~ * ~

The day was a study in agonized patience. They took shifts at the window, but there was nothing else to break the tense tedium. Thosten was on edge, growling at anyone that spoke to him and constantly throwing anxious looks out the window. When Daniel took his turn, his anxiety soared to new heights. The streets were eerily silent in spite of the crowds, the townspeople careful not to make eye contact with anyone as they hurried on their way. *Are they always like this, or do they have a reason to be on guard now?* The thought made the hair on Daniel's neck stand on end, and he imagined Malthion marching toward the inn any moment.

The room grew uncomfortably warm with five men huddled in a space meant for two. Daniel felt sweat rolling down his back, but he didn't even consider taking off his robes. He knew if they had to flee he'd need to hide, and he needed the hood for that. Adding to the tension was the fact that his arm screamed at him. It was the worst it'd been in several days, sending electric jolts through his shoulder with every move.

Dusk came and went and traffic on the street thinned, but still there was no sign of their friends. Nearly an hour after full dark they heard men moving stealthily down the hall, and Daniel's heart jumped into his throat. Clem pushed Daniel behind him as he pulled out a hand axe. Total silence fell and they waited in a semicircle around the door. Daniel was just beginning to believe he was hearing things when a board creaked and they heard the muted jingle of leather armor. Adrenaline prickled Daniel's skin and every labored heartbeat made his right arm buzz bitterly. After an eternity, the quiet footsteps stopped and Daniel all but bolted for the window when he heard Soren's hoarse whisper. "Dragon's Tooth." As one the men sighed, and Thosten opened the door.

Regnar stepped inside, and Soren looked down the hall before following him. He looked at the relieved faces and quietly said, "We may have been followed." Just like that the anxious tension returned tenfold.

Clammy talons of panic sank into Daniel as he whimpered, "*What?*"

"At the last intersection some people noticed us. I didn't see them following, but I couldn't shake the feeling that someone was."

"What do we do?" asked Thosten. His eyes darted from Soren to the closed door.

Clem glanced at the large warrior and said, "Yeah, do we run?"

Soren shook his head. "It might have been thieves, thinking us an easy mark."

Daniel's jaws clenched. "Or it might have been Imperial spies."

Soren looked at Daniel and gave a single shake of his head. "We couldn't leave now anyway. Not with the streets abandoned." His hand stroked his chin as he considered their options, the men on pins and needles. "Clem and I will stay across the way…we'll watch the hall. If they *are* Imperialists, we'll have a surprise for them."

Clem clenched his jaws and nodded. As he stepped forward Thosten shook his head. "No, you need rest. I'll watch the hallway."

Soren shook his head once more. "Many thanks, Thosten, but no. You need to defend Daniel. And lead the men if…anything happens." Thosten opened his mouth to argue but Soren cut him off. "Clem, you take first watch and I'll rest."

"Aye." The villager grabbed his pack and walked to Soren's side.

They turned to leave when Daniel could remain quiet no longer. "Wait! Did you find your contact?" He felt trapped in the town, in the room, and wanted to leave both as soon as possible.

Regnar grunted. "We'll have to search again tomorrow."

Daniel tried to hide his disappointment when Soren looked around and asked, "Any more questions?" After a minute's silence he said, "Try to rest, but keep a watch on the window." He tipped a salute and murmured, "Until morning." The two left and Daniel took in the remaining men. His fear and anxiety were mirrored in all their faces, save perhaps Thosten. He doubted very much there would be any rest that night.

~ * ~

The night was long and sleepless, and the next day passed much as the one before. After Soren and Regnar left, their close quarters only intensified the men's anxiety. They were scared, tired, and surly, so they collectively resolved not to speak to one another. His mood souring and his nerves on edge, Daniel saw Imperial troops everywhere when he manned the window. Was that beggar lingering overly long? Wasn't that shopkeeper just at her door a minute ago? Why was everyone staring at the inn?

He stuck out his two hour shift, trying hard to stay focused. *Where* are *they?* he thought for the hundredth time as his eyes panned across the street. He was finally relieved and laid down on one of the beds, closing his eyes. Sweat beaded and rolled down his forehead, and his robes felt uncomfortably warm and itchy. He sighed, knowing he wouldn't sleep but craving release just the same.

The day dwindled and shadows grew across the floor as they stared out the window, at the ceiling, or at nothing. As dusk came and the streets began to empty, stealthy footsteps approached once more. They just as stealthily gathered weapons and arranged themselves as before. ."Dragon's Tooth." The door opened to admit Soren and Regnar, but this time there was no jubilant release of tension. Everyone braced themselves for bad news.

Thosten stepped forward and clasped Soren's forearm. "What news?"

Soren returned the grip, his eyes alight with success. "We've found him!" Their fear and anxiety melted away, the change in mood almost palpable. Clem offered Daniel a goofy smile, similar to the one Daniel was sure he wore.

"Thank God," Daniel muttered under his breath before saying out loud, "Terrific!"

Soren turned a beaming smile on Daniel before motioning to their bags. "Pack up. We're going."

Daniel felt a pang of unease. "But is it safe? Won't we stand out?"

Soren glanced out the darkened window before nodding. "You're right, but we've been here too long already. The risk of being seen is less than the risk of staying another day."

Far from reassured, Daniel tried to ignore his sense of foreboding. "Oh, okay." He helped pack and hid his face within his cowl, and within five minutes they all stood at the door, weapons concealed but in easy reach.

Soren cracked the door open and peered out before throwing the door wide. "Thosten, the rear," he said as they filed out.

As quietly as possible they moved down the hall, Daniel's heart roaring in his ears. They passed through the smelly storeroom, pausing for Soren to lock the door behind them. The night's coolness was a blessing after two days in the hot room, and if not for Daniel's fear, he would have groaned in delight. As it was, the cool air barely registered as they crept down the alley. At its mouth Soren told them to wait. "What are you doing?" Daniel hissed.

"Returning the key."

"Won't that raise questions?" Daniel tried and failed to keep the fear from his voice.

Soren's eyes never left the street as he shook his head. "I paid good coin for no questions. Besides, I've used The Kettle before." He darted to the inn's door and disappeared within, leaving Daniel practically hyperventilating in terror. Within seconds he was back and Daniel was able to breathe again. He pulled everyone close and whispered, "We move. Stay around Daniel. If anything hap--well, let's go."

Daniel glanced at Regnar and saw the carpenter shared his thought. *If anything happens, we're dead.* When Soren moved, he followed and soon he was once again lost in the maze of streets and alleys. Few people were still out and Daniel couldn't help but feel that there was a large target painted on his back. He tried not to stumble as he followed on Soren's heels.

After a time they passed through an unmanned gate into another section of the city, and then through yet another. They were in a district filled with the huge homes of Namtrah's wealthy, and as full darkness fell, the streets were completely deserted. They passed mostly darkened homes as Daniel ducked his head low, expecting to feel an arrow pierce his back any second. Finally, Soren halted in front of a handsome home made of off-white bricks, its lower windows awash in light.

He murmured, "Dalen, stand guard." The villager nodded and took up a position in the shadows by the door. The captain gave one soft knock and almost immediately the door opened. Warm light spilled out, framing them all in its glare.

A deep voice from within said, "Quickly, quickly!" and Soren ushered everyone but Dalen into the foyer. A man with dark skin and eyes stood before them. He looked to be in his late fifties and was completely bald, his square jaw framed by a well-groomed gray goatee. He wore black trousers, a white blouse with frilly sleeves, and a dark purple vest with gold buttons.

He studied the men as Soren stepped forward, but before the captain could say anything, he murmured, "Hold the introductions, please." He led them into a study with plush chairs and a crackling fire in a small fireplace. The walls were lined with bookshelves overflowing with leather-bound tomes, and a large oak desk filled the far end of the room. Heavy curtains were drawn over large windows, hiding them from prying eyes.

The older man's well-toned body flowed fluidly as he walked to his desk, where he half-sat, half-leaned on it. The smooth interplay of muscle belied his age, giving the impression of a much younger man. His dark eyes studied them once more, and in a deep voice he said, "Well met, Captain Soren. Many thanks for coming to my home." He looked to the others and said, "I am Alaric. Please, be welcome."

Soren clasped his forearm, smiling grimly. "It is indeed a pleasure, Alaric. Many thanks for your hospitality."

Alaric shrugged and replied, "The pleasure is mine. Now, please tell me, Captain. Why have you come all this way after our relationship has been faceless for so long?"

Soren motioned for Daniel to join him. "This is Daniel Marten." Alaric's thin eyebrows rose as he turned to Daniel's shadowed face. Daniel grasped the edge of his hood and hesitated. Soren murmured, "It's alright, Daniel."

Daniel tightened his grip on the hem for a second before he faltered and let his hand drop to his side. From the darkness of the cowl he said, "No, wait." Soren's brow furrowed, but Alaric continued to look at him with polite interest. With a sigh he said, "I'm sorry. I know you've helped Soren in the past, but I need to know why." Daniel paused, but when Alaric didn't immediately respond, he continued. "I mean, the Empire gave you all this." He motioned to their plush surroundings. "You seem to be doing well under the Emperor. Why do you help those who wish to defeat him?"

Alaric's eyes narrowed, but when he spoke his voice was just as cultured and polite as before. "The Emperor did not *give* me any of this, Master Marten. What is mine I have worked long for, often times in spite of the Empire, not because of it. Why do I help the Resistance? I love this land. Any can see the Emperor will be the death of Enialé unless we stand together against him." A slight smile played across his lips as he asked, "Is that satisfactory?"

Daniel bowed his head in defeat. He blew out a heavy sigh, bracing himself for the inevitable reaction as he reached up and pulled back the hood. Alaric took in his appearance politely at first, but then he did a double-take on Daniel's scars and gasped. He came off the desk and glided across the room, stopping only when Regnar stepped between him and Daniel. "Is it possible?" he whispered, his eyes wide in surprise.

Daniel clenched his jaws and his ears burned at the close examination, knowing and hating what was coming. Soren stepped beside Alaric and offered Daniel a reassuring smile. "Perhaps...perhaps not."

Daniel appreciated Soren's support, but he could see in the older man's face that he'd already decided who Daniel was. Anything he said to the contrary would be wasted effort. He cleared his throat and said the only thing that came to mind. "Pleased to meet you." Alaric's chin trembled and he began to sink to his knees. Daniel pushed Regnar out of the way and pulled him up by his shoulder. "No," he barked. "None of that."

To the side Soren said, "We need your help, Alaric." The man couldn't take his eyes off of Daniel as he stood before him, slack-jawed. "Alaric?"

He turned his head toward Soren, but his eyes stayed on Daniel's face. "Hmm? Oh, yes, anything!"

Soren motioned to Daniel. "Daniel needs to return home."

Alaric frowned, finally looking away from Daniel. "What?"

Soren looked to Daniel. "Tell him, but be brief."

Daniel nodded and told Alaric the high points of his story. He explained how the Emperor promised to send him home, leaving out the children they tried to make him murder. Even being brief, the tale took time and Alaric bade him to stop at one point to offer mugs of ale, for which Daniel's dry throat was grateful. When he finished, silence fell over the room. Alaric considered all he'd heard and murmured, "Fascinating."

When he said nothing else, Daniel blurted, "Can you help me?"

Alaric's dark eyes took in his face, constantly returning to his scars. At last with a sigh he said, "I am a purveyor of knowledge." He raised his hands and indicated the full bookshelves. "I collect information, share it with those who would find it useful…for a handsome sum." He allowed a modest downturn of his eyes at the last. "I have traveled far and learned much, but I have never heard of anything that could return you to your home, Daniel. I am sorry."

He lowered his eyes. Even though he'd only known him for a few short hours, he didn't realize until then how much hope he'd pinned on Alaric. His words were like bitter medicine and he had a hard time getting himself to swallow. In a quiet, defeated voice he said, "So there is no way."

"I am sorry," Alaric said again, glancing at Soren as he did so.

The captain cleared his throat. "There is something else. You know the Prophecy." His tone made it a statement, not a question.

Alaric nodded and looked back to Daniel. Hesitantly he asked, "You are...He?"

Daniel was lost in heartache. Alaric's words peripherally registered, but in his mind's eye he saw Ashley. The children were huddled against her as she tried in vain to protect them from the dark of night. Daniel's voice was a dry whisper when he replied, "No...I don't know."

Soren's eyes never left the dark man. "Do you know where it originates?"

"The Prophecy?" Alaric still stared at Daniel's face, but when Soren rested a hand on his shoulder, he nodded. "Well, it is widely known..." He was lost in thought for a moment as though he were accessing the huge volumes of data that filled his shelves. "Maybe..." He stopped again and shook his head. "In my travels it seems to be more...involved...in the Northern Provinces."

"Here? In Enialé?"

Daniel came to himself long enough to ask, "It's not Naphthalian?"

Soren shook his head. "Most countries have the same or similar prophecies. It has been whispered all over the Empire for years."

Alaric grunted. "Yes, there are similar prophecies nearly everywhere, but I believe it originated here."

Daniel slipped into sadness and heartache once more, leaving the men to their conversation. Soren turned to Alaric. "Can you lead us?"

Confusion clouded his face. "I...I don't--" but with another look at Daniel's scars he gave a firm nod. "Yes, I can."

"Good. How long do you need?"

Alaric sprang to his feet, his indecision forgotten. "Not long. I need some things...a few maps, and a pack...I'll be back." He glided to the shelves and grabbed several sheets of rolled velum before walking out of the study.

Soren parted the thick curtains and the first light of day shined in on his face. He studied the street before turning to the villager standing near the door. "Get Dalen," he ordered. The man left and Soren rested a gentle hand on Daniel's shoulder. The captain winced when he saw the despair in his eyes. "Are you alright?"

Tears welled as he breathed, "I...no,"

Soren sighed. "Many apol--" He broke off when the front door slammed shut. The men spun toward the sound and saw the villager stumble into the room. Blood flowed between the fingers covering his belly. He fell into the wall and slowly slid down to the floor, leaving a bloody smear behind him.

Regnar jumped to his side. "What happened?" The man was already past hearing, his glassy stare confirming that he was gone before he'd stopped breathing.

"Alaric!" Soren roared. "Now!"

They spilled into the hall as the older man rumbled down the stairs. He leapt to the landing, a silver-sheathed saber banging against his leg and a fine leather pack strapped to his back. "What?" he asked before he saw a trail of blood leading from the front door to the study.

"Is there another way out?" Soren asked. Alaric grimly shook his head. The captain rested his hand on the door knob and looked back. "We move quickly. Away from the house, back to the other district...we'll lose them in the streets." He glanced at Daniel and snapped, "Get your hood up!" When Daniel complied, he glanced around once more. "Ready?" He threw the door open and launched himself down the steps, everyone racing behind him.

Daniel glanced to the side at a bloody stain on the wall, the headless body of Dalen lying on the ground beneath it. Soren took one step and froze when a man emerged from the shadows across the street. Daniel froze also, his legs nearly unhinging and dropping him to the ground. He recognized the red robes and his heart skipped a beat before he even saw Malthion's face. Without a word, the sorcerer raised his arms and crossed them, making an "**X**" with his little fingers and thumbs extended. He lowered his head for a split second until a pulsing ball of light grew before him. He threw his chin up and arms out simultaneously, and the light launched toward Daniel, moving almost too fast to follow.

Daniel closed his eyes and cringed, but just before impact, he was pushed from behind as Regnar vaulted in front of him. The light hit the carpenter in the chest and he was instantly engulfed in flames. He never cried out as the intense flames seared away flesh and melted bone. Regnar managed two steps before falling face-first to the cobblestones. Daniel froze as he stared in horror at his friend's corpse. "No!"

Navy-clad troops streamed onto the street as Soren all but carried Daniel up the stairs, slamming the door behind them. His eyes were wild as he looked around the foyer before shouting, "Up!" They raced up the stairs two at a time. There was a large window on the second story landing which Soren shattered with his A-blade before leaning out and looking up. He'd just climbed back in and taken off his pack when a concussive blast rocked the front of the house. The building shook and all the windows on its front exploded, engulfing the interior in flames.

Soren didn't even look up as the heat wave washed over them. Flames roared out of the study and Alaric moaned, "My books!"

Soren stood with a grapple and rope in hand and yelled, "Forget them!" Alaric groaned as the captain leaned out the window and threw the grapple to the roof. When it was secure, he sent Clem up before turning to Alaric and forcing him to turn from the destruction. The man gave a final groan as he grabbed the rope and climbed nimbly to the roof. Soren hugged Daniel to him with his left arm and used his right hand and feet to pull them to the roof, followed by Thosten.

The roof's front edge was fully engulfed by that time, sections falling away to oblivion. They ran along the back of the house to the edge and looked to the next building. Space was limited within Namtrah's walls and even in the wealthiest district the buildings were closely packed. The gap between Alaric's roof and his neighbor's was no more than three feet, and everyone safely jumped across.

They continued over three more roofs, the heat at their backs blistering as each house caught fire in turn. When they reached the last house in the district, they pulled up short. Daniel's heart would have dropped if it wasn't pounding so hard.

The wall that separated the districts rose twenty feet above their heads. Only then did they realize they left Soren's grapple on Alaric's roof. Soren cast around wildly and spied a skylight off to one side. Without hesitating he jumped feet-first through the heavy glass. He rolled to absorb the impact before bouncing to his feet and motioning the others to follow. When Daniel jumped he slipped on broken glass and fell sideways, landing on his right arm and sending pain exploding through his body. He surely would have blacked out then if not for Regnar. He kept the image of his immolated body at the fore of his mind and forced himself to his feet.

They dashed through the empty house to the front door. Soren cracked it open and looked out on chaos. Namtrah's elite milled around the boulevard, looking more like beggars with their faces and expensive nightclothes stained with soot. They looked on with wide eyes as their estates burned, sending thick clouds of dark smoke billowing down the street. Imperial troops picked their way through the crowd, intent on getting down to the remains of Alaric's home. They were in such a mad rush that they didn't bother guarding that end of the street.

Soren led them out the door and made for the gatehouse that jutted from the wall. He motioned for them to wait as he darted to the gate itself, but came back within seconds. The gate was closed. There was no escape. Daniel

Ron Hartman

moaned and allowed despair to overwhelm him. No words came from his smoke-ravaged throat, but inside he was screaming his love for his family. He missed and needed them so much, but he was going to die alone in a smoky ruin. He didn't hear Alaric speak, or even realize they were moving again until Soren grabbed his left arm and shook him. "Move!"

Daniel turned dull eyes on the captain. *What's the use?* When Soren gave his arm another rough shake, he shrugged. He followed Alaric as they crept down a narrow alley that ran between the last house's foundation and the wall. At the very back of the alley there was an iron-bound door.

Alaric armed soot from his face and walked up to the door, knocking a complex combination of rapid and interspersed taps. When he finished, a bolt was thrown on the other side and the portal swung open. A guard stepped out and started in surprise when he saw who stood there. He spun back toward safety, but only managed one step before Alaric's saber lanced through his throat.

"Come, quickly!" They rushed through the door and Thosten pulled it shut, throwing the bolt in place as he brought up the rear. Alaric led them through many dark tunnels that ran along the base of the city walls. Finally, they came to another iron-bound door where he paused before carefully unlocking it. He peaked through the crack and whispered, "Let's go."

They left the wall and darted into a stable. Alaric said, "Get horses," before taking Thosten with him out the stable's front doors. They gathered horses and waited nervously until Alaric threw open the doors a few minutes

401

later. "Let's go!" he shouted as he and Thosten ran to their mounts. The five galloped out of the stable and under a portcullis that they'd raised just high enough for them to escape. Smoke rolled from the upper class district as they fled the burning city. They raced to the west, putting many miles behind them before finally slowing to rest their horses. The five survivors had escaped Malthion's trap, but at a price they could scarcely believe.

Chapter Sixteen

A cool breeze drifted across the overcast sky, buffeting the men as they stood in the foothills. A mountain range loomed before them. It wasn't as tall as the Cloudspeaks, but its sheer cliffs and jagged peaks were daunting just the same. Daniel took a deep breath, and as it sighed out, he rolled his ankles, stretching sore muscles. Soren smiled at him. "You ready?" His tone was almost giddy.

Daniel rolled his neck from side to side and grumbled, "What the Hell." Soren chuckled and Daniel sighed again. *That damn map.* He shivered as a cool autumn breeze ruffled his hair.

Alaric joined them, pocketing the small spyglass he'd been using to study their back trail. He'd been frowning, his shoulders slumped, but when he saw Daniel, a spring lightened his step. His once spotless white blouse was gray and dingy, and a . blood-soaked bandage was wrapped around his upper arm. "Are we ready?" he asked.

Daniel shrugged as his eyes scanned the horizon behind them. He could see the ever-present smudge that darkened the land, but from that distance he couldn't make out the Imperial troops. He jutted his chin toward them and asked, "How far?"

Alaric's smile faded when he looked back that way. "I'd say no more than a half day," he answered.

Soren grunted. "I expected as much." He turned his back on their enemies and studied the peaks. "We'll make it to the mountains...then they won't keep up."

Alaric glanced at the captain then back toward the Imperialists. "Yes, I'm sure you're right," he murmured.

Clem shouldered his pack and joined them, his face an emotionless mask. *Well, at least* his *attitude hasn't changed*, Daniel thought. He gave the villager a half-hearted smile, but Clem ignored him and turned to the peaks.

Thosten joined them, rounding out their quintet as Soren said, "Sooner begun, sooner done." Daniel looked back at the dark smudge a final time. With a frown and a sigh, he followed Soren into the rugged mountains.

~ * ~

They'd been running from Imperial troops for nearly a month, heading due north across the Empire. Their enemies were always right on their trail, and three times they were nearly captured. The last time was a few days before, when Alaric was wounded and they lost their mounts. He'd been studying one of his vellum maps when he noticed something near the top edge.

Mountains criss-crossed the Empire's northern hinterlands, but one chain in particular caught his eye. It skirted the edge of a large lake, the bulk of which lay off the map. The mountains and the lake were unremarkable, but the name scribbled over the lake, almost as an afterthought, snared him. In smudged and faded ink was written "Sea of Sorrows" and under that in parenthesis "the Dredlen Sea". He gasped when he saw it, his eyes round, a dark hand covering his gaping mouth.

"What?" Soren asked as he studied the map. "Sea of Sorrows? What's that?"

Daniel had been drifting off to sleep when their voices roused him. He glanced over at the same moment Alaric looked his way and their eyes locked. "What?"

"I don't know," Soren said. "Alaric, what does it mean?"

The older man shook his head. "I cannot be sure…" He was lost in thought for a moment before turning back to the map. He pointed to a village a few miles east of them and said, "We need to go here." When Soren frowned, he added, "The answer lies there."

Daniel shrugged when Soren looked at him, so the next day they turned east. They were two miles from the village when Soren ordered Thosten, Clem, and Daniel to stay behind while he and Alaric pushed on. They met with a village elder who offered Alaric an old book filled with ancient writings. He just started leafing through the tome when Imperial cavalry charged into the village, slaughtering the peasants.

Soren and Alaric barely escaped, with Alaric taking an arrow in his arm as they fled. They pushed their mounts to the limit, and soon Alaric and Soren's horses tired and slowed. They had no choice but to leave them behind and ride double until all the horses were exhausted. They left them and continued on foot rather than running the beasts to death. They'd been fleeing north ever since, the Imperialists never far behind. Their only advantage was that the army moved more slowly, so they were able to stay ahead, but they never truly lost their pursuers again.

Every night Alaric studied the ancient book until the light failed. Finally, the night before he located what he sought and crowed in triumph. Soren stared at him. "Now, tell me," he commanded.

Alaric pointed to the lake at the edge of the map, his face aglow. "*This* is it, my friend! This is what we sought!"

Soren held the map close to his face and squinted. He hesitated before asking, "Deddin Sea?"

Alaric shook his head, his excitement building. "No, *Dredlen* Sea. I knew when I first saw it that it was an ancient dialect. I wasn't sure of the translation until if found it in this tome…" His voice trailed off as he beamed at Daniel, who cringed inwardly, his gut twisted by a stab of fear.

Soren lost his patience. "Tell me!" he growled.

Alaric looked back to him. "'Dredlen' literally translates as 'to burn'." Soren rocked back on his heels, a frown on his face. Just as realization dawned, Alaric shouted, "Yes! The *Burning Sea*!" He looked back to Daniel and said, "We found the Burning Sea!"

Soren's face was transformed with joy. "The Burning Sea!" he crowed. "We did it!" He gave Alaric a rough hug, the two barely able to contain their excitement.

Daniel was stunned. *Oh, damn…the Prophecy*. It had been the furthest thing from his mind for so long that he'd actually forgotten about it. When it came back so suddenly, it caught him off guard and unsettled him. Clem looked at Daniel and gave a blank shrug. He'd retreated into himself since the last of his kinsmen died, and he rarely spoke anymore.

Thosten had been on watch and came rushing into camp with the commotion. "What is it?" he growled.

Soren beamed at his friend, but Thosten's anger dampened his excitement. "We head for the mountains." The tall warrior turned without a word and returned to the watch. Soren's eyes followed his friend as he trudged away. He'd also changed since Namtrah. He was always on edge, always irritable and unapproachable, even by his old friend. The captain sighed and turned to Alaric, grinning and hugging him again. He walked to Daniel and dropped beside him. "I *knew* it!"

Daniel turned a wary eye on him. "I haven't done anything, Soren." He threw his hand up in exasperation. "I'm not that guy!"

Soren shrugged. "Perhaps…" Daniel opened his mouth to argue, but the captain's happiness turned to seriousness as he held up a hand. "You've got mettle in you, Daniel. You can be the steel we need. You can lead our people to stand and fight together! I *know* it!"

The words of Naphthali's first king rolled through his mind. *Only by combining all our talents may we become Steel.* He looked to Soren, but his objections died in his throat when he saw the hope blazing in his eyes. He sighed. The Prophecy weighed heavily on him once more.

~ * ~

By midmorning the foothills were behind them and the trek was getting steadily more difficult. Daniel's body had toughened since he'd arrived in Naphthali, but in spite of that, he was soon breathing heavily. The others wheezed shallow breaths as well, the steep climb and thinning air taking a toll. They stopped for a brief rest and Daniel sat down, gasping both from the thin air and from pain. His right arm screamed at him, and he did his best to control his breathing, trying to keep the hot jolts at bay. When the pain started to recede, he saw Alaric studying the map once more. With a groan he climbed to his feet, and he and Soren gathered around. "What's the plan?"

"Hmm," Alaric murmured, tapping the top of the map with his finger. At its very edge he pointed to a small peninsula that jutted into the Sea of Sorrows. Inverted triangles ran its length, indicating the mountains continued to the sea. "We have to avoid this, but if we stay along the mountain's main spine, we should reach the north end of the sea. Hopefully, we will leave the mountains behind as well." He traced a line through the mountains and off the map in an arc to the northwest.

Soren nodded. "Once we clear the mountains, we'll find a transport to ferry us across the Burn--" when Daniel winced he amended, "--the Sea of Sorrows." He looked away from Daniel's burning cheeks and asked Alaric, "Any idea how far the Empire stretches?"

The older man shrugged. "I've never been this far north... Who knows?"

Soren grunted and they all spun when Clem cursed. He was on his belly at the edge of an overhang, looking back the way they'd come. "They're moving fast," he growled when Soren joined him.

The captain nodded, surprised but not overly concerned that the Imperial troops had already reached the mountains. He studied them for a moment and was just turning to ask Alaric for his spyglass when the wind gusted and thunder rolled. He looked into the mountains and saw towering thunderheads climbing over the peaks. "Let them come," he murmured to Clem. "That'll slow them down. How'd you like to climb a cliff in a storm?" He chuckled, trying to raise Clem's spirits, but the last man from Standing Stone just grunted and crawled back from the edge.

Soren joined the others and studied their trail. Ahead lay a relatively easy incline before a sharp cliff loomed. "Let's gain more ground before the storm hits," he said as he shouldered his pack. When all were ready, he added, "Sooner begun, sooner--"

Before he could finish Daniel grumbled, "Yeah, yeah. Let's go." He blew out a heavy sigh and followed Clem, ignoring Soren's grin as he passed the captain. His right arm gave him an angry jolt, and he redoubled his efforts to hold it as still as possible, his breath coming in ragged wheezes.

~ * ~

The next three days were the most miserable of Daniel's life. The storm struck just before they reached the top of the cliff face and almost washed Alaric to his death. The wind howled and massive raindrops fell like icy missiles, exploding all around them. At the top of the cliff the climb wasn't as steep, but there was no shelter from the dangerous lightening that blinded them with its intensity.

They had no choice but to continue, pressing on toward a distant alpine valley that offered scant shelter.

With every flash Daniel cringed, seeing the Elite Guardsman that died from a lightning strike on the way to Stonefall. The lightning was chased by deafening explosions of thunder, making Daniel cower and his right arm scream. *Dear God, please see us through this.* Daniel's plea was answered and no one was harmed, but they were all soaked by the nearly freezing rain in spite of the tanned water-resistant cloaks Alaric had given them. By the time they reached the valley, Daniel couldn't feel his feet and his left hand was almost as dead as his right.

A narrow cave in the valley's wall provided scant protection as they huddled together. When the storm lessened to a freezing drizzle, they continued, Daniel shivering and gritting his teeth against the pain. He moved with exaggerated slowness, trying to hold his right arm steady. It wasn't long before he slowed everyone down. Soren and Alaric flanked him without complaint, but Daniel caught irritated glares from both Clem and Thosten as they ranged ahead and had to double back to keep the group together.

Evening found them in another damp cave. The unrelenting storm still hadn't ended, and travel in the darkness would have been too dangerous. Soren tried for nearly an hour to start a fire until he finally gave up with a curse and the men huddled together with wet blankets thrown around them. As steam rose from their bodies, eventually Daniel stopped shivering. It was impossible to sleep in the cramped quarters though, and he dozed fitfully throughout the night.

The next day showed no improvement. Cold rain fell throughout the day and sometimes the wind screamed at gale-force. Daniel and his protectors couldn't afford to wait, so they slogged up rain-slicked inclines, climbing ever deeper into the mountain range. For two days Daniel fell into a pain-filled routine that would have threatened his sanity had it continued for long. He pushed himself to keep the pace set by Clem and Thosten, at the same time trying not to overtax his right arm. Inevitably he'd lose his balance on loose shale or thick mud and reflexively throw his right arm out. It always sent the dead limb screaming into paroxysms of agony. Each time he bit back a moan, once even clenching down on the side of his tongue. His vision clouded over and he retreated into himself during the worst of it, trying to hide in his own mind. Only a rudimentary sense of place kept him within the group and saved him from pitching headlong off any number of steep cliffs.

He found solace in an image of his family: Ashley, sitting in a blue sundress with the children arrayed around her, all smiling at him. As he focused on family, all his senses reinforced what he was seeing. He could smell Ashley's perfume and hear Elizabeth saying "I love you, Daddy." He felt the softness of Ethan's hair and tasted Nate's tears when he kissed away the pain from a fall. This was his safe place; where he fled, where he could be surrounded by all he held most dear. Tears coursed down his cheeks as he stared at his family, perfectly posed. *I miss you so much*, he thought, pulling in a ragged breath. *I love you.* He stumbled to his knees before his wife, wrapping his arms around Ashley's waist and burying his face in her lap. He could feel her gently stroke the back of his head, and soon

411

he felt the small hands of his children, caressing and comforting as well.

When tears ran dry and he had the strength to stand, Daniel pushed away, looking into Ashley's beautiful face as he did so. She smiled at him but said nothing as he stepped back from the foursome that was his greatest treasure. He looked at them and thought, *Foursome? But there are five in our family.* Gradually realization came to him. He recognized the way they were sitting and even the clothing they wore, right down to the yellow flowers that lined the hem of Elizabeth's dress. It was the picture that sat on his desk back in his pharmacy, in another world. With recognition came a thought that'd never occurred to him before: *Why wasn't I in the picture?*

As he mulled over the question an answer came, one that was so simple it couldn't be argued or refused: *I'm dead. My family is a foursome because I'm...gone.* He nodded. Of course, it made perfect sense. The thought that he was dead and his family had moved on without him didn't so much frighten him as make him sad. He remembered once when he and Elizabeth were running errands in town. Out of the blue she asked what happened when you died. Without hesitation, he'd said, "Well, Honey, you go to Heaven."

She looked up at the sky, imagining what Heaven would be like. After a few minutes her pretty face clouded over and she asked, "Daddy, will you ever die?"

He glanced at her and smiled, patting her leg. "Yes, Sweetie. We all die someday."

"But I'd miss you!" she replied, a plaintive tremble coming to her voice.

Daniel stopped at a red light and looked more closely at his daughter. He took her little hand in his and said, "Don't worry, Lizzie. I'll always be with you in your heart, and you are *always* in mine. Besides, it'll be a long time before I die."

That placated her somewhat, but after a few minutes she looked to Daniel one more time and said, "I'd still miss you, Daddy."

Daniel smiled back. "I'd miss you too, Kiddo."

Yes, Daniel thought again, from his new perspective, looking at the posed image of his family. *I miss you, too.* Tears flowed again, and he found that his sanctuary wasn't so comforting after all. Mentally he turned and moved away, but he looked back one last time before the image was completely lost from sight. He loved them so much, needed them, but now he wanted the pain of his arm. He wanted the discomfort of the cold and wet. He wanted the pain because nothing could compare to the pain in his heart, where he carried his family, gone but *never* forgotten.

And so, he came back to himself, back to the misery of trumping through the mountains and the electric burn in his arm. Comparably speaking, the pain and discomfort didn't seem so bad, not compared to the other, deeper pain. He gritted his teeth even though he tasted blood, forced himself to get up and push on, even when he fell and wrenched his arm. He had to get up and had to hope against hope that he wasn't dead, not really. That he *would* find his way back to his family. They were there to give him comfort and strength when he needed it, but now he needed to find the strength within himself.

~ * ~

Soren watched him carefully during those dark days. He saw the misery and agony on Daniel's face and privately wondered if the Stranger would survive the trek that lay before them. As Daniel pushed away the memories to press on, he saw the steely determination he'd suspected was there all along. While he didn't know, and couldn't even guess what comforts Daniel held at bay, he was grimly satisfied to see the One resolve to keep fighting. The Burning Sea was near. While Daniel could deny his destiny, Prophecy could never be thwarted.

~ * ~

On the third night they were on a wind-swept ledge of bare rock. There was no shelter so they huddled as best they could, holding a blanket overhead to keep out the light rain that still fell. Daniel was too exhausted for discomfort to· stop him as he drifted into a fitful doze which he didn't awaken from until morning. Soren peeled himself off Daniel's left side and stepped away from the group, rousing Daniel, who opened blood-shot eyes and winced into bright sunshine. The seemingly never-ending storm finally blew itself out during the night, leaving behind azure skies and a brilliant morning.

Daniel pulled away from Clem and stood. He closed his eyes and stretched, enjoying the warmth of the sunshine on his face. When he opened his eyes, Soren smiled at him. "Feels good, doesn't it?"

He nodded and glanced around the stony plateau. They'd stopped on the highest peak in that portion of the mountain chain. All the surrounding mountains were below them, but in the distance snow-capped peaks still loomed. "I thought it'd never end," he murmured.

Alaric joined them. "You know, that storm may have been the worst I've ever experienced." He pressed his hands into the small of his back and arched until it popped, bringing a groan.

Soren nodded. "True…but we're fortunate to be rid of our shadows. They couldn't possibly track us through that."

Daniel grunted. "*I* barely kept up." His voice was small as his eyes never left the snow-capped peaks that still barred their way. Soren and Alaric shared a look before turning to their meager camp. Thosten tried without success to start a fire as Clem rolled up the blankets. Daniel picked up a blanket and rolled it. He handed it to Clem to stow in a pack and the villager offered him a small smile. *Everyone's mood is better today*, he thought until he saw Thosten glaring at him. *Well*, almost *everyone's*. The supplies were packed and as the men sat down to cold rations, the old camaraderie returned. They laughed at inside jokes and shared funny stories. All except Thosten, who sat with the group but remained quiet.

When they finished eating, they shouldered their packs and trudged down a path that wound half-way around the plateau on its way down to the next peak. They hadn't gone far when Soren let out a loud curse. His voice echoed down the mountain as they stumbled to a halt behind him. "What the--?" Daniel started, but his voice died away when he saw where Soren looked. Their path had carried them around the side of the highest peak, so they could see back the way they'd come. In a narrow valley not far behind them was that damnable smudge: an unsightly Imperial stain. Soren cursed again and kicked a rock from the path. "How-- how is that possible?" Daniel stammered, his heart racing.

Alaric recovered enough to murmur, "It is not possible."

"No!" Soren growled, glaring at their enemies. "*No!* They *could not* have followed through that storm!"

"Magic," Clem breathed in an awed whisper.

Daniel glanced at Clem's pale face and knew he was right. His stomach dropped when he looked back in horror at the troops. "Malthion…"

Alaric's eyes were round with fear when he spun to Daniel. "Don't say that name!"

Daniel could see in Alaric's eyes the same memory that reared in his own mind: the horrible fire raging, Regnar falling to the street as his body turned to ash. "We have to go…before they see us!"

Soren's gaze snapped to Daniel. "You're right," he said, fighting to remain calm. "Let's go." He turned from the dark stain and darted down the path, back around the side of the mountain and out of view of their enemies.

When they'd lost sight of the Imperialists, Daniel moaned, "What'll we do?"

Soren growled, "Our plans haven't changed. We continue around the Burning Sea…find a way across it." Daniel was so shaken by the sight of Malthion's troops that the name Soren used didn't even register. He gave a mute nod and followed as quickly as he could, his eyes locked on the path as he dodged loose stones and protected his right arm.

With the storm over they made good progress for the rest of the day. At one brief break, Daniel looked ahead to the white-capped peaks and thought they looked a little farther away than they had that morning. He discounted the idea, figuring the rough path they followed would soon wind back in that direction. The startling truth that sealed their doom didn't become apparent until they were about to stop for the night. The sun was setting, casting the land in sepia tones as they neared a final ridge and Soren murmured that they'd camp there. He led them to the rocky face and froze, staring in horror ahead of them.

Daniel stopped behind him and just short of the hill's crest, his heart in his throat as he looked at Soren's tense form in silhouette. Afraid of what he'd see, but needing to see it anyway, he forced himself to take the last few steps on numb and shaky legs. Before them the peaks declined into a series for short foothills before reaching a rocky beach. They were surrounded on three sides by the strange green waters of the sea. The tall white-capped mountains continued along the far shore to their right-hand side. Fear and confusion welled inside him as he asked, "How--what happened?"

A fierce scowl marred Alaric's face as he dropped his pack and pulled out the vellum map. Soren rested a hand on the map and gently pushed it down. "We lost our bearings," he murmured. "Veered too far west."

Daniel's bowels turned to water at the sound of doom in Soren's voice. In a whisper he asked, "What?" Alaric raised the map and his shoulders sagged. He held it out to Daniel, pointing at the mountains and the sea. Specifically he pointed at the small peninsula that jutted into the Sea of Sorrows. "No…" Daniel murmured, realization bringing his dread to fruition.

Clem realized the danger as well. He spun around, as if expecting Imperial soldiers to appear any second. When he turned back to them, his eyes were cold, his voice dead. "We're trapped."

~ * ~

The sun set and darkness enveloped them. Soren knew it would be foolhardy to backtrack at night, so he ordered the men to bed down. In the morning they'd attempt to cut back to the mainland without being seen. His dead tone and the fire in his eyes said he didn't think they'd succeed…maybe he didn't even want to. Soren took first watch, storming back down the trail without looking at the others. Daniel looked to Clem and saw only a cold mask of anger. He met Alaric's gaze and the older man shrugged as he unrolled his blankets. Thosten ignored him and lay down, soon breathing slowly as sleep took him.

Daniel sighed, laying back and looking at the bright stars overhead. *So this is where it ends.* He was exhausted, but the horrible realization of their mistake thrummed through him, adrenaline making sleep unlikely. He thought back over his adventures since coming to Naphthali. How long had it been since he woke in that field, anyway? Two months, maybe three? It seemed like a lifetime for all that'd happened.

A muffled sound came from across their camp. At first he thought Clem had rolled over, but when he realized the villager's light snoring continued unabated, he froze. The quiet sound came again and Daniel closed his eyes down to slits, pretending to be asleep and fighting hard to keep his breathing shallow. Through the fringe of his eyelashes he saw Thosten stealthily rise, remaining hunched over as he studied the others. When he was convinced they were asleep, he stood straight, hefting his bared great sword. He padded out of camp and down the trail toward Soren.

When he was out of sight, Daniel's eyes flew open and he sat up, his breath coming in fast hitches. *Oh man. What's going on?* The rational part of his mind tried to reassure him, to tell him that Thosten was going to relieve Soren from the watch, but his instincts told him that was wrong. And besides, Soren had only been on guard duty for at most two hours. His eyes darted around camp until they landed on a hunting knife lying beside a bundle of dried meat. *It's nothing, my imagination,* he told himself as he grabbed the knife with a shaking hand and followed Thosten from camp.

The blade felt clumsy in his left hand, and he cursed himself again for being little more than dead weight on this entire trip. Any of the others could battle an enemy, but even after all he'd seen, Daniel would be more likely to hurt himself than an opponent. With that foremost in his mind, he crept forward at a snail's pace, being as quiet as possible as he stalked the warrior that seemed to be stalking Soren.

He came around a bend and could just make out Thosten in the moonlight. He moved through shadows, closing on another man that sat with his back to him, looking the way they'd come. The rational side of his mind that excused Thosten's behavior fell silent as fear and panic reared anew. He tried to speak, but his throat felt like it was filled with cotton, his tongue made of lead. Thosten raised his sword for a killing strike and finally Daniel's paralysis broke. "Soren!"

The large warrior spun toward Daniel, his hunting knife held up as a paltry defense against the man's great sword. At the shout Soren also spun, yanking the A-blade free. When he saw Thosten, blade bare, his eyes narrowed. "Thost, what're you about?" Thosten glared at Daniel for a moment, but his anger faltered when he turned an agonized stare on his friend. He threw the sword to the ground, unable to raise his eyes to the captain's. Soren moved cautiously toward him and stopped just out of arm's reach. "What is it, my friend?"

Thosten's arms raised, palms up, before dropping back to his sides in helplessness. He drew in a ragged breath and whispered, "Many apologies."

Soren's brows knit together. "Why do you apologize? What have you done?"

Daniel walked in a wide circle around the warrior until he reached Soren's side. Tears stood in Thosten's eyes when he moaned, "They…they've got Daphelle, and…and our children!"

Soren's face paled and silence stretched out until he finally asked, "When?"

A single tear tracked down Thosten's cheek. "At Standing Stone…when I guarded our trail."

As the words sank in, it was as if someone punched Daniel in the gut. He'd been betraying them ever since

Daniel first met him! "Wh--" he started but Soren cut him off with an angry growl and a flick of his hand.

He glared at Daniel before turning back to Thosten. "You led them." It was more a statement than a question, but the large warrior gave a solemn nod. "How?"

Thosten held up his right hand, fingers splayed. "With this."

Soren and Daniel both looked to his hand before frowning. "With what?" demanded Soren. "Explain!"

Daniel jumped at Soren's bark, but Thosten took it in stride. He removed something with his left hand and held it before him. "The ring," he whispered.

The two looked carefully again before frowning to one another. Soren stepped forward, but Daniel dropped his knife and grabbed his sleeve. "No, I'll go," he murmured with a meaningful look at the A-blade. The captain glanced at the weapon and a look of such sadness came over his face that for a moment Daniel wasn't sure he could trust him until he tightened his grip and nodded.

Daniel turned to Thosten and forced his shaking legs to take three strides to the giant's side. He towered over Daniel, but the eyes that looked on him with such anger so often only held sadness. He held his hand out to Daniel and at first he didn't think anything was in it, but then moonlight glinted off the dull metal of a wire ring as thin as a hair. He took it and walked back to Soren, where the two studied it. It was nearly invisible by moonlight and would have been almost as hard to see during the day.

"The sorcerer can track our movements with its magic. I think..." Thosten's voice died away and he hesitated before continuing, "I think sometimes he can hear what we say, as well."

Daniel thought back to how quickly the Imperialists closed on them at the Swordgrass, and how they followed them through the mountain storm. He saw more clearly all the traps that had nearly captured them since fleeing Namtrah. His mind flashed back to the Swordgrass and he gasped. He looked up at the warrior, barely keeping emotion from his voice. "It's because of *you* that Greggor died, and Trumble…and Regnar!"

Thosten's chin dropped to his chest. When he managed to look up, tears streamed down his cheeks. "Don't you see?" he asked, addressing Daniel directly for the first time. "They have my family! I…I can't risk them!" More tears came and he looked away as he sobbed bitterly.

His words struck a chord, and once more Daniel heard Soren's voice: *You and he have a lot in common…He has three children, like you, and a wife he adores.* Daniel raised a hand to his temple and winced. "Wait…wait a minute," he mumbled. Three children stood before him, a wicked dagger pressed into his hand. They reminded him of his own kids: a girl and two boys, all about the right age. They looked at him with terror in their eyes, afraid to even move. *Kill them.* When he looked back at the warrior, tears stood in Daniel's eyes as well. He felt so much grief and pity for Thosten that he could barely speak. "Your children…were they a girl and two younger boys? The youngest practically a baby?"

Thosten nodded, his brow creased in confusion. "That's right…"

Daniel nodded and remembered Thosten had never heard that part of his tale, one he didn't have the heart to recount since sharing with Westragen and Soren. *You don't know for sure, you* can't *know!* the rational part of his mind insisted, but he *did* know. Somehow it fit perfectly. In a choked voice he murmured, "Oh Thosten, I'm so sorry."

The warrior frowned. "What? What do you know?" He took a half step forward but Soren raised the A-blade and he dropped back.

Daniel had to swallow several times past the sudden lump in his throat before he could finally say, "They died." Thosten's eyes flew open wide as he shook his head. Before losing his courage, Daniel stammered, "The Emperor...he tried to make me kill them, to...to *sacrifice* them, but I couldn't. Then he got angry, and he...he raised his hands...and...and he killed them." Daniel raised his own hands and brought them together, unmindful of the pain that exploded in his right. Tears ran freely, his body wracked by sobs. He cried not only for the children that died so needlessly, but also for their father, who took the news as if he'd been run through with a sword.

Daniel blindly stumbled forward, jerking away from Soren's restraining hand. He could see the shocked hurt in Thosten's eyes as he towered over him, and he could see a light dying there as well. "I'm so sorry," he murmured again, knowing it did no good, offered no comfort. He pulled Thosten to him as sobs rolled through the big man. Soon Soren joined him and the two held Thosten as he wailed.

Eventually his tears dried up and he nodded to the two as he pulled away. He looked into Daniel's blood-shot eyes and whispered, "I knew. I think deep down, I knew they were dead all along. I just…couldn't face it."

Daniel understood. How could any man face the death--the *murder*--of his children? He would've hidden from the knowledge as well. Then he looked to Soren. His daughter was also murdered. *Is there anyone these bastards haven't hurt?* he thought as the fires burned brightly in Soren's eyes.

"This stops, now," Soren growled. He walked to a rock and laid the wire ring where it glinted dully in the moonlight.

"No!" Thosten shouted. Soren turned to him as he added, "Let me." The captain studied his face before nodding and standing aside. Thosten retrieved his sword and took two quick strides toward the boulder, bringing down a tremendous overhead blow. The blade whistled through the air, a roar of anger escaping his lips. When it struck, a brilliant flash of light exploded silently from the ring, and Thosten stumbled backward, his great sword shattered. All three were temporarily blinded, but when their vision returned, they looked to the boulder to see that it had been split in two, a large circular scorch mark covering the top where the ring had lain.

As they stared at the broken boulder, Daniel asked, "Now what do we do?"

After a moment, Thosten tossed his pommel to the ground and turned to the other two, fire burning deeply in his own blood-shot eyes. "Soren is right," he growled. "This ends now." The captain frowned at him as he said, "I'll go to the Imperial camp." Both men shook their heads but Thosten continued more quickly. "I'll tell them the ring stopped working, that I can lead them to you. They will take me to the sorcerer. If I can kill him, you may yet be able to sneak past his dogs."

Soren considered his friend while Daniel shook his head. "Don't do this!"

Thosten looked to him, and his rage faded momentarily. "I have nothing left, Daniel. With this, I may still be able to help you...and perhaps atone for the terrible things I've allowed to happen."

Daniel still shook his head. "N--" he started but Soren cut him short.

"He's right, Daniel." The captain's eyes shone with pride as he looked at his friend. "With the sorcerer alive, there is no escape. With his death...we just may." He gripped Thosten's shoulder and said, "It would be an honorable death."

The fires in Thosten's eyes burned brightly once more when he returned Soren's stare. "Honor is beyond me. I do this for my children." Soren nodded and Thosten looked to Daniel. "Many thanks, Stranger, for the truth of it. I owe you a debt." Daniel shook his head, wanting to yell at the man not to be stupid, to stay with them, but nothing would come. Thosten looked to them a final time before he turned and bounded down the trail, back toward the Imperial camp and his fate.

~ * ~

Thosten slowed near the Imperial lines, reading the absence of natural nocturnal sounds as a sign that he was close. After an hour he was sure eyes were on him, so he stopped and raised his hands. "Take me to your commander." The command was spoken with authority and within seconds several men spilled from the undergrowth onto the trail. As the troops nervously fingered their weapons, the captain of the watch stepped forward. Thosten towered over him, and while he tried to appear imposing, the warrior saw fear in his eyes. He chuckled inwardly. *You should fear me.*

Finally, the man mustered the courage to growl, "State yer intent." His voice cracked at the last and his face flushed.

Thosten managed, just barely, to keep a smirk from his face. "Take me to your commander," he repeated. "I have information."

The captain saw the amused glint in Thosten's eyes and flushed again. He grumbled, "'Ya aint goin' nowhere!" He tried and failed to glare at Thosten before motioning to a subordinate. "Git Commander Klarn," he whispered.

The soldier dashed off and the captain turned back to Thosten. He fidgeted with the pommel of his sword and was about to speak when Thosten dipped his head and murmured, "I will wait."

He yelped and pulled his blade free before he realized Thosten wasn't challenging him. He stammered, "Y--yeah," shuffling backwards until he was flanked by his troops.

Soon the soldier returned with an older man that had iron gray hair and a long navy cloak embroidered with silver thread. His silver breastplate was embossed with the clenched fist, a sword with a jeweled pommel hanging at his waist. His eyes narrowed as he took in the large man. "What is the meaning of this?"

Thosten studied the man in a detached way for a moment, deciding how best to defeat him. When his analysis was complete he asked, "You are Commander Klarn?"

His brows pinched together and he snarled, "Yes, now tell me your business or I'll have you staked and flayed!"

Without hesitation Thosten said, "The ring stopped working. I know where the rebels are. Are you ready?" The commander's angry sneer melted away and he froze, his mouth hanging open. Thosten fought to keep from laughing. The man was clearly torn between the glory of capturing the rebels himself and the terror of angering the sorcerer. But blind obedience was too ingrained into Imperial officers for them to strike out on their own, even when the offer was so tempting.

Finally, as Thosten expected, Klarn glanced to the captain and said, "Bring him."

He stalked away as the captain closed on Thosten. He took in his muscular frame and hesitated. Clearing his throat, the captain called out, "Milord?"

Klarn spun and glared at the man. "What?" His voice was low and deadly.

He stammered, "Beggin' yer pardon, Lord, but…did…did 'ya want 'im bound?"

Klarn also took in Thosten's physique and hesitated before growling, "No! He's one of us, now move!"

The captain motioned and two soldiers fell in behind Thosten as they escorted him through the camp.

Thosten's face was blank but inside he was seething. *No, I will* never *be one of you.* He was a veteran warrior and was no stranger to military camps, so he expected to see a flurry of activity, regardless of the time. Consequently he was surprised by how few soldiers they passed, and by how surprised those troopers looked to see someone making for the large tent that dominated the camp's center. He was unconcerned by their stares at first, but as they closed on the large tent, he felt a weight press down on him. It was as if an invisible hand wrapped itself around his heart and squeezed the vitality from it. The air was thick with despair, and when the captain of the watch glanced back at him, Thosten saw the stark terror in his eyes. Fear of punishment was the only thing that kept him obediently following his commander.

They broke through the maze of tents and into a ten-foot wide span of empty space that ringed the sorcerer's tent like a lifeless moat. Klarn hesitated before stepping into the dead space and when the others followed, Thosten clamped his jaws to keep his teeth from chattering. He was a brave man but even he felt his knees quake when they stopped before the massive tent. Guards in full dress uniform stood ramrod straight to either side of the entrance. They stared before them with glazed eyes and their skin had an odd pallor to it. Their crossed halberds blocked admittance and they stood so still they appeared frozen in place. They didn't even acknowledge the arrival of the commander.

As Klarn gathered his courage, Thosten studied the unusual guards. There was something about the two that screamed of the unnatural. Finally, as the commander cleared his throat he realized what was so unsettling: they weren't breathing. Klarn swallowed the cold terror in his throat and whimpered, "We are here to see Lord Malthion…the spy has come."

Silence stretched out and Thosten could hear the teeth of a guard behind him chattering. He forced himself to relax, to be prepared. He nonchalantly hooked his thumbs on his wide belt, resting them on hidden throwing knives. Their cold hard steel was a comfort, and Thosten was able to focus on what needed done. After two minutes the dead guards silently pulled back their halberds simultaneously. Commander Klarn swallowed and stepped forward, leading them into Malthion's lair.

The inner confines were dark and mysterious, and the smoky air had a cloying, sickly sweet smell, like rotting meat. In spite of the chill air, Thosten was bathed in sweat and perspiration glistened on the officers' necks, though they were dimpled in goose flesh. "Come." The high-pitched voice came from within the dark recesses. It reverberated with power and compelled the men forward. One of the guards whimpered as they walked down a canvass-covered hallway and into a long room lit by sparsely-placed braziers. They gave off thick clouds of smoke that reeked of rot and decay. Malthion glared at Thosten from the far end of the room. He took a few steps forward and snarled, "Why have you come?"

Klarn dropped to a knee and bowed his head. He motioned and Thosten was shoved from behind until he knelt between the commander and the captain of the watch. "Th--th--the spy, m--milord," he stammered.

Malthion's piercing gaze turned to Klarn as he snapped, "I *know* who he is!" His hot glare landed on Thosten and he demanded, "Why are you here? Where is the ring?" Thosten's face was downcast as he knelt. He could feel evil radiating from the sorcerer and he trembled, his limited human spirit spiting his limitless bravery. He closed his eyes and pulled in a deep breath, letting it out slowly. "Well?" Malthion screeched. "Answer m--"

He was cut off when Thosten whirled into action. His thumbs flicked out the throwing knives in one fluid motion. The left shot toward Malthion as he reversed his grip on the right and thrust it upward as he lunged to his feet. The blade was driven first through the bottom and then the top of Klarn's jaw, nailing his mouth shut and piercing his brain. Moving faster than human eyes could follow he released the blade and ripped the commander's sword free from its scabbard. He swung it around in a clean sweep that separated the captain's head from his shoulders.

Had he watched the left knife fly, Thosten would have seen Malthion transformed, his mouth dropping into a large "O", his eyes wide in surprise. The blade stopped a foot from him when it struck an invisible bubble that flashed as it popped, incinerating the weapon. He missed the look while killing the two officers, and when he turned back to Malthion, the sorcerer's eyes were narrowed, his mouth in a rictus of rage.

Without hesitation he leapt the three strides that separated him from Malthion and swung the sword around in a mighty arc. He brought the blade down with a wild roar of rage but it stopped inches from Malthion's hate-filled gaze. He had just enough time to crumple against the invisible barrier before the second protective bubble burst, exploding with incredible force. Thosten was thrown back into the canvass wall, falling to land on top of the immolated bodies of the guards that stood behind him.

The explosion deafened him and his body screamed agony. His mouth wouldn't work, his lips charred. He could only open his left eye half-way, his right not at all. He rolled to his side and raised his right arm, only to see smoking and charred bones where his hand was moments before. He fell back with a gasp and saw an unharmed Malthion standing over him, seething with rage. As the dead door guards swept in without a sound, their swords raised, his vision faded to black.

The darkness didn't last, though. The gloom fell away as an all-encompassing light brightened, filling the void with White. Thosten was peripherally aware that the pain was gone as he looked into the light with undamaged eyes. A small group of people stood within the brightness, watching him. As he stared back, the light simultaneously increased in intensity and shined less brightly so that he could see the people clearly. Daphelle and his children smiled, motioning to him. A grin split his face and all his earthly toils and burdens were forgotten. He stood and walked into the light, into the arms of his loved ones.

Chapter Seventeen

Daniel and Soren stayed on the trail until long after Thosten was gone. What they waited for is anyone's guess, but neither spoke, nor did they take their eyes from the path. Finally, they returned to camp and woke Alaric and Clem to tell them what had happened. Clem's jaws clenched and an icy glint came to his eyes. He lunged to his feet and paced, thinking of his friends that had died because of the betrayal. Daniel laid a hand on his arm and murmured, "He couldn't help it, Clem. He tried to save his children." His voice cracked on the last.

Clem yanked his arm away. "And what of *my* friends, *my* home? I lost everything!" Daniel's hand dropped and he stood in silence, no words of explanation coming, not that any would have sufficed for the torn villager.

Alaric looked at Soren. "What is our plan?"

Tears stood in Soren's eyes as he watched Clem pace and when Alaric spoke, it was as if he was pulled from a trance. Looking at him, Daniel thought, *Clem's not the only one to lose everything.*

The captain wiped his eyes and said, "We wait till morning. When--*if*--Thosten is successful, we'll take advantage of their confusion and sneak past." No one offered suggestions or questions, so he sighed and looked at the long-dead embers of the fire, burned away like so many hopes and dreams.

Daniel laid awake the rest of the night, thinking of Thosten and the terrible sacrifice he made. His rational mind insisted he could have done nothing for Thosten's children, but he felt guilty just the same. One more death-- no--one more *family* of deaths on his head. He let out a ragged sigh. *How much more can I bear?* The quiet voice in his mind reminded him that it was his burden to bear. Yes, it was his burden, but oh was it ever getting heavy. He glanced over and in the starlight saw Thosten's discarded bedroll. *One more*, he thought, rolling to his side and closing his eyes, though he knew sleep wouldn't come. *One more death to bear.*

~ * ~

Daniel gave up on sleep and sat up, watching the sky shift from black to shades of pink as dawn approached. He glanced across the camp and saw Alaric and Clem doing the same. Soren returned, rolling Thosten's blankets and placing them in his pack before gently resting it on the ground. He turned to the others and said, "Stay here. I'll see how our friends are greeting the day." Without another word he jogged down the path and disappeared from view.

Daniel looked to the final survivors. Alaric nodded reassuringly but Clem frowned and looked out to the rising sun, refusing to speak. When Soren returned, rage burned in his eyes once more. Their slim hope of escape died when they saw the look on his face. "They've fanned out along the peninsula." He glared back the way he'd come and growled, "I don't think we can get past them."

"Do we fight?" Clem asked, eagerness in his voice.

Soren shook his head. "They're too many." He motioned toward the peninsula and said, "We have to go to the sea…maybe there's a boat…or something." The words were dead and his shoulders drooped, scaring Daniel. Soren had never given up hope. He'd always been the rock they leaned on, the one with the plans that kept them alive. The defeat in his voice was too much.

Daniel laid a reassuring hand on Soren's shoulder. When the captain looked up he said, "Yeah, we'll find a boat." He didn't believe it for an instant. Their doom had arrived. He could feel it, but he couldn't stand seeing Soren meet it in such a sad state. "Let's go." Soren searched his face for the hope he'd lost. Finally, he nodded and stepped away, leading them toward the Sea of Sorrows. *They sure named that one right*, Daniel thought. *Sorrow is all we have left.*

As they descended into the foothills, within sight of the strange green waters, they saw a contingent of blue-clad troops marching along the peninsula's eastern shore. They knew Daniel and his friends were trapped, and they wanted to cut off their last faint glimmer of hope. Soren scanned the coastline and pointed to a dark structure on the peninsula's west side. "There." He spared a final glance to the troops in the east before adding, "We have to beat them. Let's go." Daniel's heart lurched into his throat as they jogged down the foothills to the sea.

~ * ~

Lieutenant Liesat had the worst post in the Empire. There was no one for miles, no recreation to distract the men, and the weather was always cool, the scenery always drab. You couldn't even go outside without your eyes stinging and lungs burning. A month ago his scout found a farmer, lost in the mountains. His stories were a welcome respite from the boredom and monotony of duty on the Sea of Sorrows. But what really spiced things up were his wife and daughter, taken when his stories, and life, ended.

Liesat leaned back in his chair and thought about the girl. Ah, what grand memories! That was the only excitement nine months into his first command. He and his ten men were to guard the bridge, let no one pass, and capture anyone that came ashore. He gave a bitter glance out his window at the sluggish green liquid lapping at the rocks. For the thousandth time he thought, *Right! Bloody fat chance of that happening!*

When he arrived, the previous commander handed over the post and rode away, never looking back. There was more than a little madness in his eyes after being there a full year, commanded on pain of staking not to leave the post for anything. He'd lost two men to "gentlemanly" disagreements, and one just disappeared one night when he went out to stretch his legs. They found his halberd the next day along the shore, but no part of his body was ever found. "Eaten," the crazy officer said ominously before grinning and cackling wildly.

While his men unloaded a year's worth of supplies, Liesat took a brief walk around his new command. It was brief because it didn't take long to walk around a single structure, part barracks part command post, with a small stable built alongside. He sighed and tried to look ahead; to the doors this would open in his career. At twenty-three, he had to be one of the youngest command officers in the Empire!

He didn't know that the Sea of Sorrows was given little importance, that only marginal officers were placed there. Months ago he stopped thinking about his next great assignment and focused on bearing down and surviving this one. So far he'd not lost any men, though he nearly killed two himself when they got carried away and killed the girl. Someone pounded a staccato beat on his office door, rousing him from his thoughts. "What?" he snapped. The knob turned slowly and a small man peaked around the jamb. The wideness of his face was accentuated by his closely-placed crossed eyes. Liesat inwardly congratulated himself when he tried to count to ten and made it to three before growling, "Damn it, what do you want?"

The small man bowed and scurried into the room before cowering against the door. Usually interrupting the great officer meant he'd get a beating, but when none came, he looked over his raised arms with a moan. "Beggin' yer pardon, sir! I dinna mean no harm! It's jus'…well…"

Liesat blew out a heavy sigh and leaned over his desk, his potbelly rolling over the edge of the rough wood. "Spit it out, fool." He enunciated every word, growling every syllable, bringing another moan of terror from the small man.

His bladder let go when he saw the rage in Liesat's eyes, and the odor only further infuriated the lieutenant. "Vis'ters! Vis'ters comin'!" he wailed.

Liesat pushed back from his desk, a sneer crossing his face when his chair legs squealed across the floor and made the man jump and cower even more. He took an oak club from its hook on the wall and was just rounding on the man when his words sank in. He stopped in mid stride, the excitement of bullying replaced by a much darker excitement. Maybe another girl was coming... "Visitors?" he asked, his voice hungry.

The small man was curled into a ball, crying on the floor. He flailed an arm toward Liesat's door and blubbered, "By th' water!" Animalistic hunger got the better of Liesat, and he walked right past the cowering man out the door.

His second-in-command was rushing toward his office and stopped in his tracks when he saw Liesat. "Lieutenant!" he barked with a sharp salute.

Liesat waved it away and asked, "What news, Sergeant?"

The sergeant motioned toward the north. "Troops're comin' down th' coast!"

Liesat pulled up in confusion, his hunger gone. "What?"

The sergeant pointed again. "Please, come sir! They's just rounded th' point!" Liesat marched down the hall and into the much smaller office of the Sergeant at Arms, where a dingy window overlooked the northern coast. Through the warped glass he could just make out a column of navy-clad soldiers. "Is they's gonna relieve us?" he asked eagerly.

Liesat turned an irritated glare on him. "Too many. There must be something afoot." He stepped away from the window, a hand caressing his weak chin as he considered his options. Finally, he looked at the sergeant and said, "This is important! We *must* go meet them." With an eager gleam in his eye he commanded, "Rouse the boys. We march in five!"

The sergeant snapped a salute, but Liesat had already spun and rushed back to his office, pausing long enough to kick the small man still cowering there until he shuffled into the hall. He slammed the door and ran to his armoire, taking out a leather breastplate emblazoned with the raised fist. In his mind it was expertly tooled and very expensive, but in reality it was outdated and poorly made. He strapped it on, seeing visions of him boldly marching forth to meet the troops. Oh what gilded heights his career would reach!

~ * ~

The quartet ran down the foothills, racing to beat the Imperialists coming along the shore. Daniel's eyes never left the ground before him as they ran, watching for tripping hazards. Even with his caution, he kept jostling his right arm and the pain was steadily building, shooting up his shoulder with every step. Soren slowed to a jog as they came to the last hill and an unusual odor wafted over them that Daniel couldn't quite place. His lungs burned but he dismissed it, thinking it was from the run.

They stopped at the base of the last hill, no more than two hundred yards from the building. Soren scurried to the hilltop while Daniel tried to catch his breath without jostling his right arm, wincing at the painful sting each breath caused. He glanced at the others and saw Clem's face pinched in pain, Alaric's dark face looking ashen. Soren shimmied back down the hill and pulled them together. "It's an outpost of some sort. I saw movement within, but no one is outside."

"Let us have a look," suggested Alaric. Soren shrugged and nodded.

"I'll stay," said Clem. He thumped his chest and frowned, as if he had indigestion. Soren turned a concerned eye on the villager until he waved him away with an irritated look. Daniel couldn't crawl with his arm in a sling so he stayed with Clem while the others climbed up.

No sooner had they reached the top than soldiers burst from the building. Their uniforms were messy and they assembled into a sloppy formation on the bare ground before the building. Soren cursed and pulled free the A-blade but Alaric shot his arm out to restrain him. "No!" he whispered. "Look!" A bow-legged man with a pot belly and poorly fitting armor shuffled out and shouted at the men. Soren and Alaric couldn't hear what was said, but they got the gist of it as the troops made an attempt to straighten up their formation. After a brief tirade, he led all but four troops to the shoreline, where some sort of wooden structure could barely be seen. There they turned with abysmal precision and marched to the north.

Soren and Alaric shared a look of surprise. "I don't believe it!" Alaric murmured.

The four remaining soldiers leaned on their halberds and watched their compatriots march off. Soren studied them and the building for a minute before turning to Alaric. "Now's our chance. Let's go."

The two shimmied back down the hill and everyone prepared for battle. Daniel stood among his friends as they tightened armor, feeling helpless once more. He gripped his hunting knife so tightly that his fingers turned white. When all were ready, Soren said, "We'll run for the building. No matter what, don't stop until you reach it. Daniel, stay behind me." When everyone nodded, Soren murmured, "Let's go."

The four ran up the small hill and stopped near the top. Soren made sure the guards still had their backs to them, and then they ran flat out, not stopping until they felt the rough wood of the barracks under their hands. Soren used hand gestures to indicate that he'd advance in the middle with Clem to his left and Alaric to his right. Daniel was to stay behind the three and out of harm's way. When everyone nodded their readiness, the quartet crept from the barracks and closed on the guards.

The soldiers were oblivious until the very last second, when some instinct cautioned them that their doom approached. All four spun simultaneously, bringing their weapons to bear. One tripped over the end of his halberd and met his end on Soren's A-blade as it sliced through his unprotected neck. The three remaining soldiers glared at their opponents as their comrade gasped his last, clawing at the air with panicked hands. Soren lunged forward with his short sword. A guard parried with his halberd, trying to keep Soren at bay, but the captain allowed his left hand to be pushed wide and spun behind the thrust, rolling up his enemy's staff until he was face-to-face. He punched the man's unarmored abdomen with the A-blade, driving the man to one knee. Just as that limb touched the ground, Soren countered with the short sword, taking the man's head from his shoulders.

At the same time Alaric's opponent thrust straight toward him with his halberd. The older man ducked low and spun in toward the man, throwing out his foot and sweeping the guard's legs from under him. The man yelped as he fell, throwing the halberd at Alaric as he leapt back to his feet. He pulled a dirk from a scabbard at his waist as Alaric pushed the halberd to the ground and charged on. He met the weak thrust of the dirk with one, two, three strikes of his saber, each pushing the guard's defense farther and farther out. With the final strike his saber slid up the dirk and sliced deeply into the guard's hand. He dropped the weapon and would have howled, but Alaric's saber lanced into his chest and a wheezy groan was his only sound. Alaric brought his foot up between the two and kicked the man back off the blade to the dirt, where he died in a pool of his own blood.

Clem did not fare as well. His opponent thrust out with a well-balanced strike and Clem slid to the side, not realizing it was a feint until the deadly axe blade came back in and bit into his left arm. It dropped to his side, lifeless, as he hissed in pain but pressed on. He swung with all his might at the halberd staff with a hand axe. Something in the air must have weakened the wood, because it cracked with the blow, sending the heavy end crashing to the ground. Clem roared his hatred and charged, his axe raised for a killing blow. The man was too fast. He threw aside the useless staff and pulled out a long sword, allowing Clem's own momentum to push him onto the blade. The villager gasped as he staggered to a stop, the tip of the blade bursting from his back.

He tried to swallow but couldn't as blood spurted from his mouth. The guard leered at him, which only served to focus Clem's resolve. With a silent curse he pushed the blackness away. He tried to roar but a spray of blood bubbled from his mouth as he gripped the blade and pulled himself forward. The guard's leer dissolved into panic, but he thought too late to drop the sword as Clem pulled himself to within range and sent a vicious swipe across the man's throat with his axe, opening a gaping wound. As the guard fell backwards, Clem could hold the darkness at bay no longer. He staggered a step and dropped to the ground, coming to rest on his side, the pommel of the sword propping him up.

Soren finished his opponent in time to see Clem kill the guard and was about to follow Daniel and Alaric to his side when he glanced up the coast. The soldiers that left the compound heard the battle and were now racing back toward them, the long column of Imperial troops sprinting behind them. "No…" he breathed as he desperately cast about for inspiration. He glanced past Clem's body and saw what was barely visible earlier. A rope bridge stretched out over the sea's green surface for about forty feet before ending at a stone abutment, beyond which rose a rocky mound. He lunged in that direction, toward a heedless Alaric and Daniel that kneeled beside their dead friend.

Daniel dropped to his knees beside Clem, his pitifully small blade dropping from his nerveless fingers. Tears stood in his eyes as he moaned, "Oh, Clem…" Alaric stood beside him, cursing quietly. Daniel reached for Clem's shoulder, thinking to pull him off the blade so he could lie peacefully on the ground. He no more than touched the rough cloth of Clem's bloody jerkin, though, when Soren grabbed his arm.

"No, Daniel! We have to go, now!" Barely slowing, he pulled Daniel to his feet and dragged him toward the bridge. Alaric looked up the coast when Soren charged past and saw the guards no more than a hundred yards away. He grabbed Clem's bloody axe and pressed it into Daniel's hand then saluted with his blade and turned to face the hoard.

"No!" Daniel shouted as he dug in his heals.

Soren was pulled to a stop and swore, turning on him. Before Daniel could start after Alaric, he wrapped a powerful arm around Daniel's neck and growled in his ear, "He's doing it for you, now move!"

Daniel moaned as Alaric leveled his saber at the onrushing troops. He relented and turned back to the bridge, he and the captain running across the warped and weakened boards. As he ran, he heard Alaric's roar of defiance, and the clashing of weapons as the guards reached him. He heard howls of pain that did not belong to Alaric as they reached the far side and Soren pulled him to a stop.

The captain bent and sawed at one of the bridge's thick support ropes with the A-blade. Daniel couldn't take his eyes off Alaric as he stood tall amid a sea of enemies, swinging his saber with abandon and cutting down more than a few opponents. Just when is seemed he may defeat them all, the column of reinforcements arrived and he was overwhelmed by their sheer numbers. With a final surge, he was pulled down, and all that could be seen was the chopping of weapons.

"Help me!" Soren growled as troops ran toward the bridge. Daniel looked at him and then to the axe in his hand

and lay in to the other support rope. The troops saw the danger of crossing the bridge, so Daniel and Soren had a momentary lull to finish their job before arrows rained down.

Soren's support rope separated and the bridge sagged ominously for a second before Daniel's final chop sent it falling into the sea. He jumped to his feet and roared, "Aaaarrgh!" letting out all his anger, hurt, and fear in one defiant growl. Soren spun him away from the bridge and forced him up the stone embankment toward whatever waited on the other side as missiles thudded into the ground around them.

He didn't hear the liquid rattle in Soren's chest, or the grunt from behind as they scrabbled up the short incline and dropped over to slide down the other side. The archers were then firing blind and the attack dwindled before stopping altogether. They came to a halt on a low outcropping of rock that jutted across the surface of the sea, no more than a foot above the level of the liquid.

As Daniel caught his breath, he simultaneously became aware of several things. The burning in his lungs was much worse and his eyes stung. The sounds and smells he normally associated with the ocean were also absent. No sea birds cried, nor did waves crash, and the sharp, sour tang in the air tickled his memory as well, though he couldn't place it.

He wiped his blurry eyes and considered the greenish liquid that stretched out to either side of the causeway, gasping as he recognized where he'd smelled the odor before: College Chemistry Lab. He saw in his mind the glass amber bottle with the sticker on the side that read

CAUTION: CORROSIVE. He remembered thinking, *Damn right, use caution*, fearing what would happen if he spilled it on unprotected skin. He looked at the liquid once more and saw a small wave roll over the edge of the causeway, the liquid sizzling as it ate into the stones.

He pointed a shaky hand and moaned, "That...that's acid." Soren groaned and Daniel glanced at him, his fear of the acid momentarily forgotten. The captain sat rigidly straight, the feathered shafts of three arrows sticking out of his back. "Oh! Oh, no..." Daniel gasped.

Soren looked at him with glassy eyes and mumbled, "Need...need your help."

Daniel nodded. "Okay...what do I do?" Soren tried to turn but Daniel blurted, "No! Its okay, Soren, I can see them." He latched onto his fear with a manic grip, reining it in.

"Need...to come out," Soren moaned through gritted teeth.

"Hnnn..." Daniel moaned, not able to keep in the idiot noise as he raised his shaking hand toward the shafts. He wrapped his left hand around the first arrow where it protruded from Soren's back and pressed his dead right hand against the skin, ignoring the electric fire that shot up his arm. He applied pressure as Soren moaned through gritted teeth and the shaft slid from the wound with a sickening "pop". Daniel grabbed the A-blade and cut a strip from his robe to use as a bandage to stem the gush of blood, but it quickly soaked through.

Soren gasped, "Now...the next...next one."

Daniel wrapped his blood-slicked hand around the next arrow and pulled. He had to twist with the pressure, fighting to maintain his grip. Soren screamed through clenched teeth, but the arrow didn't move. Daniel gathered his courage and tried once more before whimpering, "It's stuck!"

Soren nodded and whispered, "Alright...the other."

He tried the other with the same result, only that time Soren's screams were weaker. Tears ran down his cheeks as he said, "It's no good. That one's stuck too."

Soren wheezed a minute before whispering, "S'al...S'alright. Cut 'em off." He pushed the A-blade to Daniel, whose hand was shaking so badly he could barely pick it up. With his useless right hand, the only way Daniel could stabilize the arrows was to squat behind Soren and grip the shaft between his knees. Soren passed out and Daniel grimly pressed ahead until he was done and the feathered ends of the arrows lay on the ground. The captain came to as Daniel wrapped the wounds and whispered, "Nicely done."

Daniel sat beside him wordlessly and for the first time looked down the stone causeway, doing a double-take at what he saw. Starting ten feet in front of them was a set of iron tracks that stretched to the horizon. They were laid on wooden ties, and while it was all pock-marked and pitted by splashing acid, it looked remarkably like train tracks from Daniel's world. A wooden platform straddled the tracks on four large iron wheels. The bare platform was about three feet off the ground and had what looked like a ship's mast rising from its center. There was a boom fastened to the mast, a wrapped sail attached to it. "What the Hell is that?" Daniel mumbled.

Soren motioned to it and gasped, "Let's go. Sooner begun...sooner done."

Daniel glanced at him and when Soren motioned to it again, he sighed and helped the captain to his feet. They stumbled to the car and Soren nearly passed out a second time when he fell onto the platform. Daniel's arm screamed at him. It felt like he may soon pass out as well if he didn't rest. He pushed the thought away and studied the mast. The boom was bolted to a bracket allowing it to spin easily to capture the wind from any angle. "Have you...sailed before?" Soren murmured.

His burning eyes never left the mast as he shook his head. Soren talked him through how to raise the sail and then the basics of how to turn it to capture the wind. Soon Daniel had the gist of it and turned the sail toward a slight breeze. It pulled out tight and the car lurched into motion, wheels turning easily and offering a fairly smooth ride in spite of the acidic pitting.

Daniel tried to relax as he loosely held the boom's guiding rope in his left hand. He sat as still as possible; hoping the screaming in his right arm would lessen. He glanced at Soren who lay in a pool of blood on the deck, his eyes rolling back in his head as he fought to stay awake. It wasn't until then that Daniel realized they lost their packs somewhere and had no food or water. He blinked away tears and sighed, trying not to cough from the burning in his lungs. The futility of their situation overwhelmed him as he thought, *We're dead.*

Chapter Eighteen

Daniel's hand hurt. Drops of blood fell to the wooden deck below his left hand, which held the boom's guide rope. He soon learned that sailing wasn't as easy as it looked. The winds changed on a dime in the open sea. If his concentration lapsed and he didn't respond, the changing winds could whip the sail around and dump the whole car into the acid. He glanced at Soren, whose breathing was getting more shallow and erratic as the afternoon waned. His bandages had soaked through and blood pooled on the deck where he lay. The captain was lucid for a few hours after they'd started, but since then his eyes glazed over and sometimes he moaned things Daniel couldn't understand.

He wanted to go to Soren and change the bandages, but when he'd tried once earlier in the day the captain reminded him of their situation. They had no food, no water, and no idea how long it would take to cross the Burning Sea. If they dropped the sail, it would be suicide. So Daniel had no choice but to press on, hoping they'd cross in time to save Soren. A coughing fit overcame the captain and Daniel saw blood spurt from the holes in his back. "Y--" Daniel started, but couldn't get the words past his swollen tongue. He swallowed, thinking, *I can't, not without you.* "You okay?"

The coughing subsided as Soren slumped to the deck. "Uhn…"

A gust whipped the car and forced Daniel to take his eyes form Soren and pull on the lines with his torn hand, hissing in pain all the while. It wobbled but then settled back into its easy rhythm when Daniel found the wind once more. His eyes burned as he looked ahead, praying to see the far shore but only unending sea stretched ahead. He gave a timid sigh, afraid to breathe in too much of the burning air. *I can't,* he thought again, his burning eyes feeling heavy as his attention waned. His lids closed until a tug on the guidelines snapped him back awake. He forced his injured hand to tighten down on the rope, though it cried for mercy.

The sun set and the car rolled on. Soren's breathing became ragged, stalling for minutes at a time. *Can't be long now,* Daniel thought dully as he stared at the captain through heavy eyes. It felt like they were full of sand and salt, but he couldn't stop and rest, so he just had to…bear it. Though the burden was killing him, he had to keep on bearing it.

The moon rose, casting the green sea in shades of silver. Daniel was at his limit and his eyes slowly closed, regardless of his will to resist. He didn't know how long he was out, but after a time a weak voice whispered, "Daniel." He tried to ignore it, tried to push it away and rest, but then came an equally weak grip on his leg, shaking him. He jumped and pulled on the guideline, losing the wind for a second. The car immediately slowed, but when he found the wind, it lurched back to its previous speed.

He looked down and saw that Soren had managed to crawl to his side, his blood-streaked hand resting in Daniel's lap. Soren stared at him, and Daniel could tell that for the first time in hours he was fully there. "Soren," he mouthed.

"Daniel," Soren repeated, his voice frail and weak. "Save...save my people."

Hot tears stung Daniel's burning eyes. "How?" he whispered. He wanted to say more. He wanted to say how can I save your people when I can't even save myself? How can I be the One you think I am? His voice failed him as tears flowed.

Soren's eyes said he understood what Daniel couldn't say. He gathered himself for a few moments, pulling in shallow wheezy breaths. Finally, he gasped, "I know...The Proph...Prophecy brought you here. You are...strong, Daniel. I...believe in...in you." Daniel looked into his dying friend's face and shook his head. Soren gripped his leg once more as another coughing fit brought blood to his lips. Through a scarlet spray he breathed, "In...you." He lay back as coughs wracked his body, curling him into the fetal position.

Daniel watched in an agony of helplessness as tears traced dirty tracks down his cheeks. He couldn't do anything for his friend. He couldn't even let go of the lines and hold Soren, stroke his brow as he left the world.

Soren died an hour later. He never again regained consciousness, never looked on Daniel with the hope that had so buoyed them all through their trials. Daniel stared at his unmoving body and knew Soren was gone. He knew he was more alone than he'd ever been in his life. Tears dried up, leaving salty lines on his cheeks. His tired and burning eyes couldn't make out anything anymore as he continued through the darkness. He continued to bear his burden.

~ * ~

The sun cast a blinding glare on the acid-green water, but still there was no end in sight. The farther Daniel went the more unpredictable the winds became, forcing his exhausted mind to work even harder to focus on the sail. Daniel was traveling west, yet even though the sun was rising behind him, the glare made him squint into the brightness no matter what direction he looked. With dull wonder he thought, *I made it another day.* His swollen tongue made swallowing almost impossible, so he settled for a reflexive gag that made his throat burn as if it were rubbed raw with sandpaper.

The sail's rope had been a sun-bleached off-white but the portion that trailed through Daniel's hand was stained scarlet. He winced whenever he had to change his grip and moaned when he had to pull hard on the rope. His lips were chapped and dry, and whenever he winced, they split and bled. Had he not been so exhausted, he would have considered why he was even trying to keep going, but as it was he'd passed the point of coherent thought. His body was on autopilot and so he continued, paying little attention to the hopelessness of his situation.

Even on autopilot, though, there were limits to what he could do. His eyes were so burned by the acidic vapors that he was nearly blind, and anything beyond the periphery of the car was lost in a blurry haze. His breathing was also becoming more labored as the acrid fumes burned his lungs. Even his left hand, which had grown strong and tough when it was forced to carry the load of both arms, was nearly worn out. The flesh along his palm had been eaten away by friction. Had his mind not already been shutting down, the pain would've been excruciating.

Daniel rolled along the tracks, not realizing his eyes were slowly closing. He drifted into a light doze, sitting up and gripping the rope loosely. Had he been awake and rested, he may have seen the whipping of the waves as the change in wind raced toward the tracks. He may have been able to react in time, but as it was, he was caught completely unaware. The wind slammed into the side of the car, taking the sail with it. The boom spun and the rough rope ripping through Daniel's hand, bringing him back with a hiss of pain. He tried to tighten his grip, but it was too late. The powerful crosswind pulled the sail tight and the car tilted on its side, the right wheels leaving the ground.

Daniel's eyes flew wide as he saw onrushing acidic death and he pulled in a shocked gasp, inflaming the damaged tissues of his lungs. Soren's body rolled off the deck and splashed into the green fluid as the car continued to tip toward oblivion. At the last possible second, the wooded mast, weakened by years of exposure to acidic mist, gave way and broke off at its base. The mast, sail, and boom were all carried by the strong wind over the side and splashed into the acid, sending a wave up onto the deck.

With the countering force gone, gravity reasserted itself and the car slammed back to the rails. Daniel was thrown to his rump and he stared in horrified fascination at an acidic puddle as the car rolled to a halt. It had already created a depression in the hard wood and as he watched, it ate ever deeper into the surface. *That could be me*, he thought. *Eaten alive by acid*. Without realizing he was doing it, Daniel backed away from the puddle. His eyes remained focused on the acid as he continued until he leaned back a final time, realizing too late that he was already at the car's front edge.

He tipped over and fell to the ground, landing shoulder first before his face slammed into the rocks and rough ties. Unimaginable pain ripped through him as his body accordioned onto his right side, breaking several ribs and dislocating his shoulder. He also caught the pointed edge of a rock with his forehead, and a wide cut opened, washing his face in blood. For the first time in so long, his dead forearm was the least of the pain as electric jolts of agony rolled over his entire limb from the separated shoulder. He crumpled where he lay, unable to move in spite of the shallow puddle of acid he'd landed in, which burned into his left hand, legs, and abdomen.

He tried to cry out, but the damage to his lungs was too severe. He would have wept, but sobs wouldn't come, the blood pouring into his eyes making tears impossible. He didn't even have the energy to climb back up on the car. But why even bother? Without the sail it was just as useless as his entire adventure had been. He lay there utterly defeated, the only thought running through his mind was, *Why? Why me?* He wished he'd die. He wanted the pain to end, the misery to finally be *over!*

CONTINUE

He felt the word more than heard it. The power of it bulged against his eardrums as if it were a sonic boom. Through the haze of pain, he knew he'd heard/felt that not-quite-human voice before, one that radiated such power and couldn't be denied. He raised his head, blinking away blood and studying the tracks ahead of him. As he studied them, his eyes narrowed and the steel that Soren knew lay within him finally surfaced in its terrible entirety. He wouldn't quit. Slowly his left hand extended, nerve endings sizzling from the acid bath. He reached as far as he could and gripped the edge of a pitted tie. With a groan he pulled himself forward.

Evidently it was possible to be in even greater pain, as he realized when he slid his battered body forward. His lungs felt filled with glass as the jagged ends of broken ribs punctured them, and fractured slivers pushed through his skin. He felt hot wetness as blood ran down his belly. A fine scarlet mist sprayed from his mouth with every pained exhale. His right arm refused to be outdone, though, and his hand and shoulder battled to see which hurt worst as the abused limb was dragged along the rough ground.

Daniel lay still for a moment, paralyzed by the new pain washing over him, but then he gathered his legs and reached out again. He lunged forward, inch-worming his way along the rough acid-covered ground, whimpering with every move.

The mist that came with every labored breath soon became a torrent as blood ran from his mouth whenever he opened it. The bloody trail behind him became wider and darker as more blood drained from his punctured chest, adding to what was still spurting from his forehead. After the first couple lunges, he kept his head down, blindly feeling for handholds to press on. One thought kept going through his mind, overriding every instinct to stop, to avoid damage, to lie down and die. *Continue…continue…continue.*

His hand shook every time he lifted it, and somewhere along the way his fingernail had snagged and torn off, but he didn't stop. His breathing was reduced to coppery gasps of tainted air, but he didn't stop. A buzzing of white noise filled his mind, and a detached part of him knew that soon he simply wouldn't be able to continue no matter what, but still he pressed on, punishing his body to the very limit.

He was so focused on continuing that he didn't realize a white mist was rising around him. He continued to lunge along the tracks, slowly finishing the job of killing himself. The mist thickened and soon it blocked out the sun, cooling Daniel's sweat- and blood-slicked skin, making his back break out in goose flesh.

He reached and pulled himself along, a high-pitched wheeze replacing the moans that had accompanied the effort earlier. *Continue.* His focus was complete. *Continue.* No matter the pain, no matter the cost, he pulled himself along. He didn't realize the difference when his hand reached forward and instead of grasping a wooden tie or a sharp rock, his fingers sank into dark earth. *Continue.* He didn't realize the acrid tang of the acidic air had been replaced by the fresh, loamy scent of rich soil. *Continue.*

He lunged forward as his life's blood now left a trail on dark green grass. The mist thickened until even if he'd been able to look around, all he'd have seen would have been the patch of grass he struggled along. Finally, he reached the end. His left arm lifted and reached before falling back to his side. He sobbed in despair, his body no longer able to comply with his steely will.

ENOUGH

He felt the pressure of the voice on his ear drums again, but this time it was like a soothing balm. His body was wracked by unbelievable pain, but he took comfort in the compassion that he sensed in the voice. He rested his bloody forehead on the loamy soil and gasped a final wretched breath, closing his eyes as he did so. As Daniel lay there surrounded by white mist and enshrouded in pain, the tension in his body eased away. The pinched features of his grimacing face relaxed, and he fell into a deep, restful, dreamless sleep that carried him far from pain.

~ * ~

Malthion seethed in anger. Lieutenant Liesat lay dead on the ground at his feet, the agony etched into his face a guarantee of pain that followed him into the next world. Tendrils of smoke rolled out of his ears, and his eyes were filled with blood. It took the incompetent fool a satisfying length of time to die, but even that didn't improve the sorcerer's mood.

He escaped. The Stranger escaped! Again! The mere thought sent Malthion into ever higher planes of rage. Of course he knew the Prophecy. He and the Emperor had long ago learned of the ancient lake, hence the outpost. He never believed the Stranger would make it that far. He still didn't believe the fool was the Messiah the Resistance thought him to be, even with the repeated escapes. Yet, in spite of it all, he knew how it looked. The failure of underlings impinged on him, and he knew just how angry it would make the Emperor. That thought was enough to tamp down the fires of his rage.

He hated the man. *Man*, he scoffed. *As if He could be called something as low as Man!* The Emperor was the only...being...that wielded power comparable to Malthion's. In fact his power dwarfed even the amazing heights Malthion had reached, which made him fear the Emperor. And with fear came the inevitable hatred. For now he had to bend and scrape, acquiescing to his every whim...but plans were in place. Over the years he'd learned about the power that suffused the Emperor, and soon he would move against him.

But not yet. He wasn't ready, so this wasn't the time to raise His ire, but he saw no other option. Malthion glared down at the ignorant fool one last time before turning away with a growl. He strode into his personal meditation chamber, feeling his skin tingle as he crossed the threshold. The tingling gave him courage, helped him to relax. Not even the mighty Emperor could cross through that doorway without igniting powerful warding glyphs. This room was only for Malthion, where he could be alone with his thoughts, unwatched and unhindered.

The rectangular room was an odd sight to behold within a tent, and indeed it wasn't really in the tent at all. It had stone walls and an arched wooden ceiling that rose to a peak twenty feet above the stone floor. The walls were covered with floor-to-ceiling shelves crammed with books, scrolls, specimens, and various artifacts. One end of the room was covered with expensive rugs stitched with ornate symbols in gold thread. On the rugs sat a huge oak worktable with a scarred marble top. At the opposite end the floor was left bare and arcane symbols were carved deep into the stone. To one side of the table was a cushioned chair; alongside the chair was a trunk made of dark wood. The trunk stood out in its plainness, but the air around it was thick with malice.

Malthion sat as he perused the simple-looking lock on the trunk. He was lost in thought as he entertained whatever evil men consider when their dark minds wander. Eventually with a wheezing sigh he produced an ordinary looking bronze key and inserted it into the trunk's lock. Again the tingling danced across his skin, and it once more brought him comfort. If anyone else tried to open the trunk, every molecule of water in their body would boil as they tried in vain to scream. He forced two slaves to attempt the trunk and was fascinated by the noises the human body makes as it immolates at such a fundamental level.

Tumblers turned and the lock opened. Malthion lifted the lid and inspected his most powerful items. Some were weapons, some tools, some merely curiosities, but all had captured the attention of the powerful sorcerer, and so they were hidden where none but he could ever reach them. His bony fingers caressed several of the items as they passed over them. He didn't think of them lovingly, but rather with gluttonous glee, thinking of the power he'd amassed.

His hand stopped its wanderings and hovered over a cylinder that was covered with black velvet. He growled at his own reluctance, remembering one of the tenets of his life: Hesitation is weakness. He snatched up the cylinder and slammed the trunk lid which responded with a hollow boom. Determined to delay no longer, he stalked to the worktable, pushing vials and decanters out of his way. He removed the velvet to expose a sheet of rolled leather. It was oddly colored and didn't look like the skin of any animal. As he unrolled it, he looked at the dark symbols that covered it and a malice-filled smile came to his thin lips.

The slaves, identical twins boys, were hand-selected by Malthion. He personally oversaw the tattooing of their backs, at least until their childish wailing became too much of an irritation. He ordered their tongues removed so he could watch in silence as each was marked with exactly the same symbols. He suffused the tattoos with magic and the boys were slaughtered, their skin removed, stretched, and tanned. He studied the skin, thinking of its twin that was carried by the Emperor. He traced the arcane symbols with his eyes before focusing his will. Words appeared on the leather, as if they were written by an invisible hand.

Master, I report, he thought as the words appeared. He stared at the leather and an emotion that rarely affected him took hold of his mind: anxiety.

After what seemed an eternity, a second line of print appeared. *You have him.*

He hesitated for only a second before concentrating. *No, Master. He has escaped.* A rictus of fear gripped him, exposing the blackened stubs of teeth, while he stared at the parchment. His dark tongue darted in and out of his mouth as he waited.

His heart stopped as the pregnant pause stretched until the Emperor's reply appeared. *You have failed me.* Malthion sucked in a breath but the message soon continued. *Return immediately so we may continue our plans.*

He let out a shaky sigh. The Emperor didn't intend to destroy him. *At least not yet,* he corrected himself. He was so relieved that he nearly lost the focus necessary to keep the portal open. Had he done that, he certainly would have met a painful end. To cover his slip he quickly sent a question. *What of the men?*

In truth he didn't care one wit for them, but Malthion had no intention of failing the Emperor again...which meant no loose ends. The pause was much shorter before more words formed. *No one must know of your failure. Kill them. None survive.* The obvious "or else" was not added, but Malthion understood the ramifications, to him personally and to the Empire, if any witnesses turned up.

He shrugged and focused his will a final time. *Of course, Master.* The connection broke almost immediately as the Emperor severed the link needed to communicate via the skins. He rolled the leather and wrapped the velvet around it, replacing it in the trunk. He sat in his chair and considered the drawn-out mission. He still burned at the failure, though it was not truly his own. After all, it was his men that failed, not him. Regardless, how could a simple fool escape him time and again? He gritted the stubs of his teeth in rage before pushing the anger away.

He stood and smoothed his red robes as he made for the entrance to his command tent. A final piece of business needed attending before he returned to the Emperor, and on that he would not fail. Malthion pulled the magic to him as he crossed the hall, allowing anger and humiliation to fuel the tempest. Death would come for the many that had failed him. *After all*, he thought. *None can stand before the Empire!*

August 30, 2012

About the Author

ron_hartman@mchsi.com

Ron Hartman has had a life-long passion for the written word and is an avid reader. The Prophecy Chronicles are his first written works. Ron graduated from the University of Iowa College of Pharmacy in 2000 and lives in Ottumwa, Iowa with his wife and three children.